Tennessee Truths

A Small Town Romance

Ashley Munoz

Cover Design: Wildheart Graphics

Editing: C. Marie Edits

Proofing: Tiffany Hernandez

❀ Created with Vellum

TENNESSEE
TRUTHS

To every girl who's had her heart broken, who's ever wanted solace in someone's arms.
For the one's who lost themselves along the way.
This one is for you.

* Please Check TW on my website at www.ashleymunozbooks.com— there is a reference to domestic violence.

Prologue

Faith
Age 14

THERE WAS something dangerously exhilarating about keeping secrets.

While I only had two tucked away inside my heart, they were enough to make me feel special in a way nothing else ever had.

And as a fourteen-year-old girl, stuck in the throes of middle school, I desperately wanted to feel special. Maybe it was because I felt pathetically ordinary, although more honestly it was probably because I captured the unnerving attention of my school's golden boy.

There was nothing actually golden about him, though; he was all dark colors with angry strokes and desperate dabs...he also happened to be my first secret.

The bell rang, sending a jolt of adrenaline through my system, the ear-splitting sound like a blaring alarm repeating one word over and over:

Move. Move. Move.

I darted for my locker as fast as I could without breaking into a

1

run while catching a quick glimpse of the clock hanging on the far wall.

7:35.

I let out a silent breath, wrapping my fingers around the black dial, spinning it forcefully to the left. Hearing a few laughs and titters from down the hall, I wrangled my backpack off and moved swiftly to put my things away.

The yellow sticky note crumpled at the bottom of my locker stalled me, just like it did every time. *My second secret.* Grinning from ear to ear, I shoved the scrap into the front pocket of my jeans before anyone saw me.

Then, as if the air in the hallway shifted, I knew my time was up. His arrival always felt like the beginning of a hurricane, the few seconds I had to prepare myself like standing in the center, peaceful and calm.

Quick as lightning, I was tugging my books free and situating my English essay. The last thing I wanted to do was ruin my homework before classes even started. I was nearly ready when I heard someone down the hall call out, "Seeds!"

I forced my eyes shut, shoving the nerves down like I did every day.

I didn't have to look to know people were following him. Guys were offering their palms for high fives as girls smiled and vied for his attention. Jace divided the throng like a wave, like nothing and no one was of any consequence, at least not enough to stop him or snag his attention.

Except me.

I was the stone he crashed upon with force and destruction.

"Seeds." His Southern lilt drew my eyes up. Striking blue orbs assessed me from under dark, drawn brows.

"Jace." I exhaled, hoping he couldn't hear the heavy thud in my chest at his presence. I hated him. I prayed he would get swept away in the Mississippi River on a regular basis...but more reverently, more

2

secretly, I also wrote out the spelling of his last name in a thousand different fonts, testing to see how it would look attached to my first.

"If it isn't my favorite Bible story," he joked, slapping his palm to the locker above me.

I blushed, hating that he always did this. Everyone giggled and laughed at his loud declaration. Jace and I attended Sunday school together. Thankfully he didn't do any of this fanfare there, but as soon as we were back in school, he was merciless with the jokes. In fact, it had been after a handful of Sundays that he'd chosen my nickname.

Seeds, as in faith the size of a mustard seed.

So lame.

"Seeds, did you have a good weekend? Do any reading?" He leaned in, brushing a lock of hair off my shoulder.

He knew I had because he'd seen me at the library on Saturday. He had ignored me, laughing with his two buddies, except for when he tossed a crumpled-up paper toward my empty study table.

I hadn't even looked to see if something was written on it, because I knew whatever it was would hurt my feelings or make me blush.

I flicked my gaze to the far wall ahead of us. 7:40.

RING.

The bell announced that school was officially starting, forcing everyone to scatter. I would have let out a sigh of relief, but I knew too well that Jace wasn't done.

He smirked, bending lower and inhaling a deep breath of...*me.*

Butterflies swarmed my chest as he closed his eyes, towering over me. His lips were so close.

It sent tiny shivers down my arms, like jagged arrowheads being shoved under my skin. Unpleasant fire burned in my lower belly at his nearness, the confusion of how my body reacted to him always made me emotional. I didn't want to like him. I had someone... *someone secret, but either way,* Jace wasn't him.

3

"I need to leave." I shoved at his arm, and he moved but quickly fell in step behind me.

"Do you have any plans after school today, Seeds?" he asked as I stormed toward homeroom. *Why does he care?*

"I'm going to the library, if you must know." I inwardly slapped myself. *Why did I tell him that?*

"Right after school? Have a hot date?" He picked up my ponytail, pinching the end between his thumb and pointer finger.

I stopped, forcing him to nearly crash into me. "No. I don't have a hot date, but even if I did, it wouldn't be any of your business."

He smirked. "That's where you're wrong." Rolling my eyes, I started to turn, but he stopped me. "What kind of guy would you date anyway?"

It sounded like he meant no one would *want* to date me, so naturally, hurt slipped in through my rib cage, attacking that useless thing in my chest.

"You know...the standard is pretty low. As long as he wasn't you, he would have a shot." I smirked, turning away from him. I stormed toward homeroom, where he couldn't follow.

Thankfully.

Finally letting out a relieved sigh, I tugged the paper free from the pocket of my jeans and read what was written. In messy, sharp letters were the words: *Science fiction - The Count of Monte Cristo - Chapter 12.* I smiled, because secrets were what kept me going when Jace was a jerk to me. Secrets were what made this entire day worth it.

I counted down every second of the school day until I could walk two streets over to our public library. Throwing open the thick glass doors, I quietly padded in and toward the back.

My face was blotchy from the last run-in of the day with Jace. Like usual, he had found some way to run into me. He'd always lock eyes with me, like a missile seeking its target. I always tried to ignore him, but he'd just head in my direction with more vigor. Then, right as he got close enough, he would find a way to slam into me, and as always, it would send my books flying.

Most days I didn't mind, because I had gotten used to it. However, today was important because I had a mock interview and my fake resume required perfection. It was the last class of the day, and I had managed to protect it all day.

That is, until that last class transition when my books fell and my crisp resume landed under the boot of Clay Anderson, who had just walked through a puddle. For one single moment I wanted to cry, maybe punch Jace in the face, because I needed an A on that project, not a B or anything lower. I had to get an A.

Mr. Brooks coldly told me I'd receive a B minus and that he was being generous. So now, as I sauntered through the library, I was trying to pull on the only happiness I had found in the entire day.

My secret.

The notes left in my locker would always provide a random location and the text of choice hidden somewhere in the mix. Obviously, *The Count of Monte Cristo* was no science fiction novel, but the thrill of it being tossed in and so out of place added to the excitement.

I ran my finger along the spines of different science fiction titles until the brown, cracked back with golden script caught my eye. *The Count of Monte Cristo.*

My stomach somersaulted as I tugged it free. As always, I looked around, wondering if my secret sharer was near, if for once I could get a glimpse of who it was that had been playing this game with me for the past year.

As usual, there was no one.

Unwilling to allow disappointment to sneak in, I anchored the book to my chest and walked toward the young adult section. Plopping down into a neon orange bean bag, I gently thumbed through the pages until I found chapter twelve.

A purple wildflower lay snugly in the center of the book, marking

5

my route for reading. He'd already told me which chapter, so the flower wasn't required, but heat rose up my neck as I carefully pulled it free. I loved that he always added a flower.

There, written in the margin, was his note.

Dear Pip,

While your take on the existence of jackelopes was fascinating,

I thought we could move past urban legends...

To something a little more...personal.

Tell me, since we both go to the same school...

Who do you like?

Who is it that's in your head and has maybe captured your heart?

Sincerely,

The Fool

I smiled, tracing the letters in each shaded word. We only ever wrote in pencil because they were books and we weren't monsters. I wondered how long we would play this game. He had told me enough about him for me to know I liked him, his hobbies and interests...but he had never suggested we meet one another.

How much longer would we leave each other these notes?

I was headed to high school at the beginning of fall—what would happen then?

Once I was back home in the safety of my room, I opened the book again and wrote my response.

Dear Fool,

If this is your way of asking if I have a boyfriend,

I don't.

Now, why on earth would you be curious about who I like?

Sincerely,

Pip

I shut the book, smiling at the emptiness in my room as if it were a big, fat blob of invisible support.

I'd replace the book in the same place tomorrow for him to pick up. I hated that I didn't have his locker number. I had no idea how he had learned where mine was, but it felt so unfair. I had asked him once for his, but he'd said that would make it too easy for me to figure out who he was.

Almost an entire year of writing these notes and I was no closer to knowing who it was. The rage I had felt earlier because of Jace surfaced, forcing me to open the book. I didn't care anymore, and I was tired of not knowing. I wanted someone in my life who liked me, who didn't think I was a joke. I wanted someone to want me. Revisiting my written note, I added a bit at the bottom.

P.S. I think I might be in love with you...and I think we need to meet, because I'm tired of not knowing who you are. If you agree, set up our next book, and when I go to retrieve it, meet me.

Slamming the book shut, I sagged in my bed and relished the visions of who it could be and what their face would look like when they saw my bold suggestion. I imagined him leaning against the shelf, back turned toward me until he heard me approach. I imagined us telling our kids this story, and someday our grandkids.

My mind was getting away from me, but that's what I did. I imagined things, all the way down to the kind of house we would have. My mother called me boy crazy, but I wasn't. I was, however, enamored with the idea of love—real, true, genuine love.

I wanted the reckless kind of love that made people crazy, the kind that kept people connected over years and years, like the stars... always a part of our past, always present in our future.

Two weeks later

Thunder echoed in the distance. A blip of white light stretched across the velvet sky, acting like a beacon of terror. The low rumble of caution wrapped around me, and as always, it dared me to stay and watch.

Arms flung wide, eyes closed tight, I tipped my head back and smiled. The smell of wet earth and fresh rain overwhelmed my senses, dislodging my judgment. Instead of running for the lowest ground, I prepared my spot at the top of the tallest structure in the park. A tempest like this couldn't be merely watched; it had to be experienced.

And why not push the limits of my safety? It didn't matter anyway.

It wasn't like I wanted to end my life; I just wouldn't risk missing this storm to protect it.

It was all going blissfully perfectly until the sound of a flapping tarp tore me from my reverie. Reluctantly, I turned to inspect my shabby shelter. I had planned to take refuge on the little space of floor by attaching the cover to one pole and stretching it to the other.

It wouldn't protect the entire platform, but at least it would work to shield me from the rain—except the bungee cord I had wrapped around one corner of the tower wasn't cooperating, which had forced the entire panel to cave in. Soon it would be soaked with rain if I didn't work fast. My mind wandered for the briefest of moments to my pen pal...to the notes we'd written in Moby Dick...to the one where he'd ended it.

I can't do this with you anymore. I'm sorry.

Two weeks.

He had waited two weeks to reply to my confession.

When he had responded, he'd dumped me. It was far worse not even knowing what he looked like because I couldn't put a face to my anger. I feared it would instead soak into the classics that held our secrets, which would ruin my love of books.

I moved, grabbing for the cord, holding it steady while another big gust of wind upended the other edge. The force had me careening backward toward the ladder. I gripped the railing, trying to get my bearings, but my feet faltered a few more steps. Panic seized me, frozen in my lungs as I registered how bad of an idea this was. Suddenly a warm hand covered my exposed arm, tugging me down.

I blinked, trying to process what had just happened. No one should have been out there. No one was ever out there except...

An angry boom cracked above me, followed by a raging voice yelling in my ear. "What the hell are you doing out here?"

Him.

Flashes of rueful smirks, angry taunts, and organized debauchery flashed through my mind. Him running into me, forcing my books to drop to the floor, my papers scattering across the hall. Him watching me...always watching. Him pulling Kristen Jones under his arm during lunch yesterday...while his gaze stayed glued to *me*.

"Let me go." I pulled my arm back, seething at his presence, trying to talk my stomach out of the little flip flop routine it was doing at the fact that Jace had come.

Again.

He adjusted his squatting position to better cover us with the flapping tarp, shielding us from the rain. He kept one arm around my waist, causing my stomach to riot. I was at odds with my stupid hormones, especially after my monumental miscalculation regarding *the fool.*

Still, it didn't change the fact that my face turned into a furnace every time he was close, and every evil smirk made the butterflies in my stomach flutter. It was even worse that every time he randomly appeared somewhere that I was, I mentally took it to mean we were destined to be together.

My abductor—or hero, however you wanted to look at it—made a sound of irritation from behind me as he pulled me closer to the corner.

"Let me go," I repeated, trying to push at his arm, but at the touch of his hot skin against mine, I relented immediately. The part of my body that collected his attentive glances and smiles sagged into his chest and mentally screamed at him to hold me tighter. The other part that was angry and bitter at how horribly he'd treated me for the past two years demanded I push him away and pray he tripped down the ladder.

"I'll let you go when you tell me what you're doing out here," he said against my ear, his hand flexing at my hip, causing my breath to hitch. I was so thankful he couldn't see my face.

"It's none of your business." As if my love for storms could be easily explained to the boy who bullied me? As if I could share my wonder and awe for the sky and how detrimentally beautiful it was? My body came out here as if it was called, like the sky was a siren and I merely a lost pirate at sea. Jace would laugh, and then make fun of me for all eternity.

Then there was the little issue of being dumped by someone I'd never even met.

He chuckled, a low rumble in his chest. I smiled for a second, thinking he'd be kind, but then he followed it with, "Stupid girl."

Anger unfurled inside my chest, stretching and claiming all the places previously owned by those stupid butterflies.

"I'm not stupid—you're stupid." I elbowed him, trying to get some distance. Thankfully and regrettably, he let me go.

"Why do you always fight me on this? I told you not to come out here alone," he yelled over the booming thunder, which was significantly closer now.

Why the heck was he so mad? Why did he care at all?

"I have been coming out here since long before you moved to town," I yelled back, trying to shuffle into the corner, away from him. The white light bled in through the gaps in the tarp, followed by a crack of thunder directly over our heads.

"Shit! We need to get lower. This tower is the tallest thing around here—we're sitting ducks." He grabbed my hand, pulling me up and shoving me toward the ladder. "Climb down, stay close, and as soon as you can, get in that small doorway under the play structure."

Terrified by his urgency and the fact that logic was slowly starting to seep in, I did as he said. I climbed down and ran as fast as my legs would carry me. Ducking into the small archway, I blinked against the darkness, the only light coming from the sky in flashes every few seconds.

Being the closest one to my house, this playground was the one I frequented the most. It was designed like a castle, with wooden towers standing at each corner of the structure, and it was perfect for stargazing. Unfortunately, however, Jace was right—it was pure suicide during a lightning storm.

A few seconds later, Jace barreled in, crowding me against the back wall. "We should be safe in here." He eyed the pouring rain, which we were now shielded from.

I nodded, grabbing on to my knees, leaning back. We sat in silence for a few moments, just watching the flashes of light and cringing when the thunder boomed. Meanwhile, my mind slowly pulled at all the tiny pieces of tonight, like a fraying strand of string. *Why is Jace out here? Why did he rescue me? Why does it seem like he cares?*

The first time he'd come out, it had been a Friday night, nearly dusk. I was still reading with what daylight I had left, slowly swinging. He came over, tipped my chin up, and angrily told me he was walking me home and to never come out alone again. Thinking it was another one of his stupid tactics to bully me, I laughed in his face and went back the next week. Only, he was back that week too.

And so went every Friday night for the past six months. Even on game nights, he'd make his way to the park. He even once showed up at nearly midnight. He never spoke, but he did walk me home, every single time.

"So, you came out here to watch the storm?" Jace asked, his tone an olive branch, like he was trying to make polite conversation. I was instantly suspicious. He was sitting on his knees, making him taller than me.

I looked up, relishing the glint in his eyes. I always liked looking into his eyes. I tried to as often as possible, without him noticing.

"I like storms," I quietly confessed.

"Well they don't like you." His tone was mocking. "You'd probably die if it weren't for me."

"I would have been fine. I'm not stupid or helpless," I snapped, feeling frustrated by his presence. "Why are you out here anyway?"

He went from eyeing the storm to turning his calculating gaze on me. He stared; I stared back. Finally, he brought a hand to his forehead, letting out a small quivering sound...like he was tired. "I figured it would have been obvious by now." Moving closer, he forced our bodies to touch. We were leg to leg, but I felt it everywhere.

I inhaled sharply as his warm breath fanned out on my ear.

He whispered, "It's the same reason I accidentally trip into you in the halls, and the same reason I go to the library every Saturday and why I walk the two miles to the stupid park every Friday night." His hand went to the wet hair that was sticking to the side of my face, the pad of his rough finger brushing it aside. "I'm a fool."

Holding my breath, I watched as he leaned back, just enough to reveal his expression. His heavy gaze fluttered over my face, down to my lips, just as thunder boomed again.

His confession shifted something in my chest, making me feel exhilarated and confused.

I'm a fool.

Why did he have to use that exact phrase?

"Why are you telling me this?" I asked, raising my voice over the heavy rain.

He blinked, licked his lips, and leaned closer to me. "Because I've been watching you for two years, and if I have to watch you get a boyfriend or kiss someone besides me, I'm going to get kicked out of school. We're going into high school next fall, and I don't want to play games anymore."

I kept my breathing to a minimum, letting him continue, because he had to. I needed him to keep confirming that this burning feeling I always had when he was around wasn't just one-sided.

Hot air made contact with my neck as another shudder ran through him. His words spiraled out in a rush of breath. "I want you to be mine, Faith."

I shifted forward, catching us both off guard. I tried to take it back, reclaim the small amount of distance we'd had, but he gripped my wrist, slowly pulling me closer as I breathlessly said, "So...you like me?"

White light lit the sky on fire, showing me his handsome face: bright blue eyes, a jaw that was already starting to define, and dark eyebrows that framed his features. He laughed, bringing his thumb to my lips.

"I think we're way past that, Pip."

My heart stalled. "What did you just call me?"

His hand traveled to the nape of my neck, pulling me closer.

"Pip, I'm your fool. Please don't hate me." His whispered confession washed over me.

No. It couldn't be.

I pushed him back.

"You're..." I couldn't even say the words.

"Yes, it's me. I started writing to you last year when I realized I had no other way of getting you to talk to me."

"You could have just been nice." I sputtered, still shocked, amazed...*relieved.*

His deep laugh rumbled between us. "I was nice to you when I first moved here, but you didn't notice me—not really. When I was funny, you didn't laugh. You never tried to sit with me at lunch or be my partner in class, not like the other girls. I wanted you to look at me, to notice me the way I noticed you."

I didn't know what to say to his admission. I was too afraid to believe him.

"But you said you couldn't write to me anymore...you ended things," I reminded him.

His eyes flashed as a grin broke out across his face. It was painfully beautiful.

"I wrote that because you wouldn't have accepted that it was me, not if I showed up the way you had asked me to. You would have cried or shouted that you hated me. I didn't want to risk your rejection."

His finger trailed down my face, tucking more hair behind my ear. Goosebumps erupted along my skin, making me feel fevered. I processed his truth, realizing he was right. I would never have accepted that it was him if he had shown up in the library. I wouldn't have believed him.

"Okay." I finally breathed again, my heart jumping into my throat.

He watched me, a small smile lifting the edges of his mouth. "You serious?"

"Yeah...I mean...I-I don't know what to say," I stammered. *Am I supposed to say yes? Or that I accept? Did he even ask a question?*

"Say you'll be mine. Say you'll be with me," he harshly declared to the dark surrounding us.

Nodding my answer, I waited in utter terror for what was coming next. My friends had all already been kissed at some point in middle school, but I hadn't. I had no idea what was involved with dating and becoming boyfriend and girlfriend.

Jace wet his lips, and while he leaned toward me, the tiny shuddered breath that left his lips made me think he was as nervous as I was. I tilted my chin up so he knew I was sure, because I really didn't want him to ask. Two more thunderous booms echoed overhead before his lips descended on mine.

It was as if we were pats of butter shucked into a hot pan, melting into each other, moving soft and slow. Small fireworks went off inside my head, and exhilaration roared inside my heart as a soft sound emanated from his throat. I didn't know what to do except match exactly what he was doing.

Rising to my knees, I kissed him back, grabbing his shirt, pulling him even closer. We moved to a song birthed in darkness, illuminated by fire, all while I gracefully handed my heart over to my secret keeper, my bully, the boy I was falling in love with.

Faith

Age 18

Gold and crimson balloons littered the gymnasium, tied to the black folding chairs that sat snugly in neat symmetrical lines along the pine floor and all along the stage that had been set up for our ceremony. Letting out a heavy exhalation, I walked forward, ignoring the growing crowd of families ambling in to get to their seats in the bleachers. My eyes searched, drifting up, looking for my parents and hoping they'd chosen seats close to the Walkers.

There, third row from the top, was June Walker, smiling at me, looking as proud as my own mother. The only difference was, my mother didn't require a mask when out in public, or an oxygen tank just in case her lungs stopped working.

It twisted my stomach when I saw June brave things like this, as if she needed any more reason for the people in this town to talk about her. But seeing her in such good spirits had me smiling back and waving at her and the dark-haired thirteen-year-old sitting next to her.

Returning my gaze to my fellow classmates, I looked toward the back row of seats along the floor, where Jace should have been getting settled. His dark head of hair wasn't anywhere to be seen, which made me nervous.

Over the years, I'd gotten so close to him that when he wasn't around, it left a knot of worry in my chest. I was sure that wasn't healthy, but for what I knew of love, it made sense. His touch put me at ease, his voice always calmed me, and his eyes—they centered me.

"Faith, watch where you're going," scolded my best friend, Gemma, as she pushed me forward.

I glanced back, apologizing. "Sorry, just looking for Jace."

She laughed, or scoffed—I couldn't quite tell because she frequently did both when she caught me nearly tripping over myself where that boy was concerned.

"Look, he's right there." Her hot pink fingernail shot past my face, pointing toward the middle section of seats, where our line was headed. There in the middle of the row, likely right where I was supposed to sit, was Jace, standing tall and looking regal in his crimson graduation robe. My heart flip flopped in my chest as my face broke into a smile.

He had a massive bouquet of flowers in his fist, a sly grin on his face, and one hand shoved into his pocket. A teacher would likely be over soon to tell him he wasn't in the right spot, which meant I needed to get to him fast.

Cutting away from the line, I pushed toward the center row of chairs and started moving them around so I could get to him sooner. An audible gasp came from the people behind me with a few *Heys* and *What the hecks* thrown around, but I kept going.

His grin grew, turning into laughter as he tossed his head back. I loved him, so much it physically hurt sometimes. I didn't like being away from him, ever. Which, again, if anyone knew, they'd likely sit me down and talk about how dangerous that kind of dependency was. With my head, I knew that, but my heart slammed the door on logic and settled in nicely with obsession.

Finally, the last row between us was obliterated, and I slammed into him. He caught me, pulling me close, nuzzling my neck. Once I let him go, he was quick to capture me again, this time with a searing kiss that had our classmates erupting into hollers and shouts.

I heard them, but I also didn't, because when Jace kissed me, the whole world disappeared until it was just us. It always felt like our first kiss in that thunderstorm: booming, bright, explosive. Finally, he broke our connection, his chest heaving up and down like my own. He pinned his forehead to mine and whispered, "Happy graduation, Pip."

Standing back a foot, he handed me the flowers. Wildflowers in a variety of colors were bound together with burlap, beaming up at me. They weren't like the usual ones he found; these were bigger, more vibrant, fuller...which meant he'd paid for them.

"Jace, you didn't have to get these. I know what day it is...I know what's due," I whispered, feeling the guilt tug at me painfully hard.

His firm jaw ticked as he watched me. Leaning in, he whispered, "You were worth every penny." He pressed a kiss to my brow just as we heard, "Miss Morgan, you need to get back in line before your row sits down!"

Ms. Bevney was frantic and panting. She must have run over to us. "Mr. Walker, this isn't even your row! Please, both of you go get back in line and fix those chairs," she screeched, rushing us along.

Jace pressed one more kiss to my lips. "See you after, Pip. Don't forget about tonight." He winked and walked back down the row, leaving me with a thundering heart and a smile on my face.

***

The ceremony took forever. It was agonizingly long, and the pictures afterward were never ending. I hadn't made a ton of friends in high school, somewhat due to my lack of social skills, but mostly because every girl was in love with Jace Walker. He was gorgeous, raw perfection that belonged on a magazine cover, or an ever-circulating meme.

He'd grown into that defined chin, so sharp it could cut glass, and his dark brows were set perfectly over the darkest blue eyes, which, against his raven hair, were just godlike. His Greek-like nose was straight, and somehow, he had this natural sun-kissed glow about him that he carried all year round.

It certainly didn't help quell the female population's hatred for me that he was the cliché captain of the football team. It wasn't that he cared or had plans to venture into playing professionally, but he liked to let people know if he wanted something, he'd take it.

Bodies were everywhere, pushing against each other, sweating, swarming. It was too much. I searched faces, looking for Jace, but couldn't find him anywhere. Then a warm hand tugged on mine, stopping me in place. I spun around to find a dark head of hair already walking us out of the school, toward the parking lot. Jace had changed out of his graduation robes and back into his t-shirt and jeans, his combat boots unlaced like usual.

Once we were in the parking lot, Jace opened the passenger door and held his hand out for me. I grabbed it but kissed him before I slid in and buckled myself in the middle.

We were silent as we drove, and the sky was darkening with heavy clouds, which made my stomach flip. I loved getting caught in storms with Jace. I loved getting caught anywhere with him. Finally, after about twenty minutes, he pulled up a dirt hill and put his truck into park. Distant thunder rumbled around us as the navy clouds progressed across the sky.

Jace jumped out of the truck, pillaged around in the back for a few things, and then headed toward my door. I followed after him, helping with the backpack and cooler. Rows and rows of dense trees surrounded us as we walked along the soft ground. Thankfully I had swapped my high heels for a pair of cowboy boots, knowing Jace had something planned.

"Where are we?" I asked, trailing after him.

"McGrady's," Jace murmured over his shoulder, giving me a secretive smile.

My heart swelled. I loved this orchard because of the flowers that bloomed when the apples and cherries were nearly in season. I was shocked I hadn't already recognized it, but we must have come from a different entrance than the normal route.

We walked until Jace stopped near a peach tree; underneath was a patch of soft grass. He set down the things he'd carried and pulled out a thin canvas bag.

"Is that a..." I stuttered, but Jace flashed me a smile.

"A tent? Yeah...we're spending the night out here. Your parents think you're staying with Gemma after the party. Don't worry, I covered all the bases." He started pulling out the long poles, snapping them together. I moved to help, and together we assembled the small, two-man tent.

Once it was up, I looked around and laughed. "No sleeping bags?"

A devilish smile broke out on Jace's face. "Not a chance, Pip."

I hated blushing at that. We'd been having sex since the previous summer, but he still had a way of making me feel like a virgin whenever he talked about sleeping with me. We laid down four blankets inside the tent, Jace strung up a few battery-operated lights, and then the cooler went in with us lastly. Thankfully the storm seemed to be moving in the other direction.

After our dinner, Jace kept nervously clearing his throat, which was odd. I knew he had something planned, which I'd assumed was this little overnight trip, seeing as we never had any time alone. Now, though, I was wondering if there was something else going on.

"Everythin' okay?" I asked, not realizing my accent was peeking through. I didn't love my accent. Don't ask me why, but any time a northerner heard it, they acted like I was the gum stuck to the bottom of their shoe, which left me with lackluster motivation to let it show.

"Yeah, of course," Jace stammered, his tone nervous. I knew this boy, so I knew when he was on edge about something. I was about to address it, but he turned until he was on his knees in front of me. "It's just that...you know how we talked about going to college with each other and how we're factoring each other into our decisions?"

I nodded, grabbing his hand to help calm him. He lifted mine to his lips and kissed it.

"I don't want to freak you out with this," he whispered before letting out a big sigh. "Corvin gave me something because he's heard me talking about you and all our plans...I mentioned how I couldn't afford a ring, and how that would probably scare you right now anyway, so..." He trailed off.

I swallowed a lump of giddy anticipation. I couldn't tell him I desperately wanted a ring because I was ready to marry him, so instead, I just sat there and waited. He reached behind him for something and came back with a black velvet box. I stifled a gasp as he opened it, revealing a silver locket.

"Corvin gave this to his girl back when he was shipping out with the Navy, as a way to promise himself to her and vice versa. It wasn't an engagement ring, but it was a vow just the same. So, anyway...I was wondering if you'd accept it?" His blue eyes were so deep and so full of emotion, reminding me of how hard I'd fallen for him years before and how since then, we'd only sunk deeper.

I carefully picked up the necklace and inspected it. It was a simple oval shape with an anchor on the front, and on the back was inscribed: ***Vaster than the sea, more violent than the wind, your love is the only thing on this earth that could ruin me.***

My heart wanted out of my chest, tears begged to run down my face, and confessions of undying love wanted to be released, but I kept it all back and simply leaned up, matching his height, and threw my arms around him.

"I love you and a million times yes." I pressed a gentle kiss to his neck then lowered my hands so I could tug his shirt over his head. Jace carefully set the box aside and lowered me to the blanket, smiling against my lips.

"This is me saying I want you. I plan to marry you. You're mine, Faith Morgan. Mine alone," Jace rasped into my ear while sliding his hand up my skirt.

I nodded against his chin and swore, "I'll never take it off, not until you replace it with a ring."

His kiss nearly ended me as we came together, hot and desperate. Full of possibilities, like filling a time capsule, a memorial of someplace you never want to forget. We stripped each other bare, lay down, and made love under what I hoped was a starry sky.

Jace

Age 19

The sun reflected off Faith's necklace as she smiled and animatedly talked to her parents about our plans for the following fall. Normally it would have sent me into a panic, just thinking about the responsibilities I would be leaving behind, but this time, for once, it only brought me joy. I took a bite of melon and listened to her tell them about the apartment we planned to live in, and I didn't need to see the look on her father's face to know he didn't approve.

Clark Morgan rarely approved of much where I was concerned, but I wasn't going to let that stop me from making plans, and I was glad as fuck that Faith wasn't going to let it stop her either. She'd long since shaken off the opinion of her parents, which was a survival technique because they were judgmental as hell.

"So, when are y'all leavin'?" Julia, Faith's mother, asked with a tight smile.

"End of August," I replied, wiping at my mouth, grabbing for Faith's hand under the table. Whenever we were at her parents' house, I invariably got nervous and frequently needed to touch her— although, currently, touching her just had me thinking of the previous night.

I'd climbed up the lattice outside her window and snuck into her bedroom, crowding onto Faith's twin bed, nestling under her covers. I loved those moments because I could touch her, kiss her, say anything I wanted. I had dragged my hands up her back, slinking under her thin tank top, relishing how warm her smooth skin was. I'd surrendered to my addiction like I always did and pulled her closer. A small gasp had left her mouth as I deepened the kiss and moved my hand farther down her spine until I was pushing down her sweats and...

"Jace!" Faith shouted, moving my arm, bringing me back to the moment.

"Sorry, what?" I blinked. Her parents were eyeing me as though they'd just seen that entire thing on replay. Fuck, that would be embarrassing, although there was no way they hadn't heard at least something the night before. They weren't that blind to how often Faith and I touched or kissed each other; it didn't take a genius to assume we were sexually active.

"Do you know what time your mama was wanting us all over for brunch next weekend?" Julia asked.

I glanced toward Faith, who had that pinched worry stamped across her face. It was pity for my sick mother, who couldn't host a brunch even if she wanted to. It would be Faith over at my house putting it all together, my little sister helping her, and me standing there being told what to do.

But Julia would give me another one of those tight-lipped, fuck-you-and-your-poor-life smiles if I told her any of that. *No thank you.*

"I'm not sure." I cleared my throat. "But I can get you the details later this week." I ducked my head, snagging another piece of cantaloupe. I looked back up in time to see her deliver another tight smile, which spoke louder than any insult she could have given me. I sometimes wondered what it would be like to hear all the things Julia and Clark Morgan thought about me, unfiltered, with zero pleasantries. I'd have bet it would be ugly.

I used to worry if they liked me. They played the part for a while, hosting dinners and brunches between our families, but now that Faith and I were older, they weren't afraid to show their malice for me. I used to care. I didn't anymore.

We were getting out of Collierville. Two more months and we would be living in an apartment of our own, near campus, going to college, starting our lives.

So, as I left that day, I gave them a salute, because whether they wanted me or not, I was there to stay. I wasn't going anywhere.

Chapter 1
Faith
Five Years Later

THE SOFT CHIME of the doorbell echoed up through the house, drifting to where I sat perched in my closet. I stared down at the soft chaise lounge and dug my nails into the creamy fabric, releasing my hold a second later, drawn by the glint of gold on the tips of my French manicure. I was still hesitant to ruin something that cost as much as these did and looked as beautiful.

I lifted and rotated my nails, inspecting each one, stopping on the fourth finger to the left. My eyes drifted to the large, sparkling diamond nestled in the platinum band around my finger. The rock glittered under the low lights, as though soundlessly reminding me of the vow I was about to break.

The chime went off again, cascading up through the vast, empty house, pulling me from my thoughts. In a normal life, I could rush to the door and answer it, pull the thing open, and smile at whoever was on the other side. In this life, I had people to do that for me. I had an array of employees who worked for my husband, who'd taken over every ordinary thing there was about my life.

I was merely a puppet, my strings pulled taut by the man who'd vowed to love and protect me. For years I had moved and swayed, attached to those punishing cords, nearly strangled by their presence —but not anymore.

Not after last night.

Commotion from the hall and someone chiding our butler, Andrew, had me standing and watching the entryway. Harsh, shallow breaths assailed my lungs as I watched for who was about to enter my bedroom.

Inside, I knew it wasn't him. But still, fear rattled me, making me absently run my finger over my wedding ring and turn it over until the large diamond was underneath and could be used as a weapon.

"Faith?" My best friend's worried voice carried in from the hallway. I let out a relieved breath, wiping the fresh tears from my face.

"In here," I croaked, my voice straining against the pain blooming in my chest.

"There you are." Gemma's tall frame seemed to relax as her shoulders sagged. She walked in, all confidence and strength, until I emerged fully from the closet. Her steps faltered as a gasp filled her lungs. "Oh shit." She brought her hand to her mouth in shock, her blue eyes going wide.

I tried to ignore it all, focusing instead on her familiar face, her flawless ebony skin, and her tight curls that were currently being tamed by a pair of sunglasses balanced on her head.

"Thank you for coming," I muttered, feeling rooted to the floor.

Gemma moved forward, her black pencil skirt looking out of place against the white running shoes on her feet.

"What are you wearing?" I scrunched my nose in confusion. She normally had better fashion sense than I did; even on a modest budget, she always outshone nearly everyone in the room.

"You called me in the middle of my lunch break, and you know I walk the treadmill...I grabbed the first Uber I could find and came straight here," she huffed, stepping closer. She carefully took my face into her hands and let out a heavy sigh. "He's dead. I'm going to kill him. How long..." She trailed off, tracing my bruised eye carefully.

I flinched away, feeling my jaw go tight and my lip begin to tremble. I hated how my growing bruise made me look—like I was weak, a pathetic example of loyalty, someone who wasn't loved or cherished by the man who'd promised to protect her.

"A little while, but last night was..." I faltered, not able to form the words. I couldn't put into a sentence the terror I'd felt when my husband's usual slaps to my face and forceful grabs had turned into a full-on attack. He had punched me, and once I was down, the man I'd vowed to love my whole life had kicked me in the ribs, twice sending me down the stairs.

Gemma stepped back, knowing I needed space, and looked around the room. She eyed the queen-sized bed, the plain furnishings and generic drapes. Her nose wrinkled like mine had moments earlier as she asked, "Why are you in this room and not the master?"

I moved toward the closet. We had exactly two hours before Bryan was back.

"I moved out of our room a few months ago...came in here when he started coming home smelling of whiskey and women."

Gemma followed after me, bringing her hands to her slim hips. "He's been cheating?"

I shook my head, grabbing for a suitcase. "No...says they're just eye candy for the men at the meetings. They hang on the investors, making them feel special...he insists I have nothing to worry about, but...I went to lunch with Trey, my yoga instructor, and I got slapped and called a cheating whore. I wasn't loving the hypocrisy or the cheap perfume smell, so I moved in here."

Gemma nodded her head in agreement and began reaching for my clothes. "Yeah, that's bullshit. How much of this do you want to take?" She eyed the large walk-in closet that was probably bigger than her entire apartment.

"Just enough to fill these two suitcases. I want to leave the rest." I turned toward my built-in shelves with gliding drawers and the full shoe rack, the rows and rows of different pairs from all the top designers. The soft recessed lighting in the closet cast a dreamy glow over the precious high-heeled boots and strappy heels.

I went back in time for a second to who I'd been before Bryan, to my life as the poor girl who'd married a billionaire, digging in the Sunday paper for coupons, searching for any kind of discount code that could get me a new pair of shoes so I wouldn't have to keep using super glue and permanent marker on my Faded Glory finds from the local Walmart.

"Actually, let's do a separate suitcase for some of the shoes. See any you like?" I asked, looking over my shoulder at my best friend.

Her shoulders shook with laughter. "Girl, even if I could fit into your small-ass shoes, you know I'd never wear anything that came from that man."

It was meant to be funny, but I hated the honest vehemence in her comment. The memory of her begging me not to marry Bryan surfaced, making me feel sick. She'd been right, of course, and I hated that Bryan had treated her so horribly. He'd made a big point to ensure it had nothing to do with her being black, mentioning names of many of his partners and friends who were also of color.

It was her lack of social status. Her small-town roots that bloomed into her being a lawyer for the less than reputable, a lawyer working pro bono was a joke to him. I never rebutted his statements with the fact that she and I were from the same social class, the same schools, the same hometown. I always just let him say whatever he wanted because it was easier than icing my face in the middle of the night.

"Gem..." I started, tears welling in my eyes at how horrible of a friend I'd been to even agree to marry such a monster.

She walked over and pulled me into her arms. "We both know he didn't start showing his true colors until well after you married him. Don't blame yourself. I love you and I'm proud that you're leaving him. Let's get you back home." She nodded at me, firm and resolute. She wasn't just a skilled lawyer; if Bryan cared to do his homework at all, he'd know Gemma was one of the best attorneys in the state.

A fact that would soon bite him in the ass.

"Yes, home sounds good," I wistfully muttered, tugging a few shoes free and stuffing them into my Louis Vuitton luggage.

We packed everything as tightly as we could. Gemma called Andrew up and asked that he carry my bags down to my car.

I blinked back fresh tears that wanted to fall and slowly pulled my wedding ring free. The loss felt awkward and wrong, like I'd just removed a part of myself, but at the same time, it felt like breaking free by plucking the strings, breaking them one at a time.

I placed the ring on the dresser with a note, something as insignificant and thoughtless as our marriage had been.

I want a divorce.

Chapter 2
Faith

I WASN'T RUNNING.

I needed to be sure I believed that, wholeheartedly. I was many things, had room to grow and mature, but I didn't like being thought of as a coward.

I was simply going back home, returning to the only place on earth where I felt safe. Sure, the temptation to take millions in cash from my husband sat on the edge of my consciousness, but that was only because I wanted to hurt him. However, on principle, I wouldn't. Bryan had never asked for a prenup, saying it wasn't love if you needed one.

At the time, I had swooned, but now I shook my head thinking how stupid he'd been. By all rights, I should screw him over, clean him out—but I wouldn't. I planned on cutting all ties with Bryan, didn't want a penny from him.

I took out the money I'd brought with me into my marriage and that was that. I wouldn't be spending my husband's money, because I didn't want anything but a divorce from the man. So, I organized my thoughts to start thinking of job ideas as I pulled into the small town I grew up in.

Collierville, Tennessee, was a humble little lot full of character, history, and a mixture of the new and old coming together like a preschooler mixing paint—vibrant, messy, and a little chaotic.

There were things about this town that needed to be fixed, like many towns in the south, but slowly they were advancing forward—at least that was what Gemma said when she talked about living there. I had dropped Gemma at her office after promising I'd follow up with her the next day, vowing to her that I was going to be okay.

I traveled down Main Street, passing old brick buildings, some with new flare, some with old signs...all with memories of my life bundled inside.

I gripped the steering wheel a bit tighter as I passed clusters of people laughing and smiling near the entrance of city park. As happy as I was to be making my way back home, it did come with one caveat.

My first love and harshest lesson.

Jace Walker.

I had no idea if he was still around, but seeing the town we'd both grown up in, the place where we'd fallen in love had my stomach souring.

I pulled away from the main artery of the city and veered south, past a few sets of railroad tracks until I kept going toward the outskirts of town. Rich green pastureland greeted me with firmly rooted trees, lush and vibrant.

Dogwood trees shadowed the road almost completely as I pulled into my parents' driveway. My heart raced as I put my car in park and hunched over to take in the full view of my childhood home.

It was exactly the same.

Long green vines trailed down the red brick from the second-story windows, twisting and knotting along the side of the house. The varnished oak door with its bronzed knocker stood out between the two white columns on the porch.

This home had been gifted to my parents by one of my mother's relatives and while I had never heard which one, I did know that it was all very hush-hush.

They still had to pay the taxes on the land along with regular utilities and all the debt they still had, but otherwise they were mortgage-free in a home that should have never been theirs. We rightly should have been situated near Jace's family, down near the Greenhaven Trailer Park on the other side of the tracks.

Even still, it hadn't made a lick of difference in how little I'd had growing up.

My daddy was a poor man, having never gone to college and always needing to take care of his sickly sister then inheriting his daddy's debt. My mother had married him when she was seventeen years old, tucked alongside him in sickness and poverty. I never heard anything about her parents or much of her family in any regard, but I didn't have doting grandparents or rich aunts to take me shopping.

Things were tight, always tight. But they loved me enough that I never felt the absence of luxury. I never felt anything but happiness growing up here.

Excitement fluttered through me as I got out of the car and slammed the door shut. Within minutes my daddy would come running out and fold me into a hug so tight it might make me forget all the pain I'd endured the last few years. Maybe if I had returned home more frequently, they would have intervened and forced me to leave Bryan sooner. I hadn't been home in years, though, hadn't even seen my parents except through video chat.

"Faith? Is that you?" my mother called, pulling me from my thoughts. She was leaning around one of the white pillars on the porch, wearing a pair of soft blue pants and a loose white dress shirt.

"Hey, Mama," I yelled over my shoulder, grabbing my luggage and tugging it free.

My mother's eyes raked over me, inquisitive as always. I inwardly cringed. I looked like a billionaire's wife: expensive clothes, expensive car, expensive skin, nails, and hair. On instinct, I smoothed out my slacks and straightened my dress shirt as I closed the gap between us. I knew I didn't need to apologize for being rich, but it was a hard habit to break.

"Sugar, to what..." She trailed off as my father came barreling through the door after her.

"Pumpkin!" he exclaimed excitedly.

His salt and pepper hair was more salt these days, his horn-rimmed glasses made him look like he'd stepped right out of the 1950s, and his dark slacks and collared shirt complete with a necktie implied that he was working somewhere fancier than the insurance office. I smiled, pushing toward them, their smiles nearly a mile wide as I closed the space.

Just as I was nearly to the front steps, I pushed my sunglasses up into my hair. As soon as I did, they both froze in place, gaping at me like Gemma had.

"What...who did this?" my father asked harshly, like the air had suddenly left his lungs.

I wavered, having forgotten about my eye and the bruise that was likely blooming into something vicious and horrible.

"Oh...I-I..." I stammered, suddenly embarrassed. Thankfully I was close enough that they both just gently grabbed me and tugged me close. Tears gathered and begged to be shed, but I wanted to be indoors, away from prying eyes and listening ears. My parents lived on a secluded road, but just fifty feet from it was another private drive, and I had no idea who lived there nowadays.

"I'll tell you both inside." I kissed their cheeks and dragged my suitcase behind me, my father quickly taking over.

I walked through the living room and carefully touched photos and trinkets from my childhood, things that made me feel safe. My parents hadn't done much with the inside of the house since I was last home.

I smiled at how the thin reclining chairs faced the modest flat-screen, the same white afghan blanket tossed over the two-seater couch. The same blue and white braided rug lay in the middle of the floor, and my parents' Basset Hound, Trudy, was curled up on it. She was half deaf and never got up to see what the commotion was. I liked that about her; she was always calm and relaxed.

I heard murmuring near the front door and knew my father was asking for answers he assumed my mother had. I scanned a few more pictures and smiled as I saw the ones from my high school years. I grasped my prom picture where I sported sleek bangs pinned to the side with a hair clip, like Gwen Stefani.

I loved Gwen and had gone through a phase of wanting to be exactly like her. Bright red lipstick, dark eyeliner, pinned bangs, tiny shirts that showed my midriff and baggy pants—yeah, it was definitely a phase. It wasn't even in my era, so to speak—she was more 90s grunge while I graduated in 2014—but I didn't care.

My eyes skipped over to the handsome boy standing next to me, and it felt like a fifty-ton weight had been dropped inside my stomach.

Jace.

"Faith, honey, you need to tell us what in the world is goin' on." My father's stern voice pulled me from my thoughts, prompting me to turn around. His six feet, four inches made him seem intimidating, but I knew better. He was a total teddy bear, but still...I didn't feel ready to give voice to my situation. Explaining this to my parents was vastly different than telling Gemma.

"I think I need a drink for this conversation." I escaped, walking past him.

"Of course, get comfortable." He moved aside and started going upstairs with my things.

My parents' kitchen was the same as I remembered it: chipped paint along the cupboards and some of the drawers, thick subway tile along the counters, the same old toaster resting in the corner, and my mother's mint green mixer next to it.

Everything screamed 1975, and the nostalgia made me want to curl up in the corner with a blanket and never leave. I reached above the counter and grabbed for a glass before going toward the older fridge and pulling out a pitcher of tea.

I rejoined my mother and father, who were both seated in their recliners, pensive as they waited to hear the story of why their daughter had turned up broken and bruised.

I cleared my throat as I sank into the love seat. "I'm here because I left Bryan. I'm here to start over."

My father's face fell, his lips turning into a frown as he examined the rug at his feet. My mother stood and crowded me on the couch. She didn't hug me, just sat there. It was her own way of showing support...cold and firm as always.

"Did he do this? What happened?" my father asked carefully, like he knew how fragile I was, knew one wrong question would shatter me entirely.

"It's a long story, made up of several moments leading to one tragic ending, but Bryan hit me last night. He's been hitting me, but last night he put me in the hospital." I lifted my shirt, showing my sore, wrapped ribs.

My mother let out a small gasp while tracing the bandages with her fingers. I wanted to curl into her chest and cry. I wanted her to tell me what to do, but that wasn't her. Over the years, without June, it had been Gemma I'd consulted when I needed a shoulder to cry on. It was Gemma who had been thrust beyond her role as my best friend and unfairly cast as my maternal crutch.

I flicked my gaze to my father, hoping for a warmer reaction, but with his eyebrows drawn in tight, his lips pursed, and his fists clenched, he just looked confused.

"But he loves you." My father looked up, his eyes asking for more than I was giving him.

Pain pricked my heart.

"I don't really know what to say to that, Daddy. I think he did at one point," I admitted softly, sipping my tea.

His focus jumped back to me. "Have you two tried to work it out with a therapist?"

"Clark, he hit her," my mother chided. That prickly feeling was back; she didn't sound outraged that he'd asked, just inconvenienced.

My father's face went from pasty white to a marred, patchy red.

"I'm just saying...marriage is a big thing to just throw away. Everyone goes through hard times. I'm just wondering..." He trailed off, likely reading my hurt expression.

This wasn't exactly what I'd expected when I pictured coming home. I hadn't thought it would feel this...unfamiliar. Although, maybe deep down that was why I had stayed away...because all my life, there had been parts of my childhood that *were* unfamiliar.

"Well, we're here for you, Pumpkin. Whatever you need." My father dodged my glare and stood. I stood too, pushing away my concerns and desperately needing his hug. His arms banded around me tightly as he tucked me under his chin. My ribs ached with the movement, but I ignored it, because I didn't want to focus on the pain or the weakness it exposed.

"Come, let's get you settled." My mother grabbed my hand and led me upstairs to my childhood bedroom.

The dark sky above flashed with lightning. I leaned against the tower railing, watching as the storm unfolded, as I waited for him.

The second his feet touched the platform, I expected to be wrapped in his arms like usual, but this time it was different. Everything was different.

"Faith...look." His tone dipped in a dreaded sort of way...a way that made me feel like I had fallen down the big metal slide backward during the hottest day of the summer.

I faltered back a step, not recognizing the hard finality in his gaze.

"No." I shook my head back and forth, feeling something dislodge mentally as I considered the possibility of Jace leaving me.

It would never happen.

I grabbed my locket, to remind myself of his promise. This was something else. It had to be.

"What's going on?" I dared to whisper.

"I can't do this right now." Jace's voice sounded like gravel dropped to the bottom of a chasm.

"We made plans," I muttered, staring off into the distance, still holding my locket. He'd promised me a future.

"Plans change." He lifted a shoulder, like I was an unloaded burden, a sack of grain tossed to the side, out of the way.

"Why?" I rasped.

"We're so young, Faith. We have our entire lives ahead of us. My mom's sick, and I have too much going on right now. I just need some time," he argued, pointing at his chest, as though I was being doe-eyed and ridiculous.

"If you need to put off college, let's put it off. I'll stay here with you. I'll help with your mom's medicine. I can help." I sobbed, sounding pathetic, desperate. I was begging and I hated myself for it.

"No, it's over. We're done," he said with a firm tick to his jaw. Then he pushed me.

I woke with a start, gasping for air and fumbling with my blankets.

That dream.

That fucking dream. I hadn't had it in a few years, and now, pieces were choppy and out of place, exaggerated. In real life, there hadn't been any lighting when Jace broke up with me, nor had he pushed me off the tower.

But the dream took on new little horrors every time I had it. One time Jace was a vampire and tried to kill me; in another, he was there with his new girlfriend.

In reality, nothing that dramatic had ever happened. Jace had merely showed up in our spot and broken my heart. That was the last time I ever spoke to him. That night was our final goodbye, and I still struggled against the confusion of it all. It made no sense...

We had an apartment rented, our deposit paid...we had packed our things. Our college classes were picked. Everything was ready then, out of the blue, he just said goodbye.

I tried to go back to sleep, but being in my childhood home with all the memories hanging over my head made it nearly impossible. Kicking my legs free, I got out of bed and walked to my window. Carefully popping it open, I looked down at the white lattice and green vines that crawled along the wall.

My poor, stupid heart missed that asshole. I blinked against the darkness of the humid summer night, hoping that while I was home, I could officially and finally eliminate Jace from my memories and dreams, once and for all.

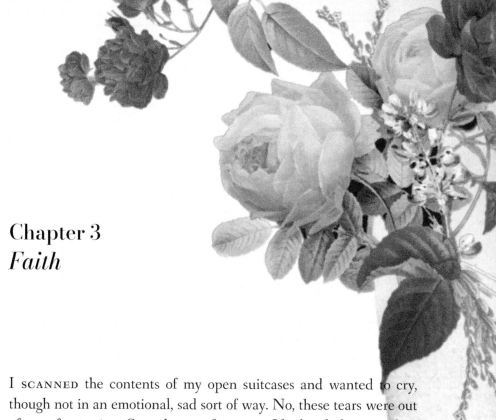

Chapter 3
Faith

I SCANNED the contents of my open suitcases and wanted to cry, though not in an emotional, sad sort of way. No, these tears were out of pure frustration. Over the past five years, I had truly lost my identity. Staring back at me was the wardrobe of a woman I didn't want to be.

She had expensive taste: high heels, dresses, high-waisted pants, silk shirts, cashmere sweaters, and pencil skirts all rolled smoothly into neat bundles. There wasn't a single pair of jeans. No ratty tennis shoes. No flip-flops, boots, or anything else I could wear on a Friday night in small-town Tennessee and stay off everyone's radar.

The urge to scream came back in full force. I needed to find a Target or Kohls...but the reminder that I was flat broke sank back in. I had $345 to my name, which I needed for gas and saving for an apartment.

Panic was pumping along with the blood going to my heart as I pictured myself standing in the backyard of Whitney Truitt's parents' house, awkwardly sipping from crystal ware while everyone congratulated her on her engagement.

My mother had given me a week to lounge around the house, watch television, and eat my weight in ice cream, but today she had wandered up to my room carrying a set of folded towels. It was her passive aggressive way of telling me she wanted me to shower and get ready for a social event.

Pushing the folded towels from my bed to the floor with my feet hadn't gone over well; it'd only urged her on in getting me out of the house. My bruise had lessened to a faint yellow over the week, now just an ugly blotch around my eye that was easily concealed with makeup.

To quote her exact words: "If you can spend an entire week re-watching that Bella and Edward, pretending they love each other, you can put some clothes on and go to a barbeque."

Naturally, I had gasped and stood immediately, insisting they weren't pretending and it was real. She'd merely rolled her eyes and left, surely thinking her mission had been accomplished.

My mother was nothing if not polite, and what we lacked in money, she made up for in her baking skills. She was polite, thoughtful, and considerate to everyone in the entire state of Tennessee—*except me.*

Because of her big fat heart, she was invited to everything—and I do mean everything. Growing up, I grew accustomed to it, but now as an adult, I had assumed I'd have a choice.

Giving up on my miniscule options for regular clothes, I pulled a black pencil skirt free and paired it with a tight red tank top. I piled what I could of my hair up into a ballerina bun, spraying the little strands that wanted to fall and pinning them with bobby pins. I put on makeup and applied dark eyeliner and red lipstick, just like Gwen. In fact, this entire look was something I'd seen her wear on *The Voice.*

I loved that woman.

I grabbed my clutch and headed downstairs, ready to join my mother for an evening with her friends. It oddly felt like I was still seventeen, not having a choice one way or another if I was dragged somewhere to socialize. I could have just said I was going out with Gemma—I needed to go see her anyway—but I loved my mother and, for whatever reason, she wanted me to go, so the least I could do was honor that.

I wished so badly I could just be honest with her and tell her how insensitive it was to force me to go to an engagement party for someone I hadn't kept in touch with, and all while I was going through a divorce. Always the perfect hostess, those kinds of socially awkward encounters didn't register with my mother.

"Okay, I'm ready to go." I huffed, looking down at my ballerina flats. I didn't need to be piercing holes in the Truitt's grass or rolling an ankle tonight.

"You forget your sweater, sweetheart?" my mother asked, pulling her own cardigan around her shoulders. My father was in the living room watching preseason football; he never had to go to these things, and I always envied him for it.

"Mama, the humidity alone will be a killer, and with all those tiki torches Beverley Truitt likes to use, there is no way I'm wearing a sweater if I have to go to this." I sauntered down a few more steps and joined my mother at the door.

She pursed her lips, eyes roaming over my chest and the small locket resting there.

"You still have that?" She raised a perfectly shaped eyebrow.

I lowered my head, cradling the object. "Of course I do..."

"I just figured you would have gotten rid of it." She gently inspected the silver pendant, speaking in a hushed tone.

"Couldn't," I whispered, watching her dainty nails hold on to something that felt like it was now a part of me.

Her blue eyes snapped up to mine, and in a quick movement she released the necklace.

"At some point you've got to *want* to protect that heart of yours," she scolded, turning back toward the front door. Sharp pain shot through my stomach as I processed her words.

It felt like she'd dismissed me, painted me with ugly, broad strokes in the ugliest color. She didn't know me, not really. She didn't know who I had become.

But it made sense. Familiar anger pulsed under my skin as I considered my past. I knew she loved me, and at times, we laughed, shopped, and joked like a healthy mother and daughter...but then, when it mattered, she'd leave me to suffer.

"We're off, Clark. Dinner is in the oven," my mother called out softly, pulling open the front door. "Honey, let's take your car." She carefully maneuvered over the gravel to my BMW.

I let out a pained sigh and followed after her. We drove toward Widow's Peak Drive, the wealthiest part of town. My parents were not wealthy by any means, but my goodness, they knew how to put on appearances and befriend the right kind of acquaintances.

"Right here." My mother indicated with her finger, directing me to the left.

I pulled over, parallel to the curb, behind a large, white truck. It was lifted with black-rimmed tires and so much chrome it made my eyes hurt.

"Are there supposed to be a lot of people at this thing?" I asked, eyeing the dozen or so cars parked along the curb, blocking the Truitt's mailbox and squeezed into their massive driveway.

"Spose so. You know Whitney has grown up here, just like you." My mother pulled down the mirror, patted her hair, and reapplied her lipstick.

"Yeah, but I didn't have the entire city of Collierville at my engagement party," I muttered thoughtlessly as I watched Shelly Breeman walk toward the back yard, grasping a clear casserole dish.

My mother froze for a moment then slowly turned toward me. "Honey, no one has forgotten that you didn't invite a single soul from Collierville to your party. Trust me."

Ouch.

Pushing past the pain of yet another zinger from my mother, I opened my door, waiting for her to join me. The heat was already swallowing me, trying to drown me in humidity. My mother took her time, grabbing the dish she'd prepared, because no one dared to cater a meal here. It would insult the fine people of Collierville if they didn't have the opportunity to show off their best and most secret recipes, allowing them bragging rights. Finally, once she slammed the back door, we moved toward the back with the small flow of bodies.

Familiar faces were everywhere, people I'd known my entire life but hadn't seen in person or talked to in five years. While they were all having babies and sharing their lives on social media, I was traveling the world, hanging off the arm of my husband, who was investing, signing checks in underdeveloped countries, and creating platforms for his technology to make him even more money than it already was.

When I married Nashville's wealthiest, most eligible bachelor, I became an instant celebrity. The king had married a pauper, and the people loved it. It boosted his image, made him seem the soft and thoughtful humanitarian. We even had a brief reality show chronicling our everyday life. We only signed on for one season, and everything was staged. It was all a lie. That's not to say Bryan didn't have his good moments, because he did, but he wasn't the man everyone saw.

I continued behind my mother as a few people looked toward us and stopped talking. Their whispered gossip couldn't be contained behind their dainty hands.

I was suddenly in desperate need of alcohol. "Mama, I'm going to find something to drink." I squeezed her shoulder, knowing she'd be perfectly fine with driving us home if needed, although we wouldn't be getting out of there any time soon.

I wove in and out of bunched groups of people gathered in small circles, laughing and joking. I avoided lit tiki torches and clung to the edges of the massive yard that was manicured with gorgeous stonework and perfectly measured mulch, until I reached the makeshift bar near the sliding doors leading into the house.

The elderly bartender offered me the specialty drink—a Whit-Whiskey Sour, created for the bride—or champagne. I accepted both.

Speaking of the bride, I finally caught sight of Whitney Truitt near the middle cluster, her left hand out, permanently holding the ring on display for all to see. Her dark hair was down in long strands nearly to her hips, her pale face was still void of any color all these years later, and her red-lined lips—which could put mine to shame— were turned down in an angry scowl.

Whitney had never liked me while we were growing up. She was always meaner than a honey badger with an ugly tongue toward anything I ever said in class. She also had the biggest crush on Jace in high school.

Her being the head cheerleader, she assumed it was her right somehow to have him. I suddenly wondered who on earth she was marrying. If it was Jace, I'd be taking a tiki torch to something, and my mother would be in serious trouble.

I hugged my champagne flute, ensuring it was ready, and sipped my Whit-Whiskey Sour until it was drained entirely. The bride-to-be cut away from the small throng of people and made her way toward me.

Shit.

She did not look like she wanted me here. I briskly wondered how horrible it would be to tell her I shared her obvious sentiment. I started in on the champagne, letting the bubbly goodness tickle my nose with a sudden swig, but it still wasn't enough of a drink to drown my awareness of how awkward this encounter was bound to be— especially because I'd shoved an entire carton of Oreos down my throat before leaving tonight.

"Faith Morgan, as I live and breathe," Whitney said, tone overly sweet, being disgustingly nice.

"Whitney." I lifted my nearly empty glass. "Nice party. Congratulations on your engagement." I smiled, trying to match her fictitious kindness.

"Thank you. Goodness, you're about the last person I expected to see here, but no matter, I'm just so glad your mama was able to drag you along." She leaned forward with another friendly smile and gently swatted my arm with her fan.

Southern compassion at its best. Most people in the south rarely knew they were being insulted, as people in the Bible Belt had perfected the art of backhanded compliments.

"I was so glad to have been home in order to tag along." My smile was so wide and ridiculous, I felt like the Joker.

Whitney looked behind her briefly, toward my mother, and that was when I noticed a small group starting to gather around us.

"Speaking of, I better get along to the other guests." She nearly walked away, and I virtually sighed in relief, but then she turned briskly on her heel and asked, "Sorry, forgive me for not keeping up, but whatever happened to you after high school? You up and disappeared. Bobby and I are designing a house and, well...I was wondering if you still did those drawings?"

Surprised by her seemingly genuine question, I was about to answer when a thick, Southern drawl cut through our conversation.

"Didn't you hear? Faith here went and found herself a billionaire...married the richest man in Nashville and sold the fuck out."

That voice...

I tried to ignore the chills that had erupted along my skin at hearing him speak, instead focusing on the mild laughter from around our makeshift circle following his comment.

I turned my head, not at all prepared to take in the mussed dark hair and the piercing blue eyes set under dark brows, all framed nicely by a deliciously firm jaw. Strong shoulders filled out a white t-shirt that looked crisp and clean.

He'd grown up. Tall and brooding, handsome and... *Holy shit, is my mouth open? Stop it. Do not ogle him. He threw you away.*

The smell of motor oil, spicy cologne, and freshly cut grass drifted over me as he drew closer. My mouth watered, but I pushed the urge back. His scent had changed. *He* had changed.

Whitney didn't respond to Jace's comment, thankfully. I blinked and realized we had a full-on crowd gathering around us now, mostly people we'd gone to high school with—mostly people who hadn't cared for me.

Two of them snapped pictures of me. *Shit.*

With him standing right next to me in the circle, Jace's masculine scent overwhelmed me, like tiny talons gripping at my memories, mocking me.

"Jace, nice to see you," I muttered, trying to be polite and start things out on the right foot. I internally begged the alcohol to hit my system, but I knew it wasn't going to happen; there were too many cookies in there. *Dammit.*

"Wish I could say the same," he joked.

A chorus of laughter broke out at his jab. I hated that we had an audience for our first time seeing each other again. I hated that he was being such a jerk, but I hated even more that I was even more attracted to him than I ever had been five years earlier.

Two more phones popped up. One girl turned so she was in the shot for whatever selfie she was taking. Her name was Kelley...something. She used to cheat off my chemistry homework.

My focus was drawn back to the man next to me. Words caught in my throat as I watched him drag a gorgeous blonde under his arm and whisper something into her ear. She laughed and wrapped her arm around his waist just as Jace's gaze lifted and fixed on my throat.

Those dark eyes narrowed into slits as he inspected my necklace while he moved his hand up under the hem of the girl's shirt. Watching the curl of his lip and the possessive way he held her next to him did something to my insides. It felt like I had caught fire, the inferno starting in my chest, making its way up my neck.

Snap—the sound of someone's phone camera sounded near my left.

I needed to get out of there.

"Well, it was nice seein' y'all," I softly mumbled, nearly positive no one heard me or cared. I stepped back, Whitney was laughing with a friend, and Jace returned his nose to the hair of the girl next to him.

The fire inside me moved, swarming my gut and flowing down my arms. I was numb, shaking all over, and entirely not ready to be around anyone.

Turning on my heel, I veered away from the group. Horrified and embarrassed, I searched for my mother. Finally finding her near the Landry family, I gently grabbed her elbow.

"Mama, Gemma called me and has an emergency—I need to go." That was a lie, of course. Why couldn't I just admit I wasn't doing well? Why couldn't I just explain to my mother that anxiety was brewing inside me, threatening to take control of my breathing and sensory functions?

"Okay sweetie, I'll grab a ride with Judy." She smiled and returned to her friends, not worried in the least bit that I was about to have a breakdown. She'd never know anyway, and I wondered if one day I would be the kind of mom who noticed that about my daughter. I hoped so.

Instead of weaving in and out of groups, I eyed the waitstaff's entrance off to the side of the house and minced along the wall, avoiding Jace, Whitney, and everyone else.

Once I neared my car, I slowed, willing my heart to do the same.

"You running away...again?" Jace muttered, moving past me toward the white truck parked in front of my car.

What kind of shit luck do I have?

He turned, waiting for my answer and squinting at the low-hanging sun that was cutting through the tree line.

I placed my hand on the door handle as panic splintered inside my chest. I wasn't ready to see him without a group around us. I wasn't ready to talk to him by myself, and I certainly wasn't ready to fight with him.

"No, I've got somewhere to be," I lied. Five years he'd had to eradicate me from his system—why was he back here, talking to me? Why was I on his radar at all?

He shook his head back and forth, letting out a heavy sigh, then pushed away from his truck. I gripped my keys, steadying myself for feeling the weight of his gaze. There was something so deliriously beautiful about being seen by Jace Walker.

He stepped into my space and ducked his head, making the

longer strands of his hair fall across his tanned forehead. I held my breath and pinned my back against the door as he gently reached toward my chest.

A thrill of memories rushed through me as I remembered him. Back when he was a tall fourteen-year-old with a backpack slung off his shoulder, smoldering at me from across the lunchroom. That time he had a gash above his brow when he was sixteen, bleeding all over his uniform during homecoming. That night he'd run across the field and kissed me in front of the entire town.

An arctic storm brewed in those eyes as he narrowed his focus on the silver pendant resting against my chest, dipping low enough to kiss the crease of my cleavage.

His warm fingers brushed against my skin as he gripped the locket. "Why are you wearin' this?" His tone was a sharp edge that caught on my poor tattered heart.

My chest heaved up and down in an unnatural rhythm.

He was too close. Everything was happening too fast.

"It's m-mine," I stuttered, trying to keep my voice from cracking. I had so much to say to him, so many questions I'd buried, so many hurts and betrayals I wanted justice for. "Besides, I don't see how what I wear is any of your concern," I sternly added, straightening my spine.

His fingers lingered on the silver pendant as his gaze transformed into something deadly. It was a look I'd only ever seen him use on his enemies, people who'd been rude to his family or spoken ill of his mama. Now he was using it on me.

"It *is* my concern when the polite thing would have been to return this when you took off. It isn't *yours*," he angrily emphasized with a cutting tone before tugging on the chain, snapping it from my neck. It didn't hurt with how swiftly he'd pulled, but it still stung my pride and the damn pit of emotions still dedicated to him, the small reserve of dreams I'd once harbored with this boy.

An astonished sound left my lungs as he turned on his heel and headed for his truck. I didn't even have time to defend myself or fight him on the fact that he had just ripped my necklace from my throat.

"Just because you're back doesn't mean people around here are going to treat you like the princess you've become. No one here much likes the rich or famous." He winked at me, climbed into his truck, and started the engine, revving it until a plume of black smoke was pummeling me in the face.

I clenched my fists in anger as I pulled my car door open with as much force as I could. Fuming and embarrassed, I held my tears in until I'd passed the party, snaked a left then a right, and hopped onto the highway. Then and only then did I let the pain battering me in the chest take hold.

"Gemma!" My fists pounded against the thin apartment door as my voice carried through the dimly lit hall. There were four doors to my right and three more behind me—if my best friend didn't open her door soon, I was going to get stabbed or yelled at. She knew how much I hated getting yelled at.

"Gemma, please open up!" I frantically cried, slapping her door as hard as possible. Maybe there was a weak pressure point some-where on the door and it would open on its own? Encouraged by that thought, I started slapping the door in various places then it flew open, and my best friend stared back at me with narrowed eyes, a tight jaw, and a look that should have killed me on the spot.

"Gem, thanks babe. Geez, took you long enough," I slurred and sauntered past her, plopping down on her two-seater couch.

"The hell are you knocking for, and why are you here at two in the morning, Faith?" My best friend crossed her arms with a deadly glare, as though she wasn't supposed to meet me earlier.

I scoffed at her theatrics. "You mean, what were you *not* doing with me five hours ago?" I counted on my fingers to see if my math was right.

She shook her head in annoyance. "It was longer than that... stop it."

"You were supposed to go out with me, so don't get mad at me for knocking." I grabbed for her remote.

"I'm mad that you knocked because you have a key. You could have just quietly let yourself in without waking up all my neighbors, or me, for that matter. I have court first thing in the morning, which is why I *told* you I couldn't go out tonight." She ripped the remote out of my hand and sauntered toward her kitchen. Grabbing a glass from the cupboard, she filled it with water from her filter and walked it back to me. "Here, drink. You're drunk as a skunk."

"Which is why I couldn't find my key...or count...thank you." I accepted the glass and sipped it, feeling my stomach tilt. "Gem, I'm sorry." I handed her the water and placed a pillow over my face.

She huffed from somewhere to my right. Since she was listening, I decided to open my heart to her and spill the entire night.

"I saw Jace." I peeked out from behind my pillow to see her sleek, dark legs carry her to my side as quick as lightning. She adjusted the silk wrap on her head and settled in for story time. I'd known that was all it would take.

Gemma and I had been best friends since the third grade, when she had just moved to the area and some Confederate ass-wipe child called her the N word. Shocked that none of the other kids seemed bothered by the situation, I walked up and threw a handful of wood chips in his eyes then pushed him to the ground. After that I grabbed Gem's hand and helped wipe her tears under the metal slide.

Our town was small and old, which unfortunately meant it had racists still lurking around. Heck, our town park was in the shape of the Confederate flag. Down here, history was history, regardless of how painful a reminder it was.

I was stuck to her like glue after that, for fear that something might happen. I knew I'd never feel the true pain of walking in her shoes, never feel the words hit my soul like they did hers, but I tried my best to be a shield, a safe harbor for when life rained and stormed on her.

She grew up learning to fight every kind of fighting style possible, because not only was she black, she was drop-dead gorgeous, Tyra Banks style with soft blue eyes and tight black curls that cascaded down her back. She drew attention and, in the south, with narrow-minded people, that wasn't always a good thing.

"What happened? Did he grab you by the arms and kiss you senseless?" she asked dramatically.

She was also a total hopeless romantic.

I half-choked on my tongue as I tried to replay what happened. Her blue eyes widened and softened, then turned hard.

"Aww honey, I'm sorry." She winced at my embarrassing replay. I had always imagined what it would be like to see Jace Walker again, and hiding a black eye I'd gotten from my husband and operating on a steady diet of Oreos wasn't the way I'd thought it would go down.

I toyed with the small pillow in my lap and nodded, still way too drunk to even process what was happening. After the Jace incident, I'd driven to a bar near the edge of town, hoping my best friend would go out with me. When she declined, I let a few men buy me drinks, let their tousled blond hair and strong jaws woo me into dancing.

Somewhere in my drunken haze, I thought I saw Jace standing against the back wall watching me. I was certain that hadn't actually happened, though, because he hated me and was probably happily married to that stupid girl from the barbeque with thirteen kids by now.

The ire in his tone when he'd tugged the locket from my neck had me thinking about why on earth he'd even care that I left back then. Maybe it was just that the locket was Corvin's and it upset him that I hadn't returned it so he could give it to my replacement; maybe he was just a selfish jerk. He had dumped me without explanation, had broken my heart into a billion pieces, and now he was acting like that entire thing was my fault. *Asshole.*

51

"How dare he," Gemma fumed, bringing me back to the moment.

I waved my hand. "I just need water and sleep, and a divorce."

I laid my head down on the armrest of her couch and burped. *Gross.* I needed a dunk tank to wash this alcohol and men's cologne off me.

"Has Bryan reached out yet?" She sat in front of me and pushed my unpinned hair aside. I didn't look like Gwen right now. I looked like a drowned cat, begging for scraps.

"He's called me about fifty times and texted about as much too." I dug for my phone in my clutch and handed it to her.

She tapped in the password she'd initially set up for me and started reading my texts out loud.

"Call me. This isn't over. Do you have any idea who I am...what you've just done? Baby, please. Is this about the woman at the hotel?" Her eyes snapped up to mine. "There was a woman at a hotel?" Her voice rose, and I wished I were sober so I could revel in that news too.

"Apparently so..." I mused, not even sure how to feel about the bomb he'd dropped.

"Please tell me you're ready to take this son of a bitch down," Gemma pleaded.

I gave her a blank look. "I don't want anything from him. Ever."

She let out a heavy sigh. "Doesn't mean you can't make him pay for putting you in the fucking hospital."

Gemma stood, ending our conversation, and walked toward the closet, where she pulled my favorite blanket out.

"You wanna come snuggle in my room with me?" she offered lightly. I knew she didn't like to share her bed, which was why she never ever had a man in it. I reached forward, grabbed the blanket, and smiled.

"No, this is perfect. Love you, see you in the morning."

She patted my head like I was a little kid and turned out the light.

Chapter 4
Jace

"It's not the drive shaft, Harold," I curtly explained while sliding back under his old Chevy.

Harold, an older man and frequent *almost* client of mine, huffed in disbelief like he always did. Thankful he couldn't see me, I rolled my eyes. The old man never took my advice, and after I worked on his truck, giving him a diagnostic, he would scoff, act like a child, and tell me he was going to get another opinion.

He never left me alone while I operated, and if I'd had an assistant who actually *worked*, I wouldn't have had this problem, but Jessie didn't. She talked and joked and said she was occupied with "bringing in new clients", which was bullshit.

My little sister was a flirt. She was barely twenty and acted like she belonged in Florida on spring break. I wanted to fire her ass, but my dad had begged me to give her the job and begged me to keep her on. Our family had dealt with enough hard hits to last a lifetime, so I just put up with it.

"Look, old man, you can take my advice and actually pay me to fix it, or you can hit the road. I have other customers to help."

Harold made some sound from his throat; I was thankful I

couldn't see his bushy eyebrows pull together and that same old look of frustration tug on that maw of his.

"Alright, fine. Go ahead and get it worked in then." He huffed and walked toward the office. I rolled out long enough to see my sister manning the counter. *Thank fuck.*

"Jessie, get Harold set up on paperwork for his truck please!" I yelled through the open fiberglass window. She looked over and nodded then proceeded to grab a clipboard and a few papers. Harold walked back through the door to the office just as my cell phone rang.

I jumped up from the creeper roller and snagged the phone from the counter. "Walker Auto Body and Towing." I grabbed a grease rag and began wiping all the muck from my hands, pinning the phone to my shoulder.

"Hey, this is Ezra from Reggie's Bar. You gave me your card for whatever cars were left overnight."

I perked up. "Yeah, that's right. Gotta car that needs towed?"

"Sure do, nice little silver BMW. Glad she got home safe, but it's almost noon and she still hasn't come to get it." Ezra's voice echoed through the phone like he was on speaker.

I'd have bet my left arm that silver convertible was Faith's, and I was about to swoop in and tow it.

I turned my wrist to check the time. "Give me twenty minutes."

It wasn't that I had a vendetta against Faith; it was just that I hadn't been expecting to see her show back up in the same shitty town she'd left five years ago. Visit her parents? Sure, but attend an actual function as small and unfashionable as the Truitts' barbeque? Not even close.

It's not like I'd had any time to prepare for her to show up again. No one had sent a town-wide email notifying everyone that Faith Vanderson, wife to the billionaire Bryan Vanderson, was back. My temper hadn't been prepared to see her face again, much less see her wearing that locket.

My locket.

It was a promise I had made to her, one she'd broken. The weight of it sat heavy in my pocket, where I'd tucked it the night before after pulling it from Faith's throat. The memory of when Corvin gave it to me had been on repeat in my head all night as I lay awake, staring at my ceiling.

Corvin was an elderly man I had met when my mother was in the hospital for treatments. Through a few turns of events, I ended up going to visit him at the retirement home he lived in. Every Tuesday and Thursday, I took a bag of pork rinds and watched rugby with the old man.

He was eighty-five, completely alone, and one of my best friends. He'd given me that locket after asking me if I was sure Faith was the one, encouraging me to give it to her as a placeholder for the engagement ring I had hoped to buy for her.

She knew the history, knew it'd belonged to a man who had been a mentor to me, someone who mattered a great deal to me. I couldn't believe she had just left without even mailing it back or giving it to her mama to pass along to me.

After ripping it from her soft throat outside the Truitts' house, I had tried to distract myself with work. But, distraction only leads to disasters in my garage, so I left and decided I'd head in the same direction I'd seen Faith going in after our little meet and greet. It might also have had to do with the fact that people were talking.

At the barbeque, more than a few people we'd gone to high school with had taken pictures of Faith and posted them on social media, even tagging me in a few of them. *Fucking idiots.* I didn't know what Faith's situation was, and I didn't really care, but it bothered me that she didn't have her security detail. Where the fuck were those guys? Where was her husband? Faith was like a lamb, prancing around in front of a pack of wolves.

They'd eat her alive.

So, I had shown up at Reggie's last night, not exactly following Faith, but keeping a close eye on where she traveled just the same. I didn't feel the least bit guilty for watching Faith flirt and drink herself stupid. I also didn't feel the least bit rueful for snapping a few pictures while she did it. I was mostly there to hand my card to the manager, because towing cars was what I did for extra cash on the side.

But the longer I stood against the back wall, the angrier I became. Something was wrong; I could feel it in my bones, partially because I knew Faith. I knew every inch of her skin, every speck of gold in her harsh blue eyes. I knew every blonde strand on her head, even if I hadn't seen her in five years.

Five frustratingly long years.

The bell on the front door caught my attention, bringing me back to Harold's truck, which I'd returned to as soon I got back from towing Faith's car. The murmurs from the front desk had me getting up and wiping my hands. I snuck a peek at the mirror above one of my rolling tool chests. Glancing from left to right to be sure no one was watching, I ran my fingers over my hair a bit to make it look a little more...something. Just...*better*.

I hated myself for caring, but I knew who was standing on the other side of that door. Unfortunately, my ex marrying someone dubbed 'Sexiest Man in Tennessee' had me a little insecure. It wasn't like I stayed current on that shit, but every so often when I went into the Quick Stop, those stupid magazines would be on display.

Bryan Vanderson was always a topic of Tennessee gossip. His abs, his money, his private jets, his orphan-saving heart—he was the state's most beloved man, and he'd married one of us, a poor girl from small-town Hicksville. Everyone fucking *loved* that.

So, it wasn't about Faith. Not really. It was more pride than anything, at least that was the mantra running on repeat in my head. But as I cleared the door, I faltered back a step.

Damn.

Time had only done her favors, even with the previous night's ensemble on. That glowing skin, those toned legs, and that smile—she was more stunning now than she'd ever been.

She flashed a quick smile at Jessie, and in turn, I scowled at her perfectly straight teeth. It'd probably cost her a pretty penny, because the girl I knew had a twisted left canine that made her smile endearing and *mine.*

I loved that little flaw of hers and that her parents couldn't afford braces. I loved that she was always confident and stunning with it. Now it was gone, and she was all refined perfection and rich. So... fucking...rich.

I pushed the door open fully and moved toward the front with somewhat of a slow swagger. I wouldn't be nice, or kind—not even decent to Faith Vanderson. She didn't deserve any of those things from me. She'd get asshole Jace, because that was all that existed anymore; she'd made sure of that when she left five years ago.

"No, I don't understand. There was no sign posted that said I had to remove it by a certain time. The only tow sign was for non-patrons, but I was there as a customer last night," Faith argued politely, probably not recognizing the raven-haired college student in front of her. Jessie was nodding her head like she understood, but I could tell by the far-off look on her face that she had no idea how to handle this.

"Jessie, you can take a break. I got this," I said, making my way toward the back of the counter and setting my eyes on Faith. Her jaw dropped slightly, and those light eyebrows shot to her forehead. I wasn't sure what I was expecting, but her doing a double take toward my sister wasn't it.

"Jessie Walker? Little Jessie...Messy Jessie?" Her voice went soft and her eyes frantically searched my sister's face for confirmation that this woman was in fact the little girl she had played dress-up with and taken to the ice cream parlor, whose hair she had braided, the child she'd played big sister to—the little girl she'd abandoned.

"Yeah...uh..." My sister faltered, looking between us.

Faith walked around the counter and pulled Jessie into a tight hug, all while Jessie looked back toward me with panic written on her face.

"It's me, Faith Morgan...don't you remember me?" Her voice came out muffled from her face being shoved into my sister's shoulder. I saw the second recognition hit Jessie as her face, which had turned toward Faith, snapped back to me in surprise.

I refrained from showing any emotion or giving my sister anything. Even though Jessie knew everything, the whole painful story, there were still days where I found her wiping tears from her face while she stared down at an old photo of her adopted older sister.

Jessie wrapped her arms around Faith, hugged her back, and started crying.

Fuck. Me.

Both women started blubbering about each other and, pulling away, Faith picked up Jessie's long black hair and gushed over it and how pretty she'd become. Jessie gushed over Faith's shorter hair (which I didn't like one bit) and how good she looked. Done with this little reunion, I stepped up and cleared my throat.

"Okay, back to business. Jessie, go take your break. Faith, if you're here to get your car, it'll be $250." I shuffled some papers in front of me and darted my eyes away from that blue gaze that was filled to the brim with judgment. Her locket burned a hole in my pocket as she narrowed those eyes on me in anger.

"No, there's no way in hell I'm paying that. You've had it for—what, an hour?" She folded her arms across her chest, which pushed her cleavage up. It seemed like she wasn't used to wearing something so low-cut, because she suddenly looked down at her chest and released her arms, a small flush creeping into her cheeks.

I laughed and leaned on the counter, toward her, invading the small space she had.

"Aren't you worth like three billion dollars? I think you can handle a little tow fee." I winked at her and gave her a seductive smile, because I hated that she'd sold out and married a rich man. I'd continued expecting a baby bump to show up in the news whenever little features were done on the power couple.

I'd continued expecting something to surface to show me why she had moved on so fast, but nothing ever did, and in every fucking clip, she was wearing that locket around her neck. Even in the special I was forced to watch of her wedding day, there dipped into the V of her dress was the silver chain that belonged to the locket I'd given her. I hadn't known what to make of it then, and seeing her at the barbeque the previous day with it still attached to her neck had caused me to feel the exact same way. *Hopeful. Confused. Angry.*

Her scoff brought me back to the moment. Faith was standing before me, turning three shades of red, fuming angry. Her crazy was about to show. I remembered Faith's crazy side—moonlit dares, her riding shotgun in my truck while we kicked up mud, skinny-dipping in the lake... I loved her daring, brazen side. Those memories surfacing made my stomach flip and my pants grow tight.

"My worth is more like three *hundred*, and this tow fee will wipe me out. Please...isn't there anything we can work out? Any kind of deal? Maybe if I pay the tow fee but not the storage fee?" Her eyes disarmed me. They belonged to the old Faith, the one who was desperate, who had to hustle her ass off to pay for art classes and supplies because her parents couldn't afford them. The one who sold everything under the fucking sun to whoever she could find just to have money for a prom dress, the one I fell madly in love with.

I cleared away those memories that got caught in my throat and turned away from her. "Can't you call your husband and have him come get it? Or wire you some money? Not sure what your deal is, but I know you can afford this, Faith." I kept my stance firm, my words crisp, driving home the point that I wasn't letting her off easy.

She bit her lip and looked around just as her eyes watered. *Fuck.*

Was she really poor? What in the hell was going on with her?

"Um...how much do you charge per day? It might take me a few days to gather up the money, but I'm sure I can get it by..."

I picked up the desk phone and started dialing what I had up on my browser page on the work computer.

Faith eyed me. "What are you doing?"

I put my finger up to indicate I needed a second.

"Yes, hello, is Bryan Vanderson available? I have his wife here and she needs—" The receiver was ripped from my fingers so fast I didn't even have time to lower my hand from my ear.

What the hell?

I stood there with my hand still in the same position by my ear and watched as her chest rose and fell as little breaths moved in and out of her mouth. She looked dazed, panicked, *cornered.*

"Dammit. I can't believe you called him." She exhaled heavily. "Shit."

I waited, unsure how to proceed. I hadn't been expecting that.

She briskly tugged at her purse. "Here, just take my fucking money."

She started rustling through her large brown purse as tears slipped down her face. She pulled a wallet free, where there were literally only two one hundred-dollar bills and a few twenties. The flap fell open, revealing a license but no other cards. I also noticed her *bare* ring finger...which shifted something in my gut, my chest, and my jeans. Like the holy trinity, Faith always affected all three.

Holy shit.

Is she single?

She threw down the two hundred dollars and began counting out the fifty. I was feeling like a dick. I felt even worse when she tried to make the last dollar with change in quarters and a few dimes.

She was broke, and I was taking whatever she had left. *Shit.*

"Happy? Now give me my fucking keys, Jace," she seethed, wiping furiously at her face. I turned, snagged her keys from the back wall, and gently handed them to her.

I wanted to say something.

I considered handing her the money back, starting all this over. I considered what a dinner date would be like, one where we sat like civilized adults and talked about what on earth was going on in our lives, because Faith had a story and I wanted to hear what in the hell it was.

But I didn't do any of those things because she was lost to me...a stranger, a means to an end, someone just passing through. Regardless of her situation, she wasn't staying here in Collierville. Best to just give her the keys and forget she was ever here.

Chapter 5
Faith

THE DISHES CLANKED TOGETHER as I added another clean plate to the drying rack. An apron was wrapped around me, rubber gloves drawn up to my forearms, and my hair was pushed back away from my face with a pink headband—exactly how I used to dress to do dishes when I was a teen. Since being home, my mother had put me to work.

So far, I had dusted, weeded flower beds, vacuumed, helped cook, and of course helped with the dishes every night. I didn't mind, the monotony of it a welcome distraction. Tonight, however, my mind was busier than normal. Jace towing my car, his anger, his eyes...those mean calculating orbs digging into me, telling me I shouldn't be back in this town. I had been here first, dammit. I wanted to say that to him, but it'd likely come out petulant and childish, things I didn't want to seem in the eyes of Jace Walker.

"Hey sweetheart, want to give those dishes a rest and come talk to me?" my dad asked over his mug of coffee. He was the male version of Lorelai Gilmore where coffee was concerned, would drink it in his sleep if he could.

"Sure, let me just dry off," I replied, pulling the gloves off and situating myself in the kitchen chair.

My father's somber eyes stayed glued to the baby blue dinner mats my mother had down at each place setting. I swallowed, toying with the napkin holder.

"I wanted to tell you how sorry I am," he started, tapping his finger on the table and watching me through his thick glasses.

My eyebrows drew together in confusion as I wondered at his guilt. "Dad, you have nothing to be sorry for. None of us knew Bryan had the abuse bone inside him."

My father's lips turned down as he ran a hand through his thin hair. Letting out a heavy sigh, he tipped his head back and muttered, "Still, shouldn't have happened to you...I just wish I could have protected you from it." The pain in his tone sliced through me, carving a path of regret through my midsection.

I moved so I was hugging him. "Thank you, Daddy. I love you so much."

He rocked us back and forth, shedding a few tears. "I'm sorry I said anything about counseling...I only said that because I know some couples who've been in your situation and saw one while they were separated. I just know if it were me, I'd do anything to keep your mother. Anything and everything."

I nodded against his chest, holding in a sob. "I know, but you can't take that on. You have nothing to be sorry for. And Bryan and I...we weren't like you and Mama. Ours wasn't that kind of desperate love you can't live without. We hadn't been close in a long while."

He hesitated for a moment, stroking my back. I looked up, trying to gauge if he wanted to say something or not. His eyebrows were drawn in, his eyes reflective and worried. I knew he wanted to say something more, but my mother came in and interrupted him.

"Faith, our show is on, honey." She grabbed the archway, eyes roaming over my father and me.

I wiped at my face and stood, kissed my father on the cheek, and followed after my mother. Design shows had always been my mother's and my favorite thing to watch together, even before Chip and Joanna Gains were a big deal. I was obsessed with interior design, and before my world had been upended, I'd had plans to study it, get a degree in it, and somehow make a life from it. The idea now sat uncomfortably in my chest. I felt like I was starting over, going back five years, to when I should have started my life; I was behind on everything.

"Stop messing with your neck," my mother chided from her small recliner, a pile of knitting sitting in her lap. We'd burned through an entire episode already, and somehow my fingers kept drifting to my throat.

I put my hand under my thigh to keep from fiddling with my naked neckline. The locket had been there every day for five years; I wasn't used to not having it. I kept tugging on phantom strings, wishing there was something to touch.

"Do you think I left any jewelry here? Any necklaces from before I married Bryan?" I looked over at my mother, who had her eyeglasses perched on her nose.

"Not sure." She reached for a deep blue color of yarn down in her basket. After a few minutes, she spoke up again. "So, Judy Masters came over this morning..."

I heaved a sigh, rubbing my temple. "What did you hear?"

Small-town gossip was more efficient than Google most days, and Collierville would put them all to shame. My mother mentioning any of her friends showing up meant they'd been here to spill secrets.

My mother thinned her lips and let out a sigh. "Well, you know my rule, sweetie."

Ah yes, the rule. "You only gossip two truffles' worth," I said, canting my head. Ever since I was little, my mother used to quote Proverbs to me and say gossip was tasty, like a chocolate truffle, and if you were going to do it, you might as well taste it so you felt the weight of your sin—literally.

"Exactly, and two truffles' worth, no matter how slow you eat it, still wasn't enough to tell me exactly why Jace Walker towed your car after bein' nasty to you last night." She was exasperated, but it seemed like it made her feel better to get it off her chest.

"He towed my car because I left it somewhere it shouldn't have been, no other reason...it was business." I flicked my hand, returning my gaze to the television.

My mother was silent, returning to her knitting. I knew her well enough to know she was feeling guilty for gossiping and hearing idle talk—and about her daughter, no less.

I decided to change the subject, hopefully making her feel better. "My neck feels empty and I can't stop reaching for my locket."

"I have a few things you can look at if you really need somethin'," she offered, adding a new column to her blanket.

More silence hung in the air. She had admitted to hearing about Jace, she knew my neck was empty, and yet she wouldn't ask about it, just like she hadn't when he dumped me. Always quiet, always silent, never speaking her mind.

I couldn't take it anymore.

"Mama, say something to me about my locket. You had opinions on it yesterday, but now you're being quiet. Just say something. I feel like I'm goin' crazy." I searched her pale face, void of any makeup. Where my father was full of emotion and vulnerable, she was stone cold.

"It isn't my place to say anything 'bout the man you love, honey. Never has been. Your heart chooses someone then fortifies the decision with walls thicker than any stone and stronger than any steel."

I rolled my eyes, feeling an immature urge to defy her. "So you'd rather me just sit alone in my misery?" I reached down to pat Trudy's head. "And what's this about love? You think I still love him?" Scoffing, I waved my hand as if to dismiss the ludicrous idea, but she only fixed me with one of her looks that was both soft and severe.

"Isn't that what love is? You carryin' another man's locket around your neck while swearing vows to a different one?" She dropped her knitting and narrowed her eyes. "You think everyone just ignored the fact that Jace gave you that as a promise and you kept on wearin' it?"

My face heated with shame. Of course, I had thought no one would notice. I'd assumed what I did and what I wore around my neck were of no consequence. Suddenly Jace's face when he pulled the necklace from my throat made a little more sense. Had he noticed I'd kept it on all this time? Had he seen any footage of my wedding?

"Do you think he knows?" I asked quietly, watching the home renovators tear out a kitchen sink.

"That you still love him? I don't think he believes enough in himself to believe you could still feel that way for him. He's...broken. He isn't the same anymore." She looked down at her hands.

"I didn't think I still did, but seein' him...it's hard," I confessed solemnly.

"We can't help who we love, baby girl. But you have a bigger problem on your hands." She pulled her glasses from her face and pushed back a few stray pieces of hair. "You need to divorce your husband. You need to find the person you were, the one you left behind when you ran off to marry him, and you need to discover who it is you want to be now. You can't jump from one moving vehicle to another."

A stray tear made its way down my face as I processed her advice. It would have been so nice to have her comfort, to have her hug me and tell me yes, you've lost yourself, but you'll find a way back.

So, I closed my eyes and imagined her arms around me tight, hugging me, like Gemma's mother always did with her. I imagined her shedding a few tears too, worried about her daughter. Then I mentally imagined putting myself back together and making a difficult phone call with my mother by my side.

It wouldn't happen, but the image I had conjured would do the trick.

I believed courage isn't something we're born with. It's something we have to dig for, and claim. So, I started my morning with a run, chasing the sunrise and digging for some courage.

I needed something to help me prepare for the phone call I was about to make. Jace had forced my hand, and my mother was right; I needed to face this.

I sat out on the back patio of my parents' house and dialed Bryan's cell.

When we were married, he never answered. Ever. He'd tell his secretary to deal with me, which was always fun because Tarryn was younger than me and acted like she was better too.

It rang a few times, and I patted Trudy's soft fur while I waited. On the fifth ring, he answered, and I paled. I wasn't ready to talk to him. Just a little over a week earlier I had been living in the same house as him, but I already felt my defenses rise just hearing his voice.

"Baby, is that you?"

"Hey..." I faltered. "It's me." I struggled with my emotions and hated that they were bleeding through my voice. At the sound of my husband using a soft tone with me, pain and misery swam through me.

I had loved him at some point, had even wondered if we'd start a family together, but over the past few months, that devotion had been replaced with derision.

"Thank God. I had no idea where you were, or if you were okay." Bryan let out a relieved sigh. I wanted to call his bluff and tell him he didn't care about my wellbeing, otherwise he wouldn't have kicked me in the stomach, sending me down the stairs the last time I pissed him off.

"I'm at my parents'." My tone came out clipped and irritated, but the more I considered what was happening, the more I realized I didn't owe him any pleasantries.

"Okay, what does that mean for us?" Bryan asked, sounding slightly panicked.

"I meant what I wrote on that note...I want a divorce."

Bryan let out a heavy sigh. "No, that isn't happening. So, take your time, go to a spa, talk to your small-town friends—do whatever the fuck you need to do, but we are not getting a divorce."

I ran my fingers along Trudy's smooth back to try to calm my heart rate. I'd known this was how it would be once I actually talked to him, but hearing his cold tone talk about us not getting a divorce provoked a sick kind of terror.

"Bryan, this isn't something I need to process. You put me in the hospital."

"Are you insane?" he yelled, and something made a hard *thwack* on his end of the call. "You tripped down the stairs and I took you in —did you forget that little bit?"

My chest was rising and falling, and I stood to try to help regulate my breathing. "I fell because your foot collided with my stomach. My ribs are still bruised, and I was approached by an advocate asking if I was safe or not and if I wanted to press charges." My voice cracked, and that was when I knew I was drowning, circling the drain just like he wanted me to. "I'm not doing this with you right now." I released a shuddered breath, bringing my fingers to my forehead to try to smooth my hair back.

"You're my wife. Mine. You'll do whatever the fuck I say you will. Now, I'm giving you a week to relax, think things over, and calm down. Then I will call you again and we will talk like the happy couple that we are."

He hung up on me, something I should have seen coming. I hated that I wasn't the one to do it. I lowered the phone and finally looked up to see my mother standing on the other side of the patio glass, watching me with a worried expression.

Come out here. Check on me. Hug me.

I internally begged her, but she turned and walked away, leaving me alone on the porch. I looked around the back yard and tried to take comfort in the vast acre of dark green that extended all the way to the tree line.

I slunk down into the patio chair and tried to remember what it was like as a child, out here with my small camping lantern, watching for lightning bugs. I used to pretend fairies lived in the woods behind my house. I used to dream about a prince coming to sweep me off my feet and show me the world. Then one day I met Jace and I started dreaming about him instead. I imagined him waiting in those woods for me, until one day he was.

I blinked to get rid of the memories and shoved myself up. This chapter of my life just needed to end already.

Chapter 6
Jace
Five Years Earlier

CORVIN NARROWED HIS EYES, watching the dark blip of color jump the counter on the security footage. He reached for his remote, hit the rewind button, and played it again. After he did this five or six times, I finally let out a heavy sigh.

"What exactly are you looking for?"

Corvin's watery blue eyes turned up, searching my face. "Reasonable doubt, I spose."

I laughed, feeling a little lighter being able to share this with someone. Corvin had become a friend to me in the strangest of ways. In my head, he was more like a priest. His small retirement room was our confession booth where I spilled all my secrets and he offered absolution in the form of wisdom.

"What am I going to do?" I leaned forward, putting my head in my hands.

Corvin brought a shaky hand to his mouth as he coughed. "Have you told anyone else?"

I shook my head. The DVD had shown up in the mail earlier that day, addressed to me. No return address, no note. Just the security footage, showing that I was identifiable in the video.

"Keep it that way. Don't bring the girl into it either, just try to sort it out before you blow everything up." Corvin patted my hand heavily.

"Faith and I...we're supposed to be leaving for Memphis at the end of the month. We're going to community college," I muttered quietly.

"Didn't realize it was already August...well then, for your sake, we might need to get ahead of this." Corvin's eyes narrowed, focusing on nothing.

I patted his spotted hand. "I'll figure it out." I tried to fight the shame settling heavy on my shoulders. As grateful as I was that I had him to bear this burden with, it didn't eliminate the sting of him finding out what I'd done.

"Sometimes life is just about lessons and how we learn them. This one I'd say you learned the hard way, but maybe the person who knows just wants you to stop." Corvin shrugged, his hunched back barely moving.

"Yeah, you're probably right." I reached for the bag of pork rinds I'd brought, trying to ease the tension out of the moment.

"Usually am," he said, sure of himself.

Present day

I sipped from my beer as I watched the sun dip into the horizon. There weren't any mountains around, but from where I was currently perched, I could see the tops of a nearby grove of trees. A wet nose nuzzled into my neck, reminding me that I needed to head back.

"Calm down, boy." I patted the head of my English Pointer and tried to shove him away. He was a rescue I'd picked up two years back. He had been discovered tied up inside a double wide, malnourished and nearly dead. Someone had posted about the dog on the news, and for whatever reason, I'd just known I needed him. He'd been my best bud ever since.

He knew it was past time for us to head back home, but I was struggling to leave. Up here I didn't have to think about the fact that Faith was in town in what seemed like a permanent capacity. But what did I know? She could have just been on some weird unplugged vacation where she tried not to spend any money. Who knew what rich people did or why they did it?

"Trevor, calm down," I muttered again as I continued to shove him out of my space. He sat back on his hind legs, staring at me...waiting. His dark grey fur looked dimmer as the sun set, and his whining finally won me over and had me standing.

"You hungry for dinner?" I rubbed his head. "That it?"

I jumped off the porch and headed down the rocky hill that would one day be a retaining wall in my backyard. Moving toward my truck, I opened the door for Trevor to jump in and looked back at my house.

It was nearly finished, a two-story, mountain-style home with nearly 2500 square feet, a massive wraparound porch, a three-car garage, and an immense stone chimney jutting from the top.

The inside was a shell. The insulation and drywall hadn't gone up yet, but the floor was down, along with all the windows and doors installed. The contractor was a good friend of mine, letting me go as slow as I needed, making payments as I could afford them.

I had a good amount saved from when Corvin passed. He'd left me everything he had, the stubborn old man. He had two kids, neither of which had ever gone to visit him, so when my friend passed away, I was notified by a lawyer that I had been named the sole heir to his life insurance claim, a few stocks and bonds, and everything in his room.

Reversing out of the lot and heading back toward town, I veered toward the local gas station.

I put on my blinker, turning into the Quick Stop, and rolled the window down for Trevor so he knew what I was doing. He was a smart dog, always needing to be included in whatever I was planning.

A part of me wondered if he was still worried I'd just up and leave him like his previous owner had.

"I'm just gettin' gas, then we'll head home and get you some dinner." I stroked his head and jumped out of the truck. Right after I set the diesel nozzle in the gas tank, I heard another car drive up. Peering my head over the side of the truck, I noticed a dark, older Range Rover.

I hadn't seen one of those make or models in quite a few years. Smirking, I thought of how Faith had once wanted that exact same car. It was her 'made-it car', the one she wanted when she became a mother to the kids we were supposed to have.

I was staring, zoning out as I walked along memory lane when someone's shriek brought me back.

I blinked and, on instinct, looked to the passenger window where Trevor was supposed to be.

"Shit." I ran around the truck, hoping he wasn't humping some-one's leg to death or, worse, trying to get into their car. He had done both—frequently.

"Trevor!" I shouted, rounding the vehicle and coming to a quick stop. Trevor was licking Faith's face, and she was on the ground, haphazardly leaned against her back tire.

"Is he yours? Can you please get him off me?" She looked up at me, nearly begging.

"Trevor, come." I bit back a laugh as I reached down to grab his collar. Trevor joined me, sitting next to me as Faith stood and started wiping her face off with the sleeve of her shirt. "Sorry, he gets excited sometimes."

"Excited...uh, yeah...I guess you could call it that," she muttered softly, still trying to clean her face.

I glanced at the car she was next to and couldn't help my curios-ity. "New ride?"

She flicked her gaze from examining her sweater back up to mine. "Yep."

We could hear the crickets chirp in the field off to the side of the station as we stood there in silence. I cleared my throat, tucking my hands into my pockets. "Hey, Faith, look...I wanted to apologize for what happened the other day—"

Her head tipped back. "It's fine." Drawing her arms in tight, she shrugged as if she didn't care. "You were just doing your job."

"Something tells me I need to be careful for a bit. I know that face—it's your revenge face."

She let her arms drop as she searched my expression, a look of surprise transforming her features. I took advantage of the moment and stepped closer.

"Let me make it up to you by taking you to dinner." My thumb grazed her elbow, rubbing a slow circle into it. Her skin was warm under my touch, sending an unexpected jolt to my system. I was assaulted by the memories of all I'd laid down, the plans I'd put on hold to appease *him*...but that didn't mean I should have been touching her.

What the hell am I doing?

Goosebumps erupted on her arm right before she let it drop.

"No. I can't. But, thanks," she curtly replied, turning to remove the nozzle and putting her gas cap back on.

I ran my hand down my face and let out an undignified scoff. I shouldn't have cared. I should have just turned, taken my dog, and walked away. But for whatever reason, her denial dug at me in a way I hadn't experienced since I first saw her on that fucking screen all those years ago, attached to that rich prick.

"So, you'll dance, drink, and kiss random strangers at a bar— while you're *married*, by the way"—I narrowed my eyes in judgment —"but you won't go to dinner with me?" I pointed at my chest, my eyebrows shooting to my forehead.

Her eyebrows jumped, matching mine. She didn't know I'd followed her. I needed to put her in her place, but she beat me to it.

"You followed me?"

"I didn't follow you—I was there to give my card to the manager in case any cars were left overnight—but someone *could* have followed you. Did you see how many people at that barbeque photographed you?"

She winced, ducking her head. I continued, hoping to make her feel the seriousness of how stupid she was being.

"Even now, you're all alone out here." I spread my arms wide. "You're in the news, on television, and whatever the fuck else all the goddamn time, and yet you think you can go on a little vacation and—what?" I gestured dramatically, looking up. "*Poof,* all your fame is instantly gone? Your stalkers and everyone looking for an easy payday just disappear? You're being an idiot, Faith, and if I were your husband..." It just slipped out. *Fuck.* It had slipped and now my face was on fire.

Her eyes turned to slits. "Well you're *not* my husband and I'm not your problem, so leave me the fuck alone. And for the record, I'm not interested in going anywhere with someone who throws away relationships and people like they're garbage." Her blonde hair shifted as she turned away from me.

I sidestepped, blocking her.

"And I'm not interested in desperate gold-digging women who cheat on their husbands. Have a nice life." I turned on my heel, taking the last word with me. I patted my leg for Trevor to follow as I finished pumping the gas, opened my door, and let him jump in.

I drove away, flooring it and leaving her in another cloud of exhaust. My heart raced, nearly ready to burst out of my chest entirely. I should have known she'd turn me down, should have seen it coming, but I'd still stupidly gone for it.

It was a mistake I wouldn't make again.

Chapter 7
Faith

"Do you even know how to drive this thing?" Gemma winced as the gears ground together. I rolled my eyes, shoving it into third and pushing down on the gas pedal.

"Of course I do. The BMW was a stick...this gear shaft is just... difficult."

"I believe you, but...ugh." The car jolted forward, forcing both of us to career against our seat belts.

"This may have been an oversight on my part." I cringed, hearing the gear grind again.

I had traded in my brand new, limited edition BMW convertible after my conversation with Bryan so I would have some extra money to live off of. It was estimated to be worth $38,000, but I only got about $28,000 for it. It was enough to buy a new car and keep some for savings.

When I'd seen the Range Rover, my teenage heart had leapt, demanding I purchase it. It was only seven thousand dollars and the dealer mentioned that a few things might need to be serviced, but I waved him off and, with hearts in my eyes, handed over my cash.

"That's it! Pull into Walker Auto Body right now," Gemma demanded from the passenger seat. I looked over, pleading with her to hang in there. I didn't want to have to take it in or accept defeat. Plus, she didn't know I had run into Jace the night before. That confusing encounter was still rattling around in my head and beating hard against my chest.

"No, um...aren't there like fifteen different auto shops in this town?" I narrowed my eyes at my windshield as if suddenly searching for said auto shops.

Gemma let out a small laugh. "There are about five, and four of them charge nearly triple what Jace charges. Besides, we try to stay loyal to the local shops that aren't corporately owned."

Of course they did.

"Well that's good for you, but I'm not giving him my business." I lifted my chin, determined to make it to the edge of town.

A loud groan emanated from the dash, making Gemma brace herself against it with a wince. "Will you at least stop in and get an estimate?"

I flicked my gaze to hers and found desperation there.

I huffed out an exasperated sigh and pulled over to the side, the car thankfully going into neutral without issue. "We'll leave it up to Google." I tugged my phone free and searched for Walker Auto Body. "If it's the nearest one, we'll go, but if there's one closer, I'm going to that one." I bit my lip and waited for the results to come up.

"You should really change your network—my results came up like three seconds ago." Gemma held her phone out toward me with a smirk on her face.

"Shut up." I grabbed the phone, scanned the red dots nearest to my location, and shuddered. "You sure this is accurate? Did you spell it right?"

"Yes, it's literally around the corner, which I could have told you if you ever listened to me. I do live here, after all." My best friend sat back and rolled her eyes.

I returned her eye roll and pushed my foot into the clutch as I shoved the gear into first. "Fine. You win. I doubt he'll help me anyway—stupid jerk hates me."

"You're exaggerating. I mean, yes, ripping the necklace off was harsh, but..."

"No, I saw him last night. He was mean. And he has a dog." I glanced over as the car jerked down the road. "Did you know he had a dog?"

Gemma braced herself with her hands on the dash in front of her. "I guess so..."

"You *guess*?" I nearly shrieked. "As my best friend, there are certain things you are obligated to tell me. Is he married? Does he have kids?"

Gemma scoffed. "Nice try, but you made me swear an oath to never tell you what was happening with Jace." Bringing her hand to her forehead with one hand and gripping the seat belt with the other, she exhaled. "Lord, you are being extra right now."

"I am not. That dog nearly killed me." I turned my nose up as we moved closer. There tucked along the right-hand side of the street was an older, single-story building with white chipped paint. Two open bay doors revealed at least three different lifted cars. Riding the roof line in red and blue lettering were the words Walker Auto.

The parking lot was mostly loose gravel and patched asphalt with faded white lines, so faint it was hard to make out the parking spaces. I pulled up in front of the door and put the car in park just as the entire vehicle jolted forward.

Gemma opened her door and jumped out. "That is a death contraption!" she yelled, heading into the shop and leaving me in the dust. I got out and blinked against the sun as I considered whether or not I wanted to go in. On the one hand, I did need a car; on the other, I could start walking everywhere. I could definitely use the exercise.

"Get in here—you need to fix this," Gemma called, hanging halfway out the door. I trailed after her, not loving the feeling that washed over me from being there the other day. I hated that Jace had this kind of power over me.

"Hey there!" Jessie greeted me as the little bell above the door jingled. The office was small, with murky glass windows covering the expanse of the front wall. The blue Formica counter stood out against the chipped tile on the floor, and messy papers and red folders littered the space where Jessie worked.

An old clock hung on the wall behind her head; it was as murky and old as the windows. The place needed a facelift, looking like it was on the brink of collapse.

"Hey, Jessie." I sauntered toward the counter, trying to sneak a peek at who might be in the garage. I wasn't ready to see Jace yet. I was positive he was going to make me feel like an idiot for purchasing the car.

"Faith, I'm so glad you're here! I have been wanting to call you." Jessie ambled around the counter and pulled me into a tight hug. I wrapped my arms around her thin shoulders, happy to be in her world again. We had been distant after Jace broke up with me. Trying to respect his wishes, I'd backed off, obliging his request for space, but it had killed me to do so.

From what I remembered, it'd killed her too. We were once inseparable. She was like my little sister, coming to me for advice about boys and clothes. Whenever I was over at the Walkers', it was always Jessie, me, and her mama, June, reading magazines, doing our nails, and gossiping about all the things my own mama wouldn't.

A splintering kind of pain opened inside of me at the thought of what might have happened to June Walker over the last five years. She had been really sick when I left, but I'd given strict orders to everyone in my life not to leak any Jace-related news to me, no matter what was going on. It was just too painful. Guess that's what happens when someone breaks your heart—they break all the sense that was once there too.

Jessie released me and searched my face before flicking her gaze to the garage entrance door. "I was wonderin' if you'd come over tomorrow? I have a date and would love it if you helped with my hair."

"Of course I will. It's been too damn long since I've done your hair." I grabbed the ends of her hair and lifted them just as Jace's voice broke into our conversation.

"What in the hell is that beast doin' here?"

Intaking a swell of breath, I turned to see him. "Hey Jace, I was wondering if you wouldn't mind looking at my car?"

I was trying to be nice. I needed to be nice.

Jace was hanging off the door frame, a black tank top plastered to his chest, showcasing all the defined muscles he'd grown into over the years. His dark hair was mussed, falling into his eyes and making him look like some model from a hot mechanic photo shoot. My eyes, of their own volition, were drinking in every inch of him. I could feel my face flush as they lowered to his waistline and lingered on his navy blue coveralls, which were turned down.

"Thought you were broke," Jace stated, as though he might be considering it.

Stepping forward with confidence, I explained, "I sold my car, which gave me some extra funds. Maybe I could just get a diagnostic, and if you don't want to fix it, I can find someplace else."

He let out a heavy sigh as he pushed through the door completely. "What's wrong with it?"

"I think it's the clutch. It's making an awful sound when I try to change gears," I answered, hopeful he'd take this on without including our personal baggage.

He let out a long sigh. "I can look at it. Leave your keys with Jessie."

I lowered my head in agreement, waiting for the other shoe to drop or, in his case, another comment to follow. We all waited in awkward silence as he shuffled a few papers.

"That all...? Or did you need somethin' else?" He looked up, indifferent, as though we were strangers.

"Jace, don't be a jerk," Jessie reprimanded quietly.

"Since when is asking our customers to leave their cars so they can be worked on considered being a jerk?" Jace lifted his hands, the sunlight from the side window catching in his hair.

"It's the way you said it, idiot," Gemma replied from one of the waiting chairs, not looking up from her magazine.

I crossed my arms, like I was trying to guard my heart. "It's fine." I turned toward my best friend. "Gem, let's just call an Uber or something and go hang at your office."

"Why can't you hang here? I'd love to catch up," Jessie argued on our behalf, hands full of folders and eyes brimming with hope. I took a second to really look at her, at the woman she was becoming. She had her mother's dark hair, just like Jace, but where his eyes were blue, hers were green, her skin fair and her features petite.

She was beautiful, and it felt like I'd just gotten to see my little sister grow up in the blink of an eye. I had no idea how high school had gone for her, or if she'd gone through her own heartbreaks. I hadn't been there for prom or homecoming; I wondered if June had been.

"No, they cannot stay here. We don't let our other customers stay here," Jace replied forcefully, grabbing for a ball cap and shoving it onto his head.

"Jessie, we'll catch up later." I grabbed her hand and squeezed.

Her lips were turned down as she watched her brother's profile. "But they aren't just customers, Jace. We grew up together. Faith and Gemma are like sisters to me...I know y'all have your differences, but there's gotta be some part of you that still cares a little bit about—"

"Jessie," he interjected harshly, "it isn't personal. It's strictly a business decision." Jace's gaze was hard as stone, warning his sister not to press it further.

"You know what? I think I'll just take my car down the street." I moved toward the door and shoved it open. I didn't care if Gemma even followed. She was a big girl, and could get home on her own. I wasn't entrusting my car to him, not when he was being such a dick. He'd probably keep it for kicks and giggles or find a thousand other problems with it and charge me everything I had left.

"You fuckin' kidding me right now?" Jace fumed from somewhere behind me.

I picked up the pace and hoped I'd somehow outpace him. Ignoring him, I pulled my car door open, and was about to hop inside when his firm hand gripped the door, stopping me.

"You honestly that sensitive? The old Faith would have fought back, given me just as good as I was giving her." Inky strands of hair stuck out from under his hat, making him seem boyish, and for whatever reason, it made my rage simmer and pop.

With narrowed eyes, I stared back at him, ignoring how sweaty he was from the Tennessee summer and how that likely meant he didn't have air conditioning in his shop. I ignored how much that bothered me and how good he smelled and how his presence felt like a soaking wet blanket, smothering me.

"You don't get to talk about the old Faith." I shoved a finger into his chest, pushing him backward. "You left her, broke her, and ruined her—you don't get an opinion on who she is now, especially after the other night at the gas station."

With the little room I had from shoving him, I turned and got into my car, pulling the door shut. He stood there with no emotion on his face, as if my words and touch were as effective as a warm breeze on an already blazing hot day. I swallowed the thick lump of frustration in my throat and started the car; thankfully, it turned over with ease.

I pushed the clutch down as far as it would go and punched the gear down into reverse. "Please don't grind. Please don't grind," I muttered uselessly to myself. Jace was still standing there with his arms crossed watching me try to pull out, but my poor, broken car wouldn't cooperate. A horrible sound emanated from below my feet. "No, no, no...please just work." I pleaded again, but it was no use. I wasn't going anywhere.

Jace stood at my hood and lifted his hand, indicating I should pop it open. Lowering my head in defeat, I killed the engine, pulled the lever to pop the hood, and got out of my car.

"Did you have this looked at before you bought it?" Jace asked while peering into the darkness of my engine. I twisted my lips to the side as I considered ignoring him, but a second later, those blue eyes slowly wandered up to mine.

"No, I just bought it because..." I trailed off, feeling more ridiculous by the moment.

"It's your dream car," he finished for me. His gaze was down on the engine, which I was thankful for, because my heart crashed inside my chest at his comment.

He remembered.

Those nights in the back of his truck half-naked, dreaming in his arms, talking about our future...about how one day when I was a mom with kids, it was an old Rover I wanted to drive around. Jace had laughed and joked about how impractical it was, but I didn't care. It was what I wanted, so he promised to make it happen. He'd give me two boys to cart around to practices and school. He'd make my dreams come true one silly hope at a time.

"Yeah, ugh...exactly," I mumbled, pulling my fingers together. The heat was swallowing us up, drowning us in stickiness. The realization that I had skipped lunch surfaced, making my stomach growl, and the reminder that he'd called me such horrible things the night prior stung. It was a horrific mess of feelings all at once, and I just wanted to hide from it all.

"Well, you're likely right about the clutch. We can start there, and I'll check everything else at no extra charge. It'll take a few days to get the parts in—this make and model are pretty hard to get." He stood back, surveying the car with a set of narrowed eyes. It was a relief that his gaze wasn't on me.

"Okay, so I need to leave it here?"

"Yeah, maybe borrow your parents' car for a bit, or if your husband has another he can send you," he added with cool indifference. A harsh retort was on my tongue, but my marriage wasn't any of his business, so I just ignored it.

"Yeah, I'll figure something out." Walking back toward the car, I pulled free my hoodie, legal papers, and a few other things I didn't want to be without for the week or two my car would be in the shop.

With my arms full, I headed back toward the entrance to talk to Gemma but paused with my hand on the door.

"Thank you for working it in, Jace. I appreciate it." I pushed out my gratitude as gracefully as one would a burp, then I moved as quick as possible to avoid any cruel remarks he might have for me. Somewhere in the back of my mind there was a small desire to pull out the comment he'd made about taking me to dinner, but it was dangerous to mull over fantastical ideas that would never and could never happen.

Now all I needed to do was get through the week and get my car back without thinking about those thoughts or interacting with Jace again.

"Dad, what on earth are you doing?" I scrunched my nose, eying my father's movements. He was in the garage, wearing his suit from work, hovering over the engine of his Lincoln.

"I just wanted to check the levels, so if you need to borrow it, it won't break down on you." He unscrewed the cap to the oil and pulled the dipstick out. My father wasn't exactly mechanically inclined, so I wondered if he even knew what to look for. I wouldn't say a word, though, because he was being sweet as pie.

"You don't have to do that, Daddy." I walked toward the hood, trying to help him.

He heaved a sigh, wiping the end of the silver stick with a thick rag. "I heard your new car is already in the shop."

I nodded silently, not wanting to drag the issue out any more than it already had been for the day. I was hot, tired, and hungry.

"Heard it's at Walker Auto..." he started, keeping his eyes on the engine. Jace was an awkward topic for us. Knowing Jace had been the source of many of my ramblings and complaints at the dinner table in middle school, it hadn't been easy for him to accept the guy as my boyfriend.

In fact, he'd spent a good six months icing Jace out, no matter how hard Jace worked to win him over. Dad didn't start warming up to him until June had a massive health crisis, requiring a week stay in the hospital.

I'll never forget the day my daddy drove us over with two huge boxes full of food for them. Dad never said why we were taking them canned goods and mac and cheese, but I had once overheard someone whisper that the Walkers were living off of grace, sweet country air, and nothing else.

Afterward, we started inviting the Walkers over for family dinner or brunch once a week, and Dad didn't mind that I hung out over there. So, when Jace dumped me not two weeks before we were supposed to leave for college, I wasn't sure how my father would react, but I assumed he was just tiptoeing around my own emotions. Both my parents knew I still loved Jace and didn't want anyone to be unkind toward him.

Gemma didn't understand that logic, but my parents supported me on it.

"Yeah, Jace agreed to look at it," I answered, toying with one of the rags on the tool table.

"That a good idea? I didn't think you two were running in the same circles anymore." He stood straight, watching me intently.

I shrugged. "It was the closest place."

He waited, watching me, looking at the engine, hesitating. He'd been doing that a lot lately.

"Just be careful. He isn't a road you want to wander down again," he warned.

I nodded, unsure why it felt so odd to agree with him. I walked over, hugged him, and left him to his tinkering.

Chapter 8
Jace

I HAD FINISHED my day with my best friend, Seth, drinking a few beers. We were at the local bar, dancing a bit with a few women, and I was essentially doing everything in my power to push out the memory of Faith being in my shop, asking for help. Sure, she was paying money for it, but she'd still come to me to fix her car.

It meant nothing, but the fact that I couldn't get my mind off the softness of her voice or how smooth her skin looked in that summer tank, how delicious the curve of her ass was in those jeans was proving to be a problem. I'd decided to move her car up to the front of my projects so I wouldn't have to deal with her any longer than necessary.

She could get her car then move on with her life or do whatever the hell it was she was here for. I still had no idea what was going on with her, but I had noticed that some of what she'd grabbed from her car were legal papers with the state seal on the front. My mind wandered over the possibility that she might be going through a divorce, or that maybe he'd died...but that couldn't be the case. In fact, neither were likely the case. Every puff piece of celebrity news and gossip portrayed the couple as happy, in love, and always together.

I kept drinking to get the different ideas of what might be happening out of my head. I had made a plan with Seth on a napkin, a plan to get her out of my mind and out of my thoughts. We were drunk as hell, but our plan consisted of fixing her car then getting a restraining order against her, so if she showed up anywhere else, all I had to do was call the local sheriff and he'd take her away. It seemed like a solid plan; all I had to do was find a way to convince the court that my heartbreak was enough evidence that she could harm me and put me in danger. Stumbling out of an Uber, barely making it into my fifth wheel was how I ended my evening.

Voices drifting through the windows woke me in the morning. I opened my eyes and blinked, trying to figure out exactly who was outside the trailer and why they were here so early. My head was pounding from my poor decision to drink myself stupid the night before.

I fumbled to the left and reached for my cell, but it tipped off the small side table.

Shit.

I lazily dove for the phone just as female laughter filtered inside.

I froze.

I knew that laugh. The last time I'd heard it, the woman who created that sound had been sidled up next to me singing at the top of her lungs to a Blake Shelton song while running her hand down my thigh. I had filed away all the minute details about Faith Morgan in my head, memorizing her. That day was supposed to be the day I proposed to her.

Her soft laugh echoed through my window again, bringing me back to staring at the faded drapes in my fifth wheel.

Why is she here?

I straightened up and tripped, hitting my head on the small overhead storage area above my bed then extracting my legs from the sheets. Trevor jolted up from his spot in the kitchen and started barking.

"Shhhh, shit, Trev. Be quiet." I brought my hand to my head, trying to rub away the ache. I walked around my bed and met Trevor, patting his fur, all while I kept trying to look through the windows that lined the kitchen.

With my eyes trained on the blurry silhouettes near the front porch of Dad's house, I flung my door open and stuck my head out.

Light assaulted me, forcing me to blink rapidly, and at my sudden appearance, the laughing and murmuring of the girls stopped.

"Uh...bro, can you put some clothes on?" Jessie seemed to choke on the words.

I looked down and realized too late that I was standing in my boxer briefs. My eyes slowly traveled back up and unfortunately clashed with Faith's sharp blue ones.

She was standing in a pair of tight jeans with a loose-fitting tank, and her short hair was braided in two symmetrical lines. Her small nose was scattered with freckles, and those eyebrows of hers, which were currently near her hairline in surprise, were shaped all feminine and pretty.

She looked like a woman. Her flowy tank somewhat hid her figure, but there was no mistaking how generous her breasts were now, and fuck me and this entire day, but it made me think of that freckle on her right tit.

"Jace!" Jessie shouted as Trevor pushed past me and ran right for Faith. She put her hands out like she could stop the assault, but we all knew that wasn't happening. He jumped on her, mauling her to the ground.

"Shit." I ran after him, pulling on his collar. Jessie was behind me with her hands over her face, covering her eyes as Faith lay on the ground, moving her face from side to side to dodge Trevor's licks.

"Dammit, Trevor, get off." I tried to assist with pulling him off her, unsure why the hell he kept attacking her.

"It's fine. Maybe he smells Trudy on me or somethin'." She propped herself up with her hands, watching as I pulled Trevor back. Her gaze wasn't on the crazy dog I was hauling; it was on my chest, or more specifically, the tattoos I'd gotten.

I hadn't had any the last time she'd seen me like this, and I wondered what she thought of them—until I realized too late that some of my tattoos were ones she'd recognize. Near my heart, scrawled in black ink were the words *Ugly truths hung around a pretty neck.*

Her eyes narrowed as she read them. Then they jumped to the scripted letters to the left of my heart. On what looked like a page from a book, *Dear Pip* was inked in black with a red line running through it.

I wanted to turn around, to end this examination and the vulnerability of the moment, but I also wanted her to see me. I wasn't ashamed that I had inked a confession on my skin, because once I'd done it, I had felt like it released something in me, freed it so there was no way I would regret it, even if it was harsh.

"Dude, I am not kidding, go put some freaking clothes on!" Jessie yelled from behind her hands, ending the moment. Faith shook her head and began wiping at her face, and I turned and pulled Trevor with me as I headed back toward my fifth wheel.

I shut the door and drew in a deep breath through my nose. I was going to need clothes, coffee, and vodka to handle this situation, because I didn't want to see Faith Vanderson—or Faith Morgan, or any other name she might go by—here at my house.

I grabbed the ends of my hair and tried to regain my composure. I snatched a pair of jeans, pulled them up, and hoped like hell when I opened the door again, the woman who'd stolen then smashed my heart to pieces would be gone.

Chapter 9
Faith

THINGS COULDN'T GET any worse. My face was prickled red from seeing Jace in a pair of boxer briefs, sans shirt. I'd married a billionaire who worked out every single day with a personal trainer, drank kale that was imported from King Trident's garden or some fancy-ass place like that, and used some moisturizer that was made from pearls found in the most remote parts of the universe—but billionaire muscle had nothing on country muscle.

Nothing at all.

Then there were those tattoos.

My body hummed with memories, like touching the button on a sleeping time machine, activated and ready to dissect every word inked onto his chest. It was a heartbreaking confession.

I'd broken his heart somehow.

He regretted me. Somehow, in my stomach, something churned, screaming that if he truly regretted me, he wouldn't have etched me onto his skin, keeping me a part of his life.

"Are you okay?" Jessie put the back of her hand to my forehead for the third time, and just like every other time, I swatted her away.

"I'm fine. Just not used to this weather—or dogs, apparently." I cleared my throat and fanned my face.

"Want some tea?" Jessie asked, perking up. Her long black hair framed her heart-shaped face perfectly, making her look grown up and not at all like the little girl I used to babysit. I had come over to help do her hair for her date and spend the day with my old friend. I hadn't thought Jace would still be living here, or rather, so near to where he used to.

The Walkers' single wide trailer sat in the same spot it always had with the white lattice covering the bottom trim and a beautiful rich blue paneling covering the outside. There was a wide, covered porch with warped, old steps leading up to the house and a small chain-link fence containing a patch of lush, green grass.

I had always loved this house. June Walker had done what she could with what she had, ensuring potted flowers littered her porch and always meticulously sweeping leaves and other debris clean from the parking space, porch, and yard.

Never in a million years would I have expected Jace to be living outside the house in a large fifth wheel, just ten feet away from his childhood home.

My mind raced, thinking over what that meant. Did it mean he didn't have a big family? No kids, no wife? At least none came out behind him when he opened the door, no wedding ring was on his finger, and no other car was parked alongside Jessie's...not even his was there.

I deflated, unsure of what that meant. Anyone could have been living in there; a woman could have been tucked away in his bed, sleeping as I sat there thinking about him. Him coming out alone didn't necessarily mean anything.

My hormones and stupid heart ignored all the discoveries. Instead they hungered for things they shouldn't hav̄ for anymore.

I followed Jessie into the house without a look fifth wheel. A hard hit of nostalgia landed square and dead center in my heart as I looked around th saw they still had that same tattered white and same blue recliner that never popped back up unless someone pushed from behind. The only change was the sixty-inch flat-screen against the far wall.

Jessie led us into the kitchen and tugged on the old fridge, its handle taped in place with black electrical tape. Five years later and it was still barely hanging on. On rusty instincts, I reached over the dishwasher and snagged two plastic cups. Just as I set them on the small island, I heard a gruff, "What in the hell do you think you're doing?"

I slowly turned around, knowing I'd see an angry expression marring Jace's handsome face, but I wasn't prepared for the red that was flushing his cheeks, betraying his embarrassment. My face turned ruddy, maybe to match his coloring; maybe I hated myself for making him feel uncomfortable.

I hated the shame that lurked behind his blue eyes, the same shame that had sat there when my father used to grill him about his future. Out of old habits that apparently hadn't died, I wanted to fold myself into his arms, soothe his worries, and promise I'd always choose him. Because I would have.

But he hadn't chosen me.

"We're getting tea," Jessie finally answered, saving me from acting like an idiot. I'd nearly forgotten what this asshole had said and done to me since I returned home.

"I can see that, but what is *she* doing in *here*?" Jace moved his arms around as though Jessie didn't know where here was.

Was I not welcome? After all these years, after all this time...

Fucking figured.

"I was just here to help Jessie, didn't mean to intrude," I softly explained with my arms raised in mock surrender. The kitchen was small with a modest-sized island in the middle, nestled into the faded linoleum at our feet. If I walked all the way around it, I'd still have to walk past Jace on the way out, unless I left through the back door. I ad done it all the time when I was younger, but now it felt too nal.

"Well, she can meet you at your house. No need for your little meetups to convene here." He flicked his hand toward me but kept his head lowered, as if hiding his face. I let out a heavy sigh and pushed forward, not caring if I bumped into him or not.

"Message received, asshole." I rammed his shoulder on my way past and kept going until I had cleared their porch steps and was almost to my parents' Lincoln.

"Faith, wait. Please." Jessie quickly ran down their rickety porch steps and hustled toward me.

I paused with my door open and watched as she got closer.

"He's been a bit of an ass for the past few years, sorry." She flushed. She wasn't justifying her brother's behavior, just telling me how it was, which was...surprising. I tried not to read too much into the 'few years' thing. For all I knew, something had happened when he dumped me, but he'd never told me.

Maybe he hadn't gotten into that college he'd applied for; maybe something had happened to his mama. My stomach twisted with discomfort at the mere idea. He'd worked so hard for her medicine, worked so hard to help her, there was no way she just...

"Jessie..." I whispered, nearly out of breath. I couldn't believe I hadn't even thought to ask yet, but now didn't feel right—not with Jace standing guard on the front steps like a gargoyle. His arms were crossed, making his biceps bulge, and the smirk that forced his lips to twist just a hair to the right made him look like he was keeping a secret.

Which of course he was. I wanted to demand answers as to what I'd done all those years ago to make him leave me, why—after everything—it was so easy for him to let me go. Instead I stepped forward, hugged Jessie, and said, "Come over to my house. I'm there all day."

I got into the car and drove away, refusing to look back, refusing to do anything but inhale short, tiny breaths. I needed answers, and I wasn't too proud to accept that the boy I'd once loved would never give them to me.

Chapter 10
Faith

THE AFTERNOON LIGHT danced along my mother's living room floor as the trees swayed in the breeze outside. I closed my eyes, soaked up the warmth of the sun, and relished not having to feel the chill from the wind. I loved these lazy summer afternoons.

"Sugar, you wanted to see me?" my mother asked, adjusting her earrings as she walked in.

"Yeah, I was wondering if you wouldn't mind gossipin' a bit with me, like we used to?" I smiled innocently.

She broke into a huge grin and ran off to the kitchen. Returning with a small box of truffles, she sat next to me and settled in.

"You have a box on hand for idle gossip?" I joked while plucking a chocolate from the box. What I meant but wouldn't say was that she had *more* on hand from gossiping about my situation the other day. A small twinge of hurt wormed through my heart thinking of my mother entertaining gossip about me. Of all the people in my life, she was the one I wanted to slam the door in people's faces, telling them I wasn't a topic of discussion—but that wasn't her.

"Honey, this is small-town Tennessee—of course I have a box on hand. Hell, it's on my grocery list every week. It's a wonder I'm not five hundred pounds yet with how often Ms. Marshall comes over."

My mother bit into her milk chocolate ball of goodness and smiled. "So, what bee has gotten into your bonnet, sweet girl?" My mother encouraged me to spill my secrets while licking her fingers.

"It's about June Walker," I explained, slightly embarrassed that I had to ask her at all.

Her blue eyes searched mine and softened. "Oh honey...I figured..." She trailed off, grabbing another truffle, a little too fast for my liking. She figured Jace had told me, or Gemma, or someone, but I had cut off all Jace-related information when I left. It was too painful. It was no secret I never gave Bryan my whole heart. I would have if I could; it just wasn't there to offer.

I had vowed to be his wife, in sickness and in health, until death do us part, which I'd meant with my whole being, like a duty...even an honor, but there wasn't any fire behind my words. I assumed Bryan never noticed, at least not enough to warrant any concern. There was no malice in the decision. I had loved Bryan, in a different kind of way.

"She passed while Jace was in jail. When he got out, he just..." My mother trailed off again, staring at the floor. Meanwhile, I felt it shifting beneath my feet.

"He was in jail? For what...how long?" I gasped. What in the hell? Jace would never break the law, ever.

A line formed between my mother's eyebrows. The way she stared down at the couch with such intensity, I wondered if she'd forgotten or was just unsure.

"Someone caught him stealing pain pills from the local pharmacy...he..." She lagged again, looking over her shoulder as if watching for someone. Sometimes she did that, as though Jesus was standing there, so I didn't pay it any mind. Suddenly she blinked and grabbed the empty truffle box. "Well, you know the rules, baby girl—that's enough of that."

I wanted more from her, needed it, but her rules about gossip were firm. Of all the times to have principles, now wasn't it. I nearly reached forward to grab her hand, but she'd already stood up and taken a few steps toward the kitchen. This conversation was over, and she wouldn't be bringing it up again.

I slumped in my chair, my eyes jumping over the webpage I had pulled up. After my conversation with my mom, I'd trudged upstairs to wallow. I'd missed too much over the past five years. My father had quit his job at the insurance firm he was at; that had been over two years earlier, and I'd never even asked where he'd been since.

My mother, I assumed, was filling the same role she always had: church receptionist, volunteer for everything that ever existed, and occasional babysitter. But that wasn't right, either, because she was leaving every morning at seven on the dot, donning blue scrubs. It was like walking through a photograph, seeing still images of a life you'd once known but couldn't touch.

Then there was Jace, and him going to jail...his mother. My fingers ached to dig for the information I didn't have, but something inside me wanted to hear everything from him. As unlikely as it was that he'd ever tell me, I still needed to hear this news from his heart.

Blinking away thoughts of him, I thought about my own journey back, and I didn't love the feeling stirred up by my examination.

I didn't like me.

I didn't like who I'd chosen to be, not five years ago and not now. Even before the abuse, I'd ignored my family, my friends, my goals and dreams, all for the sake of hanging on the arm of a man. There can be honor in laying down dreams for family, for children, and in some cases, for marriage, but that wasn't what I'd done. I ran.

I ran and kept running, and people were hurt because of it.

I shoved down the simmering shame that was begging me to just give up and hide and navigated the website in front of me. Blue and white saturated the screen, a tower of girls in cheerleading uniforms stacked on top of each other with massive smiles stretching across their faces. My heart thumped hard with anticipation.

College had always been this daunting idea that was out there, existing but not. It was as likely to happen as it was for me to get a selfie with Gwen. It *could* happen, it just probably wouldn't.

But there were online courses... I lifted an eyebrow, clicking on the blue tile for more information. This could happen. I could maybe, possibly go to college and get a degree. Dreams of applying to a few coveted interior design programs rolled around in my head as I sat there, clicking aimlessly.

I had to start somewhere, had to stop running and hiding...so I signed up for a meeting with one of the admissions counselors then shut the laptop.

Chapter 11
Jace

THE SOUND of muffled voices and laughter had me rolling out from under Faith's Rover and eyeing the office door suspiciously. I couldn't make out who was saying what, but it gave me the same vibes it had the other day when Faith was outside my house. Now, it was the middle of the week, and after seeing her nearly every day, I was hoping for a reprieve.

Monday she was at the post office. Tuesday she was grabbing water at the Quick Stop, and that one particularly sucked because she'd just finished a run and was wearing skin tight yoga pants paired with just a sports bra.

Did I mention she was glistening with sweat? I wanted to walk her back against the glass case and start things we never should have stopped. Instead, I insulted her. That seemed to be the safest thing to do when I was around her and highly aroused.

Now it was Wednesday, and I was getting tired of having to relieve myself of the stress and tension of seeing her every day in my shower every night. It would have been so much easier if she were wearing a ring, but that fourth finger had remained bare.

It didn't help matters that a few celebrity gossip networks had started running stories on their opinions regarding the tech tycoon Bryan Vanderson attending not one but two charity events alone.

It had piqued my curiosity enough to Google search everything I could on the topic, but all it led to was a bunch of images of the two of them together—holding hands, kissing, and of course, most were of their wedding. I couldn't stomach more than about ten minutes of that before I slammed my laptop shut. I just wanted her gone. I wanted the memories she'd stirred up gone. I wanted the pain and reminder of betrayal gone.

All of it—fucking gone.

I wiped my hands on an oil rag and grabbed my water, taking a big drink then splashing it over my face to get rid of the grime and sweat. The shop was mine and I was damn proud, but it was older and there were more than a few things that needed upgrading. Having air conditioning was one of them, but that would cost a pretty penny and would cut into my savings quite a bit. I made sure Jessie had a small one in the office, but otherwise I just tried to ignore the sweltering heat.

I wandered toward the office door, hearing the laughter get louder. Pushing it open, I saw Faith leaning against the counter in cutoff shorts, revealing all that tan skin and toned leg, all the way up to the curve of her ass. My dick stirred, causing me to dig out an insult to throw at her.

"Well, don't you look like a redneck's wet dream." I leaned against the door, hoping to make her as uncomfortable as she was always making me. I hated myself for still wanting her so badly.

Her face flushed crimson, but a second later she seemed to recover. "I was just coming by to check on my car and bring these over." She gestured toward a basket of muffins. They were chocolate with tiny chocolate chips, likely made with zucchini...*my favorite.*

I cleared my throat and shoved away from the door. "Too bad we can't have you bringing food like that 'round here."

"Why the hell not?" Jessie asked, twisting her face in confusion, reaching for a muffin. They probably tasted really fucking good.

"It's a policy, Jessie. We don't accept anything that's not store-bought...you know, like the schools. It's a safety measure." I headed toward the files and ignored the frown marring Faith's pretty features. There was an uncomfortable shift in my chest at seeing her react to my anger like this.

"Why do you hate me?" Faith whispered, like she'd finally hit her limit. Her chest was rising and falling with every angry harsh intake of breath. She walked toward me until her body was nearly pressed up against mine. My fingers itched to grab her hips and drag her back into my garage.

Inhaling her scent of cinnamon and sugar, I blinked, wanting to remove the memories attached to her always smelling like a freshly baked cookie. I wanted to scream at her, wanted to yell all the reasons why I hated her so much, how she'd ruined me all those years ago, then I wanted to kiss her and fuck her out of my system—but I was above that. She didn't need to know how much power she still had over me.

"Hate you? I don't hate you." I laughed, stepping closer, gazing down at her. I pulled her chin up with my finger and searched her face as I muttered, "I just don't care about you one way or the other, but more than that...I don't want anything from you. Not ever."

I let her go, laughing and stalking off toward the far wall where more client files sat. I didn't look at her expression, already knowing what I'd find there.

"Your car will be ready by Friday."

I kept my back to her until I heard the bell above the door jingle.

"You made her cry," Jessie said, crossing her arms. "Does that honestly make you feel better about all this?"

I ground my molars together and walked past her. I didn't owe her anything, and I'd have rather gone back to jail than admit that making Faith cry was like tearing a hole right through my midsection.

Tennessee Truths

Five years earlier: August

The first time I stole from the pharmacy, I was fifteen years old. My mother was coughing, vomiting, and wouldn't eat. I remembered my father talking about how there was no way we could afford her medicine. The doctor had called it into the pharmacy, but we wouldn't be picking it up.

We had sixty dollars in our bank account, and that wouldn't even cover the light bill that was due. My father was crying, sobbing like a child, while my mother coughed and coughed.

I couldn't take it anymore.

I ran out the door and hatched a shit-brained idea halfway there. A small pick of the back lock of the pharmacy door and all my problems were solved. Find the shelf that held pick-up orders, and everything would be okay.

I never took more than I needed, even though I sometimes needed to ensure it wasn't only my mother's medicine that went missing. I needed to make it look like someone there was messing up. The new guy, Drew, was easy enough to pin it on. I knew I'd figure it out as I went, if and when he got fired.

But that was it. I never stole any cash, only her medicine.

No one asked questions since I started working at a local mechanic shop for some extra cash. After that, it was easy to get what I needed, and I didn't even feel any guilt—not until I turned seventeen and I realized what I might lose if I ever got caught.

So, I stopped. I thought we'd be okay, especially since I was pulling in more money and Mom had made some progress with her health. I stopped for six months, until one night I found my mother passed out with a bottle of oxy next to her.

She had to have her stomach pumped, and she nearly died. She told me she had run out of meds, and since we couldn't afford any more, she'd found someone who could get her narcotics.

I ensured the order was called in and went back to the pharmacy that night, and I didn't stop going.

I hated not knowing who was trying to blackmail me. It had me sick. Numb. Fucking terrified. I wanted to run, but I couldn't. My mother needed me. Even if I couldn't steal her meds anymore, I could work, and then there was Faith.

The love of my life.

The woman I planned to marry.

I couldn't just walk away from her...I wouldn't, but that didn't change the fact that I had been reluctantly distant from her. I'd sneak in through her window, but only to touch her, to sink as far into her as I could and connect with her in a way that didn't require words. Sex was starting to be an outlet for me, a source of relief from the overwhelming anxiety.

I was demanding it more than normal, surprising Faith at work, driving her out to McGrady's orchard. They were quick, rushed moments of intense pleasure. It was gratifying and perfect, but Faith knew something was wrong.

We weren't making love; we were fucking, something we'd never done before. Every time we had ever been together, we were just that —*together*, intimate. We made love, but with fear beating hard in my chest, I didn't know how to be that person with her right then.

She was slipping away, each passing day and every time we were together. It was only a matter of time before she demanded to know what was wrong, and Faith was so good she'd insist I turn myself in. That or she'd agree to run with me; both were out of the question.

I was distracted, so I didn't expect anything to show up in the mail, but that day, there was another padded envelope.

My fingers shook as I pulled on the tab.

My breathing shuddered as I tugged the contents out. Photographs of me breaking into the pharmacy were tucked inside, each time stamped with a different date.

I roared in frustration. Hurrying into the kitchen to rummage for a lighter, I torched the pictures. I knew these were just duplicates, but I still didn't want them anywhere anyone could find them.

A part of me just wanted to end it, figure out who was doing this, because I couldn't eat or sleep. Everything was a massive clusterfuck, and I felt like I was losing my mind.

That night I lay awake thinking over the situation. If it was indeed blackmail, that meant whoever had sent it wanted something from me. I didn't have shit, so that thought terrified me.

What exactly could they want from a poor kid living in a trailer park?

Chapter 12
Jace

"Whiskey." I knocked my knuckles on the bar and nodded to Derek, the bartender. I liked Derek because he always knew what kind of whiskey I wanted without having to ask, and because he never cut me off. He knew I knew how to handle my drinks, and a man who knew that about another man was a good guy in my book.

"So, you tellin' me she shows back up here and you aren't even the least bit curious about what in the hell brought her back?" Seth inquired again, like he was a fucking detective and I was being investigated for the disappearance of his dick. I eyed him. He had his dark auburn hair shoved under a black baseball cap, and his pale face had been shaved recently, meaning he was hoping to get laid. He was nearly as tall as me, but he wasn't as broad. He reminded me of a professional skater or snowboarder.

He needed a life, and to stop wearing comic book characters on his t-shirts if he did in fact want to get laid.

I tipped my glass back, relishing the burn in my throat, and ignored my friend. I needed another drink if Seth was going to keep bringing Faith up. It had been almost a month since she'd arrived, and I had seen her nearly every day in some fashion.

After seeing her on Wednesday, I saw her at the dog park with

Trudy on Thursday. Trevor and I left promptly. Friday, she came to get her car. I made sure I wasn't there for that little encounter, but later that afternoon, she was sunbathing at the pool.

That shit should have been illegal. I nearly drowned the lifeguard because he wasn't watching anyone swimming, his pervy eyes fixed on Faith in a bikini. For the record, I didn't blame him, because again, she was all grown up. All woman, with curves and breasts, toned legs and defined abs. She was more than anything I'd ever imagined she'd be, and she wasn't mine.

She belonged to another man, and that reminder alone was making me insane. So, as each day hit, I became more and more annoyed. Now I was spending my Saturday night in Shelby, because I needed one day, one 24-hour period where I didn't see those blue eyes or that blonde hair or those freckles.

The ones I used to count with my lips, which would turn into a much dirtier game of trying to find all the freckles she had on her body. If I could find each one and mark it with a kiss, I'd advance in bases with her. It was how we ended up taking each other's virginity the summer we were seventeen.

"I frankly don't give a fuck," I muttered, waving my hand at Derek, thankful for his knowing nod. Seth made a sound of disapproval next to me and then let out a laugh.

"Well shit me and fuck you very much." His annoying phrase for when something surprised him caught my attention. I turned my head to see what was over Seth's shoulder and slammed my teeth together in frustration.

No. Fucking. Way.

Faith waltzed in with Gemma on her arm. The two of them were already laughing and joking like they'd been drinking. Faith was wearing a tiny black dress with high strappy heels, showing off her tan legs, and with her red lips, she looked every inch the girl I once knew who'd hoarded that specific shade of Gwen Stefani red.

She always went hunting for it in every store that sold even the smallest bit of makeup. She'd pay with nickels, dimes, and quarters, whatever she could scrounge up just to afford the cosmetic, sayin' Gwen was worth it.

Derek placed the refreshed tumbler of whiskey in front of me, breaking me away from memories still lingering at the darkened edges of my mind. I missed the sound of the stool moving next to me when Seth started walking toward the two of them. *The fucker.*

I tried to reach out and grip his shoulder, but he was too far.

So, I stayed put, drank, and watched from afar. Seth, Faith, and Gemma all went as far back as the second grade. I'd moved here before my sixth grade year, at which point Faith had landed on my radar. She hadn't known I liked her.

Like was too casual of a term. Obsessed might have been more accurate. She had these dark blue eyes set against her blonde hair and creamy skin. As a middle school boy, she was what I always imagined when I thought of growing up and getting married.

But she didn't respond to my jokes, turned her nose up when I thought I was being funny and other girls would laugh. She never looked at me in the halls. She was always in her own world. I figured the only way to get her to notice me was to break into hers.

Unfortunately, that was with cruel methods that often made her fuming mad. But that red coloring her face when I'd bump into her in the halls or steal her backpack—it became addictive. Then once eighth grade rolled around, other boys started talking about her.

They liked her long hair, her pretty bow-like lips. They liked her hips and her chest, and I couldn't take it anymore. I made my move and hoped like hell she didn't turn me down.

The song switching to some rendition of "Old Town Road" had the entire bar going crazy, as if we were still in sixth grade and not our mid-twenties. Couples paired up to line dance and started moving around the floor. I clenched my jaw as Seth grabbed Gemma by the hips, leaving Faith open for some idiot to use as a partner. Sure enough, a broad-shouldered jock with a Cumberland University shirt grabbed Faith and spun her around, smiling and holding her close.

Her blonde hair lifted off her shoulders and her legs moved like she'd been line dancing her entire life, though I knew she had to be out of practice from being on the arm of that billionaire. I endured the stupid song, and when it switched to something slower, I tried to draw in relief through my pathetic lungs, but when the jock caged Faith in his arms and they started slow dancing, I started coughing instead.

Seth and Gemma walked back toward me, reminiscing about high school and the past, all smiles and laughter. My gaze reluctantly stayed glued to the jock's hands and how low they kept creeping down Faith's backside. I couldn't see her face, so I had no idea if she was uncomfortable, and fuck, I shouldn't have even cared.

Even still, the tightness in my chest amplified like it had throughout the past week, growing and splintering. It took me back to losing her, my mom, and everything else I had going for me all at once. It was too much, too tight, too everything. I couldn't see her here, not while I was alone and especially not with her in the arms of another man. Instead of being a mature adult and leaving, I decided to make her do it.

I grabbed my phone as my eyes searched the floor, and I found Faith staring at me like she dared me to press the numbers into my cell, like she already knew.

I gave her a glare that said, *You should know better, sweetheart.* I dialed and relished the adrenaline that coursed through me. She was going to hate me, but it didn't matter. She was lost to me, and I needed a reminder that some things couldn't be redeemed.

Faith

Marrying Bryan had forced my demure and shy nature to transform into something more akin to survival. Smile big, nod your head, look your best—that way when the press came, they wouldn't be able to see through your armor.

I was thankful for the awkward shove into the limelight. It was a little bright and awkward at first, but eventually I got used to it. I acclimated to the invasive questions, the constant photographers snapping pictures left and right whenever we left our home, and my dire dependency on our security team, who'd held my life in their hands on more occasions than one. When I stepped out of the lime-light, I thought the limelight would leave me.

I was wrong.

The sound of the room shifting, people murmuring, and chairs being shoved to the side echoed in my head like the banging of a war drum. It had been the soundtrack for the last five years of my life in the public eye.

The press was here.

I didn't even have time to disconnect from the guy I was dancing with. We'd done a few turns around the floor, and the more I swayed in his arms, the less I noticed Jace nuzzling the tall brunette toward the pool tables.

"Mrs. Vanderson, is it true that you and your husband are currently separated?" asked a woman with a fat microphone that had a fuzzy red top. My gut clenched, wanting to scream at her that she wasn't allowed to invade my privacy like this, but I knew she was. She had every right because it was a public place and her camera was in plain, obvious view, which meant assumed consent by all parties.

I'd studied the laws, ready for the day when one of them stepped out of line. The only way I would get out of this was if the owner or manager asked them to leave, and I had no idea if he cared or not. The guy who was dancing had already dropped his hands and left the scene. I tried to squeeze past the reporter, but her cameraman blocked my way.

"Several people witnessed you dancing with other men on a few occasions over the past month—do you have a comment about a new fling? Are you and Bryan Vanderson separated?" She spoke as fast as gunfire. I ignored her.

A few days earlier, a few local Nashville stations had started speculating on the fact that my husband had been seen attending three different events alone, never commenting on why I wasn't there. The gossip train started, and a funny little saying emerged because of it. "Where in the world is Faith Vanderson?" started trending with a picture of me and a red hat photoshopped onto my head like I was Carmen Sandiego. It was childish and stupid, but predictable. Bryan was one of the richest men in Nashville, and after our stint with that reality show, we were a constant topic of news, so my leaving was sure to stir the pot.

But to call them on me here of all places...Jace was an asshole for this. I had locked eyes with him as he fished for his phone, as he dialed the number. Something deep down in my bones had me looking for Jace, as though he'd see how this looked, how terrible an error he'd made, and he'd come rushing in to save me.

My eyes caught on his as he tugged the brunette closer, her ample cleavage pushed up against his firm chest. He lifted his dark beer bottle in my direction as though to say, *Cheers.* Hot pain sliced through my middle as two more reporters showed up, cornering me.

Why on earth does it hurt more to see him with another woman than this horrific display of betrayal?

He had called *The Triple O: Obvious, Original, Orgasmic,* a gossip tabloid that didn't ever care about facts or clearing up any of the rumors it started. They were unsophisticated and often tried to get the most unflattering photo of whoever they were exposing. To call them journalists would be a far cry from professional. They were vultures—gross, money-hungry vultures. I didn't know who the other reporters were, but *Triple O* was bad enough.

I tried to shoulder past them again, but a second cameraman shoulder-checked me, causing me to fall to the side, back toward the center. Of course, that little move was off camera, so no one would see it. My eyes watered, and my heart raced frantically in my chest. If I ran to the parking lot, they'd have me alone. If I stayed here, a bigger group would gather. I didn't know what to do. I wanted to scream and crumble into a tiny, invisible ball all at the same time.

I looked around for help, from anyone. Gemma kept trying to get to me, but the crowd wouldn't let her. The light from the camera in my eyes blinded me. Thankfully, fucking finally the manager came over and demanded they leave, but I knew they'd be waiting for me. I knew I couldn't escape this now. They'd get my parents' address and wait for me there. They'd stalk me and make my life a living hell.

I set my jaw and walked over to Jace, who was laughing into his beer, watching someone play pool. His brunette date curled herself farther under his arm as the people around the table made little sniggering sounds at my approach.

Pulse hammering, blood rushing, I walked right up to the man who'd once held my heart and slapped him across the face. Everyone stopped laughing and talking. Jace's date straightened up, away from him, and covered her mouth in shock.

I stepped forward to make sure I got my point across. "What is wrong with you? This is bigger than you know, you asshole. You're going to feel like shit once you realize what you've done." I worked my jaw back and forth to hold off the tears that wanted to break through my defenses. "I have no idea what I did to make you hate me, but I'm done wishing you didn't. I'm done pining and letting you hold first place in a heart that hasn't belonged to anyone but you. I'm done."

I spewed and gushed all my truths in front of a group of strangers, in front of a red-faced, jaw-clenching Jace, who likely didn't give two shits that I had just told him I was still pining for him. I didn't care.

I went to the bathroom, Gemma following closely. Once we were inside, she locked the door, and I hesitantly called Tom, head of the security detail I'd left behind in Nashville. It was an awkward position I was in, still the billionaire's wife regardless of the fact that I was leaving him.

I was still tied to him in some things. The security detail was one of them, ironically enough. Bryan still wanted me protected, at least from everyone but him. So, he had told Tom to come to Collierville as soon as I admitted to where I was. He'd been staying in a hotel, just waiting around for a phone call from me.

When his firm fist pounded three times in succession followed by two short ones, I opened the door and let him quickly and safely shuttle me to his car.

I didn't look back to see if Jace saw.

Chapter 13
Jace

IT HAD BEEN five days since the scene at the Shelby bar where Faith confessed to pining for me, confessed that I still occupied first place in her heart—then ripped it all away from me in one fell swoop.

I refused to hope she still felt anything at all for me, not after she'd married another man, not after she'd started another life with someone who wasn't me. I was still so hurt and damaged from what she had done, but still...hearing her admit that she hadn't quite let me go the way I'd assumed she had felt good.

Internally, I merely accepted that it assuaged my pride, nothing more.

I was driving down Main Street, about to turn right to head into work, when a chain-link fence around an empty lot caught my attention. It was practically around the corner from my shop, a bit closer to downtown. A large blue sign hung from where the lock secured the gate, but that was the only indication that anything had happened to the empty lot. Pulling up, I put my truck in park and hopped out.

This industrial area had been vacant for years, void of any structures, just a bit of old sidewalk and dirt. Honestly it was prime real estate with how close it was to downtown, a dream spot for owning a business. I gripped the chain and tilted the sign to see the lettering better.

Future Home of Mustard Seed Auto, Tires, & Towing

I dropped the sign like it'd suddenly burst into flames.

There was no way this was happening, no fucking way, not less than a mile away from my auto shop, the *only* auto shop on this side of town. But still...

Could she?

I doubted Faith knew the first thing about running a business, but then again, I had no idea what she had been up to for the last five years. I had no idea if she opened businesses or ran them. *Better to know for sure.*

I jumped into the truck and peeled out, making a sharp U-turn, gassing it through our little town. Speeding, I took a rough right onto S Rowlett Street and swung a quick left into the Morgan driveway, sputtering rocks and gravel behind me. I put the truck in park and jogged to the front door. No one answered; in fact, I looked around and realized the only car there was Faith's Rover.

I pounded my fist against her fancy-ass door with the stylish bronze knocker, yelling at the top of my lungs. "Faith? Open up!"

"What do you want?" someone bellowed from above me. I took a few steps back and tipped my head back to see the windows on the top floor, squinting against the sun.

"Faith?"

"No, it's the Pope, you idiot! What do you want?" she yelled back, hanging halfway out of the second-story window.

"Mustard Seed Auto—really?" I splayed my arms open.

"Like that, did you?" She crossed her arms, leaning on the ledge, and gave me a side smile like this was funny as hell. When we were in high school, we did a features project where we each had to create a fictitious business name. Faith always used Mustard Seed for whatever she was creating. Mustard Seed Bakery, Mustard Seed Realty... there were a few others, and I knew her handiwork when I saw it.

"Yes, very funny. Now take it down."

She scoffed, "No. You called the paps on me—and by the way, did you see those cars on your way in? Thanks for that, asshole. They won't leave."

I looked behind me, toward the main road, and saw someone outside their car with a camera pointed at us. *Shit.*

"Sorry about that. I'll find a way to make it up to you...but this isn't payback, Faith—this is fucking bankruptcy!" I scolded, nearly losing it. If she did have access to her billionaire husband's fortune then that was exactly what would happen. I'd drown without even making a splash.

She pulled the window in, slamming it shut.

"Dammit, Faith!" I eyed the window, stretching my neck back, willing her to reappear.

A second later the front door opened. Faith reached forward, grabbing my hand, and tugged me inside.

"You idiot! They're listening. They're watching. They're going to print this entire argument online, so shut up!" She pressed her hand over my mouth. She was so close I could smell that cherry lip gloss she used to like to wear.

It was the roll-on kind I'd only ever seen in Jessie's little kid makeup kits, and Faith had always said it gave the best shine. It sure as fuck always tasted good, so I didn't care, but the fact that she was still wearing it did things to me...strange, delicious things.

She slowly lowered her hand as her eyes got big, and she took a few steps back. She likely hadn't realized how close we were, or that we were alone. I brushed a hand over my face and quietly continued.

"If you were worried about that then you should have just opened the door to begin with."

She crossed her arms over her chest and rolled her eyes. "I forgot how loud you are."

Unwilling to let it pass, I smirked and leaned closer. "I've never forgotten how loud *you* are."

As expected, she flushed pink, and it made me wildly ambitious.

"You need to leave." She cleared her throat and stood up straight.

"Is that really what you want?" I asked, toying with her. I didn't care if she wanted me to or not, but...fuck, *memories...*

She took a half-step back, conveying loud and clear that she didn't want whatever it was I was insinuating, but the fact that she didn't verbally tell me to go jump off a cliff was something.

I ducked my head, changing tactics. "You'll put me out of business, but I thought you had no money anyway." I quirked my eyebrow in question.

She watched me for a solid second or two, making me shift with discomfort.

Suddenly she stepped closer. "Tell me what happened with your mama."

What?

I blinked, keeping a stoic expression as I said, "Pass."

She let out a huff of air. "I'll take it down if you tell me." Her eyes disarmed me, and she stepped even closer, so close I could feel the heat coming off her body. She always ran warm, like a little spot of sunshine. I narrowed my eyes, telling her to go fuck herself with my gaze.

She inhaled a shuddering breath, as though she was trying to prove something. "I still have some cash left from the car I sold, and... I..." Blink, swallow—she was a mess. "I have access to more," she finished, jutting her chin up.

"That so?" I stalked closer, and my nose twitched. *Cinnamon sugar. Sunshine. Cherry lip gloss.*

She lowered her chin, and I shook my head to focus. "I don't buy it. You don't have the kind of capital to start a business of that caliber, nor do you have the brass to do it."

She cocked her hip, narrowing her eyes. "Don't question how much capital I have, Jace. You know if I say I have the money to open it, I do."

Those crystal blues stared at me, silently asking me for truths while she threw out half-assed lies. I wouldn't cave, and I wondered if she would.

Her annoying-as-hell hall clock ticked in the silence then she whispered another request.

"Tell me about why you went to jail."

Where the fuck was she getting this intel? I knew Jessie hadn't told her shit, but either way, there wasn't anything I was interested in rehashing with Faith.

"Pass."

She turned on her heel and let out an undignified groan while pinning her hands to her hips. "I can look it up on my own, I would just rather get your side of it."

"And if I don't tell you, you're going to open a competing auto service?"

"Why not? I need something to do with my time." She lifted a shoulder.

I stared at her, watching for any tells that she was lying, then ground my back molars together. I stepped closer to her, forcing her eyes to search my face for clues.

"It's awful fast, don't you think?" I grabbed a stray piece of her hair and twirled it around my finger. *Pure fucking silk.*

"N...no," she stuttered, but she didn't move back. "I called a guy, who made the sign...rushed it at no extra cost."

"So, are you saying it's just a sign?" I asked, leaning closer. With my lips just an inch from her jaw, my hand traveled to her hip, anchoring her in place.

Her chest rose, inflating like a balloon. "Um...no...what?"

This was gloriously perfect. She unraveled entirely at my touch.

I dragged my finger up her arm, pressing a ghost of a kiss to her ear. "It's just a sign, isn't it? It's fake, just bullshit...you're just messing with me?"

She leaned closer, pressing her warm fingers into my chest. If she tipped her chin up even the slightest bit, I was going to kiss her—hard.

"Maybe...but now you'll be wondering, won't you?" she whispered, her warm breath fanning out on my neck, those lips so close to my skin. I swallowed thickly, uselessly, hoping she'd close the distance and put me out of my misery—the shop forgotten, the past, all of it gone in a second. I turned my head, closing the small gap myself, my lips making contact with her skin as I pulled her into my arms.

Fucking finally.

I knew in that moment that another man's wife held my heart in the palm of her hand. With every beat, she could break it, ruin it. But as I wrapped my body around hers and slowly moved my lips up her jaw until I found that mouth, I couldn't find a reason to care.

Scorching, that's what this was. Her small gasp as I marked her skin had my fingers pulling her waist closer so she could feel me, feel what she did to me. Just as my lips were about to descend upon hers, she grabbed hold of my shirt and pulled me away from the door, making me lose my balance, forcing me to falter to the side. Within the blink of an eye, she opened the door and shoved me hard until I was tripping out the door.

Holy fuck. How...

"Enough people will see the signs and wonder if your business is even still open," she explained while her lungs strained for air. *She felt it too.*

She tucked her hair behind her ears, crossing her arms. I righted myself, still wondering how I had just gone from nearly kissing her to being shoved out her front door. Wait...did she say...

"Signs?"

A rueful smile from those glossy lips. "Signs."

Shit.

I stepped closer to re-engage this conversation, maybe with less clothing, but she slammed the door shut, and I heard the sound of the deadbolt sliding into place.

Chapter 14
Faith

GEMMA: Are you sure you want to do this?

Me: Yea...I'm ready.

Gemma: Okay, I'll send you the address and the time for the interview. As your lawyer, I'm advising you wait until we have more of a grip on him, but as your best friend, I'm advising you to kick ass.

Me: Love you. Thank you. I trust you to still get what we need regardless of my social blip.

Gemma: I like your confidence and you're right, obviously...but still. Be careful.

I lowered my cell phone and pressed the button on the right to turn it off. It was so much easier to type words on a screen than it was to walk out and make them happen, but I wasn't lying. I was ready to do this.

It was gutsy, bold, and might ruin me, but I was banking on being real and honest. It was a trend these days, and I was hoping I could use it to help my cause. I was about to do something people just don't do. It was societal suicide, but I didn't care. Society had never belonged to me, nor I to it...and this was my way of breaking up with it, of saying *Fuck you* to everyone who ever pretended to care.

This was my swan song.

That afternoon, I drove over to the Collierville Cemetery and drifted slowly along the black asphalt, winding around green earth and grey stones. I felt a heaviness in my heart, so dull and so painful that it shortened my breath.

I followed Jessie's directions on what section to head toward, parked, and then began walking reverently through the turf. Rolling hills bounded in every direction, little glints of color and white stone getting caught in stray streams of sunlight. Most graves were well tended, with plentiful arrangements and small balloons.

Finally, halfway up a hill, I found her plaque, tucked into the ground and shaded by a tall weeping willow. Pressing my knees into the earth, I focused on the white lettering, tracing her date of death with my finger. August thirteenth—I was already engaged by then, already living a luxurious, pampered life with more money than God.

My eyes stung as the wind picked up, a rare chill in the air fluttering against my tear-stained cheeks. I wanted to pour my soul out to the woman who was once a second mother to me. I wanted to throw myself on the ground and cry, sob into the grass, hoping somehow she'd hear me and know how sorry I was. Instead, I sat perfectly still, my shoulders shaking and my heart aching.

"What are you doin' out here?" asked a harsh, rumbling voice from behind me, startling me so much I cursed.

"Jesus."

Jace clicked his tongue. "Might not be a good idea to take his name in vain out here. This is holy ground." He walked softly around the other plaques and settled on his butt, tossing his arms over his knees, a bundle of purple daisies resting in his clenched fist. I hadn't seen him in days, not since he stood in my house, touching me, eliciting a response from my body so strong I nearly melted at his feet.

A lax breeze blew the willow wisps around as we sat in silence, a strange calm hanging between us. I wanted to talk to June, tell her about my life, tell her how much I missed her, but I couldn't with Jace here. I was about to stand to leave when Jace let out a frustrated sigh, kicking his leg out, looking down at his mother's grave.

"It's slightly pathetic, don't you think?"

My gaze flitted up, not sure if he was talking about me or to me. I couldn't deal with a zinger from him right now, so I waited for him to continue.

"You'd think, in death, there would be more grandeur..." He flicked his fingers toward the stone with a grimace. "The rich pricks in this place all have these gawdy headstones, as tall as a kinder-gartener. Some even have mausoleums dedicated to their loved ones, but we..." He stopped, that muscle in his jaw jumping.

I leaned forward to trace the lettering again, feeling it comfort me somehow.

"I hate having to search the ground for her. I hate not being able to just see her name as I walk up. She deserved more than a plaque in the ground..."

Finally clearing my voice, I risked asking, "The headstone cost too much?"

He sneered. "That's what I heard."

My head snapped up. "What do you mean?"

His focus was off in the distance, his hair shifting slightly with the draft, his blue eyes cold and unfeeling. "I heard from my dad, when he came to visit me in jail...they couldn't afford this. Even the fancy white lettering cost more than what they could afford at the time."

My heart seized in my chest. "You missed her funeral?"

He nodded solemnly.

"I'm sorry," I whispered, feeling my heart shred in half. He'd worked so hard for her pain medicine. He had been consumed with her getting better, with her making it. For her to die...and him missing it—it just wasn't right.

After a few silent moments he stood, hissing at me, "You should be—it was your fault."

The air whooshed from my lungs, as though he'd just hit me with a sledgehammer, right in the chest.

I couldn't form words, couldn't do anything but sit there and heave sputtering breaths. Of all the hurtful things Jace could ever say to me, that was the harshest. How was it my fault? What the hell had happened?

I spent the day cleaning, filling out applications for internships at different design firms, and waiting by the phone for my admissions counselor to call. I needed to keep my mind busy, keep it off what'd happened with Jace. It was too painful; his insults and taunts were too much. I had thought if I showed some courage with having that sign made, letting him know if I wanted to open a business that threatened his livelihood, I could, he'd back off.

Would I actually open a business like that? No.

Not in a million years, but I thought it would get Jace to soften, or retreat.

You should be—it was your fault.

His angry retort rumbled in my heart, scratching and digging into the very marrow of my bones. Needing some space from my room, my house, and especially my parents, I left.

The crickets sang to me like they used to, reminding me of home, of what I'd left behind, all the brokenness that was buried here. I pushed past the underlying feeling that I didn't belong here anymore and continued walking toward the tall wooden castle, blanket in one hand, wine in the other. If I was going to face this place, it was going to be done with alcohol—although the closer I got, the more I wished it were something stronger than wine.

The night was cloudy, no stars, no moon, just the awkward safety lights they'd put in some time in the past few years. It was almost like the sky was shaking its head at me, telling me this part of my story was over and not to come back here. There was no magic in the air tonight, just darkness and a few clouds.

I ducked my head and climbed the rickety steps, carefully walking plank by plank across the bridge that rocked back and forth under my weight. I continued forward until I got to the ladder and then crawled into my spot. Not *our* spot, but mine.

It had been mine first. Now that I was home, it was time to start reclaiming things that had been lost to the wreckage of Jace's and my relationship. I had been too timid then, too weak, but I wasn't now. I might not have been the strongest, but I was stronger than I had once been.

I laid the blanket out, twisted the cap off my wine, and took a sip, looking around, wishing the stars were out so it'd justify this awkward rendezvous. At least then I could be stargazing, but no, I was just cloud stalking. It had been three days since my breakdown in the graveyard, three days of digging through news articles and Google searching Jace's life, June's...anything to tell me how it was my fault.

I found out Jace was sentenced to six months in jail for breaking and entering at the pharmacy, no possession charges. That was it. Six months, in and out...but Jace made that decision to steal his mother's meds on his own. I had nothing to do with it...but maybe that was why he had decided to dump me. Maybe he hadn't wanted to involve me in his new life of crime, but that couldn't be right with how hostile Jace had been toward me since I'd returned, especially with his comment about it being my fault that he missed his own mother's funeral.

Something had happened, something big. I needed more information, but I wasn't sure where to start to get it.

"What are you doing up here?" That deep rumbling voice jarred me, and I jumped, just like I had in the cemetery.

"Holy shit!" I covered my mouth with one hand and my heart with the other, willing it to calm down.

"Always such a dirty mouth when you're scared," Jace muttered, crawling the rest of the way up the ladder and onto the platform.

"I wasn't expecting company," I sputtered while moving to the side so there was distance between us. It was big enough for us to lie down, but now that Jace had bulked up in muscle, the space felt a little tight, and after what he'd said the other day, I didn't want to be anywhere near him.

"Clearly," Jace said, nodding toward my chest.

Confused, I looked down and realized I was wearing a thin sweater wrap over my sleep tank. I had no bra on, and it was chilly, so my nipples were alert and saying a big hello to anyone who had a view of them. I pulled the cover around me, cutting off his view, and rolled my eyes. I hadn't been expecting to see anyone, so fuck him and his judgment.

"What are you doing here...and why do you keep popping up at places I am peacefully visiting?" I asked, tilting my head to the sky, avoiding eye contact with him. Those thin white clouds hadn't moved, the awkward safety lights creating a strange glow. Suddenly, I wanted to go home.

"I live here, come out here a lot," he gruffly explained, moving his legs until they were thrown in front of him, taking up even more space. His comment about living here seemed non-threatening, but since I'd arrived, he'd been nothing but an asshole, so I knew it was a dig.

Memories fluttered between us whether we wanted them to or not, rising from the ashes like an angry phoenix...his smile, the warm balmy air that night we lost our virtue to one another...laughter and promises made under large white moons, blinking stars and onyx skies.

Happiness rolled around inside me, somewhat dislodged and out of place, but it was quickly obliterated by the memory of his face when he ended it all, how he'd chosen to do it here, in our sacred place, our harbor against the storms that battered us.

"You trying to figure out a new way to screw me over? Maybe you could kill my dog or repossess my truck." Jace half-shrugged, not glancing at me but keeping his gaze on the sky, like he was looking for something.

Asshole.

"I was thinking of the last time we were here together and how cowardly you were that night," I snapped.

He responded by dipping his face, hiding it from me. He didn't reply for a while, and I took the opportunity to sip my wine, but the mood was uncomfortable. I kept thinking of how he looked that night in the bar with the woman tucked under his arm, how it was someone different from his date at the barbeque. The feeling soured in my gut; he'd turned into a playboy and had likely fucked half the women from here to Memphis. That sudden urge to leave gripped me, causing me to twist the cap onto my wine, nice and tight.

"This is stupid," I muttered, grabbing for my blanket. Jace reached out to stop me, his large rough hand landing on my soft one. The difference was striking. He had stains from oil and grease while mine were manicured, soft, *expensive.*

"That night..." He stopped, looking down at my hand. I watched, unsure if I wanted to hear what he had to say. Such a big part of me didn't. Such a big part of me had moved on, was over him, but there was this damn spark. It wasn't just a spark of lust or love; it was curiosity too. There were too many unanswered questions rolling around in my head.

"Save it." I pulled my hand free and stood, but suddenly he did too.

"Earlier this week you wanted answers...I'm here 'bout to give you one. Do you want it or not?" Jace asked with that same deep Southern drawl he reserved for when he was angry. His eyes looked like mercury as they searched mine, like he was out in space, searching for home.

I wanted to walk off, scoff, and flip him the finger, but I *did* crave answers.

"Fine." I relented and sank back into my spot, this time crossing my legs, criss cross- applesauce style.

Jace let out a sigh, snagged my wine, and tipped it back. I watched as his Adam's apple bobbed with each gulp.

"That night, I had planned on talking to you about something else...when I texted you that morning to meet me at the spot, I had planned to ask you to run away with me." Jace's confession wasn't at all what I was expecting. I was expecting excuses, justifications for why he'd felt right about dropping me like a bad habit.

Intrigued, I leaned closer. "What do you mean?"

Jace tipped his head back to the sky and let out a groan of frustration. "It all got so messed up. There are still some things I don't want to tell you because it wouldn't make a difference, but just know I didn't want to break up with you." He righted his head and leveled me with a serious glare, the safety lights making his blue eyes bright. "I never wanted to break up with you, Faith...but by the time I had straightened it out..." He trailed off. "Six months—that's all you waited before you were in another man's arms." He bristled, looking down again, and this time my heart twisted angrily with hurt.

I hadn't known.

I'd had no idea he wasn't being honest.

"How could you hold that against me? You broke me...my mama was so worried she nearly committed me. I didn't leave my house for weeks. I didn't have an appetite, started losing a god awful amount of weight." My tone was picking up decibels as the pain surfaced.

"Why did you do it?" He turned his entire body toward me, and I stared back, blinking in confusion.

"Do what?"

"Why did you run to him? Why did you only wait six months?" Jace seared me with his stare, showing too many of his own cards. I'd hurt him—unknowingly, but I had.

I narrowed my eyes on him. "Is that why you've been so mean to me? So cold? Because I moved on too fast for you?"

He scoffed and shook his head back and forth. "You claimed all these lofty feelings for me, but you sure as hell moved on pretty fast."

I was stunned, totally speechless for a few seconds as I processed what he'd said.

"You break my heart and then get mad and hold a grudge against me because I didn't stay pathetic and in love with you after *you* ended things with *me*?" I stood, shouting down at him with fury and hurt.

He stood too, towering over me with his jaw set and eyes in slits.

"Of course I moved on, Jace. I was heartbroken. I ran into the first pair of open arms that would take me. I wanted a refuge, a safe place to hide and heal from how badly you'd hurt me. I can't believe you have the audacity to be angry about it all these years later."

"But you didn't just move on." His blue eyes narrowed. He took a step forward, leaving barely any space between us. My chest was rising and falling fast; his wasn't at all. Typical. He was always like a fortified wall against my flimsy, caving ones. "You *married* the first pair of open arms, Faith. Fucking *married* him. You didn't rebound... you just moved on from me...from us, like we didn't happen."

"And you never came after me!" I shouted, angry that I was revealing that it mattered to me. At least I hadn't let the rest slip; I wouldn't recover if he knew what I had prayed on my wedding day.

I took a step back, needing air, needing something...anything. I searched his eyes, tried not to pull anything from them that he wasn't offering, but he looked...he looked like he was drowning in regret. I swallowed and pushed my hair off my face, a sudden gust having blown it askew.

"You didn't want me," was all I could manage to mutter out loud. The truth was, I hated how weak I had been back then, how pathetic and hurt, how right Jace was. I should have dated Bryan, sure...but marry him? No.

I should have grown up; maybe then Jace would have found me. Maybe he would have spoken his truth, or whatever version of it he was willing to give, and we would have found a way back to each other.

"I needed you," Jace whispered, so quietly I nearly missed it. It was full of pain and cracks, of just as much hurt...of all the same things I carried.

He needed me...the words rolled through me, falling like a star from the sky to the vast, open sea. It was there, but I couldn't hold it, couldn't grasp it long enough to make anything of it.

I stirred, ready to leave, my emotions running rampant, and this time he let me. I left the wine behind but grabbed the blanket and shuffled my way down and out of the castle.

I felt like I was looking at a piece of paper that'd been shredded and glued back together. I couldn't make out what had happened, but the tremor in Jace's voice when he'd said he had needed me made me feel exposed...ugly and raw—things I didn't want to be feeling, not after he had dismissed me so easily in the cemetery.

The darkness wasn't lessened by the moon shining overhead. I didn't live far from the park, so walking by myself never was much of a problem, but halfway home, I saw a pair of headlights trailing behind me. They were about three car lengths back or so, but they slowed, following me.

My insides swarmed with anxiety as they crept closer. Where I was walking, there was a chain-link fence for the high school baseball field to my left and the road on my right; I had nowhere to go but forward. I quickened my steps and inhaled steadily through my nose as I took inventory of what I had on me: a blanket.

Well shit.

No cell phone, no pepper spray or anything else to make me safe while walking home at night.

The humming of the engine got closer as the car crept along the road. Suddenly the vehicle burst into speed, heading right for me, pulling up along the curb and shoving a large video camera through the window behind the driver's seat. "Faith, do you have a comment about your separation from Bryan Vanderson?" someone asked from inside the car.

I blinked at the light attached to the top, which was blinding me.

"Faith, is it true you're reconnecting with an old flame?"

I waited only a second longer before bolting forward toward the school and away from the reporters, horrified and appalled that they'd tracked me and had possibly seen me sharing wine with Jace. I crept along the side of the school and cut through the back field. Thankfully, there was a side gate that led to a small patch of trees butting up against my back yard.

Tears stained my face as I hurried with shaky legs and a hollowed chest. I kept forgetting that this part of my life wasn't unscathed by my marriage. It was like a fat ink blob, leaking and infecting everything in its path.

Chapter 15
Jace
Five years earlier: August

THE MEETING REQUEST came similar to the DVD and pictures: via padded envelope. I was to meet my blackmailer behind the Baptist church at ten p.m. the next day. I hadn't been eating, and what I did get down came back up. Faith was so worried; her face was permanently pinched. I hated myself for lying to her. Whenever she pressed, I'd lie and say it was just my mother's health that had me stressed.

I couldn't tell her. I refused. If I didn't or couldn't comply with the blackmailer's wishes, I didn't want her to go down with me. It wouldn't be fair to her. So that night, after I climbed in through Faith's window, knowing she'd be asleep, I held her as tight as I could.

I fought back tears as I inhaled her cinnamon and sugar scent, swallowing all the words I wanted to whisper into her ear about us and our future, how I'd fix it. No matter what was going to happen with this blackmail, I'd fix it and come back to her. Instead, I just listened to the sound of her breathing until the sun came up.

The next night, I walked with my hood drawn and a gun packed into my jeans. It had been locked in my father's safe, but with how many hours he worked, I doubted he'd notice it missing.

The breeze of summer had chilled to the point of being uncomfortable. My skin pebbled under my layers as I made my way through back alleys and yards, a low hanging moon my only source of light. Inhaling short breaths, I finally ambled toward the parking lot of the church. There were no stray cars in the lot, no one awkwardly standing around, just the flood light breaking up the dark.

A gruff voice spoke up behind me. "Good, you showed."

I turned swiftly, trying to control my heart rate, and then as I took in who my blackmailer was, I immediately wanted to throw up.

"I hate that it came to this, but I'm out of time." He stepped forward.

I was so shocked I wasn't sure I could speak, but finally I choked out, "What do you want from me?"

Then the world shifted, time stopped, and my lungs failed.

The cost of my choices was a noose around my neck, one I couldn't get free from because I knew what would happen if I turned him down and just accepted my consequences. Two lives hung in the balance, but only one could continue without me.

So, as I accepted my fate, agreeing to his terms, I tried to plan. I grappled with ideas for how to turn him down, how to fix it, because there had to be a way to fix it...I just needed time.

Present day

"You're out here early," John called out to me from over his air compressor. John was a good friend of our family, had worked with my dad at the mill.

I smiled, bending down to pick up a pack of insulation. "Yeah, needed to clear my head a bit," I replied, moving from the garage to the inside of the house. I had been insulating it little bits at a time, as I could afford it and as I had the time to lay it.

"What on earth do ya need to clear your head for?" John asked, following me inside. He helped me lay the padding in between the beams. We worked quietly for a few minutes while I deliberated over whether or not to spill my situation to him.

"It's just that Faith came back." I laughed like it was ridiculous, because my reaction to her returning was just that. John had known me long enough to know the whole history behind my world melting down after she left.

"I see, and that's not going the way you planned?"

I smiled. "Not exactly."

John moved down the wall, lifting the lining and shoving it in. "How exactly did you think it would go?"

I considered that for a moment. "I'm not sure, but being a prickly dick to her wasn't what I had expected. It's just..." I let out a sigh, taking a break. "Whenever she's around, something inside me just charges up, like an electrical current, and then *zap*."

"You zing her." John nodded, keeping his eyes on the wall.

"Exactly, and I can't seem to turn it off. Doesn't help that I'm still attracted to her, or that she seems to be single now."

"Is she now?" John's white eyebrows rose to his forehead as he turned toward me.

I shrugged, hating that I didn't know her entire situation. Finishing my side of the wall, I pivoted to head back toward the garage, but John stopped me with a hand to the shoulder.

"Look, son, it sounds to me like you owe her an apology. Lord knows there's a trough full of troubled water between you two, but if you ever want to get out of the strike zone and into the kissin' one...I suggest you start being nice." He moved past me, heading toward the garage, taking the last word with him.

I pulled my gloves free and ran my fingers through my hair. I knew he was likely right, but I had no idea how to let my guard down enough to apologize to her. Flashes of how painful it had been when I saw her up on the television, pinned to Bryan's side would surface, driving me to anger.

I had hoped the day I ever saw Faith again, I'd have moved on and would be happily married. I'd be living in a big house, with my own property and a job I created with my own two hands. I'd be proud and worthy, enough to tell her to go fuck off with her billionaire life.

The problem with letting go and moving on was just that— leaving the spot you've claimed while pining and waiting. Whether it was for hate or hope, it was still a fire lit with kerosene...a dire need for completion, closure. Maybe that was what I needed with Faith— not a second chance, but just to close our book, to end it and get it all out, once and for all.

It was nearly dark when I pulled into my driveway, pushing nine at night. I supposed I hadn't really needed to restock, clean, and organize the entire garage, but I'd been trying to get my mind off the closure situation I was planning with Faith. So, now I was tired, sore, and just ready for a shower and some sleep.

I exited my truck and began trudging toward the front door but stopped when I heard a lilt of female laughter from inside. One nice thing about having thin trailer walls was the fact that I could usually get a nice heads-up about what was happening inside—hugely helpful when the parents were in arguments when I was younger.

I knew that laugh, and just like the other day, a protective anger rolled through me. I didn't want her here. I looked back over my shoulder and realized I had completely missed her dark Rover parked along the shoulder of our driveway. Exhaustion tugged at me as I wiped my face with my hand.

Shame rose up again, because I didn't want to see her face and have this unspoken reality between us. I was still shit poor and she was still married to a billionaire. I didn't want her in my life, seeing that I was still in this damn trailer, regardless of my home that was nearly built. We were still just as poor and pathetic as when she left.

I pushed the door open and found Jessie and Faith sitting around the coffee table, a big brown pizza box in front of them. My dad was reclined on the couch, laughing, holding a slice. All eyes jumped to me as I made my loud entrance. Trevor jumped up from lying in Faith's lap and ran toward me, licking and jumping on me. I ignored how it felt to see him with Faith.

Dad stopped laughing and set the pizza down. "Hey there, son. How are you doing?"

I nodded at him, showing respect, but I could feel my hackles rising over Faith sitting there on the floor, witnessing how dirty I looked, coming home from a day of work, from a job she had joked about taking from me.

"I'm surviving, for the moment." My eyes flicked to Faith's and faltered.

Her eyes were zeroed in on my forearms, and then they roamed my torso and legs until finally moving up to my hair and eyes, where they froze. Her face was flushed, and she looked...I knew that look. It was seared into my brain from the first time I ever touched her enough to provoke a response; she was turned on.

"Well, join us. Faith brought pizza." Dad waved his hand toward the box, and my eyes went to his waving hand then landed on Faith again. She wore a simple grey t-shirt that was loose but still managed to cling to her chest in all the right ways. The neckline was a deep scoop, revealing her collarbone, which—for whatever reason—was sexy as hell.

Her short hair was curled and had a piece pinned to the side. This was what I'd always wanted with her: family dinner nights where she'd just chill with us, where we could just relax and then later go home together.

An ache so far deep into my core surfaced and threatened to finish what Faith had started five years earlier when she married Bryan. It terrified me how much seeing her like this affected me.

I cleared my throat and set down my lunchbox and work gear. "I'll have to pass. I'm going to shower and then go to bed."

"Stop that. Come sit down and have some dinner with us," my dad argued, snagging a piece and putting it on the paper plate next to the pizza box. Heaving a sigh, I reluctantly accepted and took the seat next to him.

"So, Faith was just telling us what it was like to go to some of those fancy spas and how her first time, she didn't know what to do." Jessie laughed, biting down on another part of her pepperoni pizza. I didn't look at Faith, because I didn't care about her stupid fancy life, or her stupid fancy spas.

"Sounds boring as hell." I nearly winced, thinking of what John had suggested. *Be nice.*

"I don't think so, son," my dad warned, giving me the look—the one that promised he'd make my life a living hell if I was rude.

Faith dropped her piece and dusted her hands. "No, it's fine. I have an early morning anyway, so I should get going."

"Don't leave because of him," Jessie insisted, setting her piece down too. I watched both girls and continued to eat my pizza.

Faith surveyed the room, letting her gaze slowly drift to me, then to the pizza. "It's fine. It's not him—I really do have to get going. Plus, I don't want to intrude on family time."

She moved to grab her purse then my dad spoke up. "Once upon a time you were family too. You're always welcome here." He stared at her and nodded. She stared back, one hand on her purse, and I could see her eyes beginning to mist.

My father had always been as much of a dad to her as her own. I knew she loved him, and hell, maybe she even needed to be around him tonight, but I was a bastard and didn't want her in my space, didn't want her near what I cherished.

"Thank you. I'll see ya around. When I get my own apartment, I'll have to have y'all over." Faith smiled at my dad and Jessie but refused to look at me. She was about to leave, but my curiosity was piqued now, and fuck if I didn't need to know what she meant by getting an apartment.

Her getting an apartment locally seemed to almost confirm my 'Faith is single' theory. She reached for the doorknob right as I lurched forward for another piece.

"Just hang out, Faith. No one's tellin' you you've gotta leave. Plus, there's still too much pizza."

She paused and looked back at me for a second. Maybe she was remembering my mother's rule from all those years ago, the one where Faith could never go back home until she'd eaten more or stayed later, always saying there was still too much of whatever we were eating.

Jessie jumped up and reached out to grab Faith's hand. "Yeah, way too much. Come on, sit back down." Faith followed and eyed me suspiciously but sat next to Jessie while a new episode of *The Office* came back on. We all settled in and watched the television as the drama unfolded before us. It felt like slipping back in time, only instead of having Faith curled up beside me, laughing at another dubious idea from Michael Scott, she was down on the floor.

Since I was behind her on the couch, it gave me ample opportunity to watch her hair bounce whenever she laughed, and I could see her toned arms reach behind her to stretch, which made me tense in all the wrong places.

Once the show ended, Faith hopped up and started gathering the empty paper plates and the pizza box to help clean. I joined her while Dad and Jessie stayed put, talking about the semantics of the British version of *The Office* versus the American one.

"Thanks for cleanin'," I muttered while facing the sink and washing out the cup I'd used. She stayed quiet behind me, wiping down the counter and stacking the rest of the paper plates we kept above the oven.

"It's no problem," she gently answered.

I turned and crossed my arms over my chest, watching her. She had on black leggings that molded to her legs, and that deep scoop shirt exposed her soft skin. I didn't see any straps on her bare shoulders, which meant she was wearing a strapless bra. Memories of the last time I'd seen her in any kind of bra ran through my mind and made me nearly delirious with need. She'd always had the most perfect breasts, and now that she was grown... I eyed her chest, curious if her husband had made her get them done, like her teeth and everything else that was shiny and expensive about her.

Slowly my eyes drifted up, risking that she might be watching me, but she was busy looking around. Having her seeing my house made me feel exposed, vulnerable. It was too much. I cleared my throat, thinking of a way I could be nice instead of saying something mean, but that charged feeling was just too damn much.

"It's just that I know you're probably used to people doin' this stuff for you."

She flinched at my rude comment and let out a sigh. "You know what?" Placing her hands on the counter, she leaned forward.

I stepped closer to her, not sure what the hell I was doing. "What?"

Rising up on her tippy toes like she was going to kiss me or whisper in my ear, she carefully placed her warm hands on my chest for balance and murmured, "Sometimes I daydream about putting superglue in your baseball caps then watching you put them on that gorgeous head of yours." *She thinks my head is gorgeous?*

She spun in a circle and started to walk away. I tried to clear the attraction I felt so intensely out of my throat, as if that was where it gathered instead of in my pants. I saw Faith go back into the living room and say her goodbyes, grab her purse, and head out the door.

Before thinking better of it, I quickly stalked after her, because as I stated, I couldn't very well clear the attraction because it was currently sitting ramrod straight in my jeans. Also, I thought this might be a good opportunity to get closure. Trevor perked up from his spot, thinking it was time to go to bed. I shut the door behind me, hearing him barking and jumping up on the couch to see me through the window.

The frail, warped steps creaked as Faith jogged down, eager to get away from me, but she wasn't going to get far. She walked briskly past my fifth wheel, but just as she was nearly free, I reached for her shirt and pulled her back, dragging her into my humble home.

Be nice.

She let out a little yelp as I grabbed her rib cage and maneuvered her inside. Once she was in, I shut and locked the door then spun her around to face me. She was so close her warm breath mixed with mine. Her forehead was at my chin, and all I had to do was take a step back and give her some room and a good explanation as to why I'd just pulled her in here, but I couldn't. Instead I let my fingers slowly trail up, under her shirt. The feel of her smooth, warm skin under my fingertips was like having someone place an air mask over my face. She was here. With me. My pulse raced as my heart rioted in my chest, screaming, *Mine. Mine. Mine.*

She let out a hiss and gripped my shirt. "Jace, what are you doing?"

I didn't answer, just let my fingers trail over her toned stomach and abs, stopping at her bra line. I drew a boundary in my mind, because attraction was one thing, but suicide was something entirely different. She'd already ruined me once. I didn't want her to push me away, so instead of trying to get the closure we both needed, I asked her the first question that popped into my head.

"How did he propose to you?"

The lights were off in my trailer, so all I could see were the shadows in her hair and the silhouette of her face. She was looking up, those perfect lips accessible, and I wanted to take advantage, so fucking badly. But I wouldn't. I didn't know what this was or what I was doing, but reconnecting wasn't it.

"Did he plan some intimate dinner with low lighting and an orchestra, or were you out on a boat and he did it under the stars?" I whispered, running my hand over her hip and to her lower back.

She inhaled sharply and turned things around on me.

"How were you going to do it?"

"What?" I froze in place.

"How were you going to propose?" Her voice was soft, with genuine curiosity peeking through.

I was suddenly so glad she couldn't see my face, because I was

137

positive there was a myriad of emotions flashing across it, ones I wouldn't be able to hide even if I tried.

"Or were you never actually going to..." She trailed off, looking down and loosening her hold on my shirt.

I lifted her chin and stepped closer, hoping her grip would return.

"I was going to wait for one of those nights when the moon was just a tiny sliver, so we could easily see those stars you love. I had this plan to dance to that soundtrack you love so much, the one with the two girls who sing in the show, Nashville or somethin'... Anyway, we were going to drive out into the middle of nowhere, no lights, nothin' to dim the light of the sky. I was going to pack a tent, like we did after graduation, and we were going to dance just like you always loved doing in our castle. Then I was planning to get down on one knee and ask you there, spill my guts about how much I loved you from the first moment I saw you, how back in middle school I would follow you to class, even if it meant I was late to mine, because I had to know how you looked sitting there at that table so I could daydream about you.

"I was going to tell you how perfect you were, how in high school I tried to make you a ring in shop class, how I considered asking you to marry me then...and then I was going to make love to you under the stars."

I couldn't read her expression well, but she cleared her throat, something she used to do when she was getting emotional. I still wouldn't give her any space and relished how warm her body was pressed up against mine.

"He threw a big party, invited nearly two hundred people... proposed in the middle of it all. Everyone was watching." The sadness in her tone stripped me and made my ribs feel too tight.

If there was one thing about Faith that was essential, it was her deep need for privacy. She hated big parties that were centered around her. All her birthday parties from middle school on were small, tiny affairs. Just me, her best friend Gemma, and whoever Gemma was dating at the time; that was it. Occasionally she'd allow Jessie to tag along, but only if Jessie swore not to let any restaurants sing to her or tell anyone it was her special day. I could only imagine what a big public engagement like that must have done to her.

"I would have loved the way you were going to do it. Although, I was so infatuated with you that you could have dropped to one knee in the Quick Stop and it would have been the best thing to ever happen to me." Her hushed confession made my heart beat erratically. Hearing that she'd prefer my hypothetical proposal to her actual one was...confusing, exhilarating... horrible.

I had this need to touch her, so I leaned in, my hands on her hips, and skimmed the side of her face with my nose. Her breathing hitched, and her hands wrapped around my neck, pulling me closer. She still wanted this. It was clear in the way her body responded to mine and what she'd admitted the other night in the bar...and just now with the proposal.

She still wanted me.

Pride surged in my head and hope propelled me forward to grabbing her chin and tilting it up. In the darkness of my trailer, I pressed my lips to hers, feeling a fire surge between us. She pushed up, kissing me back, pulling my shirt into a firm hold.

I wanted to make her remember how good we were together, but the reminder that this wasn't real slowly trickled in. She was married. She belonged to someone else. We needed closure.

I let her go, took a step back, and then did what I did best—I deflected and turned things around on her.

I opened the door and said, "He sounds like an asshole, yet you still chose to marry the prick." My heart thundered in my chest, telling me to stop being a dick to her, but it hurt so badly, this life she had without me. Every time I took one step forward, it was like I took twenty back.

She ambled backward, but I ensured she didn't trip. Once she was safely on the ground, she looked up at me and sternly said, "Fuck you Jace." She swept a finger under her eye and stepped back, like she was headed toward her car, but stopped a few steps in. "You want to know why I married him?" she asked angrily, stalking forward a bit.

I wasn't ready, not with her angry like this.

"I went on four dates with him, just four then I was ready to break it off. But I drove into the Quick Stop the night I planned to do it, and I saw you with Jessica James. I couldn't breathe. I couldn't fucking see straight, so I went back to Bryan." Her desperate glare was slicing through me like glass. "I said yes to him because I thought you'd finally see what was happening. I thought you'd come...I thought for sure an engagement would make you snap out of it. I kept thinking you'd show up. Even on my wedding day, Jace—that's how fucked up I was over you. I was more eager to see you on that day than I was to see the man who'd put a ring on my finger," she spat.

I was so thankful there were no lights on because I was barely holding it together.

"It was always you, Jace, until you were nothing but a memory, even when he started..." She stopped and looked down, shook her head back and forth, and backed up. "But it doesn't matter anymore," she whispered, and she might as well have taken her heart out of her chest and tossed it at my feet. As it was, her words cut through me, ridding me of any more pride and any more anger. She'd taken it all right out of my veins.

Chapter 16
Faith
Five Years Earlier: November

"You're a zombie, Faith. Come on, go out with me...you haven't been out in weeks," Gemma begged, like she had nearly every Friday since the breakup...since he left. I'd watched *New Moon* about a million times, feeling a kinship with Bella after Edward ditched her. Jace was no immortal vampire, but he was the rock dividing my insane river of a life into manageable pieces. He was firm, rooted, secure. I saw my future with him, and without it...without him...I had no idea what I was doing or where I was going.

"I don't want to," I muttered while watching the fields behind my parents' house. I was terrified of seeing Jace with someone new. I'd barely left the house because I knew my heart wouldn't be able to take it. I'd fall apart on the spot.

"We won't even be local. Let's go to Memphis, make a weekend of it," Gemma pleaded, her hands coming together like she was praying. She probably was.

My mother had been praying the last few weeks, and each week she'd been getting louder. "Jesus, help the girl. Jesus, give the girl purpose." And my personal favorite: "Jesus, take the wheel. I know it's a song, but I think we could really use some direction right now."

Getting out of town wouldn't be so bad. I wouldn't see Jace in

Memphis...but it was already five in the evening. "With what money? Sleeping in your car isn't exactly a good idea." I lifted my head from my knees to catch her bright smile.

"My cousin Jade just got an apartment there and I've already asked if we could stay the night." Gemma waggled her eyebrows and began grabbing my duffle bag from my closet.

"Don't you have classes or something law-related?" I turned my head and raised an eyebrow in question.

She rolled her eyes. "It's Thanksgiving break."

"But your job..." She worked herself stupid during the breaks to save up for whatever her student loans didn't cover during the school year.

"I have the next three days off. Isn't that insane?" She pulled open my dresser drawers, pulled out two thongs, and threw them in my bag. That was enough of that. I stood and took the bag from her.

"You should have led with that, idiot. I would have gone with you if I knew you had a long weekend."

"Pshh, you would not. You've been in a funk, girl. Rightfully so, considering...but I miss you and really want to hang out with you." She folded her arms across her chest and narrowed her gaze on me.

I loaded up the rest of my things and nodded my agreement.

I felt my spirits lift marginally as we left the city limits. I tried to ignore how the last time I'd gone to Memphis was when I was with Jace. I tried to ignore how it'd been nearly four months since I had his arms around me, kissed him, or even saw him.

We stopped at Jade's apartment, dressed in tight dresses and tall heels, utilized all the fancy makeup her thirty-year-old self was able to afford, and headed out, fake IDs in hand.

Memphis was a different world from what we were used to. We were easily swept up in the frantic beats that thrummed through the darkened room, the moving bodies that swayed to the music. It was amazing but also a little too much for my small-town self. I took refuge in a large, circular booth, sipping on some sort of blue liquid in a tall glass. I knew the word adios was in the title, but I'd missed the rest.

We weren't twenty-one yet, so drinking made me nervous and awkward as hell. I hadn't built up the courage to go to the dance floor without Gemma yet. She'd found herself someone who wanted her on the floor with him with every change in song, so I sat tucked away in the dark booth, wishing desperately that I'd downloaded *New Moon* onto my Kindle.

"Any chance you'd be willing to share this big booth?" a velvet voice asked from above me. I snapped my head up and met a pair of electric blue eyes. They were firm, resolute...not the same kind of blue I was used to.

I shrugged, unsure of what to do.

"It's just that I've been trying to find somewhere somewhat quiet to sit, to enjoy this drink, but there aren't any booths left." He smiled wide, looking like my own personal knight in shining armor. "You seem like you don't want to be disturbed, so I was content with standing, but it seems your beauty keeps distracting me." He splayed his empty hand open, like he had a legitimate argument in it.

I giggled, the alcohol making me lighthearted and giddy. "I wouldn't stop you from scooting in, but...like you said, it's big, so maybe stay on your side and I'll stay on mine?"

He smiled, he was so well put together and grown up it made me swoon a bit. Maybe I'd been reading too many vampire books, but his smile made my pulse race. His suit was nicer than anything I'd ever seen on a real-life person.

He slid into the seat across from me as smooth as butter, all the while keeping his gaze locked on mine. We watched each other in our own kind of silence in the midst of the chaos and noise around us.

He appraised me from over the brim of his glass of amber liquid, and I liked his eyes on me. I liked how they made me feel. I liked how much better it made me feel compared to how I had been feeling. I'd been dead and now had someone offering me the chance to live again.

"What's your name?" he asked, loudly enough for me to hear over the music.

I rubbed my finger around the rim of my glass, unsure if I should tell him. "Not ready," I muttered in response, smiling like an idiot at the prospect of someone wanting me.

"Hi Not-Ready, I'm Bryan. It's nice to meet you." He sipped his drink and slid an inch to the right, closing the distance between us.

Present day

The fluorescent lights in the Collierville library flickered, nearly ready to go out as I hurried in through the front doors. They were going to close soon, but I'd requested a few books and wanted to grab them before the weekend hit. I needed distractions.

Big, heavy ones that had clever, unsuspecting love, dragons, and fairies. Vampires, werewolves—I'd take it all as long as it kept my mind in a different world. I needed fiction to fix me...and distract me from the fact that my husband wouldn't stop calling and texting and my ex-boyfriend wouldn't stop being an angry asshole. It was all wearing on me something fierce.

I kept expecting Bryan to show up like the boogie man. It had made me so nervous I was picking at my nails in fear, nearly every day. He'd said I had a week, but it had now been over a month and he still hadn't shown up, nor had he given any more clues as to his decision on granting me a divorce.

Thin, stained blue carpet quieted my steps as I made my way to the holding shelves. If memory served, all I had to do was find my name on the printed slip of paper, grab my book, scan it, and go. There were about ten books total on the hold shelf, but once I got to the end where my books should have been, I saw there was a note taped there.

Faith Vanderson,

Please see me.

Gloria

I peeled the note off, inspecting it for clues. Why on earth would Gloria want to talk to me? I kept my gaze focused on the note as I turned and ran right into something solid.

"Ouch, sorry," I muttered, bringing my hand to my forehead. *Did I just hit a chin? Holy hell.* I blinked, taking a step back, and inspected what or who I'd run into.

Jace stood there in his heavy boots, a pair of navy jeans forming perfectly to his thighs, and a black t-shirt plastered across his firm chest. His dark hair was slightly askew, like he'd been running his hands through it. My stomach tightened at the sight of him, and I hated myself for it. It had been a full week since I'd seen him, since he'd said those hurtful words and his touch had branded my skin.

I thinned my lips and tried to push past him but he put his arms out, like he was ready to stop me.

"Oh, good. You're both here." Gloria beamed at us as she rounded the corner. Her white hair was wound up into a tight bun on her head, her weathered face relaxed and her thin lips painted a coral pink color.

Jace and I looked at each other, confused.

"What exactly do you mean?" I asked, following her frail form toward the back of the library. Jace followed too, huffing out a frustrated sigh. I resisted the urge to roll my eyes at him like we were twelve.

"Here we are." Gloria stopped at a table full of at least fifty books.

Jace stopped next to me, gently lifting one of them, but Gloria reprimanded him.

"I don't think so, Mr. Walker." She lightly slapped his hand.

His eyes went wide as he dropped the book. I stifled a laugh.

"I had planned on fining you two for the damage done in this library, but now that you're both back in town, this is better." Gloria smiled, stacking a few of the books.

Jace's gaze snapped over to mine, likely thinking the same thing as me. We'd done a lot of things in this library so there was no way to know exactly what she was referring to, but I wasn't admitting anything.

"What exactly are we fixing?" Jace rubbed a hand along his chin.

"There are fifty-three books we've found over the last few years that have your notes written inside. Pages and pages of correspondence between you two, written into the margins, just ruining these books." She shook her head in disappointment. *"To Kill a Mockingbird* is a classic!" she said forcefully.

Jace winced, and I wanted to die. Truly, I wished the earth would open up and swallow us. Jace had said they were decoded books. He'd said no one would ever know.

"No matter." She breathed through her nose, seeming to calm down. "You're here to fix it. That's all that matters. You aren't leaving until you've erased every single page." She held out a box of Pink Pearl erasers and gestured toward the two wooden chairs.

Jace scoffed, "Not to be rude, Miss Gloria, but how do you know these were from us?"

Hope fluttered. *That's right—we never used our names.* Suddenly a smug feeling settled in as I crossed my arms and quirked a sassy brow, practically shouting for her to prove it.

Gloria rolled her eyes. "You two honestly don't think we knew what you were doing? You left a trail messier than a pig rollin' in a pig pen during spring!" She moved closer to the books. "That and we have security footage."

Shit.

Jace laughed. "There's no way you can force us to sit down and do this. Can't you just charge Faith for it? She married a billionaire, didn't you hear?" He smirked at me, and I nearly launched myself at him.

"I know you'll do it because regardless of this horrific act of vandalism, you two were good kids. I know you'll do the right thing." Gloria softened and patted her hair. "Now, the back door locks on its own when you exit." She grabbed her coat and purse, sauntering away.

The lights in the front half of the library shut off, leaving just the few lit up over our table in the back. I hesitated a second, not sure if Jace was going to take off or stay, then realized Gloria was right. Regardless of what he chose, I needed to fix this.

I stepped forward and pulled a chair back, taking a seat, then flipped through the first book. I heard a huff of breath before I saw Jace plop down next to me.

"I can't believe you're agreeing to do this." Jace grabbed *The Catcher and the Rye* and began thumbing through it.

"I can't believe we continued writing in these even after we realized who each other was," I muttered while reading one of the notes I'd written.

Dear Fool,

What's your favorite thing about the sky?

Dear Pip,

The stars are literally history, and we get to see a piece of it every night.

"Honestly, I'm shocked there aren't more. We kept going until... what, tenth grade?" Jace quipped, holding an eraser between his fingers, leaning over the desk. For whatever reason, I was terrified of him actually erasing any of our history. I hadn't even known it still existed before today, but now that I did, I couldn't bring myself to remove this little part of our past.

"Are you going to erase it?" I whispered, terrified.

"Should I?" he whispered back.

The pain slicing through the space between us made my eyes burn.

"Doesn't seem right...all this stuff," he whispered, moving to another book.

I grabbed one, eager to read what our younger selves had written.

His not-so-manly giggle had me leaning over and trying to see what he was reading.

"It's about that one time after we got to second base in sophomore year and you started freaking out." He turned those laughing eyes on me. I smiled, remembering, but gently grabbed the book so I could see what we'd written.

Pip, why are you sitting so far away from me?

I'm kinda freaking out I guess.

I couldn't tell...

Make fun of me all you want, but I'm not used to having a boy's hand up my shirt and on my...you know whats.

Do tell. On your whats, Pip?

Fool, stop.

Why are you freaking out about it though?

I don't know...guess I just feel a little awkward now that you've seen them and felt them.

And their perfect...actually, I can't wait to do it again. Want to meet me behind the back wall?

You misspelled they're...and no. Are you crazy? The library is full of people.

All the more fun. No one will even see us.

But once they read these notes, they'll know. God, this is so embarrassing.

You're Pip and I'm Fool—no one knows who we are.

Gloria is walking over—if she catches us, we're in so much trouble. Fool, seriously, stop looking at me like that!

Like what? Like your beautiful and perfect and I want to kiss you?

You misspelled you're. And yes, stop looking at me like you've seen my you know whats.

I may become the world's worst speller if it makes you blush like that...

I'm blushing for other reasons and you know it.

"We were so reckless," I murmured, feeling my face flush.

Jace let out a heavy sigh as he shut the book and moved it away. "No, we were in love."

"Same thing." I met his stare and watched as his eyes lowered to my lips. My heart pounded so hard in my chest I wondered if it'd break through altogether.

I hated how desperate I felt for his touch, how deep my hunger went. There was a void in my soul where Jace Walker had once been, and now that he was so close, it was as though my entire being beckoned for him to fill it.

"I couldn't come after you," he said, barely above a whisper.

He was so close, I could feel his hot minty breath on my face. A lump was stuck in my throat at what he was about to admit.

"I would have if I could have...but I was in..." He hesitated, carefully capturing a stray piece of my hair between his fingers.

I closed my eyes as he brought his forehead to mine. His scent surrounded me, tugging me deeper into the emptiness he'd left me with.

"I would have started a fucking war for you, Faith. I would have burned down the church, given my soul to the devil just to break in and stop your wedding, but I was put in jail a few months before." He let out a weighty sigh, and my heart felt the heaviness in his unstable timbre. Tears stung my eyes, battering them for what I owed him. "You were mine, Faith. I was yours and you just walked away. You married someone else." His eyes closed tight, like those words had accidently escaped the locked confession box he'd buried in his heart.

I wanted to speak, to say something, but he didn't give me a chance.

"Burn 'em for all I care. I'm done." He shoved his chair back and sauntered off toward the back door, leaving me alone with our past. Just like last time, he'd discarded it like it was nothing.

Chapter 17
Jace

"So, what's going on with you two anyway?" Seth asked while he thumbed through a comic book. Based on how careful he was with the edges, it must have been a rare one. Seth kept all his comics in plastic covers, only taking them out every so often.

I continued cleaning the grease off the motor I was working on. It wasn't really needed, but the thing was so old, it would be a nice gift for Mr. Stein, who was getting too old to see under the hood well anymore.

"I don't know. I keep trying to be nice, but every time I'm around her, I just..." I tried to shut out how I'd left things the previous night in the library. She had been right there, our history laid in front of us, and it was getting all too easy to forget why I hated her.

"You're a dick?" Seth peeked up from his spot on the counter, across the garage. He was the only one allowed in here with me while I worked. So far, I hadn't had to hire another mechanic or anyone who could help with custom work because regular oil changes and towing services kept us plenty busy, but one day...

"Yeah," I muttered, spraying the Simple Green along the caked-on grease around the gas cap and battery.

"Well man, I'm tellin' you all you have to do is kiss her. You aren't really mad, you're just pissed that..." He trailed off. "Well shit me and fuck you very much."

I looked at him from around the hood, trying to gauge what had caused him to use his ridiculous phrase.

He had his comic pinned to his chest, his other hand on his cell phone, his eyes narrowed as he read something. I waited, the soft sound of the band Chevelle playing in the background, grounding me until my friend explained what was going on. My gut churned on instinct, already assuming it had to do with Faith. *What if something happened?*

Suddenly I was reaching for an oil rag so I could grab my cell.

"You were wondering what her situation is?" Seth yelled, clearing the music.

I stalled, my hand on the rag. "Yeah..."

"An interview with her just popped up on the internet. Gemma sent me the link." His green eyes jumped up, boring into me, waiting for my reaction.

I wouldn't give him one. In fact, on pride and principle, I waited until I had finished the truck, washed up, and gotten home before I finally tugged out my cell and clicked on the link Seth had forwarded to me.

Patting Trevor's head, I watched as the interview started. Faith sat in a red chair across from some talk show host, her yellow skirt like melted butter over her knees. A black fitted shirt went up to her neck, the sleeves short, and there on her lips was that red stain.

"I can't thank you enough for coming in and talking with us today," the host said, shaking Faith's hand.

Faith smiled in response and crossed one leg over the other, her long skirt covering her legs. She looked poised, ready, and completely comfortable being on television.

"Thank you for having me." She smiled.

I got up, snagged a few chips, and began preparing Trevor's dinner as they talked through a few more pleasantries. When I heard,

"...your impending divorce from Bryan Vanderson," my eyes darted back to the screen.

"Yes, people have been speculating for a while now, but I'm here to put the rumors to rest. Bryan and I are currently going through a divorce."

The host winced, nodding her head. "I know this is such a private matter and a sensitive subject, but would you be willing to open up about the details surrounding the split? Our viewers are all so curious."

I shook my head in irritation. These guys were all out to make an easy buck.

Faith gave her a tight smile. "Nothing to tell. Sometimes people just don't click. We're going our separate ways, an amicable separation." She blinked twice in succession, causing her long lashes to flutter. *She's lying.*

Faith had an easy tell. It made playing any kind of game, especially poker, with her hilarious as hell. She couldn't lie to save her life.

So why was she lying about the divorce?

I lowered the phone, knowing Faith wouldn't give any more details, but suddenly I was filled with a surge of confusing emotions—elation that she was free, frustration that she was still married at all, and curiosity about what on earth she wasn't saying. Either way, I finally had an answer to what in the hell Faith was doing here. She was getting divorced, and soon she'd be a single woman—and I'd been nothing but a dick to her.

Fuck.

Chapter 18
Faith

I KNEW my time with my parents was running out. My father's disgruntled throat-clearing and heavy shaking of his newspaper while eyeing me with pity had been a regular routine every morning since I arrived. My plans for my apartment were nearly in place; I just needed two more nights and the space I had gone to see would be mine. Two more nights of tolerating my father's glare and passive aggressive comments about not needing to air my dirty laundry on live television.

He didn't like that interview at all, regardless of the fact that I'd lied through my teeth about the divorce, taking the higher road—*much* higher.

"So, you plan on getting a job?" He stared me down with those horn-rimmed glasses.

I smiled sweetly at him over a glass of orange juice. "Yes, eventually I do. I need to get settled into my apartment before I look for work."

He answered me with a firm clearing of his throat, which generally meant he was ready to give a lecture. Folding his newspaper in half, he said, "I'm sure I could find a place for you at the office." Dad was working at the bank as a loan officer now, giving him just the smallest bit of seniority over the tellers.

I stood, pushed my chair back, and smiled at my father's sweet attempts. When I was a teenager, he had wanted me to try to get a scholarship to college, seeing as they couldn't afford it. My grades were fine, but not stellar. I'd joined cheerleading but had missed two out of the four years of high school because of fees, and because I didn't exactly get along with the girls on the squad. I had planned on going once I married Jace, which was never a fun conversation topic with my father. Now, as a twenty-five-year-old with no college education and no job prospects, I felt ashamed of his offered handout.

"It's okay, Dad. I've got some ideas."

"Just don't keep hiding out," he pleaded, sitting up tall.

I stopped mid-step, confused. "What do you mean?"

He let out a sigh. "I see you checking the curtains for the press and news folk...I don't want you hiding out because of them, especially now that your interview has aired."

This part of my life wasn't something my family was exactly familiar with. Being tucked away in Nashville had kept the press away from my small-town upbringing, but now that I was back, it was like a big spotlight hanging over us all the time. My throat was dry as I tried to clear it, wanting to convince my father I wasn't hiding out, but the truth was, a part of me was hiding, too afraid of being chased or watched. Now that the interview had gone live, the talk shows and news outlets were going crazy.

There would be more photographers than ever, no doubt, but I was banking on them focusing more on Bryan since I'd painted him as the jilted husband. I had seen a few gossip tabloids already printing that I had cheated, leaving him in the dust. A few others were commenting that he was licking his wounds and cradling his broken heart in the Cayman Islands.

"I promise I won't." I bent low to kiss my dad's cheek.

I jogged upstairs and pulled on a pair of dark skinny jeans, paired them with a white t-shirt, and tugged on my thrift-shop-find cowboy boots. It felt good to get back to myself. As much as I adored all the expensive shoes, there was nothing like sliding on a pair of cowboy boots.

My day was mostly spent with Gemma in the office, prepping, planning, and getting divorce papers ready to serve Bryan with. He'd mostly been quiet, giving me the space I'd asked for except for a few texts here and there. At night, it was usually the worst. He'd text me pictures of us, telling me he missed me. I never replied. After the interview aired, I assumed he'd call me or something, but it was as if he hadn't seen it.

I kept busy with Gemma for the most part, minus the few times she took calls and had to meet with a few other clients. I'd procure myself a notepad and begin doodling. For some reason, I found myself drawing the inside of a garage lobby.

"You haven't sketched like that in forever!" Gemma gasped, pulling the notebook from my fingers, tracing the shaded lines I'd created. "Faith, this is gorgeous..." Her blue eyes widened as they flitted from the straight lines and shaded shapes. I blushed and looked away. "Why his auto shop?" Gemma asked accusingly, pointing her manicured nail at the sketch.

I drew in a sharp breath, knowing it wouldn't do any good to try to lie to my best friend. She saw places in me I didn't even see, so she'd definitely see this.

"Because that was always the dream. Whatever it was we were going to do, we were supposed to do it together. I'd help him draw and inspire ideas, then we'd manage and create it together. I'm so proud of him for his shop...guess for a second I just wanted to know what it felt like to dream with him."

"Even if he never knows you're dreaming?" Her eyes narrowed while her hold on the paper slackened.

I shrugged. "Even then."

She shook her head like she didn't understand it. I didn't either, but some small part of me wanted to stay tied to that girl I used to be, the dreamer who chased goals and larger-than-life plans with the boy she loved.

Gemma cleared her throat and shuffled a few papers in front of her. "We're all set. They're all filed. He'll get served by Friday, but because of your segment, he could—"

"I know." I cut her off as nerves snaked their way under my skin.

Gemma sat forward, her tight curls framing her face. "He could still spin this, delaying the divorce—"

"He can't." I cut her off again with my nose flaring.

Gemma set her papers down and leveled me with a stare. "Honey, he can, and he will. He has to protect his image. You know this."

I watched her grey-blue eyes move over me, watching...assessing. "I didn't say anything bad about him. I think he'll see it as an olive branch."

"Don't get me started on that shitshow you put on. I can't believe you did that." She shook her head, perching on the edge of her desk.

My face exploded with heat. I hated explaining my choices to her when, in my gut, I knew she was always right. Gemma was my role model. She didn't know it, but I looked up to her in everything.

"I know, but I just want to be done with it. I just want a divorce, and maybe now he'll give me one." I shrugged.

Her eyes were furious, frozen orbs. "You're my best friend and I love you. You know that."

I nodded, readying myself for whatever she was about to say.

She waited a second, thinning her lips.

"Just say it!" I yelled.

"Grow the fuck up already!" she yelled back.

I inhaled a sharp breath. "What?"

She stood, towering over me. "I begged you not to marry him. I told you that you were still in love with Jace, that you hadn't healed. I told you it was a mistake—but you ignored me!" She raised her voice, pacing like she was in the courtroom.

I held my breath, feeling my chest shudder.

"Bryan beats you and puts you in the hospital, you come back and are treated like shit by your ex, and you just keep lying down and taking it. Stand up for yourself. Stand up to Bryan. Don't settle for a divorce. Sue him. Take everything from him. Make sure he knows he can't mess with you!" She glared at me.

I knew she loved me. I knew if our roles were reversed, I would be yelling this at her, but it didn't soothe the sting.

A sob worked its way out of my throat. "I can't."

"Why?" Gemma begged.

"Because I'm scared! Okay? I'm scared he never actually loved me. I'm scared he'll win and I'll be stuck with him while he hurts me. I'm weak, Gem. I don't know how to be strong."

Silence echoed loudly between us as tears cascaded down my face. She crouched in front of me, carefully cradling my jaw. "Once upon a time, you were the strongest girl I ever knew. She's in there still. He's just been pouring dirt on your spirit, hoping to bury you for the last five years. We'll get you back. I promise."

I launched forward into her arms and let her hug me. I let honest tears of regret and shame fall to her shoulder, let something inside me break open without any hope of being put back together again.

Fat raindrops fell from the darkening sky. I winced as my wiper blades screeched and groaned, reminding me they were old. I was traveling back to my parents' house, calling the day to a close when the sky opened up and dumped itself out onto the highway. The only good thing about this weather was that it kept the paparazzi at bay.

"Shit." I put my hazards on, slowly pulled to the shoulder, and turned my car off to sit and wait the storm out. Every so often there was an intense storm system that would sweep through the area, and the safe thing to do was to pull over. After about five minutes of solid downpour, it started to taper off.

"Finally." I breathed out and turned the key over to start the

157

engine. Nothing happened. Panic swept through me as my face pinched in worry. "Come on." I pushed the key over again and waited. The clicking sound of a dead battery met me and seemed to echo in the emptiness of the car. Groaning, I leaned forward and rested my forehead against the steering wheel. I had no idea what was wrong with my car, seeing as Jace had looked everything over when he fixed the clutch.

Pulling my cell free, I searched for the number to a tow company, avoiding Jace's auto shop. I was in Collierville city limits and his shop would be the closest one, but I didn't want to see him, not after the night in the library.

Placing the call and getting an estimated wait time of about thirty minutes, I decided to read over the paperwork Gemma had given me for the divorce. My heart still beat rapidly every time I considered what I was about to do, when I considered how Bryan would react. Fear snuck inside and threatened to crack me open when I imagined his impending outburst. A sharp knock on my window caused me to drop the papers and jump.

"Shit." I pressed my hand to my heart.

Dark hair matted over a set of icy blue eyes met me. I swallowed down my confusion and opened the door.

"What are you doing here?"

"Well what a nice greeting. Is that how rich people say thank you?" Jace crossed his arms over his chest and turned that sexy grin on me.

The rain had lightened, but it was still sprinkling. I swiped at my face and tried to ignore his lingering stare on my white shirt. "It's just that I didn't call your shop...I was expecting a different towing service to come."

Jace let out a sigh and dropped his gaze. "I have an arrangement with a few of the other companies for any tows if their roster is filled up or there's bad weather."

I darted my gaze to his tow truck, which was parked behind me, and let out a small sigh. "Okay, looks like you get to tow me home then." I opened my door and pulled out my jacket and purse.

"Spose so, unless you'd prefer I just leave you here?" Jace opened his arms and began walking in front of my car. "Wanna pop it open?" he yelled right as the sky opened up again.

I brought my purse up to cover my head while Jace tipped his face back and blinked at the sky.

"Never mind, let's get out of here. Go ahead and jump into the truck," he shouted over the rain as he began getting my car hooked up to the tow chain. I ran forward, jumped into the cab like he suggested, and tried to stop the chills running down my arms. Trevor was sitting in the middle of the bench, and instead of the frenzied greeting I usually received, he merely nudged my arm with his nose and then settled his face into my lap. Feeling the extra weight in the back of the truck shift and move the cab around had me looking in the rear-view mirror.

Jace's biceps tensed under his white mechanic shirt. His hair was in his eyes with little drops of water falling from each strand. My heart was riotous in my chest as I watched him work. So often I would let my mind wander to what it would have been like if Jace and I hadn't been interrupted. If he'd have proposed and married me, if he would have dreamt up this life he was living, my dreams blossoming alongside his. If we were together each day, beginning them together, ending them together...

Jace's door opened, and he briskly slid into his seat and slammed his door. I cleared my throat and buckled up, jostling Trevor until he rose, spun in a circle, and readjusted his body to lean against mine. I wrapped my arm around him and patted his side until he closed his eyes.

"This storm was supposed to clear up by now," Jace muttered, putting the truck into gear and pulling us forward. I didn't reply to his sentiment, too caught up in the past. His scent overwhelmed me, drowning me in memories, demanding that I stop and pay attention to the fact that Jace hadn't moved on. Whatever his reasons were for leaving me, after all these years, he was still single. Something odd and exciting was churning in my gut as we made our way down Bentley Road.

"How long were you waitin?" Jace's Southern accent peeked through his question, and it made me smile.

"I'm not even sure, got caught up in reading over some papers." I tucked a few wet strands of hair behind my ears and watched Jace's forearms flex as he gripped the wheel.

"Why didn't you call my shop?" His gruff question made me squirm. I liked that he cared whether I called him or not, but I didn't want him to know that.

"Why would I?" I looked over and raised an eyebrow at him.

I watched as he kept his gaze focused on the road, not sure if he'd respond. Silence hung between us as he turned onto my parents' road.

"You know I would have helped you...I wouldn't have charged you or whatever." He put his blinker on to turn into my parents' drive. "I want you to know you can call me...if you're stranded and shit...I don't want that."

I watched my lap as a small smile crept across my lips.

"I think maybe we need to talk," I confessed, hoping he wouldn't turn me down. He'd confessed something to me the other day, and I hadn't stopped thinking about it; we needed to talk. There was just too much history between us that didn't add up.

"Looks like no one's home," Jace lightly quipped, ignoring my request. He pulled around the gravel circle and put his truck in park.

I tangled my fingers together in apprehension. "Want to come in for a few minutes to dry off?" I offered.

He didn't look at me, but quietly said, "Wouldn't hurt to get warmed up a bit, I guess."

I gave him a half-smile as we both exited the truck, the rain lightly pelting us.

I watched as Jace let my car down and unhooked it from his truck, setting it down carefully. Once he was finished adjusting everything, he brought his hands to his hips and stared me down. *Is he going to change his mind?*

The icy rain hit us at an angle as he waited one second...two... then his steps started toward me and I didn't wait. I walked ahead of him, listening for his steps behind me.

Once we made it to the door, I felt his body heat directly behind me as his fingers dug into my hip. My breathing came out in harsh and heavy breaths, eager for his touch to settle my nerves.

I opened the door, walked in, and turned. Jace shut the door behind him and pressed his back against the polished oak. His blue eyes searched my face and tracked my movements as I stepped forward.

I tipped my chin up and approached until my toes met his. His chest was heaving, like mine.

My lips were traveling slowly to meet his as he carefully grabbed my jaw and splayed his fingers into my hair. Maybe we didn't need words. Maybe we just needed to speak the other language our souls were versed in, the one where our fingers danced along each other's skin, and when our lips met, our strangled gasps would heal and mend whatever we'd broken.

Our breathing mingled for only a second before we were interrupted by the sound of my name being called.

"Faith, baby, is that you?" Bryan's sickly-sweet Tennessee drawl carried from the living room.

No.

Steps echoed on my parents' old floors as the boards bore his weight. I smelled his overpriced Creed Aventus cologne before he even made an appearance. It had always smothered me, even before my bruises carried the scent. I turned my whole body toward the sound, taking a step back toward Jace.

Bryan's tall frame filled the arch in the foyer, his slate grey suit perfectly tailored and without a single wrinkle. His clean-shaven face revealed a firm jaw, and light eyebrows framed warm blue eyes— deceiving eyes that covered up the monster lurking beneath.

"Bryan...what are you—"

He cut me off, flicking a quick look at Jace then back at me. "I'm here for you, babe."

He leaned in, grabbing my waist with force. He pulled me away from Jace and planted a firm kiss on my lips. It was quick, too quick for me to even push him away. I ducked my head and tried to push the bile down.

"Your parents went into town to run a quick errand, wanted you to be surprised for dinner. I didn't want them to tell you I was coming." He smiled brightly, showing those gorgeous teeth of his.

His gaze landed back on the man behind me, the one I was desperate to reach for.

"Oh, was there trouble with Faith's car?" His eyes narrowed on Jace's shop logo, near the breast pocket of his shirt. "What do I owe you?" He reached into his back pocket to grab his wallet.

"No, this is my—" I tried to explain, but Jace cut me off.

"$130 even, for the tow."

I turned to see the expression on his face.

"Jace..." I pleaded—for what, I wasn't sure. His lips were thinned into a firm line, his glacier stare glued to my husband, who was digging through the sea of green in his wallet.

Bryan placed a few bills in Jace's ready palm. "Thanks for getting my girl here safe."

Jace let out a scoff, "My pleasure. Glad I could get her where she belongs."

I swallowed, wanting to scream. Why was Jace so willing to leave me here?

"Jace, wait—it's not—this isn't..." I tried again, but he locked his jaw, giving me a death glare. It made me falter a step.

Jace turned without saying goodbye, leaving me alone with my husband, my abuser.

I shut my eyes tightly when the door clicked shut, but as much as I needed to let him go and walk away, I couldn't.

"I need to grab something from his truck," I muttered to Bryan then ran after Jace, shutting the door behind me.

Jace was already to his door, opening it with force. I ran to it and held it with my hand. "Jace...can you let me explain?"

"What's the fucking point?" He turned away from his truck and brought his hand to his hair. I hated the look on his face; it matched the look he'd given me at the barbeque when he was angry with me. "You know...I actually believed that little segment about you getting a divorce." He laughed, shaking his head.

Rain hit my face like little pellets from an airsoft gun. "Let me explain. I wasn't—"

"Get back inside, Faith. Your husband is waiting for you." He ended our conversation, moving his body to get back into the truck, which put me slightly off balance.

"Jace, please...just listen," I begged again as he slammed the door shut. I hated how those words sounded coming out of me. They sounded so similar to when I'd begged him not to dump me, begged him not to end us. He'd left anyway, just like he was now. I swallowed the thick lump of fear in my throat and let out a shuddering breath as I watched the tail lights of his truck disappear.

My car didn't work, so I couldn't just drive away. There was no other car available, and the rain was still pouring, so I walked back inside.

Bryan was back in the living room, nursing a small glass of amber liquid in his left hand, his cell in his right. I had no idea how long he'd been drinking. He was high functioning but still liked to get mean whenever any amount of alcohol was involved.

He looked up at me and smiled, like he hadn't driven me away from our marriage with a hospital visit.

"No kiss for me?" Bryan asked, patting the seat next to him.

"We're technically separated right now, Bryan. Do my parents even know you're here?" I peeled my coat off, taking the farthest seat across from him.

"The fuck we are." He laughed, taking a sip. "And yes, they do...

in a way." He tossed his head as though considering the question. "Now come over here and give your husband a proper greeting."

I didn't move, just crossed my arms protectively.

"I've missed you, babe. But you know, based on that interview, it almost seems like you've missed me more. What was it you said?" He leaned forward. His blond hair was a little longer on top, so pieces of it fell across his brow. I hated how handsome he was, because it covered up how ugly he could be. "I still love my husband, and a part of me will always love him," he mimicked.

"But we're over," I said, finishing the sentence he was trying to use against me.

"Of course, now that I've given you the time you asked for...it's time to come home."

I kept my gaze on the floor, unwilling to engage with him.

"Baby, what's going on? You were so sweet in that interview, so sweet it won't be hard to convince people we decided to work it out." He got up and stalked toward me. My heart thrashed violently in my chest. "Get up," he demanded.

I breathed through my nose. The urge to comply to avoid pain was right there on the edge of my movements, but my desire to make things difficult for him was stronger.

Cold fingers wrapped around my left bicep, yanking me to my feet. I let out a pained sound as he seethed in front of me.

"I said to fucking get up."

"Bryan, please—"

His lips landed on mine, harsh and demanding. His other hand gripped my chin, pinning it in place as his lips moved over mine and his tongue invaded my mouth. Whiskey assaulted my taste buds, warming my mouth, drowning me.

"I gave you everything, Faith," he rasped, breaking the kiss. "You were nothing when I met you—fucking no one. You will not make a fool of me." His grip on my arm intensified as his voice escalated in volume. "Do I need to remind you who I am?" he whispered harshly near my ear, biting the sensitive flesh there.

I let out a whimper, terrified of where this was headed. Bryan had never raped me before, but I had no idea what he was capable of. My insides began to shrivel up in fear just as the front door jingled and the sound of keys interrupted my husband's tirade. He let me go and sat down, pulling me to his side and sweetly kissing the top of my head right as my parents sauntered in.

"Faith?" my father asked, stopping dead when he saw Bryan. "What are you doing in here? I told you we would call you." His angry tenor shook the room.

My eyes watered as I fought back the emotions clawing at my insides. My mother gawked, pushing forward. I got up immediately and went to her side. Bryan's jaw ticked as he watched.

"Clark, nice to see you. Julia." Bryan canted his head as he stood, buttoning his jacket.

My father's face was blotchy. "We agreed to arrange this meeting, not have you here when we weren't." He turned, inspecting me. "Faith, are you okay?"

"Of course she's okay—I'm her husband," Bryan boomed, shoving his hands in his pockets.

There was an awkward silence hanging in the air, but I refused to speak until he was gone. My father seemed to be trying to regain his composure; my mother lightly held my wrist.

"Just the same, I think it would be a good idea for you to go. This wasn't a good idea," my father declared, gently dropping his brown paper bag. I could see green veggies and a carton of cookies sticking out.

Bryan looked down, clicked his tongue, and went to retrieve his long jacket. "There's more to the story. I wish you'd let me explain, but I can understand where you stand. I'll go, but I'm not leaving town yet. I would like the opportunity to treat everyone to dinner if that's okay?" His blue eyes were deceptive and cunning. They pleaded and begged with my parents, who I could see visibly soften.

"We'll be in touch after we get a chance to settle this evening," my mother said, surprising me. I whipped my head around to see her expression, because surely a body snatcher must have stepped in. There was no need to touch base or settle. This was an open-and-shut case. He hit me. I was done. We were getting divorced. End of story.

Bryan tipped his head to the side, gazing at me with a pathetic lilt in his tone. "I love you, Faith. I'll call tomorrow. Just, please...please come back to me." Tears actually welled in his eyes as he departed. It took all of my strength not to start clapping at his performance, but based off my parents' red, watery eyes, his presentation was utter perfection. I swallowed thickly and softly padded upstairs to pack a bag for Gemma's. I wouldn't risk them letting him back in, thinking they were helping in some way.

Five years earlier: January

The light on my phone blinked, indicating that I had another new message. Pushing the device under the sweatshirt balled up in the passenger seat of my old Honda Accord, I flicked my gaze back to my windshield. I was spying, like a creeper, but in all fairness, I couldn't exactly move. Another ping reverberated from under the sweatshirt, reminding me that I shouldn't be staring at the couple across the street. I continued to ignore it, though, like I had the other few text messages from Bryan, because I was surely in shock.

Jace stood, tall and rigid in his dark jeans, black hoodie zipped up to his throat, his snapback covering his dark hair, leaving little pieces sticking out on the sides. Dipping his head, he whispered something into Jessica James' ear, causing her to laugh. They huddled under the covered station near her fancy Audi, which was white, the color of the gum she'd spit in my hair in the tenth grade. My teeth clicked together on instinct as I remembered how she had flirted with Jace, slipping her hand up his shirt while he was distracted and then feigning innocence.

Her thin frame was angled toward Jace as she turned her phone toward him, laughing and touching his arm. Then he ran his arm up along her side, touching the skin under her shirt.

Tears swam in sync with the drizzle hitting my window. Childish assumptions swirled inside me, making me feel foolish and starry-eyed. When Jace had let me go, I'd truly believed he'd never move on, unless it was coming back to me. I had thought he'd take the time he needed for his family, for his mother, sort it out, and then he'd be mine again. My heart wouldn't even consider the idea of him moving on, but now under the fluorescent glow of the gas station lights, I could see how horrifically wrong I was.

Without thinking, I swiped at my face and reached for my door handle, shoving it open. Questions about why he'd left me scratched at my throat, begging me to run over there and demand his attention. He'd been completely silent since we broke up, no accidental texts, no friendly check-ins, nothing. He had just evaporated into thin air, like Edward did to Bella. *Fucking men.*

I wanted to make him see me, and since I couldn't go to his parents' house and bother his mama, now was my chance. I stood, letting the rain pour over me, running into my shirt, soaking it through, along with my thin Keds and jeans.

Jace dipped his head down, close to her ear, and from the angle I had, it looked like they kissed. I couldn't tell from this far away, but my stomach tilted with anxiety and shock just the same. He was moving on. Without me.

Clinging to my survival instincts, I got back in my car and peeled away from the lot, not caring if he noticed I'd been sitting there, watching. I drove for thirty minutes until I was standing dripping wet in the lobby of a five-star hotel in Memphis. I waited as Bryan ran down to meet me. We'd only been on four dates, and I'd been distant after our last one because he had told me he was already falling for me and was already picturing a future with me.

I had recoiled instantly because my heart was sworn to someone else. There wasn't a chance in hell I'd sacrifice my chance at having a future with Jace. Now, knowing he was already moving on and doing whatever it was he was doing on top of the fact that he'd harshly dumped me out of nowhere. My fight was gone.

I let Bryan tuck me under his chin, wrap his arms around me, and wordlessly lead me upstairs to his room. He didn't say anything as he tapped his key fob to the scanner on the door and it blinked green. He didn't mention the burly security guards standing outside, and I didn't ask. I knew he was rich; he said he'd developed some tech that caught on quickly and from that built up a nice nest egg. When we entered, there was a soft glow from the desk overlooking Memphis; otherwise the lights were off.

He left me standing in the middle of the room while he went to start the bath. I aimlessly drifted toward the window and watched the lights of the city cast a blue glow for as far as my eyes could see. My heart pinched as I tried to see past the city lights and peek into the darkness, where my past was, where the boy I loved was falling in love with someone else. Bryan stepped behind me, grabbing my hand, he led me to the luxurious bathroom.

White marbled floors expanded beneath my feet, a massive jacuzzi tub rested near the corner, and across the room was a large walk-in shower, all glass and white tile. It was beyond opulent, beyond anything I had ever witnessed in person. So distracted by the pain hollowing out my chest and the beauty surrounding me, I didn't even notice when Bryan stood in front of me and began slowly peeling off my shirt.

He tugged it above my head, running his warm fingers up and down my arms, and he removed my jeans and shoes next. I kept expecting shame or caution to surface. I kept expecting an objection to leave my tongue or some sound of protest to come out, but nothing came. Once I was naked, he gently led me toward the tub and helped me in.

He was going to leave me, let me have privacy, but as I sank into the delicious heat, I tugged on his hand, silently asking him to join me.

He gave me a heady look, arousal clear in the way his eyes dipped to my chest. He slowly discarded his clothes. He was all hard edges and smooth skin, no hair, and perfectly tanned with zero awkward tan lines. He looked like one of my Ken dolls from when I was little. A different kind of heat began to unfurl within me as he crawled in behind me. He tugged me to his chest, still not asking any questions.

It was there in the rapture of his embrace, when he whispered "Stay with me" in my ear that I nodded my agreement and sealed my fate. I had muddled through almost five months of heartbreak and I wasn't healed or ready for another relationship, but I was ready to put the Jace chapter behind me once and for all. Maybe with enough time, I could grow to love Bryan the way he deserved. I could love him in a different way, maybe a more powerful way.

I just knew I wasn't going back to Jace Walker.

Chapter 19
Jace

"You in the mood for some lunch or what?" Seth leaned forward and scanned the thin, plastic menu in front of him. We were in Memphis, settling in at the hotel restaurant. Seth wanted to get me out of the city, get my mind off what I'd explained to him. I wanted to get wasted, to forget the fact that Faith wasn't single, forget she was still very much married.

A UFC fight was scheduled here, so later tonight, we'd go watch two grown men beat each other senseless. I'd spend that time imagining it was Bryan in the ring, getting his face pummeled.

Seeing Bryan Vanderson in person, touching, kissing Faith three days ago was too much. I blanched as humiliation swam through me, thinking back to that day, how it had felt like Faith was about to kiss me...how she'd asked me in, how down deep I knew what I felt, how that look had crept into her eye when she took a step back when she saw her husband. Still, I'd left because that look wasn't any of my business. She wasn't any of my business. Not anymore.

It was all the reminder I needed to stay as far away from her as possible, and maybe this weekend, I could find someone to fill that space in my heart that had always belonged to her. It was a long shot, but I'd take it.

"Yeah, any ideas on what's good here?" I eyed the double bacon cheeseburger and aimlessly looked over beer options. I wasn't really in the mood for beer. I liked to indulge at night if I was relaxing, but otherwise I was a water or iced tea kinda guy. Seth took a few more seconds to look over the menu, and while he did, I let my gaze wander to the large television over the bar.

It was playing some local station out of Nashville; the clip was labeled breaking news or some shit. I looked around for the bartender or anyone who might take pity on me and turn it to sports highlights, but I couldn't seem to locate anyone who could help.

I let my eyes wander around the bar for a bit instead of watching the gossip segment—until a familiar name caught my attention.

Faith Vanderson.

I narrowed my eyes and watched intently as the blotchy-faced reporter leaned forward, looking at her tablet. "We're told someone anonymously leaked these, just moments ago."

I watched, curious as to what the hell they were talking about.

The reporter nodded to someone off camera then warned, "The photos we're about to show are disturbing. We encourage anyone with sensitive viewers in the room to be aware."

My heart nearly gave the fuck up on me.

Images of Faith with a black and blue eye were now blown up on the fifty-five-inch screen. Another image of her ribs was on display; they were a deep purple and yellow, and there were a few more bruises on her arms.

"Now, we know Faith just released her own interview saying the divorce was amicable and they were separating on good terms, but then these were released. The dates of the hospital visit line up with the window of time we all noticed Mr. Vanderson showing up alone attending a few events, and take a look at this footage. This was filmed just a week after her hospital visit."

Choppy footage of the Truitt's barbeque was on the screen— someone had recorded a video of my conversation with Faith. It caught my angry glare on her necklace and Faith's eyes turned down like she was a damn puppy getting in trouble. The face of the person recording appeared in selfie mode, saying, "That was Jace Walker and Faith Morgan's reunion after their brutal breakup five years ago. Broken heart much?" It was Shania Deegan, an avid hater of Faith from high school.

Guilt settled hard in my stomach. I tightened my fist and breathed through my nose.

I blinked to try to keep it together, but I was itching to get in my truck and find her. She had been trapped in an abusive marriage all this time, had been hospitalized because of it, and I had been nothing but an asshole to her.

Fuck.

I was pretty sure tears were running down my face, but I was too fucking numb to feel them. I peeled out of the parking lot and floored it toward Collierville.

Five years earlier: March

"Mom, can you hear me?" I frantically pushed my mom's eyelids open, scanning her pupils, pushing my fingers to her throat to check her pulse. My heart was racing as panic and adrenaline shot through me like a piston. With shaky hands, I grabbed my cell phone, dialed 911, and began to spout off details of what was happening. My mother had thyroid cancer, and it was slowly eating away her throat. She did have some medication for it, but her insurance had dropped her a year earlier. She had a fighting chance, except one of the side effects of her medication was that her bones grew weak.

So weak that tripping over the comforter on the floor and landing on her wrist had broken it. She was constantly in pain, which led to an opioid addiction, which then led to withdrawals. As long as I was able to get her the meds, she wouldn't turn to the harder stuff, but after the blackmail, I had been trying to do right by the system and work for it. I was exhausted and desperate, though. I made shit money, and at the end of every day, it still wasn't enough.

I'd even found myself trying to flirt with Jessica James a few weeks earlier, just so she'd invite me into her car. My plan was, once I was close to her purse, I would rob her blind. Thank fuck I saw Faith pull away from the other side of the street. It brought me out of that bad head space and gave me perspective.

I'd work and get the money the honest way. I'd figure it out. Faith was always like my guiding light, except I had no idea what she'd think of me if she knew I'd stolen medication for my mother. My gut told me she'd understand, but my head whispered little lies that it was too late.

Once we were in the hospital, they set my mother up in a room and connected her to an IV. Her veins were nearly bone dry from dehydration. They had high hopes that she'd be fine once they regulated a few things with her vitals and checked in with the doctor on call. Relieved, I sauntered toward the coffee machine, which was in an open waiting room. A few tables were scattered throughout the vast space, along with a few televisions and snack machines. I grabbed my thin paper cup of caffeine and sank into one of the chairs, tipping my head back to watch the news.

I didn't particularly care about what was going on in the world, but I needed a distraction—except the clip wasn't a news segment. It was an interview on some talk show.

In the chair across from the host was a businessman, likely richer than God, with some metallic-looking suit, slicked-back blond hair, and a clean-shaven face. I smirked at the loafers on his feet and the lack of socks showing; always thought that looked ridiculous on grown men. The woman next to him was a cliché blonde, holding on to his arm as a megawatt smile graced her pouty red lips—

I sat up quick as lightning as my exhausted eyes took in and finally registered who that woman was. Creamy skin, deep tan from too much Tennessee sun, hair so golden it looked as if she'd plucked rays from the sun and braided them into her hair, and eyes as deep and blue as the ocean.

Fuck.

Why was Faith holding that man's arm? I stood, pushing the chair back, and stalked closer to the mounted television. My heart thrashed in my chest, aching to be calmed.

"So, this is new for you, Bryan, right?" The host lifted her hand toward Faith and smiled.

Bryan, whoever the fuck he was, turned his head to look down at Faith. "It is...but it's serious. In fact...we have some news." He gave the camera a big smile and tugged Faith's hand free to place it out in the open for everyone to see.

I wasn't sure why until I realized she had a diamond about the size of my fist on her left hand. Shallow, hollow breaths were coming out of me in small bursts.

What the fuck am I watching? What is happening?

"We're engaged," Bryan said excitedly as the host leaned toward the diamond with her mouth open. My eyes moved to Faith's. Her blue eyes looked dead and didn't match the smile cresting on her beautiful lips.

"Wow, congratulations. This is very exciting, but some might say it was rather fast—would you agree with that?" the host asked, crossing one leg over the other and sinking back into her chair. Faith resumed holding on to Bryan's arm.

He shook his head back and forth and looked down at Faith. "Not for us...we just knew. When I know I want something, I don't wait for it to possibly be snatched up by another man." His words felt like a punch to my face, like they were aimed directly at me, like he fucking knew I'd let her go.

Maybe he did, but shit...this hurt. It hurt more than...

"So, when's the big day?"

My eyes snapped back up to see what they were going to say.

Faith smiled again, looked up at the man next to her, and said in her honey-soft voice, "Six months from now. We want a September wedding."

Tears burned the edges of my eyes, and my hands had gone numb. It didn't feel real until she spoke, until I heard her voice say she was marrying someone who wasn't me. She was moving on. Permanently.

If she thought she was marrying that rich prick, she was wrong. I'd fight this. I'd fucking fight for her. There was no chance in hell this was happening.

Just as I tightened my fists and headed toward the main hall, looking for the exit, I saw two officers heading my way. Dressed in black uniforms, one spoke into his walkie, the other moving his hand to his belt as he got closer to me. I stopped, wondering if they needed help finding someone.

"Jace Walker?" asked the officer to the left.

"Yeah, that's me." I quirked a confused eyebrow.

The second officer removed a pair of silver cuffs from his back, and then everything moved in slow motion.

"You're under arrest. Hands behind your head," one of them barked with authority and a little bit of disgust.

Confused, I just stared at them. I had no idea what the hell was happening, but my hands went up and I did as they said because I didn't want to get shot. I knew there had to be some kind of mistake, because...

No. No fucking way did he...

He cut me a deal. We made a deal! I wanted to scream it, wanted to shout it and cry it, run and sag away from the cuffs, beg the officers to hear me, but I already knew who had orchestrated this.

I already knew I was condemned and there was nothing I could do. While they cuffed me, they rambled off my Miranda rights, but my eyes went back to the television.

Faith leaned over and kissed Bryan on the lips. He brought his hand to her chin, flashing a watch worth more than my entire existence. My stomach dropped, because I'd lost her regardless of my deal. Regardless of what I did, what I said, I was still losing her, and I was about to lose my mother too.

Chapter 20
Faith

IT WAS the perfect day to officially move into my new place.

The apartment was a two-bedroom open floor plan on the fourth floor of a building in downtown Collierville. It had a doorman and keycard access only, so I felt safe. I felt free and, for the first time ever, I felt like me.

My dad helped me haul my things up, even though there wasn't much. I unpacked my duffle into my new closet and made up my new bed with new sheets, but otherwise my apartment was empty.

I needed to drive to IKEA and pick up an entire apartment's worth of stuff this weekend. I would have gone today, but my Rover was still at the mechanic. I'd called and had a different shop pick it up and look it over to ensure there wouldn't be any more surprises. I couldn't handle Jace having to pick me up again.

So, with nothing left to unpack, I walked aimlessly around my empty apartment, set up my laptop, and decided to sit on my new bed and watch a few episodes of *Superstore*.

One episode turned into four, my Chinese food came, and I ate alone then eventually fell asleep, but I woke a while later to a sharp knock on my door.

I jumped, my heart racing.

My first thought was that it was Bryan, but I had shown my doorman a picture of him and told him under no circumstances was he ever allowed into my building. I'd even tested him to see if he could be bought, but he was an older man, said he had daughters and granddaughters and would be honored to watch out for me. So, I believed him.

I jumped off my bed, ran to the door on my tiptoes, and carefully, cautiously peeked through the glass in the tiny hole.

A flustered, angry-looking Jace stood on the other side. *How the hell did he find me?*

Confused, I slowly opened the door and stuck my head out. "What do you want?" I used my serious tone, showing I meant business, because after him leaving me with my abuser the other day, I wasn't sure what to feel. Sure, he didn't know Bryan was abusive, but still. He had just left me—again.

His blue eyes were frantic, searching my face back and forth, his lips thinned into a frown and his jaw covered in day-old scruff. He was handsome as always, but my attraction was tempered by his abandonment.

"Can I come in?" Husky darkness swam through me as I processed his words.

I hesitated, and apparently that was all he needed. He pushed the door open, lightly forcing me back, and walked in. He secured the door and stared at me from his spot in front of it.

"What are you doing here, Jace? How the hell did you—" He cut me off, stepping forward. My words caught in my throat as he knelt before me, gripped my shirt, and shoved it up. My stomach was on display, revealing my light grey sports bra and my still faintly yellow ribs.

He ran his oil-stained finger down my fading bruise and swallowed. His Adam's apple moved, and I nearly touched it in fascination. I concentrated instead on his eyes as they scanned my torso. His muttered "Motherfucker" made angry goose bumps erupt along my arms.

How did he know?

My body was thrumming with need at his closeness, at how his finger kept skimming my skin. But his actions from the other day—from every encounter—came back, crashing through the walls of my heart, reminding me.

I shoved my shirt down and stepped back.

"H-he hurt you—why didn't you tell me?" Jace sputtered, standing...staring. Misty eyes met mine, and it nearly made my heart wilt.

"I tried, but you left." I lifted a shoulder, hating the weight of his stare on me.

He winced and pulled his hands through his hair. "Fuck."

"How did you find out?" I asked, curious and embarrassed.

"It's been leaked. I saw it while I was in Memphis, blasted across the television."

My stomach clenched. "What?"

No...no, this can't be happening.

I ran to my laptop, punching my name into Google, and sure enough, the images were there, picked up by various gossip and media outlets. I clicked on a YouTube video of a news clip and saw it already had thousands of views.

"Oh my god...I'm going to be sick."

Jace was next to me in a flash, his long arms coming around me. I inhaled his motor oil, spicy-clean scent and held back the tears that wanted to fall. Someone had leaked private photos, images that had been taken by police officers and filed away for if and when I decided to press charges. How was this possible? How could this have happened?

"It's okay, Pip. It's going to be okay, I'm here," Jace soothed, and hearing my old pet name...it felt so good, but I knew better. This wasn't right.

He hadn't wanted me until he found out Bryan had hurt me. That was some conditional shit I didn't want any part of.

"You need to leave, Jace." I leaned back, leveling him with a weary look.

He met my stare, fear mixing in so beautifully on his features, nearly driving me into his arms. He looked like he was about to burn the world down.

"Hasn't it been long enough that we've been apart? Haven't we both gone through enough?"

I stood, needing space.

He followed, nearly about to cage me in again, but I put my hand out to stop him.

"Did you not hear anything I said?" I searched his crazy eyes, which were studying my face, searching for some weakness.

"I did, but—"

I shook my head and stepped back. "You chose to push me away. You chose to be cruel and punish me for what you did to us. You didn't ask."

"I did ask. I tried to take you out when we talked at the gas station, remember?" he pleaded, grabbing me by the hips and pushing me toward the wall. *Oh no. No, no, no, no.*

I wasn't emotionally strong enough to stop him if he started kissing me or doing anything else with me against the wall. I pushed against his chest.

"Jace, just stop. Yes, I refused a date with you, but you still didn't have to be such a dick. I refused because of how mean you were and because you *dumped* me!"

I put my hands on my chest in desperation. I hated how frivolous the words sounded on my tongue, as if I could wrap five years of pain into those six letters. Dumped made it sound like we were fifteen and my best friend told me he didn't want to date me anymore. It wasn't nearly harsh enough for what he had made me feel.

"Faith, I'm begging you to stop this shit. It's been long enough. Let's just..." He pushed his lips together, his sapphire eyes assessing me with frustration. He wore a thin black t-shirt, which shifted with his arms as he tightened his hold on my hips. Memories swam through the small distance between us, fusing into the pads of his fingers as they pressed against my sweats. They begged me to wrap my arms around his neck and give in. They sang of a time when he was my whole world.

I closed my eyes, inhaled through my nose, and slapped at those images, tossing them to the dust-covered floor, where they'd been for the past five years.

"No." I shook my head, keeping in my tears, my hurt, all the nicely folded things I'd carried for so many years. "Go. Please." I stepped out of his grasp and headed to the door.

"Pip, please," he begged again. Hearing that name after five years, now two times in a row...it was a cruel move that made my anger rage.

"You can't just walk back into my life and suddenly want me because you feel bad for me. It doesn't work like that," I angrily explained, opening the door.

He stepped closer to the exit, and he was nearly through the door when he gripped the frame with one hand.

"No."

Bereft of words, I stared, unsure of what to say. He turned until he was facing me fully.

"I didn't fight for you back then. I just let you go because..." He trailed off, looking down. All it did was serve as a reminder that there were still secrets and lies between us. I crossed my arms in frustration.

"This isn't the way you fight for me, Jace. You don't—"

"I was trying to be honorable. I thought you were still with him." He leaned closer.

"Why didn't you ask?"

"Why didn't you tell me?" His eyes softened, a gleam now sitting inside them. My heart beat hard in my chest, begging me to close the distance between us.

He stepped closer.

"Why didn't you come up to me at that barbeque and tell me you were going to be single, tell me it was over and you were coming back?" he whispered, running his fingers along my jaw.

"Jace, you ripped my locket from my neck without even hearing more than a handful of words from me."

"I'm sorry." His voice hitched, and I knew if I dared to look into his eyes, I'd find those tears falling.

"I need you to go," I whispered.

"I tried to come after you, after I got out..." he started, forcing my eyes to jump to his. He stepped closer, cradling my jaw in both hands.

My knees nearly gave out. *He came for me?*

"What stopped you?" I whispered, heat spreading from my face, dipping to my chest.

"You."

I scrunched my brows together in confusion at his answer.

"The way you looked at him, the way you kissed him...you looked at him with a devotion you've never had with me."

"That's not true." A tear slipped free. "I've never loved anything or anyone as much as I loved you." I shook my head as much as his firm fingers would allow. They splayed into my hair, moving back to wrap around my neck.

"That may be true, but that look was still enough to stop me. You loved him, and I wasn't so selfish that I'd take you from that."

That humbled me. It didn't make me jump into his arms and kiss him, but it did make me take a step back and consider what he was saying. After a few seconds of heavy breathing, I finally responded.

"Just...give me tonight. Let me think about this. I hate how mean you've been. I hate how horrible you've made this. I'm confused. Just give me a little time."

He moved out of my doorway, watching me from the hall, as though waiting for some other reaction, something other than what I was offering. He finally nodded, lowering his head as he did so. Just as I was about to shut the door, he dug something out of his back pocket. I held the door between us and watched him curiously as he grasped a stack of white letters tied together with a piece of white string.

"Here. These..." He cleared his throat, his eyes searching the parchment in his hand. "I didn't want you to see these, but..." He shoved his free hand through his hair. "But I had a feeling you'd shut me out. I just need you to know..."

He placed them in my hands, turned on his heel, and walked away. I shut the door and tried to regulate my breathing. *Did that just happen?*

I settled into bed and carefully opened the letters. I gently unfolded the first one and began reading.

Dear Pip,

For so long, all I wanted was to erase you, but I realized you're stitched within me. I would have to cut you out, remove you surgically, but I'm not sure I'd survive.

Love, your fool

I drew in an unsteady breath as I pored over his words. The letter was dated five years ago, August...during the time he would have been in jail.

I went for another.

Dear Pip,

Do you still hear it? The thunder that broke open our souls that night? It's still inside me, like lightning trapped inside a bottle. Except there's no light in my soul, Pip. It's all darkness and loud cracking thunder. You broke me, love. I'll never work right without you.

Love, your fool

I fell asleep reading letter after letter of his confessions, his love, his heartbreak. Tears stained my face and clogged my throat as darkness invaded the world and left it cold and empty of light.

Knocking woke me, again. I blinked against the sun that was already invading my bedroom because I had no defense set up yet. I leaned toward the empty side of my bed where my phone was charging and pressed the side button. Eight in the morning and someone was knocking.

I trudged out of my room, peering through the tiny glass eyehole, and was met with a blurry version of the man I'd kicked out the night before. Confusion muddled my choices as I tugged the door open.

"Jace, what are you doing here?" I swiped at the matted hair that fell into my eyes. Oh, right, I was in my pajamas. *Shit.*

Before I could cover my shirt, I saw a generous grin break out across his face.

"I was wondering where that t-shirt went."

Heat overwhelmed my face as I stammered a response, finding that nothing was coming to my mind as a good justification for stealing his oversized shirt in high school and still wearing it at night all these years later. I walked back toward my bedroom, letting him in behind me.

I heard him laughing as I quickly pulled on my sweats and traded his shirt for a bra and tank.

Once I came back out, I found him in the kitchen, opening all my cupboards and peeking into my fridge.

"You've got absolutely nothing in this house. You're basically a squatter." His voice echoed as he peered into a lower cabinet.

I walked to the pillar, near the edge of the counter, and crossed my arms. "I haven't gotten out yet because of my car." I tried to push past my knowledge of the letters, of all the tiny pieces of his soul that he'd shared with me. He wasn't acting like he wanted to talk about them, so I tried to follow suit.

He stood from his squat and eyed me skeptically. "What's wrong with your car?"

I flushed and looked anywhere but his face. "It was still stuck at my parents' house, dead battery and all." I moved away from the pillar and headed toward the fridge where I knew I had leftover

Chinese. "By the way, why are you here? Didn't I kick you out last night?" I stood up with my white takeout boxes and handed him one. "Or did I dream that?" I quirked a brow as I opened my container and dug into it with the plastic fork that'd come with it.

"You did." He nodded and lowered his head to look into his box then glanced toward my fork. In a flash, he leaned forward and grabbed it from me.

"Hey," I whined around a mouthful of kung pao chicken.

He dug into his box and shoveled a large scoop into his mouth, stepped closer to me, and gave me the fork back.

"So, you had it towed to a garage?"

"Yeah, Ace's Auto." I stared at the green pea he had stuck in his teeth. "Gross." I waved my fork at him.

"You don't have anything to drink!" he argued while digging for more food.

I furrowed my brows, searching my kitchen. White, blank space met me. There was an empty sink and a white older-style fridge, but nothing else. The kitchen was small too, such a stark change from the one in my house in Nashville, which I hadn't even been allowed in because we had a chef who made all of our meals, including my coffee. I could do nothing in that house, and it drove me insane.

"Suppose you're right," I conceded.

"I am, so go get dressed. I'm taking you shopping. We're getting this apartment furnished and buying groceries, so you don't die." He shoved my shoulder with his.

Butterflies took flight in my stomach at the contact, at the realization that I was getting a glimpse of the boy who'd rescued me during a lightning storm then gave me my first kiss.

"You don't have to help me." I cleared my throat and moved away from the counter.

"I know." He assessed me with those eyes and dark eyebrows drawn in. I waited, not sure for what, but I was certain he was going to say something else to explain why he was doing this. When nothing came, I let out a heavy sigh and headed toward the shower.

"Fine. I want to go to IKEA."

"IKEA? That's all the way in Memphis!" he yelled at my back.

"You want to help me or not?"

"Yeah, yeah...fine. Just hurry your cute ass up," he joked, and I nearly tripped into the door frame with how it made my pulse jump.

I knew this might be a colossally bad idea.

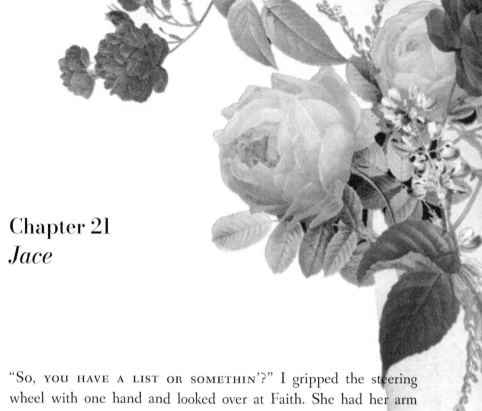

Chapter 21
Jace

"So, you have a list or somethin'?" I gripped the steering wheel with one hand and looked over at Faith. She had her arm resting out the window and the summer heat hitting her face.

"Yeah, it's pretty long though, so if at any point you decide you can't handle it, just head to one of the staged bed areas and take a nap." She smiled at me with those red lips slung to the side.

I wanted to pull over, drag her toward me, and remind her exactly where she had always sat in my truck—where she belonged. The urge was especially strong after seeing her that morning, wearing my old football shirt with those bare legs on display. Shit had me hard as hell.

"I think I can handle a little furniture shopping, plus they let you refill at the food court and stuff. It'll be fine."

She glanced over at me and smiled. "Okay, just don't say I didn't warn you."

We pulled into the vast, ridiculously packed parking garage and settled into a rhythm, an oddly refreshing one I strangely didn't mind at all. I had imagined what being with Faith was going to be like a million times when I was younger, but nothing could compare to how delicate she looked standing next to me and how normal it felt grabbing a shopping cart and following her around a store.

"Jace, you've got to follow the arrows, or we'll get all messed up." Faith eyed the floor and held her hand out to gesture at the path.

I resisted the urge to let out an annoyed sigh because this place was packed with people. "Fine, lead the way." I smiled.

I watched as she maneuvered her cart toward the display rooms and slowed to watch as she took down little notes about different things she liked. I paused at one display in particular that had dark leather recliners with fur throws and a fake fireplace. It looked like a little winter setup, but I liked it. It was masculine and nice, something I could picture in my house.

"I love those recliners!" Faith exclaimed next to me, her warm shoulder brushing against mine. It sent a jolt of excitement and nervous energy through me.

"Yeah, I was just thinking how nice they'd be one day," I mumbled then wandered toward a different part of the store.

"Did you ever end up going to college?" Faith quietly asked while moving down the row of open displays of living room sets.

I picked up a random magazine a staged coffee table and contemplated not telling her, but I'd done this. I'd showed up on her doorstep saying I wanted to be back in her life and her to be in mine. So, I heaved a sigh and said, "No. Everything changed after jail...then Mom. I ended up just taking a few business courses and opening the garage."

We walked ahead until we'd transitioned into the staged kitchen area. Faith walked toward the middle where there were bins and shelves of different glassware, silverware, and other items. She started piling things into her cart, and I stood ready to help but not sure what she was looking for.

"What happened with June?" Faith was standing near her cart and watching me with those eyes, the ones I'd fallen into, drowned in, and nearly died in.

I took my empty extra cart and headed toward a new section of the kitchens. "Couldn't keep up with the meds, insurance wasn't covering it. She was in too much pain, and I was..." I trailed off, hating the feeling of that memory slicing me down the middle, hating how attached it was to Faith and to *him*.

"Jace, that's plenty. No need to keep goin. I'm so sorry..." She pulled me by the arm toward the wall so we weren't facing all the other people passing by. I didn't hate the feel of her hands on me, so I let her guide me.

"She couldn't take it. I was in jail for six months, and by the time I got out, she was gone. Dad said she'd overdosed...said she'd found a way to get her hands on drugs without me there to get her the meds she needed." I murmured my story close to her ear, because it wasn't meant for everyone to hear. I wished we were at her apartment, in private, so the world didn't have a front-row seat.

"What on earth happened, Jace? I mean, I know some of the specifics because I asked, but I know you...you'd never break the law."

You happened.

"That's a long story, one for another time." I shifted my weight and moved the cart back toward the path everyone else was on. Faith followed with her basket and we continued shopping.

Things went smoothly the rest of the trip as she picked out things to fill her home with. She found a decent couch and chairs, an entertainment center, and little side tables. She found two stools for the bar area in the kitchen and said she didn't want a table. The way she said it, though, was sad, like she didn't need it or didn't expect to use it.

We laughed a lot, especially when we went to the bed display area and I tried lying down on every single one. Faith plopped down next to me on a few, and it took all my resolve not to roll on top of her, store full of people and all.

We transitioned to the end of the store where we had to pull out the larger pieces that were boxed up. We soon realized even with our two carts we'd need a larger, flat roller cart to get the rest of her things. I tried not to blink at the total amount that showed in green against the black register screen. She was dropping close to $3500 in just a few hours. It was money I'd only ever dreamed of spending at one time at a store like this.

I had saved a good nest egg to use as a down payment for the shop, but otherwise I'd never had that kind of money.

We loaded the back of the truck together, which was hilarious because Faith was scrappy as hell. She heaved the flat boxes over her head like they were nothing but always made this cute little sound like she was exerting all her muscles to do it. She explained that Dwight Schrute said to make extra noises when carrying heavy things and it'd make you stronger.

She made me laugh, real laughter with real smiles, and I wasn't ready for our day to end.

"Okay, we've got your apartment covered. Now all we need to do is get you some food," I said while getting on the freeway toward Collierville.

"You've done enough, and I can just order more takeout. Uber Eats is a thing now." She smirked at me from her seat. Her hat was off, and her blonde hair was tied back into a low bundle at her neck. Little strands were falling across her forehead, and my fingers itched to tuck them behind her ear.

"I'm getting you groceries then I'm eating dinner with you," I promised. She chuckled and shook her head but didn't refuse.

We walked around the grocery store, and again that oddly normal rhythm fell back into place. We had just one cart this time, so her shoulder bumped mine every so often, and when she couldn't reach something on the top shelf, I'd reach over her and get it, feeling her warm body press against mine for the smallest of moments.

She was laughing about organic bananas being more of a rip-off because they were smaller when someone walked up to us and snapped a picture. It took me by surprise, so much so that I didn't even realize what was happening.

"Is this the guy you left your husband for?" asked a large man in a loose hoodie from behind his camera. His curly brown hair was stuffed under a beanie and his protruding nose had acne scattered across it. I wanted to punch him there just so he'd leave us the hell alone.

"No, this is my friend from high school. Please excuse us." Faith lowered her head and moved to the side. I was about to reach for the idiot's camera to take out his damn memory card when Faith stopped me by touching my arm. "We can't touch their equipment...just leave it. Let's get out of here." Faith gave the man a glare and shouldered past him.

We walked down a few more aisles in silence, and I checked over my shoulder to be sure we weren't being followed before I asked, "Does that happen a lot?"

It was a stupid question, because of course it did. I suddenly felt sick over doing that to her. I hated myself for putting her through that shit.

"Yeah...you get used to it after a while, but since I left Bryan, it's been worse." She gently picked up a box of dryer sheets and placed it in the cart.

"So, you basically don't have any privacy?" I grabbed a thing of laundry detergent and tossed it in.

"Nope." She let the P pop and moved down the aisle.

We finished shopping, and I thought we were out of the woods where the media was concerned, but on our way out there was an entire group of camera-wielding men and women waiting for her. As soon as the glass doors slid open, we were bombarded.

"Faith, have you moved on? Did you reunite with your old flame?" asked one red-haired woman.

"Faith, is it true what Bryan said about your addiction problem?" yelled a man with a blue visor.

Faith didn't falter for a second. She straightened her spine and plowed through the crowd without saying a word. They followed us, continuing to yell questions and accusations at her, some aimed at me. I followed her lead, clenching my jaw in anger. I wanted to yell at all of them to fuck off, but I didn't want to make things worse for her.

I helped Faith unload the cart into the truck, and people took pictures of it, which wasn't ideal because now they knew what I drove. They also had a good view of all Faith's new furnishings.

Once we were done, she tried to return the cart, but I gently grabbed her by the arm and settled her into the passenger side of the truck, shut the door, and locked it. I walked the cart back to the little return area and heard a few more comments about Bryan and Faith—about their supposed baby, their upcoming trip to Martha's Vineyard, and if they were still doing the charity auction in England this summer.

The reality of what she'd left behind settled into my bones so deep I nearly faltered, tripping to the ground. She'd had a good life with Bryan, at least in terms of financial security. It was something I wouldn't be able to give her...not on the level she was used to.

I climbed back into the truck and began reversing, not caring if the idiot reporters were smart enough to move or not. Faith didn't say a word as we drove out of the city limits. I saw her swipe at her face a few times as the day waned to night. I wanted to be sure no one was following us, so I drove around aimlessly for a while. We listened to a country playlist I'd made, no news clips to interrupt us, no media or gossip for her to hear.

I just wanted her to be okay, and for the first time since letting her go, I realized she might be as broken as me.

Chapter 22
Faith

Driving around in the cab of Jace's truck, listening to slow country songs and getting lost in the summer breeze was everything I needed. I'd had my fair share of surprise paparazzi follow me and snap pictures at the most awkward moments, but having them bring Jace into it felt dirty, wrong, like he was somehow tainted by the poor choices I'd made all those years ago.

His words about how quickly I'd moved on ran through my mind again. They'd been on repeat for the past few days, but it was worse now that he'd come to my rescue, helping me today and then having to witness that shitshow at the grocery store. It was embarrassing.

We'd turned off onto a backroad some time ago, and I had stopped paying attention. The truck slowed as it turned down a narrow dirt road, moving along at a snail's pace, and tall trees created a curtain of green as the headlights reflected off them. We drove for a little while until we finally slowed to a stop. Jace put his truck in park, turning his key and clicking the headlights off. We were thrust into even more darkness, and for whatever reason, I loved it.

"Don't freak out, but we're both exhausted and we need a reprieve from what happened back there," Jace slowly suggested. In my ears it sounded husky and warm. The moon was out tonight, so

I was slowly letting my eyes adjust and pick up the shadows and little details I could make out. "The ice we bought will keep your food for the night. I've got a cooler back there in the bed, so I'll throw the perishable stuff in there," he offered, unbuckling his seat belt.

I copied his actions but furrowed my brows in question, not fully understanding what we were doing. "Then what?"

He waited, shifting around in his seat. "Then we sleep."

"In the truck? Out here?" I looked around, hearing my voice pitch higher.

"Well, the way I see it, they've pieced together who I am by now and likely have people watching my place. They've probably got people watching around town for you, and even if we did go back to your place, we've got a full truckload of apartment stuff that can't be left overnight in that parking lot." He reached behind the seat and pulled something free. A soft fleece blanket landed in my lap. "Out here, your stuff is safe, and no one is going to find us. As for where we'll sleep—no, not in the truck. I thought maybe we could sleep in the house tonight."

He didn't give me time to argue, just hopped out and started sorting the groceries out of the back seat and into the cooler. I jumped out to help him, and we worked quickly, moving the perishables into the cooler and the dry goods to the bed of the truck, freeing up the back seat. Once we were finished, I stood there, unsure what to do next.

"If you prefer to sleep in the truck, we can. I can sleep up front and you can have the back," Jace offered, tone somewhat awkward and nervous.

"That depends," I said, looking back toward the dark house. It was two stories, but that was all I could really make out in the darkness. No lights were on inside, and there seemed to be a few tools scattered around the property, ladders and some tables out and ready for a slab of wood to be laid across them.

"On what?" Jace hesitantly asked, walking closer.

"On whose house this is and whether or not we're going to get shot for trespassing tonight."

Jace laughed and moved ahead of me. "We won't be getting shot. This is...uhhh..." He hesitated and went quiet for a moment. "It's mine."

Shocked, I stopped where I stood and clung to the blanket in my arms.

"What?"

Jace stepped forward, moving ahead of me. I was losing track of him in the darkness, so I scrambled to keep up.

"Yeah, it's not finished, but it will be soon." He used a key from his keychain and unlocked the front door. More darkness greeted us, save for the moonlight that streaked in through the back windows.

My mouth dropped open in surprise—the place was enormous. My eyes narrowed, searching for what little details I could glean from the dark space. A massive kitchen sat snugly against the back part of the house, windows facing whatever view was out there. A gigantic room was next to it, and a small wall divided another compact space near the front door. There were stairs off to the side, leading up to where bedrooms and bathrooms probably were.

"Jace..." I was in awe of what he had done.

"It's not too bad, I guess," he said humbly.

I walked over and grabbed his arm. "Not bad? Jace, this is beyond incredible. Can I have a tour?"

"In the dark?" He laughed and took his hat off.

"I can use my cell phone light," I eagerly offered, holding up my nearly dead phone.

"How about in the morning? I'm pretty tired, and I imagine you are too." He moved away from the open space and headed toward a side door. I trailed after him. The door led to a garage, and he had his cell phone light out until he found a small space heater. He turned and led me back through the house until we were heading upstairs.

I tried to take in what I could of the space, but it was too dark to really see much. He led us toward the end of the hall, to a bedroom from the looks of it. He shut the door, which was without a doorknob, so it sat slightly ajar. As I walked around, I noticed it felt softer under my shoes and the floor was lighter up here. I kneeled down, pressing my fingers into the surface, and sure enough, the space was carpeted.

Jace walked over to an outlet and plugged in the small heater then turned to face me. "Don't ask, but one of the crew guys was left unsupervised for the day while my contractor was out sick. He decided to put electricity and carpet in this room." He shook his head back and forth, bending down to remove his boots. "We haven't even painted yet, so yeah...it was a massive clusterfuck. But, it hasn't been fixed yet, so for now it'll work to our benefit." He scooted back until he was resting against the wall.

I was already feeling warmer with the heater going, so I toed my shoes off too then stood there awkwardly.

"You gonna sit down?" Jace laughed, looking up at me. I shifted from foot to foot.

"Yeah, it's just that...uh, could you turn around or something?"

He let out a laugh. "I can't see you as it is. Why, you gettin' naked?"

A nervous laugh slipped free as I tried to control my shivering. It was warmer in here, but it was still cold. "No, I just have to take my bra off. This one I'm wearing is all kinds of uncomfortable."

"Plus, you have that theory," Jace said, adjusting his back into the corner.

I turned my back to him and began unhooking my bra from under my shirt as I laughed at his remembering my theories.

"The wiring messes with the shape of your boobs, right?" Jace laughed from behind me.

I pulled the bra through the sleeve of my shirt. "All I know is it seems unnatural to sleep in anything but your skin."

"Does that include clothes too?" Jace rasped with heat in his voice.

"Sometimes," I joked, getting on all fours and dragging the

blanket closer to the heater. "How did you want to do this tonight?" I asked, lifting the blanket like an offering.

He leaned forward and pulled his sweatshirt off, up over his head. Folding it a few times, he stuffed it behind his head. "I'll sleep in this corner, and you can sleep there in front of the heater."

I let out a sigh and offered him the blanket. "Truce, for one night?"

I couldn't make out his face, but he sounded amused when he asked, "What do you mean exactly?"

"You use that sweatshirt as a pillow, spoon me, and let me use your arm as a pillow, that way we're warm and both covered by the blanket?" My voice pitched with question even though I was trying to make a statement. My fingers twitched.

My offer was greeted with silence...awkward, heavy silence. I was about to move and lie down, ignoring him, when I heard, "A truce sounds good."

He lay down behind me ever so carefully, his back up against the wall. I tugged the heater a bit closer and swallowed the fat lump of anxiety in my throat while cautiously adjusting my body until I was lying prone in front of him.

His large arms came around me, caging me in, until we were spooning. I held my breath for a second, until I heard his rumbling voice say, "Want me to let you go and find somewhere else to put my arms?"

I shook my head, because his arms were warm, and they felt good. *So right.*

"It's okay," I whispered.

The silence was somewhat stifling, but it was also peaceful. I closed my eyes, ready to drift off to the rhythm of his rising and falling chest, but reopened them when he asked, "Do you miss it?"

I pressed my lips together and watched the shadows dance across the moonlit wall.

"That life, the money...do you miss being rich, having everything you could ever dream of?" His husky voice rumbled in my ear, making goose bumps erupt down my arms from how close his lips were.

"Not at all actually. I hated that life. Maybe if I'd had it with the right person, but still...it was exhausting." I yawned, feeling more and more drained by the second.

He kept still behind me, but I swore I could feel him tighten his hold on me.

"You ever going to tell me what happened after I left?" I muttered, sinking further into his firm chest.

His torso moved behind me as he situated his body again, this time bringing one of his hands to my hip. "Well you know my mom died while I was in jail..."

I nodded, irritated that he wouldn't just explain the entire story to me. "Yes, but what put you in jail? What on earth happened?" I urged him on.

"It's a complicated story..." He heaved a heavy sigh then changed the subject. "When did he start hitting you?" Jace's voice was so soft, so tender it made my eyes water.

I was at war internally about my response. My heart thrashed in my chest and all I wanted to do was tell him, but a part of me still wanted to keep a few things hidden. He'd abandoned me and now he wanted me to talk about the abuse I'd endured with my husband?

I shifted in his arms to get more comfortable, and I unintentionally brushed up against something hard at my back. I froze, wide-eyed and a little surprised. I slowly pulled forward, not sure what to do.

He laughed behind me and pulled me back against him. "Sorry... looks like I can't hide what it does to have you with me like this. Don't worry though, I'm not going to try anything."

For whatever reason, that turned me molten. My face flushed as arousal and memories flushed my body. He was hard for me when we hadn't even done anything, hadn't kissed or touched...I mean, I was lying back against him, but still.

I cleared my throat, determined to move past the awkwardness. "It was about ten months ago." His arms tightened around me as I began to open up. "He...he had these big business deals that were falling through left and right. He'd lost millions, and he was stressed." My explanation was choppy and awkward.

Jace started rubbing my arms, dragging his palms up and down my bare skin. After a few times of him doing that, my t-shirt had ridden up, exposing the skin on my abdomen. I blinked, trying to focus on my next words.

"We'd been distant much longer than that...to the point where I started sleeping in another room. I think a part of me wanted him to cheat on me, just get it over with so we could divorce and be done with it." I dipped my head, feeling shame flicker inside. "I should have left him within the first year. He knew..." I paused, not sure I wanted to reveal this part of the story.

Jace placed a careful kiss to the back of my ear, silently urging me on.

"He knew about you...knew I wasn't over you. He knew it when he proposed and when we said our vows. I'd never kept it from him, but it strained things once we were married. After the first year, things between us just fizzled and faded. He worked constantly and I slowly became a shell of who I once was. So, I essentially set up my own room, slept separately from him...we hadn't been intimate in months when he started hitting me."

I whispered my confession, feeling my resolve begin to crumble. Explaining this to Jace was horrible and the worst kind of absolution. It felt good to talk about my life with someone, and it felt good to have someone care.

"He came home one night, drunk...started talking about you... about how he didn't want to be my second choice anymore, how he wanted to sleep in the same bed at night and for me to be his wife again. He kissed me hard, pushed me against a wall, and then..."

I held my breath, not wanting to relive it.

"That's enough," Jace whispered breathlessly against my ear. Pain reverberated in his tone, sinking into my chest.

His arms were like a band of steel around me.

I watched the darkness, seeing nothing but, for the first time in a long time, feeling entirely safe. Warm air hit my skin as Jace began to mutter something, but I was so exhausted I didn't hear all of it. The only thing I caught was "...mistake and should have never done it..." Then I was asleep in the arms of the one man who'd hurt and somehow healed me.

Chapter 23
Jace

EARLY MORNING LIGHT cut through the window above me, the reflection hitting me right in the eyes. It woke me and brought back the entire evening in one harsh moment, reminding me of the reckless thing I had asked the night before, about the abuse...to hear Faith talk about her life with another man. Thankfully she hadn't been able to see my face, I'd hid it—or at least I had tried to.

It wasn't easy to picture her with another man, but it was worse picturing her being forced and beaten. I'd lain awake for hours, with her sleeping silently in front of me. I had debated telling her the whole story, about why I left her, why we ended. Apprehension had stalled me, and when I'd heard her soft breathing and felt her go lax in my arms, I had let it go.

Faith was quietly snoring against my chest, hair mussed, shirt pulled taut against her chest. Her pert nipples showed through the fabric, and the blanket pooled at her waist. I was already rock hard against her, painfully so, and this just made it one hundred times worse.

I tried not to watch the rise and fall of her chest, but I couldn't tear my eyes away. They kept going to the curve of her breasts on their own. My arms tightened, my fingers desperate to find purchase somewhere on her skin. I was battling this silent war when Faith stirred, opening her eyes.

A slow smile worked itself across her face, making the skin near her eyes wrinkle and stretch. Her arm shot up as she stretched against my chest, and there was absolutely zero chance of her not feeling my hard-on.

The second she did, she paused.

"Jace," she whispered softly, like it was a secret she was too ashamed to address out loud.

"Faith," I whispered back.

The silence that followed was heavy. The lies I'd been carrying for the past few years, the things that had ripped us apart...it all sat sandwiched between us. I wasn't sure what she was thinking, but I knew I wanted to start unraveling some of these strings that had bound us in dishonesty these last few years.

I was ready to start talking, admitting, explaining, but the timing just didn't feel right. Her fingers gently grabbed the hem of my shirt and began to push it upward. Goosebumps broke out along my skin at her delicate touch. She continued to push up until she had a view of the tattoos. Tracing them with her finger, she finally said, "Those letters were beautiful..." She let out a soft sigh, which made my gut clench tight. "When did you get these done?"

Propping my head up with my hand, I gazed down at her. "After you left."

Her eyes darted up to mine and stayed glued there for a few silent seconds, at which point I took the opportunity to cover her hand that was on my heart with my own hand.

Those gentle blue eyes lowered to my lips as she asked, "So...the Dear Pip one?"

I moved my hand down to her hip, where I lifted her shirt up an inch and traced circles on her skin. "It killed me, Faith, fucking ruined me that you moved on, married him so easily, so fast. The first tattoo...I started after I heard you were dating him. I had no extra cash, none, but I knew a guy. Then I got the rest after I got out of jail." I watched her, ensuring she wasn't recoiling or moving away from me. Moving my fingers, I continued. "I'm sorry I've been so mean...it's just...seein' you back here, it was difficult not to react and be hurt over everything that happened."

She nodded slowly, carefully.

"I wish you'd tell me everything that happened."

I wanted to. Fuck, I wanted to so badly, but how could I spill it all now? She'd think I was just trying to capitalize on the fact that her husband was an abusive dick. She'd assume I just wanted into her pants. I needed to show her I was better than that, show her I could take my time, build this thing up, and then explain it all.

"I will, in time, I promise."

She nodded while seeming to fight a few tears. I pushed my hand from her hip to her back and rubbed the skin there, bringing her a centimeter closer to me. She brought her hand up to my face, examining my hairline and the space close to my ears.

"You're still so handsome. You've always been good-looking, but you grew up to be somethin' else entirely." A bit of her hidden drawl broke through in her examination.

I wanted to laugh, make a joke about it, but my throat was tight as she continued stroking my hair and slowly, ever so softly moved the pads of her fingers down to the corner of my eye and farther to the bridge of my nose, until she was tracing my lips. "Jace, can I ask you for something?" She leaned into me, nearly pushing against my hard-on, which almost made me groan.

"Anything," I whispered.

"Kiss me? I know what I said yesterday, but I feel like I need to just see if..."

I cut her off, smashing my lips to hers. She let out a small sound of surprise then relaxed into it. It was an unhurried, measured kiss, like time slowed down and stopped just for this moment. Her hands went into my hair as she pushed further against me, increasing the speed of our kiss.

"Jace..." She exhaled against my lips. My name was a plea, a moan, something she had said when we made love as teenagers. I moved until I was hovering over her. She was flat beneath me, hands still plunged into my hair, lips sealed to mine. She bucked her hips upward, eliciting a groan from me.

Our chests heaving and begging for air spoke the words we couldn't...or wouldn't. They said what we were, what we still had wasn't just a spark—it was the whole damn fire, burning down forests, billowing smoke and steam. We had the entire thing still locked inside each other, and all we had to do was let it out.

"I don't want to do something you're going to regret," I muttered against her skin as I made my way down her throat, kissing every creamy, soft inch.

"I could never regret you, Jace, not anything we do or have ever done. Never," she rasped harshly as she pushed those fingers into my hair and pressed her lips to mine.

I lifted her shirt, exposing her breasts. Sitting back for a moment, I tugged it over her head and relished how perfect she looked.

"This fucking freckle..." I leaned down and traced my tongue over the dark spot on her right breast. My hands were everywhere, gripping those heavy, perfect globes and pulling the hardened nipples into my mouth. "You're still so fucking perfect," I whispered as I lowered myself between her legs, licking my way down her flat stomach. Once I traced my tongue near the waistline of her jeans, I looked up to see if she was okay with how fast we were moving. I expected reluctance but found something else entirely: *desperation.*

Just as I put my fingers to her copper button, we heard a loud shout from downstairs. Faith's eyes went wide, and I jumped up, looking at the door then quickly running to hold it shut while she got dressed.

"Who is that?" she asked while scrambling for her bra and t-shirt.

"My contractor. I forgot what time they get here in the mornings." I ruffled my hair, feeling like an idiot. How could I have not remembered that John was coming with his crew this morning? I didn't want Faith to be embarrassed and in turn regret our night, or worse, our morning together.

Once she had her t-shirt on and was digging for her shoes, I grabbed for my boots and tugged them on. Just as I laced them up, someone shoved the door open.

"Jace? Oh good, you are up here. John was just asking for ya." Gavin, one of the foremen, raked his greedy eyes over Faith, who was slowly standing up, grabbing the blanket we'd slept beneath. I ground my teeth together as his eyes stayed glued to her, a warm smile lighting up his face. "Hi, I'm Gavin. I'm—" I shoved him out the door and down the hall before he could finish. "Hey, what the hell?" he argued as I kept shoving him.

"She's not available," I muttered through clenched teeth, looking toward the stairs, slowing down the shoving. "I'll be down in a second." I turned back to see Faith trailing us, clutching that blanket to her chest. I grabbed her hand and smiled. "Hey, want that tour?"

She smiled up at me and nodded.

I tried not to make more than I needed to of the tour. It was just a house; it didn't matter that I had imagined her in the bed or soaking in the tub. It was nothing that I had been picturing her bare feet on the floors, swollen belly, that sinful smile and those lips on me as I kissed her against the bedroom door, that left ring finger wearing *my* ring.

"So, upstairs, we've got three bedrooms, one you've seen..." I cleared my throat, walking toward another bedroom, slightly bigger than the one we'd been in the previous night. "All have smaller walk-in closets, and there's a bathroom across the hall." I walked out, toward the back of the hall, until I approached the master. "This is the master." I moved aside and let Faith walk past me. It was spacious, with a massive walk-in closet and attached bathroom. She took measured steps across the floor until she got to the floor-to-ceiling window that took up half the back wall.

"Jace, I'm so proud of you," she said on a sigh, tracing a finger down the side of the window. "This is just...incredible." She turned and smiled at me. I tried not to soak it up, but my damn heart took it and latched on, eating up her praise. She moved to the bathroom and took in the double sink, huge soaking tub, and walk-in shower. She gazed at, ran her finger along, and smiled at each small thing she found. I found myself watching and waiting for that small crinkle near her eyes.

We moved downstairs, where John and Gavin were putting up drywall, something I was supposed to be helping with. I winced and waved at them, and they each gave me a thumbs-up with winks and bouncing eyebrows. Faith admired the bottom level the same way she had the upper, smiling and gasping over the view from the kitchen.

"Jace! Oh my gosh, is that McGrady's tree farm?" Her eyes lit up, blazing with questions.

I blushed, hating that she was remembering that time we'd talked about where we'd live one day, when'd she said, "Right in the middle of McGrady's tree farm would be nice, that way I can eat all the peaches I want." It was the reason I'd taken her there after graduation. We'd had such big plans, and I hadn't meant to build my house here, but maybe it was fate. It had just been a good-sized lot for a decent price.

"It's no mansion, Faith. Nothing that special...I'm just ready to get out of that damn trailer park." I resisted the strange feeling that was worming its way through me at her excitement.

She walked over, standing in front of me. She threw her arms around my neck and looped her fingers into my hair. "Jace Walker, don't you dare downplay this. I hated living in a mansion. I moved into the smallest room available because it felt less lonely. It wasn't a home. This..." She looked down, her face flushing pink. "This is a home." She let me go and walked toward the front door. "We should probably head back."

Chapter 24
Faith

THE FLASHING green light on my phone caught my attention, causing me to lurch to the side and grip the device in a deathlock.

I pressed the side button to bring the screen to life and eagerly opened my texting app.

Jace: Did you fall asleep on me?

I cracked a smile and swiped my response.

Me: It was two in the morning—don't you have a business to run?

Jace: Yeah, about that...I found two more signs around town yesterday. I'm getting tired of tearing them down.

Me: Well maybe they'll stop going up if you bring me some breakfast.

I watched the little dots appear and disappear for a few seconds, a little blob of guilt simmering in my belly. I'd had the Mustard Seed auto signs made up, paying extra for a few to be done quickly, but I had no actual plans of opening an auto shop in Collierville—or anywhere, for that matter. My only future goals were to get divorced. Still, I wasn't ready to fold with Jace. I'd been burned one too many times by the men in my life to hand over all the cards just yet.

Jace: You're lucky you're beautiful.

I closed the app, rolled over in my bed, and stared at my ceiling. The smile on my face wouldn't budge and hadn't for the past three days, since our morning at his house.

After our moment in the kitchen, Jace had driven us through a drive-through to get breakfast. I hadn't been through one in years, so I'd ordered a big fat breakfast platter so I could taste a little bit of everything. Jace had made fun of me, but I didn't care. I felt like Rapunzel finally being let out of her castle tower, getting a chance to experience the world for the first time.

He had called Seth, and the two of them had unloaded the back of his truck into my apartment. I'd called Gemma, and she had come over and helped me sort the groceries. She'd also kept giving me the look, the one that said *Spill!*, but I wasn't ready.

We'd all eaten lunch together, after which Seth and Gemma left, leaving Jace and me all alone in the apartment. As sexually charged as things had been in the bedroom that morning, we were surprisingly shy with one another in the apartment. Jace kept smiling and dipping his face, like we'd just met and he was trying to flirt. It was the cutest thing I'd ever seen and caused an eruption of fluttering in my stomach. We ended up exchanging numbers, and since then we hadn't stopped texting.

It felt like we were in high school again.

I slid out of bed and headed to the bathroom to start the shower. Sunlight spilled in through my large bay windows and warmed the wood floors as my toes padded across the open space. Now that I had furniture and curtains, the place felt like home.

I wanted to invite Jace over for dinner, but I was still hesitant with everything hanging in the void regarding my divorce. Also, if I was honest, I was having a few trust issues with Jace. What if he just ripped the rug out from under me again? What if something just clicked in him again like it had when we were nineteen and he just left? I couldn't go through that again.

I was drying my hair with a white fluffy towel when I heard a knock at the door. Still cautious from what had happened with Bryan, I carefully peeked through the privacy hole and was pleasantly surprised by the array of color I found there.

Swinging the door open, I smiled and watched for that slow grin to break out on Jace's face. It was something I was getting reacquainted with.

"Flowers for you," he murmured while moving past me into the apartment. I carefully wrapped my fingers around the burlap that contained the bundle of wildflowers. Memories slammed into me from when he'd tuck them into the spines of our books.

I shut the door and smiled as I took in his appearance. Wearing a thick-navy t-shirt with his shop logo in the corner, black hair slicked to the side, and day-old scruff running along his jaw, he was the good dream you have after waking from a horrific nightmare; he was my entire undoing.

I took the assortment of flowers and held them to my nose as I sauntered toward the counter. "Thank you," I whispered, trailing him as he made his way to the kitchen. He set down a plastic bag and two coffees. I moved toward them and reached for one of the cups, but Jace slowly moved it to the right, forcing my arm to cross his body.

"I brought you breakfast," he rumbled, drowning me with that cold stare of his.

I swallowed my nerves and matched his smile. "And what do you want for it?"

He twisted toward me and dipped his head, watching me from under his long lashes, then let out a little laugh. "Kiss me."

I smiled and felt that fluttery feeling come back with full force. We hadn't kissed since that morning in the room, so I wasn't sure what would happen if we did. I had been ready to have sex with the man that morning, and we nearly had, but now I felt nervous. He must have sensed my hesitation. He muttered a soft "Small steps" against my temple as he kissed my hairline.

I tipped my head back, stood on my tiptoes, and dared him with my own stare. Gripping his shirt, I pressed a kiss to his mouth.

His arms shifted me until I was sliding to the right along the counter, putting me in front of him and allowing his long arms to cage me in. My arms went around his neck as he deepened our kiss.

It was like we'd never ended, like we'd never broken each other's hearts, never walked away from the one true thing in both our lives. He let out a groan as his hands moved up my sides and dug into the flesh that barely showed where my shirt had risen. I flushed and leaned my head back, breaking the kiss, because if I didn't, I'd give away the entire farm without finding out if the farmer had any intention of keeping it.

I also couldn't help that annoying thing that kept scratching at my consciousness. As much as I hated to even consider it, I wanted this Bryan chapter behind me before I started having sex again. I didn't know why it mattered, but after reflecting for a few days, I realized it did.

"So, what's on the agenda today?" Jace asked, handing me my coffee and kissing the small space beside my eye. The intimacy of it made my breath hitch.

"I have a meeting with Gemma. Bryan gets served today, and now that those pictures were leaked, we aren't sure how it'll go." I moaned as I bit into the sugary donut he'd brought me.

Jace cleared his throat and asked, "So you're really going through with the divorce then?"

I eyed him, confused. "Yes, of course..."

"It's just that the other day at your parents' house, he seemed so..."

"Full of himself? In love with me?" I offered, trying to help him fill in the blank.

"Confident—not like a man about to go through an ugly divorce. By the way..." He leaned closer to me. "I'm so fucking sorry I didn't hear you out that day. I'm so sorry I left you there."

I swallowed the remainder of the donut and watched his throat bob.

"Did he hurt you?" he whispered, running the pad of his thumb across my hairline.

I lifted my shirt sleeve higher so he could see my arm. "Just grabbed me hard, but I got out of there before too much damage could be done."

Jace's hard stare traced the small bruised indents from where Bryan's fingers had wrapped around my upper arm.

"I still can't believe I just left you like that..." His gruff statement came out cold and full of regret.

I shook my head. "You didn't know. I would have done the same. Let's forget it and just focus on this...on us." I blushed, spreading my arms wide, not sure why I'd just put myself out there like that. There wasn't an 'us' to focus on, just a few kisses and heated moments.

"Hey, when did these arrive?" Jace asked, moving toward the living room. I smiled and met him near the soft leather recliners he'd eyed in IKEA, the ones I'd ordered the next day.

"Yesterday."

He rubbed his hand over the leather in reverence. "Nice choice."

I wanted to lay it all out there, because I wasn't good at holding my proverbial poker hand this close to my chest. I wanted to tell him I'd bought them because he said he liked them, and I was already picturing them set up in his living room, facing that massive window, overlooking the orchard.

Instead of saying all that, I merely hummed a response.

"So, dinner tonight?" I asked, smiling up at him. He still had to go to work, and I wanted him to know it mattered to me that he'd driven here, knowing he had to go back, but again, I didn't want to be that pathetic girl he used to know, the one who was a love-sick puppy. So, I kept that little piece of gratitude to myself.

"What time?" Jace asked, rubbing my wrist with his thumb. Maybe it wasn't such a good idea to have him at my house so late. Maybe I needed to lay down some boundaries.

"Sex?" I replied, mortified by what had just slipped out of my mouth. "I mean six! Six o'clock!" I blushed intensely, and he smiled, holding back a laugh.

"I'll be here." He dipped his face and kissed me chastely on the lips.

"Are you okay?" Jace softly asked while we moved forward in line. I swiftly nodded, not realizing I hadn't responded with words...again. He'd asked me a few questions since we pulled up to the theater, but my mind was somewhere else.

It was on memories, past moments with Jace when we'd snuck into this very cinema...dark, secret moments when we'd huddled up in the back, pulled out a blanket, and felt each other up while watching some thriller. He'd stolen more of my innocence here than anywhere else, and now I was standing in line, ready to go back into that same dark room with him.

He'd texted me earlier, asking if I wanted to go to a movie with him. Since the previous night's dinner had been such a success, I figured why not? We were learning how to be around each other again. We were occasionally kissing, but nothing more. *It's fine.*

Except now all I could think of was if Jace planned to do something tonight and whether or not I was ready. I went over the facts in my head again: Bryan hit me. Bryan cheated. I didn't owe him anything...and yet, I just felt like I couldn't be with someone again until my divorce was final.

"Two, for *Fatal*," Jace requested through the small circle in the plexiglass window. The girl taking tickets blushed and pushed her chest forward. I smiled, thinking of what it must be like to be a seventeen-year-old girl and have to deal with Jace up close.

Tonight, he was wearing dark jeans that molded to his thighs perfectly, and he had on dark combat boots and a black t-shirt. His hair was askew and gorgeous, his blue eyes dancing as he smiled and retrieved the tickets. My heart bounded behind my breastbone as though it was screaming at me to claim him, but he wasn't mine to claim, and I wasn't his.

He reached for my hand and pulled me along toward the concession stands. "Want anything?"

Just you. "No, I'm okay," I said in a slightly watery tone. *What is wrong with me?*

He skipped the lines and kept walking us toward the large hallway that led to the designated theater.

Before we reached the door, he tugged me hard toward a dark alcove.

Planting his hands on either side of my head, he caged me in and stared down at me.

"Look, I hate feelin' like somethin' is wrong with you...did I do something?" He searched my eyes, worry slipping through his expression.

I brought my left hand to his throat and moved my fingers up until I was pushing his hair back. "No, you didn't. I'm just nervous...I keep remembering what we used to do here."

I blushed, ducking my head.

He lifted my chin. "Is that right?" He held my face in his palm so I couldn't look away then ever so slowly closed the gap between us. "Like this?" He softly kissed my lips and, a second later, gripping the back of my head, he deepened it.

I moaned into his mouth and pushed against him. "Yes, and more..."

The hall was getting more populated, and while no one could see us unless they really tried, we were still next to a stack of booster seats. It would only take one parent to need one and come over for us to be discovered.

"Like that time I snuck that blanket in with us?" His husky voice danced along the flesh of my earlobe, hot and sweet. I closed my eyes and let him drag me under the tide of our past. I nodded as he pushed his hips into mine, and I felt him hard and ready for me.

It caused a rush of heat to pool in my belly, low and deep and primal.

I pushed my hips forward and tipped my head back to have him claim my lips again. He did so with fire on his tongue, like he was aware of the war that had raged against our hearts, like he was planning to fix it all with merely one kiss.

The danger in his touch was that he could.

He seared me, pressed into me impossibly hard, causing my hands to push up under his shirt and my nails to sink into his skin. I wanted him. I *needed* him.

His rough hands went to my neck and carefully tilted my head to the side as he devoured my mouth, groaning and rumbling dirty things near my ear.

"I loved how wet you always were for me." He kissed the space below my ear. "Always so receptive and ready." His kisses went lower until he was sucking on the skin at the base of my neck. "Everything inside me is fighting the urge to fuck you against this wall right now." More sucking and his right hand went around me to my ass, where he pulled me closer. "Would you like that?" He lightly bit my shoulder, pushing my bra strap aside. I had no voice, nothing left in my lungs to give him. My legs were weak as he let each word leave his lips, leaving me with a promise and a hope for what might be building between us.

His words, although tantalizing, were devoid of any heart. There were no promises of love, which sobered me a little too quickly for my liking. I'd been led by emotions before, and it had taken me to dangerous places.

"Let's go watch the movie," I said, raspy with need as I tried to calm down. I smiled up at Jace, heaving in extra air, hoping he'd get the hint without being offended.

He smiled down at me and nodded. "Just walk in front of me so no one sees this." He looked down at his legs and I laughed. I tugged his hand and did as he asked, staying plastered to his front until we settled into our seats, not in the back, but in the middle.

I wasn't sure if I had ruined things by calling off our grope session in the hall, but when he slipped his hand into mine and held it for the length of the film, I felt maybe I hadn't ruined anything at all. Maybe, just maybe, we weren't tarnished by what we'd done, weren't too far gone for redemption. Maybe we could still find our way back to each other.

Chapter 25
Jace

THIS NEW EXISTENCE I had with Faith was something I couldn't seem to get used to. It felt like it used to with her, back when we were kids—less sexual, more aware of how we treated each other. I both loved and hated it.

After the movie theater, things had only gotten worse with our groping and make-out sessions, but every time I started falling into old patterns with her where I'd explain in graphic detail what she did to me and what I wanted to do to her, she'd pull away. I was starting to think my girl had turned prude over the past five years.

Another part of me just wondered if it had to do with her still being married. I didn't love that she still legally carried someone's last name, but I also wasn't about to let that small technicality stand in my way. I wanted Faith. I wanted her heart, her soul, her body, and every single future kiss from those delicious lips.

It was Saturday and I had my arm around Faith's shoulders, tugging her along with me down at the local Collierville market. Ever since the movie night, she'd stopped looking over her shoulder as much. If it was because of her fear of the cameras or of Bryan, I wasn't sure, but I liked that she seemed more at ease now.

"This one." She grabbed a wooden frame in awe. It had an

engraved wildflower sticking up out of the dirt that looked 3-D against the stained grain of the wood, especially with a light dusting of red over the petals. It was spectacular...and nearly two hundred dollars. I winced and tugged on her arm on instinct, but she stayed rooted in place.

She talked passionately with the artist who had made it, asking questions about the process behind each piece. Scattered throughout her booth were dozens more like the one Faith had in her arms. I saw her eyes go big as she began inspecting the other items.

One had metal infused with the wood, outlining a very detailed carving of a mounted motor. It looked cool as hell. I peeked at the price on it, just out of curiosity, and saw it was $350. *Holy shit.*

I wandered away from the booth but stayed close enough to see Faith. She was digging in her wallet, pointing at several pieces. I watched her smile as she handed over her card to the woman in the tent, watched her transform into the billionaire's wife that she was underneath. My chest burned as the reality of our lives and the difference between our worlds came into focus. This was who she was now. *Rich. Entitled.*

She'd grown accustomed to walking into any situation and just laying down her card. I didn't have the strength to look and see if her card was black, or if it had her husband's name on it. I didn't know enough about the details surrounding their marriage.

I'd heard bits and pieces in the room that night, heard enough to make my stomach sour, but that didn't mean he'd cut her off. It certainly didn't mean she wasn't still living off of him in some capacity. Sure, she'd shown her self-sustaining status that day she couldn't pay for her car, but maybe that had been too much for her.

I knew one thing for sure: she wouldn't be able to settle with a guy like me, someone broke, still stuck in debt. My fingers were raw from how many times I'd had to rub pennies together to make my loan payments and cover Jessie's college tuition. Faith didn't belong with a guy like me, and I'd be damned if she settled. It'd go somewhat like her marriage—she'd stick it out, miserable, lonely, until one day she just left.

"Ready to walk around some more?" Faith asked excitedly, slipping her fingers into mine. I looked down at her, saw the afternoon sun reflect in those blue eyes, and I wanted to drown. For one second, I wanted to be someone else, anyone else—not the poor kid from Collierville who had to really consider if he could afford a piece of art before just laying down his card.

I nodded my agreement and followed after her, swallowing my pride one horrible piece at a time.

"So, what's your plan after everything?" I asked while we slowly sauntered down Main Street, hand in hand. A few people glanced our way, pulling their phones out, pointing them directly at us. Faith had sunglasses perched on her face, her hair curled with a few pieces framing her features.

I had sunglasses on too, hoping to at least marginally guard my identity. Faith tipped her head back, smiling up at me; chocolate ice cream was smeared along her lips, making me insane.

"I had a meeting with my admissions counselor the other day," she said happily while swinging our arms.

"College?" I asked, unsure why that excited me so much.

"Yeah, I mean...I know I need a job too, but..." She lifted a shoulder and let it drop while her eyes went back to the sidewalk. She seemed to ignore the people who were stopping to film us, but it made me uneasy. In fact, I couldn't stop looking over my shoulder.

"Maybe we should head back to your house..." I suggested, seeing a few women from the hair salon pressing their faces to the window, watching us.

Faith let out a sigh. "Sorry...I'm used to it, but you probably aren't." Her face flushed red, making me feel guilty. I pulled her under my arm and pressed a kiss to the top of her head.

"What happened to that big burly guy who bailed you out that night at the bar?" I steered us toward the diner, where a side alley would take us back toward Faith's side of town.

"Tom? He's still around, usually lurking in the background. He likes to give me my space. In bigger cities, he's closer. Here, he's relaxed a bit, but he's there."

I stopped, turning her toward me. "You mean...the other night at my house?"

She laughed. "No, he doesn't follow if I go somewhere with you— he knows you'll protect me."

We started walking again. "How do you pay his salary?" I threw my arm around Faith's shoulder as she tossed her cone away.

She let out a heavy sigh, which meant I was probably not going to like the answer.

"It's your business, sorry..." I muttered, wishing I hadn't asked.

"No, it's fine...it's just that I don't like that I still live off of Bryan. Tom is still on Bryan's payroll, because Bryan wants me protected."

My stomach felt like it was filled with lead. It was the only redeemable thing about the asshole.

"I'm glad you're letting him pay for the extra security," I replied, hoping she knew I didn't have a problem with it.

She nodded. "Gemma wants to push for money in the divorce... for assets." Her withdrawn tone made my stomach twist.

"You don't want to?" *Please say no.*

"I don't want anything to tie me to him...I just want my own life." She tipped her head up again. This time I stopped. Leaning down, I cradled her jaw and gently kissed her. The whole town was still there, buzzing around us, snapping images, capturing our private moment and offering it to the world as if they owned it.

"Whatever you decide to do, I support you," I whispered against her ear, kissing her neck. She sagged against me, nodding into my chest.

We made our way to Faith's apartment, where we planned to invite Jessie over for dinner. We took the elevator up to her floor, for no other reason than to just stay connected and tucked together. When we stepped into the hallway leading to Faith's door, there was a man swiftly mincing toward the stairwell.

"What the heck?" Faith muttered.

"Do you know him?" I asked, stepping away from her, closer to her door, so I could ensure it hadn't been tampered with.

"No, never seen him before, but didn't it look like he was moving away from my door?" Faith dug for her key in her purse.

"It did. No one else has a key, right? Does Tom?" I narrowed my eyes as we carefully opened her door.

"Tom does...but I trust him with my life."

Faith's apartment looked the same as it had when we left earlier that day. Not even a single piece of paper seemed out of place, the throw blanket still folded the same. "Anything look off to you?"

Faith's brows scrunched together. "Not that I can tell."

I locked her door, unable to shake the feeling that someone had broken into her apartment. I decided right then I wasn't leaving her alone that night.

Jessie came for dinner and stayed through a movie, and while it was a fun evening filled with laughter, the mood from earlier hadn't quite dissipated. I couldn't shake the feeling that someone had been in this apartment.

It didn't help matters that Faith had been getting text messages all evening. She'd run into the kitchen to refill a glass or the chip bowl, but every time she'd have her eyes narrowed on her phone, her fingers furiously typing away to whoever was talking to her.

"Everything okay?" I asked from across the room, unwilling to keep letting this little charade slide.

She hurried, bustling around the kitchen. "Yeah, just Gemma with some lawyer stuff." She waved her hand around, but I knew there was something more to it. Problem was, I also knew she didn't trust me enough to share it with me.

Once the movie ended, Jessie hugged each of us and headed home. Faith went to the bathroom, and I started cleaning up. Just as my hand brushed up against the blanket that had been on Faith during the movie, her phone buzzed.

I picked it up, ready to place it on the coffee table for her, but the screen lit with a message. My jaw clenched shut.

Bryan: Don't forget about Christmas—remember that trip I promised you? I got the confirmation last night. The place in the Netherlands is ours.

Fuck me if it didn't feel like these two were playing some kind of game. She'd been texting someone all night with apprehension on her face. She'd been ducking and hiding, and why wouldn't she? She'd been playing me like a fucking fiddle.

I tossed the phone back on the couch and ran my hands through my hair, trying to remember. The images of Faith's bruised body flashed through my head as I tried to calm down. She wouldn't just let him back in. No way. I knew her better than that. There had to be a different explanation for this.

"Hey, I'm glad you stayed." Faith smiled, walking over to me. Her hair was tied back at her neck, leaving little tendrils free around her face. I tucked one behind her ear as she leaned into me.

"Of course I stayed." I bent down and kissed her. I wanted to lift her, walk her back to the bedroom, and own her, claim her like a caveman, staking his territory—but she'd hate me for it. Sure, I could probably kiss her, make her feel something enough to want that, but tomorrow she'd hate me or herself, and for that reason, I wouldn't push.

"I was wondering if I could cook you dinner tomorrow?" She gripped my t-shirt and leaned back a fraction. The gravity of it made me want to scoop her up by her ass. "I know we've been here a few times, but I could come over, either to your dad's place or yours. We could spend time there." She beamed, biting her lip.

My heart kicked hard in my chest, terrified. I was so insecure. The text about Christmas in the Netherlands had me turning her down.

"We can do it here. I like your place better."

"Okay. Bring Trevor." She kissed me hard and then let me go with a smile.

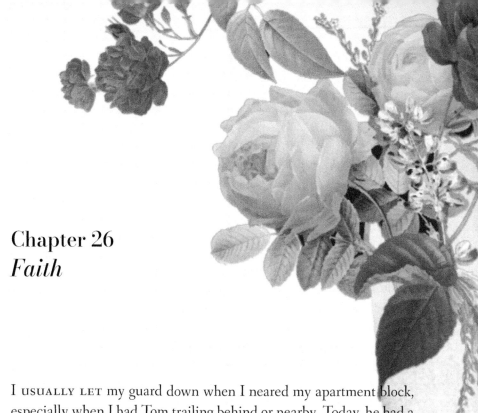

Chapter 26
Faith

I USUALLY LET my guard down when I neared my apartment block, especially when I had Tom trailing behind or nearby. Today, he had a family emergency, and since I was sticking close to home, I told him to go. I was wearing a pair of jean shorts, a tank top, and flip-flops, swinging my cloth grocery bag back and forth as I made my way home.

The sun kept playing peekaboo in between the trees that lined my street, and because I was feeling nostalgic, I tipped my head back and smiled. I was a bird set free. I was home and I was happy. Things with Jace were going so well it had me smiling, ducking away from the sun. Butterflies took off in my stomach whenever I received a text from him or heard his voice on the phone. I was falling for him so easily—too easily. We still hadn't talked about anything from our past, but maybe we didn't need to.

Curiosity dug into my veins, though, hungry for the miniscule details he hadn't shared yet.

Then there was the previous night. Gemma had gotten an email from Bryan's lawyer with a few testimonials about my drug abuse—my *nonexistent* drug abuse. Apparently, there were videos, which

223

caused Gemma to go into freak-out mode, texting me every five minutes to ensure there wasn't anything I was keeping from her.

Then out of nowhere Bryan had texted me about Christmas. It was so odd and out of place that I had stared at it for an hour after Jace went home. He'd made sure he talked with Tom about the guy who'd been seen in my building earlier that day before he left. I had wanted him to stay with me but refused to ask him.

The text almost felt like code in some way...but why would he text me as though we weren't currently going through a divorce? I would have almost wondered if he'd sent it to the wrong number, but I *had* mentioned the Netherlands. I had picked out this beautiful place to spend a magical Christmas, but that had been almost two years ago. It confused me. I knew he was trying to throw me off my game, which he'd done successfully, because I had no idea what to expect from him.

I had just walked past the dumpster area near the side of my building when a hand grabbed me by the wrist and tugged me into the alley.

My stomach flipped as fear shot through me. I didn't have time to move before a hard body crushed me against the brick wall and a large hand covered my mouth.

"Did you honestly think you'd get away with it?" Bryan rasped hot, anger into my ear.

I blinked and tried to grasp what was happening. Bryan stood over me, wearing an Armani suit. His imperfect hair covered half his forehead and was wild, as though he'd been running his fingers through it manically. His knee was pressed between my legs, his hand firmly closed over my mouth. I took in air through my nose and tried not to panic.

"Now, I'm going to lower my hand and let you breathe, but I need you to promise you aren't going to do something stupid like scream," he muttered calmly, like he was helping me out of some barbed wire and just needed my cooperation in order to get me free. "You promise?" he asked, his blue gaze pinning me to the wall as much as his body.

I nodded my agreement and relished the air once his hand was gone. I wasn't going to scream, because I was playing the long game with this fucker. I'd known he was going to freak out over my interview, but the leaked photos were probably what had sent him over the edge. As if I had any control over those.

"I want to talk over dinner tonight. There seems to be a lot of misconceptions about what actually happened in our home, and I think we owe it to one another to clear things up." He brushed his hands down the length of my arm. I resisted the urge to pull it away and shove him out of my space.

"I agree that we do need to talk, but I'm only interested in talking to you with my lawyer present," I replied boldly, trying to keep my head held high. He was a dragon, maw open, ready to devour me—except he wouldn't end me quickly. No, he'd lock me away, keep me there to do his bidding, punching and hurting me when he needed a release.

He slapped the brick above my head and let out a sound of frustration. "Dammit, Faith, this isn't a joke. I need to talk to you without an audience. Do you think you'll get anything from me? You think you'll get a dime? Tennessee isn't a community property state, which means you get shit, because you came into this marriage with shit." He fumed, moving his face closer to mine.

My heart raced, desperate for safety and a place to hide. I didn't give anything away, just kept my chin held high and my gaze locked on his.

"If you think I'm going to let you ruin me, let you fuck some country boy while you carry my last name *and* give you half of what I own, you're fucking delusional." He searched my face, and *shit*, I must have looked surprised when he mentioned Jace, because he smiled and leaned in closer. "Didn't think I knew about your small-town boyfriend?" He laughed and ran his fingers through my hair, toying with the ends. "I know everything about your little lover. I know he's in over his head with his auto shop, and I know the tuition fees he owes for his sister are overdue. I know he'll be bankrupt in a few years if he doesn't get some steady revenue, which will force him to sell his house."

He leaned in, pressed his lips just under mine, and smiled again.

"You can make me forget him, Faith. Make me take his name off this ugly little list that's in my head. Because if you don't, who knows what kind of calamity could befall that sweet little family."

He straightened, causing me to lurch forward.

"Dinner tonight, six o'clock. I'll be out front waiting."

———

"What the hell am I going to do?" I groaned into my arms, which were folded on top of Gemma's desk.

"For starters, you're going to move your ass. You're messing up all my case files." Gemma poked at my arm with her chopstick, and I slumped into my chair, leaning away from her desk.

"If I don't go with him, he's going to ruin Jace—*and* Jessie, for that matter. He threatened their entire family." I leaned against my fist, laying my concerns out there for my best friend to fix. She gazed at her box of chow mein, ignoring me. I liked to think she was just contemplating a solution, but I knew her too well—she was trying to calculate calories. "Gemma, now is not the time to worry about your ass!" I slammed my hand down on her desk.

"Bitch, you know how I feel about my ass—how dare you!" She leaned forward to snag her phone to input the calorie intake.

Once she was done, she finally met my crazed glare and cleared her throat. She stared at me with her hands steepled like a badass lawyer and then smiled at me. Her lipstick was still flawlessly in place on her lips, a deep purple, making her white teeth look even more glorious.

"Oh my god, stop with the evil smile." I huffed an exasperated sigh and rolled my eyes.

"Don't you dare steal my evil smile from me. You know how much I live for knowing more than other people." She laughed, lowering her hands and adjusting her back into her ergonomically correct chair.

My chair was a piece of shit, zero lumbar support whatsoever—kind of like how my best friend was currently acting.

"Like it's hard to know more than me, Gem." I rolled my eyes again. I was smart in my own way, but I wasn't lawyer smart.

"Look, he's panicked, which is good." She checked her phone, disengaging from my panic.

"Okay." I held up my palm for her to continue.

"Okay—nothing. He's panicked. It's good." She said each word slowly so I'd understand.

"For fuck's sake, Gem—tell me why that's good."

She let out another evil laugh, and my eyes twitched with how badly I wanted to reach across the desk and tackle her. "Okay, sorry. It's just so much fun. Look, you embarrassed him by talking about your divorce publicly, and then with the photos being leaked, it'll compromise business deals, stockholders, shares—I mean the list goes on and on. He wants to strong-arm you into admitting you're on heavy drugs, you need rehab, and the photos were fake. He wants the world to think you're still madly in love with him." She leaned forward to snag a piece of paper. "But!" She put up a finger. "We have leverage." She flipped a few pages over and slid them my way.

I read over the proposal she'd already written up for if and when Bryan fought us on the divorce.

"Shit," I whispered as I read over her ideas. She was purely diabolical.

"There's more where that came from, baby." She winked. "So, you can go to dinner tonight, show up, and slam this down in front of him, get him to back off. Or you can wait him out, stand him up, and see what happens. It's up to you." Gemma checked her nails like she didn't have a care in the world.

Her confidence put out all the fires burning in my chest.

"Okay, so this is the plan?" I shuffled the papers so they were in order.

"This is the plan." She nodded and I sat back, brought my fingers up to a steeple, and returned her smile.

I tried to call Jace, but his phone went to voicemail. My meeting with Gemma had taken up more of the day than I'd realized, so I was running on nearly no time to get my game plan together. My nerves were raw, my brain in overdrive as I wrestled with the fight-or-flight instincts that were firing off like little flare guns in my head.

They were telling me to stay safe, stay the hell away from Bryan, and not go to dinner with him. It was like dining with the devil himself, my poor soul begging me to see the light and repent.

But I had to do this. I couldn't risk Bryan messing with Jace's job, his new home, or Jessie's school. I wouldn't allow it.

So, as I fumbled with my sling-back heels and black dress, I voice-texted Jace.

Me: Rain check on tonight?

He responded fairly fast.

Jace: What's up?

I hesitated, wanting to tell him, but not with a text where he could misconstrue the situation.

Me: Nothing, just have to meet about some legal stuff. I'll call you later tonight

Jace: I could come with you. I don't mind hanging out while you go over stuff

The text nearly made my heart explode. The idea of having Jace next to me made me feel immediately at ease, but the words Bryan had uttered earlier about their life and business came rushing back.

Me: It's okay. It's something I need to do alone.

I added a heart emoji to hopefully get the message across that it wasn't what he thought, that I wanted him there, but I also wanted to protect him and Jessie. Bryan was a devious monster, cunning and quick on the draw. His money made him a very serious threat, one I wouldn't take lightly where Jace or his sister were concerned.

Seeing that Jace hadn't started typing anything new through the text thread, I exited the app and called Tom. He was ready for me downstairs, under orders to take me to meet Bryan. At least I didn't have to ride there with my husband. At least I had a few minutes of reprieve before I had to see him again.

The drive to the restaurant in Collierville was quick. It still made my skin crawl that Bryan was in the city I lived in, but at the same time, I didn't want to travel anywhere he could get me alone or away from my new life.

The low lighting of the restaurant took a second to adjust to as I walked forward, back rigid, stomach tense. I moved around a few sequestered tables with nicely dressed couples seated at each one. The music was quiet in the background, and the piano serenade seemed so poetic as I walked toward my abuser. At the back of the room was a small table hidden by tall plants and statues, perfect for a private conversation. *Fuck.*

I held my chin up, putting on the front that this didn't affect me in any way.

Once the server assisted me with scooting in my chair, took my drink order, and left, Bryan showed his colors.

"I said six." He scanned the menu.

I didn't touch mine. I knew he'd order for me anyway, as he'd done since we got married. It had started when I didn't know what to order at the five-star restaurants he'd take us to. I was thankful for it, but he never tried to educate me, never offered to help. I knew he liked the control.

I sipped the water in front of me and channeled my inner Gemma, trying to pull that evil smile out of my arsenal. It was in there somewhere; I'd practiced it enough before this meeting. I cleared my throat. "I had things to do."

It was 6:15—the idiot was honestly whining about fifteen

minutes? Gemma had said it'd put him off his game. It'd be throwing a juicy piece of meat in front of that monster living inside him.

He slowly set his menu down, and our server came over like a little lap dog. Bryan ordered the braised lamb for both of us, which seemed fitting as I currently felt like I was being led to the slaughter.

Once the server flitted away, taking our heavy leather menus with him, Bryan landed his clouded gaze on me. His eyes were irritated, slightly red, like he'd been drinking. He was a high-functioning drunk, but there was a limit to his façade of sobriety.

"Are you ready to talk about this bullshit divorce?" he asked, sipping his scotch. I eyed the movement, darkness tugging at the edges of my memories, threatening to take me back to those nights. The smell of liquor on his tongue as he forced angry kisses on me... the horrible burn as he tossed his glass of amber anger in my eyes... the feel of his fingers against my neck as he forced me to the ground... I blinked and pushed back the bile that threatened to surface.

"I told you—I am more than happy to discuss it with our lawyers. What is it exactly that you had to discuss with me in private?" I leaned back, desperate to get as much space from him as possible.

"This is fucking bullshit, Faith." He raged, spit flying from his lips, but no one would see.

We were hidden. He could hurt me, and no one would know.

"Here's what you're going to do." He leaned forward, his metallic red tie gleaming under the lights. The lighting was getting more pronounced in the room as daylight waned outside. "You're going to admit you're an addict. You're going to admit you're checking your-self into rehab, and we're going to have a very public makeup. Hugs, kisses—we're going to act like the fucking couple we *are*." He jabbed his pointer finger into the table, driving each point home. Desperation was leaking through every single pore in his face. He had bags under his eyes, the blue color of them was less vibrant, and his hair looked greasy.

He was off his game, probably drinking more than normal, which meant he was easier to mess with. I smiled at him, watching him from under my lashes, like I was about to flirt.

Instead, I reached into my purse and pulled out the paper I'd gotten from Gemma earlier. I slid it in front of him and leaned back.

"Here's what *you're* going to do. You're going to sign the divorce papers. You're going to leave Jace and his family alone and never look into them again. You're not going to fight me on the divorce or drag it out. We'll handle it quietly, quickly, and be done," I said, my tone light and easy, like he wasn't scaring the shit out of me.

His angry gaze left the paper and landed on me. Hurt, fear—it all swirled in those irises I had once loved, but like most of our marriage, anger overshadowed those other emotions. It was always more potent.

"You're going to go to the cops and press charges against me?" He said it like I'd been the one beating him.

I leveled him with a serious glare. "Yes. Those are my terms. As you can see, they already have the report from when I went to the hospital. I merely have to let them know I want to press charges." Gaining steam and feeling powerful, I leaned forward and pressed my finger into the table. "Then I'm going to war with your investors. I'll be on every talk show from fucking New York to California as the spokeswoman for female empowerment. You'll lose millions. Think of how many people won't do business with you once they learn you're an abusive dick."

I leaned back again just as our meals arrived.

I retrieved the paper from in front of him. He seemed to be thinking over my words, or he was just in shock. Either way, it made me feel powerful.

When the server left, I stood and looked down at my husband. "I think we're done here. I look forward to seeing your signature on those documents as soon as they're delivered to you." I went to turn away, but he grabbed my wrist.

His fingers dug in deep, and pain shot up my arm as he tugged me back toward him. I landed in his lap, and he didn't waste any time. He tipped me back and kissed me—hard.

I pushed against him, and tears sprang to life in my desperate eyes once he finally let me up. I went to slap him across the face, but just before I did it, I realized there were two people standing along the wall of the restaurant with cameras aimed at us.

"Go ahead, hit me. I've already paid them to edit it to make it seem as though you lost it." He smiled wide. "You forget, sweetheart —this country was built on hush money, ugly truths, and dirty secrets. I own more people than you think. Take your story to the cops...see what happens." He tucked a stray piece of hair behind my ear and leaned in to kiss my swollen lips. Tears trailed down my face as fear settled into my chest.

Bryan had just earned a TKO. I was lying flat on the metaphorical mat with nothing left.

Chapter 27
Faith

"Jace, please open up," I pathetically pleaded with the paper-thin door on his fifth wheel. I'd knocked at least ten times and was positive his sister or father was going to overhear from the mobile home any second and come to check on who was making the noise.

It was past eleven at night. After the dinner with Bryan, I'd driven all the way to my favorite lookout point and parked. I had crawled onto the hood of my car and watched as the sun dipped below the horizon, on its way to start a new morning in a different part of the world. I sat and watched the stars as they came out one by one. It wasn't until I began to shiver uncontrollably that I realized I needed to head back, but the idea of going home wasn't something I could stomach.

Bryan knew where I lived, and was probably watching me. What I'd felt was a new start for me now felt like an hourglass. I was on display for him to watch as the sand poured down on top of me, smothering me and leaving me free of choices.

So, I had driven to the only place I'd feel safe. It alarmed me that it was Jace I'd thought of, that it was Jace who, deep down in my bones, was the person I knew would keep me protected against what-ever scheme Bryan had cooked up.

Finally, on my eleventh sturdy knock, the door was flung open. Jace stood there in his boxer briefs, a scowl on his handsome face and a death grip on the door.

"What the fuck do you want, Faith?" he growled, his gruff tone chipping at me. Angry Jace was back. I knew I'd bailed on dinner, but that didn't explain why he was being so mean.

"Can I come in?" I asked, voice barely above a whisper, terrified he'd shut me out.

Jace looked over his shoulder for a second before letting out a heavy sigh. "I'm not exactly alone."

Pain so shallow and so dull socked me right in the chest. The heaviness of it nearly made me trip backward. He'd already moved on from whatever it was we had done, whatever moment we'd allowed ourselves. We hadn't made a declaration or anything, but it was more than I'd given anyone else since Bryan...since him.

"Oh..." was all I could supply.

"Figured you'd be with him tonight anyway, and we don't owe each other more than that, right?" Jace's dark eyebrows drew together in question, quietly waiting for my confirmation.

"Why would you think that?" I shook my head, confused.

"Someone was kind enough to forward this to me a few hours ago." He huffed, reaching behind the door, toward the counter.

A second later he shoved his cell phone in my face. On the screen was an image of Bryan leaning me back in his arms, kissing me. The angle made it look like I was kissing him back, and the headline read: **Lovers reunite in small-town Tennessee. Faith Vanderson comes clean about the lies of divorce and photoshopped evidence.**

I let out a shaky huff of air as tears burned the edges of my eyes. This was all it took to shake whatever the fuck it was we had together?

"The asshole forced himself on me." I swallowed thickly, real-izing I needed to tuck my emotions away and save face. He didn't need to hear any more; it wouldn't matter. "I'll let you get back to your guest." I turned on my heel and headed for my car. I didn't want to stay and talk or explain myself, I didn't want to do anything. I just wanted to go somewhere and hide.

"Faith, wait…" I heard Jace call from somewhere behind me, but I was already moving, nearly to my car. As soon as I opened the door, a large hand slammed it shut from behind me. "Fucking wait," he seethed. His hair fell across his forehead, slicing into his eyes, creating a dark mask, and in the murky midnight air, it made him look beautiful.

"For what, Jace? You already made your decision—there's nothing to wait for," I half-cried, half-yelled at him. Hurt was hammering away at my heart, removing any resolve I had left.

Those cobalt eyes may as well have been a scale with how he was weighing me, measuring something, but I didn't know what.

"What were you going to do when you came here tonight?" His question somehow made him seem more vulnerable than standing there in his boxer briefs did.

I let out an honest laugh. "I was going to ask you to hold me, to let me sleep in your arms because it's the only place I've felt safe since I left Bryan." That took him off guard, enough to let me open my door and slip inside.

I gently shut the door to my parents' house, trying to be quiet enough that they wouldn't wake.

"Faith, that you?" My mother's voice carried from the kitchen.

"Yeah, it's me, Mom," I whispered, carrying my heels in my hand, moving toward her.

"Haven't seen you in a little bit, sweetie." My mother's flowered robe was pulled tight, her hair in curlers. She only wore curlers at night when she had somewhere to go early the next morning.

"Sorry, didn't mean to wake you," I said, feeling my toes press into the cool hardwood floor.

"I was up getting some water, you're fine." She waved me off.

I followed her around the kitchen, ready for some water myself. I realized I hadn't eaten any dinner once I saw the platter of home-made chocolate chip cookies my mother had made. Pulling back the saran wrap, I snagged one.

"Where are you going in the morning, Mama?" I chewed, crossing my arms over my chest.

She blinked, looking surprised. "Oh..." She pressed a hand to her curlers. "Just heading into work." She moved toward the stove.

I furrowed my eyebrows. "Since when are you working?"

"Since your father isn't in the insurance business anymore," she muttered, her lips thinned into a lifeless line.

"Why on earth did he get out of the insurance business anyway?" I asked, feeling guilt tug in my lower belly. I should have been finan-cially taking care of them. I should have checked in. I should have grown the fuck up.

My mother shrugged. "Just came home one day with his box of personal things, looking haunted, and said he was job hunting." She was quiet for a moment. "Why are you here, honey? Did Bryan finally convince you to go to dinner with him?" she asked, filling a clear glass with water.

Shock splintered through me, slowly leading to hurt.

"How did you know?" I whispered, terrified to hear her say she knew. If she did, it would change everything between us.

"Well," she started, letting out a heavy gust of air like it had been trapped inside her lungs. "Your father and I met with him. It was the right thing to do, to hear his side too, see how we could help you two out. I told him he needed to take you to dinner, just sit down with you and start there." She smiled at me, fucking beamed.

I faltered back a step.

"Faith, honey? You okay?" She reached for me.

Tears clogged my throat so badly it felt as if I'd stuffed three big fat taco shells inside it. My mother and father had talked to my abuser about how he could get me alone, how he could talk to me?

I turned away from her, pushed my feet back into my heels, and grappled for the front door. I ignored her questions, her calling my name. Blood rushed through me, pumping so hard it blocked everything else out.

I swung the front door open only to find Jace there, hunched over, his hands propped up on either side of the door frame.

His blue eyes snapped up. *That look...* His face held a thousand apologies. I inhaled the twilight air as I pushed into the darkness. I shut the door behind me, cutting off my mother's words.

He gently grabbed my hand and pulled me toward his truck. I didn't know why I followed. At this rate, I should have just headed to Gemma's—she was the only person who hadn't let me down—but I was numb. My parents had talked to Bryan behind my back. They had suggested he take me to dinner.

"Come home with me," Jace muttered, opening the passenger door of his truck.

I merely nodded, climbing inside.

Something hard was poking me in the back. With my eyes tightly shut, I shifted backward, closer to the warm spot behind me.

A soft groan erupting from the other half of the bed had me freezing and straightening my spine. The previous night came rushing back: Jace's face, his trailer, his arms...this bed...*my mother.*

My eyes flew open. The sun was peeking through thin white curtains and hitting the brown paneling enclosing us in a tiny room. Something warm covered my feet; I looked down to see Trevor curled up at the bottom of the bed. There was a firm, flat hand on my stomach and that hard length grinding into my panties from behind.

I turned my head slightly, but Jace's face was shoved into my shoulder. He wasn't awake, not enough to really register what was happening. I took the silent moment to remember what had happened.

Come home with me.

That was what Jace had said. I'd crawled into his truck on numb legs and sat there with my face in my hands, so out of touch that when walking up to his fifth wheel door, I hadn't even registered that he'd said he wasn't alone.

As I had climbed in behind him, I'd briefly wondered if he'd kicked whoever it was out, until I saw Seth stretched out on Jace's couch, snoring.

"He's been here with me since we left the bar earlier...he had too much," Jace had grunted as he led me to his room.

"So, when you said you weren't alone...?" I'd quirked an eyebrow at him, utterly confused as to why he had let me think that.

He had blushed, actually blushed. "It was Seth. I just figured you were here to tell me you were gettin' back together with your husband, and I wanted to hurt you in some way."

Jace's grip on my stomach brought me back to the moment. Feeling reckless and emboldened by the privacy of his room, I rocked back into him.

He let out a small laugh, followed by a gruff, "Don't start with me unless you're willing to finish."

Heat simmered in my core and crept up my neck.

I considered it for a moment, and after the previous night, I didn't want to do anything but spit on, burn, and disgrace my vows to Bryan. So, I pushed back farther into him, gaining me a low groan from his throat.

"I'm serious, Faith. I'm hard as stone right now, and if you start teasing me and pull the plug, I'm gonna die of blue balls."

His hand danced along my ribs, tracing ever so slightly toward the edge of my breasts. My breathing came out labored as I allowed myself to enjoy his touch. I'd slipped out of my dress and into one of Jace's t-shirts before we got in bed, and his scent was everywhere.

"So, what's it going to be?" he mumbled tiredly into my ear, his hot breath fanning out on my hair. I squirmed again, hating the ache growing between my legs. He froze and slowly dropped his hand until he was tracing the inner part of my thigh. "You're wet?"

I made some sound of acknowledgment and waited for him to make the choice for us, because I was too much of a coward to do it. He was hard, I was wet—things couldn't have been more perfect if we tried. Instead of taking charge like he used to, he let out a pained sigh and rolled away from me.

"What are you doing?" I asked on a deflated whisper.

"Waiting for you to tell me what you want." He looked at the ceiling, and I kept my gaze away from the pitched sheet clinging to his waist.

"I want you..." I half heartedly responded.

"You aren't ready for sex," he declared, shaking his head against the pillow.

I swallowed, knowing he was right. "It's not because of him." I needed him to know that.

He looked over and quirked a dark eyebrow. His tan chest was bare except for the trail of dark hair leading down from his belly button to his boxers.

I cleared my throat. "I just don't know where we are with all of this...I'm still hung up on a few things with how we ended and what happened last night. So...it's not that I don't want to have sex because of him or the marriage. I just need you to know that." I didn't even realize I'd turned to face him until he matched my posture, propping his head up with his hand.

His blue eyes danced with laughter as he scanned my pink cheeks. I wanted to do something bold and brazen to get that look off his face. I didn't want him to look at me like I was a funny joke, or some girl too shy and vanilla to know what she wanted in bed. I knew.

Blinking harshly against the light in his room, I leaned away from him and watched the ceiling, like he'd just done.

His fingers brushed aside the hair sticking to my face. "What just happened?"

"You looked at me like I was amusing." I turned my head to see his expression.

"You *are* amusing." His lips twitched like he was holding back a laugh.

"I am not. A girl wants to be sexy, desirable, but not amusing. I want you to look at me with fire, like you can't keep your hands off me...like..." I trailed off, hating where this little tirade was taking me.

"Like I used to?" Jace finished for me.

I waited, not sure if I wanted to admit that. After a few seconds, I nodded.

He let out another heavy sigh. "But you aren't mine, Faith. I can't look at you like that."

Painful honesty—it sliced through me like a freshly sharpened knife.

I wasn't his because *he* had let me go. I didn't belong to Bryan. I hadn't ever really belonged to anyone but Jace, so to hear him dismiss me...it just hurt. I wanted him to fight.

I wanted him to rectify what had happened to us all those years ago, to finally put us back together.

"The other night in the movie theater, you acted like that didn't matter," I said, reminding him that he had been on the verge of fucking me against the wall in a public place.

Jace rubbed his jaw and stretched. "Sex is one thing. I can fuck you, Faith, no problem. It'd be like every other girl I've been with over the past few years—meaningless—but that look you want...I can't give you that until you're mine. No strings, no drama. Just mine."

The branches outside swayed, creating a shadow across the bed. I closed my eyes and swallowed the burning sensation that hit my chest. The silence ate up the angry retort that was on my tongue, the hurt that he'd moved on, the fact that he had left me, that this was on him. But I swallowed all the words and shut my eyes until I had tamed my tongue enough to leave him with this thought.

"I've only ever been yours, Jace." I forced confidence into my tone, like he had when he talked about the other women he'd been with. "But you keep letting me go." I rolled away from him, pushing the blankets off and grabbing my clothes. I hated the images that had crept into our conversation regarding him and other women. I hadn't thought he'd been a monk—I wasn't stupid—but it still hurt.

Cold water poured into my cupped hands from the bathroom faucet. I splashed my face twice, hoping to rid it of the tears that had started back up. I grabbed a folded towel from the small cupboard above the sink and dried my face. My throat burned as emotions clawed to get free. I needed to get home, get somewhere private and away from where Jace would hear me or ask. That was assuming he'd even care.

I pulled Jace's shirt over my head and grabbed for my bra right as the thin door opened.

"What the fuck...?" Seth dropped his jaw, squinting from the light. Trevor started barking, trying to get through.

I grabbed for Jace's discarded shirt to cover my breasts right as Jace stumbled into the cramped space.

"Fucking Seth! Don't look at her," he yelled, grabbing his friend by the shirt and pulling him back. Next, he grabbed Trevor's collar and pulled him back.

Jace quickly stepped into the spot Seth had stood in and shut the bathroom door.

His chest heaved as he stared at my bare arms clutching the shirt to my chest. "Sorry...I forgot he was here," he mumbled, running a hand through his hair.

A laugh bubbled up from my throat before I could stop it, and Jace's stoic expression transformed from stunned to amused.

"You think it's funny?"

I laughed harder, clinging to the shirt for dear life as he advanced toward me. There wasn't much space, so in a single move he'd crowded me toward the thin shower. His hand wrapped around my waist as he pulled me toward his chest and shifted us into the stall.

"No! Jace, no!" I begged, but it was too late.

He lifted me and drenched us both under the hot spray while he laughed. "Not so funny now, is it?"

I turned in his arms, watching the water pebble on his firm chest. His head was lowered, forcing the water to pull his hair forward. I pushed my fingers into the soaked strands and nearly crumbled when those icy eyes opened on me. Words were there...unspoken, vulnerable...raw. I reached behind him and tethered my fingers together at the base of his neck, letting the sopping shirt drop to the shower floor.

I was still hurt from the comment he'd made earlier. I was still broken about the fact that he'd lumped me in with the other women he's so easily had and discarded over the years, but having him like this—it was strangely powerful. Regardless of our past, I knew deep down that in our future he would be mine. *Only mine.*

The pads of his fingers drifted down my rib cage and back up, across my collarbone and down to my aching nipples.

I let out a small gasp just as a fist pounded on the door. "You two realize this trailer doesn't come with that big of a water heater, right?" Seth yelled through the door.

We waited, and Jace's gaze didn't leave mine as he continued to palm my breasts, his lips traveling closer to mine. It took all my resolve not to hurry the process up, but I wanted him to come to me, to want me.

"Seriously you guys! My place is over thirty minutes away, so I have to get ready here. Hurry up and *do not* have shower sex. I am begging you not to have shower sex," Seth continued, tapping his fist against the door a few more times.

Jace let out a small laugh and reached for the shower knob, turning the water off. I felt like he'd just ripped the plug out of the socket, ending whatever charged moment we'd just had way too abruptly. He stepped out first, grabbing a towel and covering my shoulders with it.

"I never let you go, Faith." He stepped closer, lifting my chin. "Never once...I just had to figure out how to fix it all without losing either of you, but instead I lost you both." His stoic expression lifted to mine, nailing me to the wall. I knew he was talking about his mother, but I had no idea what he'd had to fix. I wanted to push him for answers to force this overdue conversation, but he was already turning to leave.

Chapter 28
Faith

A SHARP KNOCK on my front door had me snapping my head up from my laptop. I'd left Jace's trailer a little after ten in the morning, calling Tom for a ride. Once we arrived at my building, I asked him to stay near the perimeter and watch for Bryan. I had also asked him to install an extra deadbolt on my door for me. When I'd unlocked my door, I'd noticed right away that someone else had been in my space. Papers on my counter had been askew, and a few books on my shelves had been out of place. Tom had been inside within seconds and checked everything over, but no one was there.

Now it was nearing dinner time, and the sun dipped low, casting an orange streak across my hardwood floors, meaning night was nearly here. I was jumpy.

Another rap on the door had me scooting away from the counter on shaky legs. I hadn't talked to Jace, via text or in any other form. When I'd left the trailer, he had seemed withdrawn. In fact, after the shower, it had been like the Jace I was reacquainted with had returned. He'd remained silent while I waited for Tom, just browsing through his phone while he chewed on an apple.

Another knock sounded, causing me to jump up. Peeking

through the view hole, I let out a heavy sigh and pulled the door open.

"Hey." I leaned against the solid frame, watching as Jace gave me a tight-lipped smile and sauntered past me. He carried a black duffle bag in his left hand, and a fluffy white pillow was tucked under his right arm. I quirked a brow in confusion as I secured the door. "What are you doin'?" I asked, nearly joking with my tone.

"Thought it'd be obvious," he muttered, pulling a big blanket out of his duffle and laying it down on the couch. His tone was ice cold, and his demeanor was stiff.

I walked closer to the living room, crossing my arms. "Well it's not. What are you doing?" I leaned my hip against the tall bar stool I'd been perched on moments earlier.

Jace looked up with that frozen glare of his. "I'm here makin' sure you aren't alone. You seemed to be pretty shaken up last night." His Southern twang cut through the space between us as though I was being reprimanded. Something like pride and shame mixed together like a dangerous cocktail in my stomach.

"I don't need any favors. I have Tom outside—it'll be fine." I wished my tone was stronger, more resolute, but I was nervous about my situation. Bryan had shifted the game board and I was insecure about his next move, but I didn't want Jace here just because he felt obligated.

An irritated huff left his lungs as he fluffed his pillow on the couch. "This isn't a favor, and I already told your bodyguard to head to his hotel. I've got it covered until tomorrow." He stood from the floor where he was crouched, setting everything up. "What's the dinner plan?" he asked, stalking toward the kitchen, pulling the fridge open.

Irritation burned in my chest, causing me to clench my fists. I already had one man manipulating me; I didn't need another.

"Jace, just go home. I don't need—"

"Why did you meet with him?" His glare cut through me like a hot knife in butter, and I felt like I needed to grab on to something with how angry he sounded. He stalked closer. "Why alone? I keep trying to add it all up, Faith, but it doesn't make any sense. You said it was legal stuff, so I assumed that meant Gemma."

I grasped any word I could find in my head, anything that would assuage his anger, but nothing was coming. I couldn't tell him Bryan had threatened him because his pride would take a hit and he'd leave. I couldn't say what game I was playing at because he'd be angry that I wasn't already pressing charges.

His scoff brought me out of my thoughts. "Regardless, you came to me last night, for some reason, even after meeting with him alone." He pointed at his chest forcefully. "Me, not *him* or Gemma, but me. You want to be honest about the feelings behind why you did that, or would you rather I just set up shop and stay?"

Frozen and confused, I stared him down as he stared right back. Honesty wasn't something either of us was versed in since there was clearly still a lie sitting snugly between us. I certainly wasn't going to be the one who made the first move or the first declaration. We'd kissed, touched, but words? We hadn't shared those yet, not one about what this meant, what it would mean long term, or if it meant anything to him at all. He'd so carelessly talked about fucking me like I was the other girls, and that reminder burned like a quick shot of Listerine, wrong and horrific.

No, he wouldn't get my truth first. Not until he shared his.

"That's what I thought." He shook his head back and forth, likely in disgust, and returned to digging through my freezer. He pulled a frozen pizza free and flipped it over, scanning the instructions. A moment later he leaned over to my oven and started the preheating process.

Needing some space from his frustration and his motor oil and fresh laundry smell, I walked back to my bedroom and shut the door.

Tears slipped down my heated face as I climbed into my bed. Jace was angry at me, and knowing he would never harm a hair on my head made his anger somehow worse than Bryan's. Bryan had hurt me because his ego was bruised, and I had no problems fighting with him, knowing it was always a battle of pride and will. With Jace, it was a battle I could never win, because I didn't need to fight him. No, in order to hurt him, all I needed to do was exist.

An hour later, a rumbling stomach had me leaving my room in search of the source of the Italian sausage smell that had invaded my apartment. Opening my door, I heard the sounds of laughter from the living room, along with clapping. Scratching my wrist, I tried not to be affected by the sight of Jace reclined on the couch with a fat smile on his face as he watched the television.

I walked toward the kitchen, eyes on the TV screen as I went. A tall man leaned over a large wheel and spun it as hard as he could. The small planks rotated, hovering too close to the bankrupt slot. The man cringed as it landed on the black plank at the last second. I smiled. "You still watch Wheel of Fortune?"

Jace didn't look at me as he replied, "Every weeknight if I can make it home in time."

I snagged two pieces of cold pizza and minced toward the opposite end of the couch from where Jace sat.

He didn't seem to notice or care that I had adjusted my body against the soft leather of the couch and was digging my feet under the blanket he'd put on the sofa earlier.

We watched in silence as the new category and blank tiles popped up on the screen. I loved this part, when no one knew anything, when no vowels had been purchased or guesses made. I knew Jace loved it too; he'd always been so good with words.

The first contestant bought an O and spun the wheel again, creating a symphony of applause. I peeked at Jace over my pizza. Ever so slowly, I dug my feet closer to him, hoping he wouldn't push me away.

He didn't acknowledge it or respond, so I waited and watched the screen again.

Another spin ended in two more vowels and three consonants revealed. All I saw was a bunch of letters, and I had no idea what it could be when Jace blurted, "Miss America Pageant."

The contestants hadn't guessed anything yet. They were still draining all the vowel purchases they could, regardless of how much of the puzzle was showing. I swallowed my pizza and dared to scoot my feet closer to his legs. He still didn't seem to notice what I was doing. Maybe I could get close enough to kiss him and start there with an apology.

I hadn't been wrong, but at the same time, if the tables were reversed, I'd be hurt too.

A few more spins finally had someone guessing the puzzle, and sure enough Jace was right. He turned a megawatt smile on me while clapping his hands together. "It's so easy—why do they drag it out like that?" he asked, scoffing a bit.

It wasn't easy. I'd had no clue what those random letters would reveal, but I had always loved how good he was at this silly game show.

"You should go on the show, win a million dollars."

He rolled his eyes at my remark, which made me feel foolish.

"If only it were that easy…" he muttered under his breath.

I wasn't stupid; I knew it wasn't that easy. I hated that he acted like I had changed that much over the past few years. I hadn't. I was still bargain bin Faith, still that same haggle first, apologize later girl.

His gaze lowered to the couch, where my feet were slowly making their way toward him. I froze for a second, unsure of what he was going to do. A second later he let out a huff of air and stood up. He walked to the kitchen, grabbed a glass of water, and when he came back, he avoided the couch altogether, opting for one of the lounge chairs instead.

My heart sank.

My appetite dissolved in a moment, causing me to stand and discard my pizza on the counter. I poured a glass of water as the sound of the wheel spinning ricocheted around the room amidst more applause, laughter, and more small-town stories about the contestants who had wives and husbands waiting in the audience. I watched the boy I'd once loved smile at the television as he sipped his water. A tear slipped free, which was my cue to head to bed.

The boy I'd once known was gone. Whether he had let me go or I'd given up too easily...it didn't matter. A monster had found me, and now I was nothing but a walking nightmare.

Chapter 29
Jace

THIS APARTMENT WAS TOO BIG. It was too bright and too cold.

I shifted on the narrow couch and tried for the millionth time to fall asleep, but like it had done for the past few hours, my mind went back to that moment when Faith texted me about needing a rain check. Maybe I was too close to the situation to see clearly, or maybe I had been waiting for that other shoe to drop...but I'd known then she was meeting Bryan. So, when those images of the two together had shown up, it'd hurt more than I had expected it to. That paired with the text about Christmas...it was too much. It only proved that she had gotten too close, and I was being too careless with what was left of my heart.

It had thrust me back into that moment in that waiting room when I saw her on the screen attached to his arm, back to when my entire world fell apart.

Last night, when Seth and I were out catching a quick bite at the bar, I had thought...I didn't even know what I'd thought. Maybe she'd asked me to dinner because she was feeling what I was feeling. Maybe we'd keep kissing and that thing that kept trying to click into place between us would finally connect. Then the fucking television —that, again, wasn't on a sports channel—showed the exclusive:

250

billionaire Bryan Vanderson out in Collierville, Tennessee, and reconnecting with his wife.

My gut tightened, my throat went dry, and my fucking heart flipped me the middle finger with an *I told you so, sucker*. He'd thrown her back over his knee and kissed the hell out of her. Camera flashes went off, a few people seemed to clap...she was in a tight black dress, looking gorgeous and very much the billionaire wife that she is. More than fifteen different people were kind enough to forward me the link after it aired, too. *Fuckers*.

Then she'd shown up on my doorstep, looking like she'd seen a ghost, knocking like the hounds of hell were after her. I hated the way I reacted to her, how childish and immature I turned when there was even a chance of heartbreak involved. After she left in her car, some invisible thread shit was at work, pulling me to her. If there was even a chance that Bryan had forced himself on her, there was no way in hell she was spending the night alone.

I knew she was going to her parents' house, knew she'd be safe there...and yet I couldn't leave her there. I needed her with me.

That was when I realized I was still in love with her, and it felt like I'd never fallen out of love. It was like someone had just picked up a dusty picture and blown all the dust away. We were still there, still alive...still beating.

But I was angry with her too. She'd lied to me. She'd pushed me away, then all this shit came out and I was just supposed to believe the best of her.

My pride wasn't built that strong.

I rubbed absently at my chest as the thoughts turned over and over in my mind. She was too close, had too much access to me. She could ruin me with one quick text to her husband. One open thread on her phone to him, talking, communicating with him, and I would be done for.

I needed to know what I was to her, who I was to her. I needed her words, her promises, her body...I needed more from her than what she'd given me so far. Maybe that was why I had lied to her.

When she'd asked about that look while we lay in bed in my trailer, I had lied about how Faith could be like every other girl I'd been with over the last few years. There'd only been three women, and Faith could never fall into a category any other woman had ever been in. Not even if it was a quick fuck, not even if it was a regret, not even if it was an accident—she would always be in a league of her own.

Huffing out an exasperated sigh, I sat up and ran my hands over my face. I thought of the look on her face when I'd chosen to sit on the lounge chair, when I'd distanced myself from her. I just couldn't do what we'd done the night before, pretending there wasn't this huge void between us.

Standing, I walked across the room. A sensible white bookshelf sat between her large bay windows, the sleepy town of Collierville dark outside them save for the few lights from the freeway and street-lights. Curious and bored, I checked to see what kind of reading selection she had.

From what I understood, she hadn't brought any books from Nashville, but maybe she'd brought some from her parents' house. I traced my finger over the book I remembered Faith last reading when she was with me.

I pulled on the dark glossy cover and held it, the pale pair of hands holding a red apple so achingly familiar. I thumbed through the pages and smiled at the memory of Faith tucked under a blanket in the back of my truck, her black-rimmed glasses balanced on her nose while she pored over the pages like her life depended on it.

I blinked dry eyes as memories of her curled into my chest, reading and talking about her favorite stories rattled through me. It was why I'd chosen books for us, because they were a great love in her life and I just wanted to be a part of it.

I moved my fingers over a few other titles and stopped. *The Catcher in the Rye* was there with a white library label on the spine, and next to it was *To Kill a Mockingbird*. My eyes took in the other books, all classics. Beyond the first shelf of Faith's personal selection, they were all library books, all the books we'd written messages to each other in.

She kept them. After I had left her there to erase our history alone, she must have brokered a deal to keep them.

Something like hope mixed with fire burned inside my chest; it was uncomfortable and exhilarating. Maybe she did feel the same way about me.

I turned from the bookshelf and, without thinking more about it, headed toward her room. Her door was cracked open, revealing a bedroom bathed in moonlight. It illuminated her sleeping silhouette. The empty spot next to her called to me as I considered all the details of the evening. I considered my anger and how harsh I'd been, but the feelings that had just cracked open inside of me from finding those books caused all the other emotions to dissipate.

Shuffling forward, I took a few steps into her bedroom then a few more around her bed, until I was on the opposite side of where she was sleeping. Without thinking any more about it, I pulled the covers back and crawled inside, the heat already pulling me under.

Her bed was soft, and her cinnamon and sugar smell invaded my lungs. I inhaled deeply and, on instinct, pulled her into my arms. Because she was mine. Because at night I wanted to pretend time didn't exist and our past had never been forced to end and our future was never contrived to begin without the other.

Four years earlier: October

"Big brother." Jessie hugged me tight. I wrapped my arms around her and tried to gauge the reaction of my father, who was picking me up from jail. My six months were finished, and I was free.

"It's good to see you." I ruffled her hair and moved on to my dad, who wrapped me in a big bear hug. We left the facility in my dad's old truck, all three of us squeezing in on the bench. I watched as buildings flashed by, the sun bright and high in the sky. I should have been enjoying the freedom, the wind blowing in my face, but I only had one thing on my mind.

Revenge.

Being double-crossed, losing one's mother, and losing the love of one's life all within the span of a year will certainly mess with one's head. Mine was currently riddled with ideas on how to get back at the motherfucker who'd betrayed me.

"It's been so lonely without you," Jessie started.

I looked over and saw how she tugged on the sleeve of her sweater, pulling it down over her fingers. She'd started wearing baggy sweaters around the time I broke it off with Faith. The two of them were close, but with what I was dealing with, I needed them to have the same amount of space as I had with Faith.

"It wasn't easy when Mom passed, and you weren't here. We had to bury her without you...that was..." My dad's throat clearing had her looking up and trailing off.

I knew it was hard to talk about, but I wanted her to feel like she could talk about it, so I squeezed her knee to continue.

"Anyway, it was hard. I'm glad you're back. We both are." She looked up at my dad again. They both seemed like they wanted to say something but weren't saying it.

"Just spit it out," I huffed, hating how irritable I already felt.

Jessie ducked her head again, not meeting my gaze as she continued. "Guess what I'm tryin' to say is that if you get your revenge on him...you'll go back, and you can't go back. I missed you, Dad missed you. We need you here."

My dad chimed in, keeping his eyes on the road. "It ain't worth it, son."

How they both seemed to already know my motives bothered me. They only knew about what had happened because I'd told them during their visits over the past six months. I shook my head, looking out the window.

"Have either of you heard from her?" They knew who I was

talking about, and I was grateful for it. I just needed to put to rest the questions that were fluttering around inside my chest with wings of hope.

Did Faith hear about what happened? Did she know about my mother?

It was quiet in the truck as we continued toward our humble trailer park. Jessie was the first to speak. "I haven't heard from her... nor have I reached out."

"Don't think she knows what's goin' on, son...I don't rightly know what she knows, but I do know she loved your mama, and if she'd known she had passed, there's no way in hell she would have stayed away."

"If she'd known you were locked up, she wouldn't have stayed away," Jessie rambled on. My heart clenched tight. I had made my sister swear not to reach out to Faith or say anything around town about what was going on. I didn't want Faith coming after me out of pity, but still, I had assumed someone would have leaked that I'd gone to jail or that my mama had died.

If she did know, maybe she was done caring. She had a new husband, after all. I had been privileged enough to see the spectacle during a television special that had come on in the day room. Ironically enough, there should have been about zero chances in hell that I saw that special given that there were only certain people who made the decisions on what we did and didn't watch in there. There was one television, the remote welded to the tray.

They split us up into different types of shifts in the day room. Not wanting any fights to break out, they sequestered us according to the color of our skin. I was thrown in with a bunch of white suprema-cists, skinheads who were the worst motherfucking people I'd ever met. I usually kept to myself, trying not to make waves. Jessie had brought me a few books, so I read, but that day Arnold oversaw the day room. Arnold happened to like celebrity gossip.

That was the one and only time I spoke up. I walked over and asked him to change the channel, nearly begged the fucker, but he only smiled that wicked smile of his and turned it up. I threw up my dinner after I saw how beautiful she looked, how perfect she was, how expensive the entire thing seemed.

During one photo they showed the couple standing side by side, and I noticed hanging delicately from her neck was that silver chain, the one I had given her. *The locket.*

That was when I stood and pushed Arnold, forcing him to fall out of the chair next to the remote. I didn't get a chance to change it. I had my hand twisted back until it nearly broke and then someone came up from behind and put me in a chokehold. I blacked out before the guards came in to break it up.

Now I was free, and I could go find her. I could go disrupt her perfect life the way she'd upturned mine.

Except...

"Jace, whatever you're thinkin', just leave it. Let her live her life, live yours, move on. You don't need anything more from either of them...not him or her," Jessie begged, grabbing my hand.

We parked the truck and filed out. I'd leave her alone...right after I snuck a look at her. Just once.

I waited a week at home, trying to readjust to life, but jail had rightly fucked up my head. It wasn't exactly a friendly place, or a safe one. At home, I found myself having nightmares. I'd be in my cell, back in jail, with people trying to hurt me. It was a clusterfuck, and I was more than a little messed up.

My dad noticed first, and after a few angry arguments, he demanded I attend therapy. There was a program that helped people who struggled with the readjustment period, no matter how long they had been in the system. So, I finally caved and took him up on his suggestion to see a therapist.

It sated my anger and need for revenge, but it did nothing at all for my desperation to see Faith.

Finally, after a few months had ticked by, I made my way to Nashville where the princess lived.

She was easy enough to track, not paying attention to her

surroundings because of her security detail—something I would have made sure she changed if we were to get back together. After a spin class and yoga something, she went shopping.

She wore large sunglasses, black high heels that wrapped around her ankles, a tight black dress that had a slit at the thigh, and those classily red lips. She made me weak. People say they go weak in the knees, but mine felt right as rain. It was my heart that was weak, my resolve—my soul.

Her dress, the diamond ring on her hand, the way she seemed to glow—it was all nothing compared to the confidence she wore. She held her head high, walking with sure steps and a poised smile on her face, like she knew a secret no one else was privy to.

As I followed her throughout the day, there was one thing I couldn't shake, one thing I couldn't take my eyes off of, and it was that same silver chain attached to the locket I had given her. She still wore it even though she was married to another man.

That had to mean something.

It meant everything.

I was going to pull her aside, find an in, and just grab her hand, pull her to my chest, and demand answers. She was edging her way toward a brunch place that likely charged fifty dollars for a plate of pancakes. I snuck in through the side door, telling the hostess I was meeting a friend. She let me pass without question.

I waited in the alcove near the bathroom, watching as she walked in and looked for someone. My heart raced, for some reason thinking and imagining it was me she sought. It was easy to pretend she was always looking for me.

But she wasn't.

Her face nearly exploded with the most beautiful smile I'd ever seen in my life. My gaze left her body to scan the room for who she was looking at, and there in a suit worth more than my entire life was him.

Her husband.

The man who took her from me. His smile was something of

equal measure to hers, then they connected, and it felt like the whole room shifted. He held her like he owned her, searing her with a kiss, and he didn't give a single fuck as to who was watching.

She giggled a second later, realizing they were creating a spectacle. He leaned back just a fraction and brushed some of her hair aside, searching her face as though she was the most precious thing in the world to him. I'd have walked away if I were the better man just based off that look alone, but I wasn't the better man. I still had plans to pull her aside, to try to steal her...until I really looked at the expression on her face.

Tears welled in her eyes as she held his face in her hands. I could hear her say, "I missed you." Then she was throwing herself at him again, kissing him like she needed him for her next breath. That was when it hit me. That was when I knew I had to walk away, because I loved Faith and I'd do anything for her, even let her live the new life she wanted and love the man she needed.

Chapter 30
Faith

"So what should we do?" I asked Gemma, feeling conflicted and distracted. She huffed out a frustrated sigh and stacked a pile of papers.

"We issue a statement. Get you back on camera, maybe answer some of these requests from press who have reached out to you about what they saw the other night, and you tell them what happened—that he forced you against your will, that he's not right in the head." Her blue eyes narrowed on something on her desk. I looked down, trying to see it, but I didn't know what to look for.

Her half-eaten salad was there, bits of boiled egg having fallen onto a legal pad, and her shaker bottle had a half-finished smoothie inside it. Otherwise her desk was occupied by neatly stacked piles of paper.

"What is it?" I asked, still unsure what she was seeing. When she didn't move, I continued, "Was it the eggs? I told you not to get the salads from the back. You have this theory that they're newer, but sometimes they get lazy and stuff the new ones in front, shoving the old ones in back." I waved my hands toward the salad and grimaced.

She waved her hands. "No, stop. What?" She blinked at me,

confused. "I was just thinking about some other options we might have."

I sat down in the chair with a heavy thud. A week ago I'd have been excited at the prospect of having one up on Bryan, but after the dinner, I didn't think it was possible to be a step ahead of him. A buzzing sound caught my attention, and I flipped my phone over to see that my father was trying to call me again. He'd been trying to call me ever since I left the other night.

"Faith, don't give up. Don't you dare give up." Gemma reached forward and grabbed my hand. I let out a sigh and held back a few stray tears.

"I'm not. It's just...everything is so screwed up. I just want a divorce. Why can't I have that?" I held my hands close to my chest, as though I could somehow tend to my heart through my shirt.

"We need to get you in front of a judge—privately. I have connections with one...I might be able to set it up, just act like we're looking for some advice on what to do, because at this rate, Bryan could have fabricated evidence that you were on drugs or God knows what else."

I nodded, knowing that was likely true. The urge to sob was stuck in my throat. I wanted to yell at the man, scream at him, and demand he let me go. He'd obviously never wanted me in the first place, otherwise why would he have hurt me? Why not let me go and find someone else?

The idea of another woman going through what I had slowly started to sink in. I blinked away the images and let out a resigned sigh. "I have to go to the cops about this. I have to press charges...I don't have a choice. What if he does this to someone else?"

Gemma leaned back, her toned arms coming up behind her head to stretch. "Faith..." She let out a sigh and leaned forward a moment later. "It's the only leverage you have on him."

"He called my bluff with it..." I shrugged my shoulders. "So what's the point?"

Gemma searched my eyes frantically. "But—"

"Gem, I have to do this. I have to." I stood, not wanting to talk about it anymore. She'd originally told me to do this anyway; it was my own stupidity that'd had me holding off. I needed to do this, if only for the small chance that it would spare someone else in the future.

Tom had shadowed me the entire day. In fact, two other guards had appeared as well. I had pulled him aside and told him I couldn't afford to pay them, but he'd laughed and reminded me that the bill was being paid by Mr. Vanderson. It concerned me, wondering if they would just step aside at his arrival should my husband pop up somewhere, but Tom assured me that no one was going to talk to me alone unless I requested it.

I had gone to the police department and submitted everything. The officer who helped me assured me everything would get passed along to the proper authorities in Nashville, but I pushed to ensure it wasn't passed along to anyone except the original officer who'd been there the night I went to the hospital.

She had been sweet, concerned for me in a motherly way, talking to me about how she'd gotten free of an abusive relationship herself. I knew she couldn't be bought by Bryan. I knew if he did have cops in his pocket, she wouldn't be one of them.

I was opening the third deadbolt on my front door, ready to shower and call it a day, but as the door swung open, apprehension gripped me. Had someone been here again? Would Jace be here?

I peered around the corner and called out, "Hello? Jace?" I walked farther in, secured and locked the door, and kept moving through the space. This morning had been slightly awkward...I'd woken up early to his arms caged around my middle. When I'd fallen asleep the night prior, he had been on the couch, so I had no idea what had happened, but I was too irritated to let myself sink into his warm chest. Instead, I pushed away from him, showered, and left.

I hadn't received a text or call from him all day, which was fine. We weren't buddies. We weren't lovers. We weren't anything.

Relief and reluctance swept through me as I realized Jace wasn't in my apartment. It wasn't like he'd said he'd be back, and I wasn't his obligation.

Frustrated with myself for wanting him there regardless of how he'd made me feel, I tugged my shirt over my head and peeled my jeans off, kicking my shoes forcefully into the corner of my bedroom. I stalked to my shower and stood under the spray for as long the hot water would allow. I cried angry tears of uselessness and regret. I sank to the floor and wrapped my arms around my legs as I let the heat sink deep into my skin. I just wanted a fresh start. That was it. No shadows from my past, no danger in my future. Just a clean start.

Once I was finished, I wrapped my hair in a white towel, piling it on top of my head, and tugged my silk robe on. Padding into the living room, I pondered dinner ideas but stopped cold at the sight of Jace standing at the desk near the large window in the living room. He had a few white papers between his thumbs, and his eyebrows had formed a determined shelf on his handsome face. I wasn't sure what he was looking at, but it had him confused.

"Hey," I muttered, pulling the towel off my head, slightly self-conscious about whether or not he was still mad at me.

He lifted his head, pulling one sheet of paper free from the rest. "Hey." He turned, that look staying in place as he assessed me. "What is this?"

I stepped closer, closing the gap between us, and surveyed what was in his hands. It was the sketch I had made of his lobby and logo while I was in Gemma's office. I'd thought it was still tucked inside my notebook, but I must have taken it out and forgotten.

I turned and laughed lightly. "Nothing, I was just doodling in Gem's office the other day."

"But why did you draw my lobby and my logo? Are you planning on buying out my loan in addition to opening your own auto shop?" he accused with a menacing tone.

I spun on my heel, confused. "What? No..." I stammered while he drew closer. He knew that whole auto business thing was a joke, total bullshit. So why was he acting like it was a serious threat?

"Faith, tell me the truth. Why did you draw this? Don't give me some bullshit about signs and just pretending." He held the paper up, close to his face. His dark eyebrows rose, but his full lips shifted into a firm line, waiting for my response.

With a heavy sigh, I dropped into the lounge chair closest to me. "I was thinking about you, okay? I was thinking about how proud I was of you...of how, if we'd been together when you started the shop, I would have sketched something like that." I swallowed thick humility that was lodged in my throat. "Because we'd always planned that. Remember? You and me against the world...whatever we planned to do, we'd be in it together."

His face transitioned to something softer, something placid. He turned and headed toward the kitchen, as though I hadn't just shared a massive piece of truth with him.

"Um, do you have any thoughts on what I just shared?" I slowly stood, following after him.

He started picking ingredients out of a bag, but his clear-cut answer rang out between us. "Have you removed all the signs from around town yet?"

He was demeaning in his question. Sure, I'd done the signs as a joke, but I thought he knew that. "Yes, they're all gone."

And they were. After he rescued me and we started our friendship again, I'd removed them all and hadn't put any back up. I would never threaten his livelihood.

"Good. Just stay away from my business, Faith," he muttered, stomping out my door, letting it slam shut.

The lack of regard for something so personal that I'd shared hurt. It frayed the patchwork of squares and fabric I'd stupidly thought we had started weaving together again.

At his departure, I locked all the deadbolts on the door and went to bed. This time, I locked my bedroom door.

Chapter 31
Jace

"No THANK YOU, BABE," I muttered to the petite blonde in front of me. She had asked if I wanted to do shots with her in the dark booth, near the back.

I was out with Seth again, because I lacked friends and balls, apparently. Tucked in my back pocket was the sketch Faith had drawn. The honesty she'd shared had ripped the proverbial rug out from under me. I hadn't been expecting that. Not in the least.

"Okay, I have to say somethin'," Seth declared, dropping to the stool next to me.

I quirked a brow.

"Why are you two doin' this?" He leaned in toward me, trying to quiet his voice. I appreciated that, and since I'd dragged him into my bullshit, there wasn't any reason to pretend I didn't know what he was talking about.

"She isn't telling me everything," I replied, grabbing my tumbler, tipping it sideways.

Seth made a disgruntled sound. "So, she's doing exactly what you're doing then?"

My gaze jumped to the side, eyeing him. "What?"

"You still haven't told her shit about what happened, and you wonder why she's not cluing you in to all her drama? Come clean with her, lay it out on the table—all of it. Then she might do the same, and if not, at least you'll know."

I could feel the tension in my shoulders grow and my jaw go tight. *Fucking hell.*

He was right.

Enough was enough. I just needed to come clean—there wasn't anything left to lose anyway.

"You outta here?" Seth asked, turning toward me on his stool, his eyebrows jumping in surprise.

"Yeah, I gotta go have that talk. You okay gettin' home?"

"You know I am." He returned his eyes to the front, laughing, shaking his head. I stood, clapped him on the back, and headed back to Faith's apartment.

I had originally told Tom to take the night off, but when I went to the bar, I made sure one of his guys headed over. I doubted Faith even knew the exchange had happened.

I pulled the key free from my pocket and started unlocking each deadbolt. She didn't know I had swiped her key and made myself a copy, but I figured she'd assumed as much after I let myself in earlier in the day.

The apartment was dark, just a few lights from outside peeking through her large windows. She didn't want blinds because she was on the top floor, but if it were up to me, she'd have them. Four stories up wasn't enough to keep the nosy masses from spying.

I slowly walked toward her room and twisted the knob, only to find it locked. I let out a small laugh and walked back to the kitchen to grab a small flathead, something I'd left there the week before. In seconds, the lock popped open. The moonlight wasn't as prominent as the previous night; instead darkness covered her sleeping form.

The only light came from a few street lights outside, muted by her curtains.

I pulled my shirt over my head and shoved my jeans down, crawled in behind her, and pulled her to my chest. *Fuck.*

She was nearly naked. The only piece of clothing separating us was her thin cotton underwear, but her breasts were bare, ready for me to palm.

I was desperate to feel her; my fingers itched to go lower and feel between her legs. I pictured her writhing against my fingers, moaning, desperate for release. I pictured her head thrown back, her breasts out, pushing against the cold air, pebbled and hard, aching for my touch.

I was growing hard behind her as she slept, which made me feel like a creep, so I ensured my fingers stayed at her hip and didn't go anywhere they shouldn't.

"Jace?" Faith asked, tilting her head back to rest against my chest.

I brushed a few strands of hair off her face and watched as her full lips parted. She was tired, likely not trying to be sexy, but I had one thing on my mind at the moment.

"Do you believe people can fall out of love?" I asked quietly. The darkness covered enough of the room to hide how much I was revealing in the question.

She waited a breath before answering. "I think so..."

I shifted my left hand until it was resting on her side. "Why?"

She hummed and leaned into me, and her soft skin sliding against mine felt like hearing my favorite song or eating my favorite food. She was an addiction.

"I honestly don't know. I mean...you would know better than anyone." She sounded confused, as though I'd just asked her to rotate the tires on my truck, like this was something I was the fucking expert on. My chest tightened with the same regret it had harbored for the past five years.

"Faith," I whispered, sharing in this tiny cocoon we were creating. My lips fell to the shell of her ear. "I never stopped loving you."

She stilled. My nerves thrummed with energy at what she might say.

I'd just blatantly thrown my heart out in front of her, and I wasn't sure what I expected her to do with it.

"Don't say things like that," she muttered, her voice thick with emotion.

I turned her until she was lying flat on her back, staring up at me. The darkness covered us, like a blanket of secrets, like the lies that had shrouded our past and still clung to the edges of our future.

"Why not?" I searched her eyes, desperate for some kind of hope to still be lingering there.

"Because"—her eyes went wide, her voice stripped thin—"you ripped my heart out, Jace. I was so in love with you and you...you just stopped loving me back. Don't make light of it when it hasn't happened to you."

She tried to wiggle free of my hold, but I wouldn't let her go. I moved my hand to cup her hip more tightly while lowering my face until my lips hovered over hers, until I could see the light from outside gleaming in her blue eyes.

"It did happen to me. I had to watch with the rest of the world as the girl I loved walked down the aisle toward someone else. Do you have any idea what that did to me, Faith?" My voice was harsh, desperate for her to understand.

She blinked, causing a few tears to slip free. "Then why? You still haven't ever explained it to me. Why did you do it?"

I shook my head and locked my jaw, refraining from spilling all the things that had torn us apart over the years—but enough was enough. After silently letting out a steadying breath, I finally confessed.

"Someone caught me...they had video footage, timestamped pictures of me breaking in, stealing my mother's meds." I shook my head, leaning back a fraction, but Faith wasn't having it. Her hands cupped my jaw, keeping me close. "They sent the video in August... before..." I trailed off, hating how all this was coming out. "When he showed up, he gave me a choice: break it off with you or go to jail. If I went to jail, I wouldn't be able to get my mom any more meds. Even if I didn't steal, it was still my income with Dad's that helped get her what she needed."

Faith let out a shuddered breath, but I wasn't finished.

"So, I let you go, knowing it was the only choice that could save my mother's life. I was planning, though. I figured I just needed a little time to figure it out, get leverage on him—which I did end up getting. Got the asshole fired, but it was all too late. You were engaged, and by the time I found out, I was getting arrested."

"He...but..." she stammered, trying to grasp what I hadn't said.

"Double-crossed me...yeah. He still turned me in, despite me breaking it off with you."

Faith sat up, pushing at my chest, her breathing erratic and strained.

"Who did this to you?" Her voice cracked. "To us..."

I shook my head in disgust. I still, after all these years, couldn't stomach that he'd done it to us, to *her*.

Too much time had passed for an answer, which must have made it seem like I wasn't going to give her one. Maybe I shouldn't have. Did it really matter anymore?

She thrust at my shoulders. "Who?"

Venom laced her tongue, gouging somewhere deep inside me.

Her eyebrows drew together, her face just inches from mine as she again demanded, "Who?"

Finally, with a heavy sigh, I relented. "Your father."

Chapter 32
Faith

IT WAS two in the morning, but I didn't care. For years I'd wondered why the boy I loved left me. I'd lost countless hours of sleep, my appetite, my heart. I had blamed myself and discounted my worth over how easily Jace left me. It never made a lick of sense, how we could be so insanely in love, with plans and ideas, then one day it all just ended. No explanation except that we were too young, and he had too much going on with his mama.

It hadn't been enough then, and it still wasn't, which was why after Jace made his confession, I threw the covers off, pulled on some clothes and some flip-flops, and stormed out of my apartment, leaving him behind. I wanted answers, and I wanted them now.

I used my key, let myself in, and started a pot of coffee. The bubbling brew was atrociously loud, which I knew would wake my father.

I pulled out a chair and situated myself in the old kitchen chair as the aroma of the dark roast filled the space. Moments later a soft glow emanated from the stairs, and my father cautiously wandered down in his striped pajamas and robe. Nice to know if I'd been an intruder, he'd have been properly dressed when he died.

"Pumpkin?" His bushy brows drew together as he assessed my

posture. I pushed the chair back, minced to the coffee pot, and poured two cups.

"Daddy, I think we need to talk." I handed him the steaming mug.

His eyes assessed me warily, but he accepted the cup and sat down.

"What happened between you and Jace all those years ago?" I started, hoping he wouldn't drag this out with any lies or bring up what had happened the other day with my mother. I didn't need to hear his side of that; I just needed answers.

His face paled for a brief second, and he tried to hide it by sipping from his cup. "That's a bit of a complicated story, honey. I think it might be best if we left it in the past."

Anger took hold of me and shook my soul so hard I wanted to scream. I wanted to throw my coffee at him, because that admission was enough to show he'd orchestrated something.

"Tell me," I insisted through gritted teeth.

He winced at my tone and stared down at his mug.

"When I married your mother, we were so poor we had to live with your mother's parents for a while. While your mother was perfectly happy about the situation, I was miserable." He stopped, taking a small sip.

I leaned back and tried to stay patient as he took the longest route possible to get to his point.

"I was ashamed...and every day I'd come home from job hunting, your grandfather would scold me and tell me how pathetic I was. One time in particular, he told me how much he wished his daughter had married someone else."

I noticed his eyes misting as he recounted his story. I stayed quiet.

"I was weak back then, so weak. Your grandfather was harsh, both verbally and physically. When I'd get turned down for yet another job, he'd smack me around. All while your mother wasn't watching, and he knew I wasn't going to say anything, but it slowly broke me down. I began to agree with him after a few months of failure. I wanted to leave your mother, knowing she deserved better."

"And did you?"

"Leave her? No. Maybe I should have, but I stuck with it. Finally found a job, saved every penny I made, and right when I was about to rent a small apartment, her father bought us a house—this house... actually, and one we hadn't even had a chance to look at. And that's how our relationship went. Her father would buy us things, undermining my position of authority until it wore on our marriage so much we almost divorced."

I sat back, arms crossed and totally confused.

"What does this have to do with Jace dumping me?" Maybe before the Bryan thing, I'd have softened and shown him some compassion, but after him hearing Bryan's side of the story and encouraging him to take me to dinner—not a chance.

My father sagged in his chair, his pinstriped pajamas perfectly ironed, not a wrinkle in sight. "At that brunch...the one where you two were telling us all about your plans for college...I knew I had to do something."

"What is that supposed to mean?" I leaned forward, feeling a fire start to burn in my belly.

"It means he was no good for you. He was dirt poor. If I let you two get married, have kids...it'd be the same exact cycle I fell into with your mother. You'd end up living here with us, I'd resent him for not providing for you, and you'd eventually hate me for undermining your marriage."

"Dad you have no way of knowing that would have happened!" I stood, shoving the chair back.

"Your mother hates her father, hasn't spoken to him in years because he was so unkind to me. Her loyalty stood with me, and after we nearly divorced, it only became stronger. That was the final straw for the two of them. He made her choose, and she chose me."

He stayed seated while I paced around the kitchen. "So, let me get this straight..." I brought my fingers to the bridge of my nose. "You

271

sabotaged my relationship? What exactly did you do?" I was breathless, nearly on the verge of a sobbing meltdown. My hands shook and my stomach churned as I waited for him to explain.

"One of our clients had filed an incident report about some missing prescriptions. We had to look into it. Their assumption was that it was an employee, and I was put in charge of reviewing the tapes. I found Jace in several of them, stealing from the pharmacy, and suddenly it felt like a gift had been dropped in my lap."

"You blackmailed him?" I whispered, disgusted that I shared DNA with this man.

"I merely told him to break things off with you, and yes, I used the tapes as leverage." He stood, moving closer.

"Do. Not. Come any closer to me," I snarled. The rage simmering in my veins could have leveled an entire city. I crowded the counter, holding it to keep myself stable as sharp breaths rattled my chest. "But why..." I tried to force the words out. What he'd done was so terrible. "How could you send him to jail after he'd already broken up with me?"

My father, the man who'd been gentle and kind to me, who'd bandaged my skinned knees and kissed away my tears when I fell from trees, blanched. A lump formed in my throat as I waited for him to deliver the final blow.

His eyes dimmed, hip lips turning down as something like shame twisted his features. "You had met Bryan, which was good, but I knew as soon as Jace saw and found out you were engaged, he'd ruin it. I knew you still loved him, and if he showed up, you'd leave Bryan. So, I sent the tape to the police, made sure he didn't have a chance to ruin what you had going for you."

An anger so raw, so violent swept through me. It rivaled anything I had ever felt when being abused by Bryan. This was different. This was a man I'd loved for so long being ruined...this was betrayal.

"You ruined his life." My voice was a low hiss as I clenched my fists. "You ruined my life...you..." I hiccupped on a harsh sob that was cutting into my windpipe. "How could you?"

"I thought I was doing the right thing. You were better off—"

I put my hand up to stop him. "I can't... You need to stop talking." I took a calming breath, which did nothing at all for me. "We're done. I don't want anything to do with you. I can't ever look at you the same after this...you disgust me."

I stormed out of the house before he could respond.

"Jace, it's me again. Please call me back, I really need to talk to you." I pressed the red end button on my phone screen and lowered my hand. I'd driven back home as soon as I left my parents' house, hoping Jace would still be at my apartment, but when I got home, it was empty. It was still early, so I knew he'd likely gone home to get some sleep, but I couldn't help the disappointment I felt at knowing he wasn't here.

I walked toward my coffee Keurig and pushed in another pod, gearing up for my fourth cup of the day. I was restless, desperate to talk to him about everything I had learned, and more than anything, I wanted to finally close the horrific chapter I'd been stuck in for the past five years.

Jace *had* wanted me. He had never stopped wanting me.

His anger toward my return suddenly made so much sense. He had been blackmailed, trying to find a way back to me while I just ran into another man's arms, marrying him and removing the possibility of us ever getting back together. I'd unknowingly betrayed him, just like my father had done to me.

I was too keyed up to sleep, so I passed the time reading through the rest of our books with all our correspondence written in the margins. I held a few close to my chest and hoped like hell that Jace would give me another chance. I knew he was still angry about me going to dinner with Bryan alone, but there had to be a way of fixing it. He just needed to give me a chance.

Chapter 33
Jace

THE EARLY MORNING air was balmy and crisp against my skin as I exited my truck. I eyed the three men who were wandering around outside my building suspiciously. Two of them looked like contractors, but the third had on a tailored suit and held what looked like a phone up to his ear. Each of them had their backs turned to me, so I wasn't exactly sure what they were doing.

I walked up, surveying the man with the notepad and measuring tape suspiciously, and put my hands to my hips.

"Can I help y'all with somethin'?"

The businessman turned and ended his call. I took a step back instinctively when I realized it was Faith's husband.

Did he know I'd been kissing and holding her at night for the past few weeks?

"Jace Walker?" He stepped forward with a money-making smile.

I was wary already.

"That's me. What the fuck do you want and why are you here?" I was on edge. He'd hurt Faith and now he was smiling at me like he'd just found his next winning ticket.

"Faith mentioned you might be a little bristly." He laughed, shaking his head back and forth while he reached into his back pocket.

What the fuck does that mean?

I still hadn't had a chance to listen to my voicemails from Faith since I told her to go talk to her father the night before. I hadn't felt right about staying in her apartment while she wasn't there, so I'd headed home, passing out the moment my head hit the pillow, and then was late getting up.

I had dashed out the door, barely buttoning up my work shirt, grabbing only a banana as my breakfast on the way over. I had an early oil change scheduled for one of my regulars and had never been late a day in my life; I didn't plan on starting now.

"Look, I'm not sure how much Faith told you, but it's all here." Bryan handed me a check. I gripped the thin paper, drawing my eyebrows together in confusion. The amount was written out for one point five million dollars.

"What the hell is this?" I lifted the slip of paper, eyeing the other men, who were watching in silence.

Bryan observed me with a line drawn across his forehead, clearly confused. "Faith didn't tell you we'd be here today?"

It honestly felt like my heart had turned to stone with how heavy it was thumping inside my chest. She wouldn't go behind my back. I wouldn't accept that she was playing me. But then again, that had been my fear when I'd found the drawing of my shop logo. Also, the Christmas text was still without explanation, and she'd lied about going to meet him at dinner. Tiny seeds of doubt began to blossom inside my head.

"She didn't mention it," I mumbled curtly. Whatever his point was, I wanted him to make it fast.

Bryan's expression was pinched as he considered me. "I'm sorry, I would have had more tact if I'd known she hadn't told you. We drew up some papers the other night at dinner, and she mentioned her idea for Mustard Seed Auto but said we'd be better off investing in your brand, taking it national. She wants to grow roots closer to her parents once the baby comes."

Maybe it was possible to actually go weak in the knees—I felt the entire fucking world shift under my feet.

"What?" I whispered, trying to regain my composure.

To his credit, he seemed surprised by my response.

"Again, I'm so sorry. She mentioned you two were friends, that you'd been catching up this last month, so I assumed she told you. She's due in February. Anyway, all this drama around our domestic issues has really put a damper on things, but we're eager to move past it, especially since talking things through the last few days."

He smiled at me like I was the poor destitute kid asking for a handout. I wanted to punch the smug look off his face, but I wouldn't give him the satisfaction of pressing charges against me.

"So, you're...what"—I shrugged—"wanting to buy me out?" I tried to seem unfazed by the bomb he'd just dropped. Faith had said he'd pushed himself on her that night; why on earth did it feel like I was being set up?

"Yes. Would you accept that amount?" He gestured toward the check.

"Sorry, I guess I'm a little slow here. Faith mentioned havin' a different experience the other night at your dinner. She's mentioned quite a few things to me, in fact." I wanted to flip this around on him and make him feel off balance, like he'd done to me.

His armor didn't crack; he merely looked down and let out a sigh. A second later, one of the men with the notebook walked over and held out a file. I wondered why he seemed so familiar...then realized he had the same build and hair color as the guy we had seen leaving Faith's apartment building that day.

"I'm sorry, I was concerned she might be leading you on. She set up the dinner, wanted to talk business. Regardless of our marital status, we're still business partners."

A flash of color met me with a few pictures of Faith and Bryan at dinner. In the images, they had a few papers between them, lifting and examining them. In one photo, Bryan was examining one paper, and in the second, Faith was smiling and pointing down at another.

I felt fucking sick to my stomach.

"This was her idea. She even drew a few mockups for our business." He pulled out the images Faith had traced of my business logo, the ones I'd found in her apartment and accused her about. "So, what do you think? Feel like getting rich today?" Bryan asked, shoving his hand out, like the devil ready to make a deal.

Chapter 34
Faith

I TUGGED on a fresh pair of clothes, still eagerly waiting for a phone call from Jace. Worry began to gnaw away at my stomach. Had something happened to him? My mind was racing relentlessly about what it could mean that he wasn't answering my calls.

A knock on my front door jolted me out of my thoughts and had me rushing to open it.

I jerked it open with a hopeful "Jace!" on my tongue. The tall, brooding man on my stoop pushed his way inside and shut the door behind him.

I inched my way backward toward the kitchen.

"Sorry to disappoint, but your boyfriend is probably off spending the million dollars he just accepted from me." Bryan slid out of his suit jacket and laid it across the back of the lounge chair. He began rolling up his sleeves to his elbow, his signature move for when he was about to get his hands dirty.

I inhaled a sharp breath and tried to stay calm while I took inventory of my surroundings. I had access to weapons. I had a taser in the drawer next to my bed, pepper spray in my purse, and knives in the kitchen. I wasn't going down without a fight. To distract him, I tried to entertain whatever game he was playing.

"He wouldn't take any money from you." I strategically shuffled closer to the counter.

Bryan walked away from me, turning his back and wandering around the room. "He would if he didn't think there was any reason not to, especially if he thought you had betrayed him."

My heart sank. *What the hell does that mean?*

"What did you do?" I held my hands behind my back, gripping a steak knife.

"Nothing you didn't already start...I merely played on all the things he doubted in you to begin with." He picked up a framed picture of me with Gemma from back in high school. "You never brought any photos with you after we got married," he muttered, surveying the photograph closely.

"Are you really going to start complaining that I didn't bring anything personal with me into our fake marriage?" I stayed rooted in place, terrified of what his goal was with his faux interest.

He snapped his head toward me. "It was real." Putting the picture back carefully, he moved on to the books.

I bit back my retort about how it wasn't real, not any of it. The love, the attraction—all of it was a lie fabricated by my father. I should have never met Bryan Vanderson.

"Quite the collection here." He moved his finger across the spines of each of my books. "Would these be the books you paid the library to keep, to help amend for the vandalism inside?"

"How do you know about that?"

He smirked, taking out *Of Mice and Men*. "Same way I know about the logo you designed for your redneck boyfriend's shop, and how I know about his house, and the Saturday market." He cracked the spine and began reading out loud. "Fool: So we're together now? Pip: Of course we are. How many other boys go around kissing you?" Bryan let out a scoff, shaking his head. "If only he knew."

"So, you've been following me?" I glanced down briefly at my cell and pressed the record button, just in case he slipped and shared something incriminating.

"I paid a private investigator to follow you and lover boy. Quite boring intel, actually, but I loved the juicy bits about him sleeping over. Looks great for me, you sleeping around before we're even divorced. Funny thing is, every time you've left your house, I've had one of my men come in and stage things so it looks like you're an addict. They've also been collecting things for me." He moved away from the books and toward other photos on my television stand.

Curiosity clawed its way out of my throat. "Why? You could give me a nice quiet divorce, start over, be free of me—why the dramatics?"

I had no idea why he was making this so ugly when it was really quite simple. I didn't want anything from him, and I'd sacrifice whatever Gemma had requested in the divorce filing if he just left me the hell alone.

He let out a heavy sigh as he lifted his head, eyes cast upward toward the ceiling.

"Believe it or not, Faith, I'm a prideful man, and I loved you. In whatever fucked-up version of love was true for me, I did." He laid his hand over his heart.

"Then why hit me? Why hurt me like you did? That's not love." I pushed my phone closer while tightening my grip on the blade at my back.

"Because you wore the necklace of a poor loser who'd once promised you a future. When I actually provided that future, you still couldn't deign to give me enough respect to remove it and try with me. You were never in this all the way." He shook his head back and forth, and the smallest twinge of shame flickered alive inside me.

He was right. I just hadn't known I'd hurt him; I'd had no idea he even cared.

"Why not tell me in a loving fashion then? I would have stopped wearing it...I would have chosen us—"

"Because that's not love." He pointed at me.

Shit. He was right.

Releasing the knife, I stepped forward. "I'm sorry. For the record, I'm so sorry for ever hurting you. It wasn't my intention."

Shoving his hands deep into his pockets, he regarded me for a moment before stalking toward me. "I appreciate that, but as I mentioned, my pride was wounded more than my heart. So, I've hurt you back in a way you won't recover from, and I had every intention of doing it. Buckle up, buttercup—we're even now, and we aren't getting a divorce."

He came closer, which had me retreating, feeling weak, pathetic.

"Don't come any closer to me," I demanded, clearly enough for my recorder to pick up.

"You're my wife, Faith. State law says I can do whatever I see fit with my property." A wicked smirk twisted his cruel mouth. My heart sped up and beat frantically as I considered what to do. He was going to hurt me.

A generous smile broke out on his face as he began to loosen his tie.

"What are you doing?" Fear shook my voice, betraying how scared I was.

His blue eyes danced as he drew closer, undoing the top button of his shirt then moving farther down.

"You want to know my favorite thing about you, Faith?" He tilted his head to the side.

I didn't answer, because I knew that look in his eye, and he wasn't even drunk. The demon had come out to play.

"You were always so willing to please me. You were like clay, so perfectly moldable, so functional for everything I needed. You were so happy to be saved from your trainwreck of a life that you looked at everything with such awe and wonder." He peeled his shirt off and tossed it to the floor. "Every time I fucked you, it was with this knowledge between us that you loved another man." His belt went next, and he wrapped it around his knuckles.

I watched his feet as they drew closer; he was nearly to the refrigerator.

"I promised myself that when I made my move after all the sleuthing and discovery, once Jace was out of the picture for good, I would fuck you like you were truly mine, with you being aware of every evil piece of me. I'd fuck you like you were without any remnants of your old life. No locket from your ex, no promise of salvation hanging over your head—just me. Only mine."

He stopped just as his hip brushed the counter. I was fixated on his closeness, and had missed how he was devouring me with his eyes.

I kept expecting adrenaline to kick in like they talk about in the movies, something to surge through me to protect me, to get me moving from this spot to doing anything else...like stabbing his chest with this knife, maybe? But nothing was coming. I was completely frozen in place.

"You ready to dance, baby?" His voice dripped with lust and promised torment.

I stepped forward and tried to prepare my soul to dance with the devil.

Bryan's moves were mostly predictable, and while I hadn't taken self-defense classes during my stretch of freedom like I should have, I could still mostly forecast what he was going to do next. I knew if he saw me hold the knife in front of myself, he'd dodge or do something to catch me off guard, maybe even take it and use it against me.

At present I'd backtracked enough to grab it, keeping it tightly held behind my back. He was still making his way toward me, in measured steps. I'd been holding him off with conversation, but it was wearing thin.

I had mentioned that Jace was coming for me, and Bryan had launched into an entire tirade.

"Do you know how fast he took that money? He finally gets a chance to break free from this shithole and you're going to hold him back?" He laughed at me, pointing his finger like he was accusing me of something terrible. "That coward isn't coming for you, Faith. No one is. Because I own everyone in your life who could or would ever come to your aid." He flicked the black button of his slacks and slipped them off, now standing in just his black boxer briefs.

Gemma would come and she'd kick his ass, except she had a deposition this morning that would tie her up for hours. I was screwed, and my only hope was to surprise him with a knife to his chest...or stomach. Some resigned part of me didn't want him to die. I just wanted to live.

I lowered my head and began to plead with him. "Please, Bryan... please just let me go."

"Why? So you can charge me with more abuse allegations? Those went nowhere, by the way—fucking nowhere, because I own Tennessee."

"You said you did love me in some capacity," I reminded him through a stream of tears. The reality of what was about to happen to me was starting to sink in.

"Would a rough fuck really be that bad for you, baby? You're going home with me either way. This part is just foreplay." He took measured steps closer, now an arm's length away. I could smell him. "You aren't going to hate what I'm going to do you. I'm just going to remind you who we are together, who I am underneath this disguise. Then we're going to start over. You're going to come forward and admit to being in and out of rehab, we're going to have a baby, and it's going to be perfect." He grabbed my chin and sucked my earlobe into his mouth while pressing his erection into my stomach.

My heart was thumping so hard I could feel it everywhere, my head, my throat, my hands. It was thrumming with fear and awareness. This was it, my chance.

My fingers felt numb from how hard they'd been gripping the wooden handle on the knife. I blinked and counted down in my head. *Three.* His lips traveled to mine as he tugged on them with his teeth. *Two.* More tears surged. *One*—

The front door burst open, wood splintering and shattering across the floor as my father barreled through. His tall frame was covered in pieces of wood, his shoulder jutted forward, and his eyes...those gentle eyes were wild.

My heart leapt into my throat.

"Daddy." The word was a garbled sound coming from my mouth.

Bryan narrowed his eyes, grabbed my wrist, and pulled me to his chest. "Clark, this is a marital manner. I'll kindly ask you to leave."

"Get away from my daughter," my father said, seething, stepping forward.

"You heard my side of this—you know what is really going on," Bryan continued, pulling me closer.

My father shook his head, his jaw tightening. "We were trying to pay you a kindness, but don't think for a second that we believed you."

Bryan was distracted; his hands were still on me, but my wrist was free. I dropped the weapon at my back, realizing I didn't need it. Instead, I used my free wrist to plant a hand on his chest, twist my body, and knee him in the groin.

Finally, Bryan released me, staggering against the counter. I ran toward my dad, letting him pull me away. Dad pulled out his cell phone and put it to his ear, rapidly talking to the cops about what was going on. I couldn't catch my breath as I watched Bryan lean over, sliding against the lower cupboards until he was on the floor.

He groaned, veins protruding from his neck and forehead as he turned his head to look at me. "I loved you, Faith...how could you do this to us?"

"Just stay put now. The police will be here any second to sort this out," my dad said, trying to calm the monster. I was amped up. I suddenly wanted to make him feel as pathetic and weak as he'd made me feel. I wanted to punish him as he'd punished me. I didn't even realize I had started to surge forward until my dad laid a hand on my shoulder.

Moments later, the sound of sirens echoed loudly, and police and paramedics were running up the stairs and invading my apartment. I complied with the police and gave my statement. Then I passed along my phone as evidence so they could hear the entire conversation that had been recorded.

On the way out of the apartment, I saw a few paramedics hovering over a body in the hall. I couldn't make out who it was until Dad spoke up from behind me. "It was that man on the ground...it's how I knew something was wrong, why I barged in through the door."

Gasping, I lurched toward them. "Is he okay? Tom?" I tried to get his attention, but my dad and two officers held me back.

"Let them help him, he's okay." We made our way outside, where I assumed I'd be able to leave, but because I'd married Bryan fucking Vanderson, I was put into the back of a cop car and taken in for questioning.

My dad called Gemma, who raced over to meet me. She ripped the police a new one for how they had treated an innocent victim. She demanded a few seconds alone with me, at which point I explained about the recording.

"Tennessee law," Gemma said, smiling at me.

"Tennessee law," I muttered back, proud that, for once, I had retained something useful from one of her lectures.

When the police came back in, we complied with their questions as there was no reason not to. Bryan's attorneys showed up, demanding my recorded conversation not even be entered as evidence. But Gemma reminded them that in Tennessee, in order to be recorded, only one of the participating parties has to agree to said recording. Since I'd agreed, there wasn't much more to fuss over.

Once we were finished with questioning, Gemma walked me out the station doors with her arm around me, and we found my father waiting for me in the courtyard. My back stiffened, remembering what he'd done. Gemma hugged me closer to her side, likely trying to gauge what I wanted to do. I had told her everything.

"Give me just a second, please." I smiled at Gemma and turned toward my father.

He stood from the bench he'd been sitting on and hesitantly walked toward me.

"How are you holding up?" his soft voice inquired.

I hated this new existence we found ourselves in. He had always been my protector, my friend, but what he'd done to Jace was inexcusable.

"Dad, thank you for coming to my rescue." I smiled up at him, and the hope in his eyes nearly drove me to my knees. I knew he'd acted out of love, but I couldn't get past what he'd done.

"I'm going to stay with Gemma." I held his hand, squeezed, and let it go.

His downcast gaze was quick, there and gone, replaced by a placating smile. "Okay, I understand. Just...come home or call me when you're ready to talk." He hesitated for a second. "I just...I need to tell you how sorry I am, about Jace and everything."

"So, you've told him you're sorry then? You've apologized?" I asked, daring him to contradict himself. He wasn't sorry, because if he were, he would have made things right years ago.

Just as I expected, he winced.

"That's what I thought." I shook my head. "I love him. He would have been in my life if you hadn't ruined that, and Bryan wouldn't have been at all."

My father stepped closer, his eyes brimming with tears. "Just remember, honey, if it was that easy for him to leave this time around, he wasn't ever supposed to stay in your life." He leaned down and pressed a kiss to my forehead, squeezed my shoulder, and walked away.

Chapter 35
Faith

I DROVE toward McGrady's tree farm, not really knowing where I was going. I knew Jace lived somewhere close to it, and after going to his trailer and seeing that it was gone, I knew he had to be up here. Jessie had given me the address, and I just hoped like hell my phone GPS wouldn't get it wrong.

After the police station, Gemma had taken me to her house, but I was restless. I needed to talk to Jace. I needed to see him. All my calls and texts had gone unanswered, and I needed to know why.

Bryan's words had been on repeat in my head for hours, causing me to get in my car and find him.

The faded streak of orange and purple scattered across the sky as dusk settled in. I was thankful I'd come in partial daylight as his place was going to be hard enough to find. Finally, after a few twists and turns, I found the road.

Minutes later, I was slowly making my way up a long drive, and the fifth wheel parked in the driveway told me I was in the right spot. My heart swelled.

Unbuckling, I slowly made my way toward the door. Nervousness had crawled in and lodged itself in my hands, forcing them to cramp into fists. Awkwardly, I knocked.

I could hear Trevor barking on the other side of the door. There were beautiful sconces on each side, illuminating the stoop. I knew if I were to walk around the side, I would see the porch wrap all the way around the house. This place was absolutely gorgeous.

Finally, the door swung open. Jace stood in a pair of white socks, faded blue jeans, and no shirt. My breath hitched at how striking he was.

"What are you doing here?" he asked, accusation rolling off his tongue.

I stepped forward, pushing past him into the house. He surprised me by letting it happen. I shut the door until it clicked behind me. Trevor calmed, his nails clicking against the floor, the sound echoing through the empty space. I could smell something cooking and the soft sounds of a television going.

"You moved in, or...?" I looked around. The foyer was still unfinished, but the walls beyond it were painted a beautiful soft grey with a dark stain on the trim.

"Faith...what are you doing here?" Jace asked again, this time crossing his arms.

"What are you doing here?" I turned the question on him, stalking closer.

His eyes roamed my face, searching for something. "I live here."

I walked past him, slipped off my shoes, and padded farther into his house.

His kitchen was nearly finished. There was dried glue on the wall where a backsplash would go, but otherwise the cabinets were installed, along with the range and white Quartz counters.

"These are beautiful." I ran my finger along the surface and walked toward the window. Jace had moved a couch into his living room and had mounted a seventy-inch flat-screen on the wall; otherwise the space was bare.

"Faith..." Jace drawled from behind me.

I turned, eyeing him.

"You didn't take the money." It was a statement, not a question.

He grunted. "Does it matter?"

"It does to me," I whispered, walking closer to him.

His stormy eyes were fortified and unyielding. "No, I didn't."

"What did he tell you? Why are you looking at me like you hate me again?" I risked asking, wrapping my hand around his bicep.

"Doesn't matter." He shrugged. I could tell he was lying.

"Tell me." I stood on my tiptoes and pressed a chaste kiss to his lips.

Jace was quick, fast as lightning with his hands. He grabbed my hips, walked me back to the island, and lifted me.

Leaning his face toward my neck, his lips pressed against the shell of my ear as he rasped, "He told me what I needed to hear in order to finally let you go."

His words fell like shattered pieces of glass around me.

"What?" I pushed against his chest, no longer willing to be nice or chaste.

"Just go, Faith." Jace released me, bringing a hand to his face.

I contemplated fighting him, but we'd both had enough fight for the past five years. We needed peace. So, I gently folded my plan together inside my head and jumped down from the counter. I patted Trevor's head, whispered a promise into his ear, and left.

If Jace thought this was over, he had another thing coming.

I needed supplies for my plan, so I headed out early that next morning to hit up the hardware store. Now I was exiting the elevator and nearly to my apartment, and I stopped at the sight of Jace leaning against my door. He wore his grey hoodie under his leather jacket; his hair was rogue, being pulled in every direction; and his black boots were untied, the laces drooping next to him on the polished floor. He looked up at me with torment in his eyes.

My heart pitched, rioting in my chest. I had to keep it together and act cool.

I walked with confidence, but then my ankle twisted to the side. *Shit.*

"Are you okay?" Jace leaned forward as if to stabilize me.

"I'm good, thank you." I cleared my throat and began unlocking my door.

Jace didn't wait for me to offer for him to come in; he just followed after me.

I walked toward the kitchen, grabbing a glass and filling it with water. Having Jace's presence behind me felt like turning my back on a dangerous animal. I wasn't sure if it would still be there when I turned around or if it would devour me while I waited.

Finally, he spoke up, spilling his gravel-like words. I turned toward him, watching his half-crumpled form on the bar stool while his eyes bored holes into my counter.

"I heard about what happened yesterday." He looked up at me with a sad smile. "I'm so sorry he touched you, sorry he nearly did more. I'm thankful your father got here..." He trailed off, looking down at the counter. "What did you think of your dad's confession?" he asked quietly, drawing a circle on the counter.

I cleared my throat. "It crushed me. I tried calling you...several times, actually."

He nodded his head. "I saw." His blue eyes flitted to my lips briefly before homing in on my eyes.

Of course he had. He was just ignoring me.

"Why are you here, Jace? You made it clear last night that you were letting me go." I grabbed hold of my arms, bracing them against my chest. Plan or no plan, his rejection terrified me.

"I realized something last night." His lips turned up as his eyes darkened.

"What's that?" I whispered, wishing I could pull on my locket or something to feel grounded.

"I owe you an apology." His eyes warned that another breakup was coming.

I turned around, facing the sink, muttering, "Don't want one."

"Well, you're getting one," Jace insisted from behind me.

I spun around, storming past him, moving to the boxes scattered around the room. I started packing, ignoring him.

"What are you doing...?" He looked around with furrowed dark brows and a ticking jaw. I didn't answer. "Where the fuck are you going?" he asked again, frantically looking around.

"Don't worry about it," I said, clutching a few books, shoving them into a box.

Jace stood, hands on his hips, jaw hard as granite.

"So, you're just leaving?"

"Yeah, I am," I retorted.

"College?"

I shrugged. "Something like that."

He clicked his tongue and scoffed before stomping out my door and slamming it behind him.

This plan better fucking work.

Chapter 36
Jace

THE SUNRISE from my bedroom window was stunning. I stood and stared, mesmerized that I had gone my entire life without a view like that. I had never traveled anywhere grand enough to see something that brilliant. I'd hiked a few times, but with work...life just got in the way.

Trevor slept peacefully in his bed in the corner, and everything else was silent. The house was finished enough to move in. All the last-minute details I'd finish up on my own. It was the only part of my life that felt untouched by the shitstorm that was Faith, her husband, and her shitbag of a father.

I'd made the decision after Bryan offered me the money that I didn't need this shit in my life. I didn't need Faith, unsure who she wanted...didn't need her undecided ways endangering my heart. So, the only thing to do was try to move on. Fucking finally, after five years, I needed to let her go. She'd figure out her drama at some point, but I didn't need to be a part of it.

One day she'd settle down again with someone new. She'd fall in love, hold hands, kiss...I blinked harshly against the sun and brought the cup of coffee to my lips. I had things to do around the house, so I started on a few of them before needing to leave for work.

The day went by painfully slowly. Each vehicle was torturous to work on because my mind wouldn't shut off. As much as I wanted to not think about Faith showing up at my house then leaving the first time I asked her to without even fighting me, I couldn't manage to make the loop in my head stop. She had believed I hadn't taken the money.

That has to mean something...

Doesn't it?

I closed up an hour early, not even caring that Jessie hadn't shown all day. My company wouldn't exactly have been cheerful anyway. I headed toward the grocery store on my way home, trying to shove away the way Faith had looked in her apartment surrounded by boxes. She was leaving.

College, pregnancy, divorce—whatever it was she was doing, she was leaving.

I just needed to move on, let my heart once again mourn the loss of Faith Morgan.

I had just turned the corner into the breakfast aisle when I spotted two familiar women, their heads close together, laughing about some box in their hands. I wasn't going to approach her; she was with my little sister, and they seemed to be having fun on maybe their last night out before Faith moved away.

I could have just left, but that didn't stop me from watching.

Faith flipped the box over, leaning back as she laughed at something Jessie said, and that was when I noticed Faith's neck.

What in the hell?

That had me stalking toward her. Both women paused their laughter and jokes at my approach. Jessie ducked her head, while Faith examined the box in her hand with renewed interest. The silent treatment—nice.

"What the hell is on your neck?" I asked, gripping my basket.

Faith tipped her eyes up, her mouth already curved into a sultry smile. "Whatever do you mean?"

I scoffed, "*Hilarious.* How did you get the locket back?"

She let out a sigh, putting the box of cake mix back. "I'm so glad you put it that way, as *back* refers to the fact that it belonged to me and I merely reclaimed it." She smiled, red lips, white teeth...my stomach tightened.

I didn't even have a response. That locket had been in my house at home, in a locked box...along with my dads' gun and Faith's engagement ring...the one I'd never given to her.

My eyes flitted to Jessie. "Did you...?"

Jessie shook her head. "Leave me out of this." She raised her hands and stepped away, looking at the wall of cake mix to our left.

"You know, Jace, I'd love to stay and chat, but I have places to be, things to do. Have a nice evening." Faith smirked, linked her arm with Jessie, and sauntered off.

I stood there watching, unsure what had just happened but feeling a shift in my chest.

Chapter 37
Faith

"Mr. Vanderson has written into the divorce settlement what he'd like to offer his wife, Faith Vanderson," said one of the stuffy, dark-suited attorneys in a sharp, crisp tone. They'd been speaking legal jargon for the past hour, and I had never been more thankful for Gemma and her ability to interpret.

"How sweet," Gemma mocked, shuffling a few papers. "But we've written up our own settlement, and to save us both time, why don't we start there." She handed them each a copy. Bryan was on the other side of the table, an officer standing guard in the corner. From what I understood, he was battling jail time, having been charged with assault, abuse, and a few other nefarious things after my recording was heard by a judge.

But that wasn't my problem.

"Forty percent? That's insane!" yelled Dark Suit Number Two while looking through the papers. I had no idea what Gemma had written in; I was just there to get a divorce. I didn't care what else that meant for me, so I'd given Gemma free rein to ask for whatever she wanted to.

"These are the companies that were started while my client and Mr. Vanderson were wed, and she assisted with the startups. In fact, she was the point of contact on every one of the ventures, entitling her to more than half, but we decided to be generous." Gemma folded her hands.

Meanwhile, my heart was kicking into overdrive. There were at least five companies I'd helped start while married to Bryan. Five at forty percent was...too much money for me.

"Give her one hundred percent of each. She basically started them and maintained them herself. She can have the houses in Aspen, Germany, and South Africa as well," Bryan muttered morosely, his eyes trained on my neck. I fought the urge to hide my locket. I didn't want to hurt him further, but I also had to stop worrying about his feelings.

His lawyers all stared, gawking. My jaw had dropped too. Bryan's eyes moved from my neck until they were trained on the table, but his voice was hard as stone.

"I fucked up. My apology doesn't matter, so I won't give it, but if I can try to make it right, I will." He stood, pushing his chair back. "You get the companies, and everything they yield going forward. They're yours." He faltered for a second, his jaw ticking. "For what it's worth...I'm sorry. I loved you in my own twisted way, but I shouldn't have harmed you. I shouldn't have done a lot of things."

I swallowed down the pain that was being unleashed and the confusion that was bubbling in my chest. That was heartfelt, almost sweet even. It didn't change the fact that he was an abuser, but I could appreciate that he at least gave me an apology. His eyes locked onto mine before he turned and left the room. His attorneys gave Gemma one last look, me a passing glance, and then followed suit.

I sat back in my chair, unsure what exactly had just happened.

"So, does that mean I'm divorced?" I whispered, afraid to shatter the moment.

Gemma laughed. "After the judge signs off, but yes...he signed the papers." She let out a sigh and then another chuckle before turning to face me. "Faith...do you have any idea how much money you just received?"

I did, but it hadn't registered yet. HypeT had brought in five million the previous year, GTerics X a little over fifteen the year before that, and my favorite smaller startup, NefferLeaf, over eight million; the others were all hundreds of thousands of dollars in yields.

"This is a huge loss to his bottom line—why did he agree to give all of it up?" I asked, almost to myself.

"Because he's trying to repair his image," Gemma muttered thoughtlessly as she began piling papers together. For some reason, her comment stung. I knew it was stupid. It didn't make sense, but I had imagined he really did love me, thought he really was sorry. She turned toward me. "Hey...I'm sorry." She pulled me into her arms, and a slew of tears fell down my face.

"I don't know why I'm reacting like this. It's so stupid." I sniffed, swiping at my face.

"Honey, you're allowed to grieve your marriage...you did love him, after all." She rocked me in her arms, and I couldn't help but wish it was my mother who was rocking me, my mother who could talk to me about the pain of losing someone or something that was once a part of me. But that wasn't her. It would never be her.

"Thank you." I sniffed again, swiping the final tears out of my eyes and letting out a sigh.

"It's done, babe. I say we celebrate tonight." Gemma smiled and stood.

"Yeah, that sounds good."

Gemma deserved to celebrate after everything I'd put her through; after all, she'd stood by me for so long. I wanted her to be proud of me, and while I knew she was in some ways, I also knew it had broken her heart to see I'd settled in with an abusive asshole.

―――――

Gemma leaned against my shoulder while the sounds of the nightclub thrummed around us. Gemma had wanted to go dancing, and I'd realized it had been too long since I had indulged in something as fun as dancing in a nightclub. These clubs were vastly different than the smaller bars we frequented in Collierville and Shelby.

After our feet were aching and our bodies sweaty, we collapsed into a booth.

"I have something to tell you," I yelled into Gemma's ear. She sipped a tumbler of water, starting what I called her cooldown process. She wanted me to get drunk, but since she was the one who'd done all the legal work, I bought her all her favorite drinks.

Her blue eyes lit with excitement as she moved her head to the beat. "Hit me with it, babe!"

I laughed and put my arm around her. "I'm officially enrolled in online classes, and I've already talked to one of the design firms in Shelby...they agreed to let me intern."

Gemma squealed, leaned back, and threw her arms around me. "I'm so proud of you."

"It's not much to be proud of..." I shrugged, already feeling a little self-deprecating.

She shook her head. "You're rich. You could ditch college, design —all of it—but you're going through with college, and for that, I'm damn proud of you."

"You're my role model...did you know that?" I tipped my head up, watching her.

She snorted, shaking her head.

"It's true. If I had posters on my wall, you'd be on all of them. I love you, and I'm so glad I have you in my corner, so glad I've always had you." I started choking on a small sob.

"Oh my god! Stop, you're going to make me cry." She shoved me away but swiped under her eyes before grabbing her water. "For the record, I love you too. It's going to work out, okay?" She threw her arm around me, hugged me to her side, and then jumped back up. "One last song on that floor—let's go!"

I let her grab my hand and pull me up, and then I danced.

Someone knocked on my door close to noon. I was busy packing, not paying attention to who was there. Now that the divorce was final, I was a little less worried about things. I yelled, "Come in!" and moved toward the kitchen.

The door opened slowly, and I already knew who it was by how gently the knob turned.

My father was here again.

I heaved a sigh. "Dad..."

"Just hear me out, honey. I just..."

I shook my head. "It's not going to change my mind. Dad, I need some space." I shrugged, moving around the room.

"We messed up..." His voice cracked.

"We as in two of you, and yet the only person who has reached out a single time is you," I harshly snapped. It hurt that my mother hadn't reached out like he had. It hurt a lot that the last time we'd spoken had been about how she'd had dinner with Bryan and suggested he go out with me. She hadn't called or texted, nothing.

"Your mother is trying to give you space," he muttered, sounding defeated.

Ironic. So fucking ironic. I wanted space from her, but I wanted her to at least try. I wanted her to want me.

"I'm moving. I won't even be in the city anymore." I sighed.

"I know, and you can go, do whatever you need to do, but I'm just asking if you'd come to the house...have breakfast with us," my dad pleaded, slowly moving around the scattered boxes.

I considered it. At some point, I'd want to forgive them, but it was just too soon.

"You both crossed such a big line. You should have stood by me—only me. You should have rooted for my life with Jace, should have stood by my choice to love him and my choice to leave Bryan," I lectured, folding my arms across my chest.

"I know, and I'm so sorr—"

"No, just stop. I...I need space, Dad. I don't believe that you're sorry, not yet. I need some time away from you both. I hope you can understand that."

Tears welled in his eyes, shredding me in half. I hated this. I hated it so much, but it was the truth...the only one I had to give. I needed to stand by it.

"Okay...I love you, sweetheart. Just...come back to us, okay?" His voice cracked again as he leaned in, kissing the top of my head.

As soon as he left, I crumpled into a tiny ball and cried.

Chapter 38
Jace

WORKING HAD BECOME a mundane task that brought me little joy. I didn't listen to music...it was playing, but I didn't really hear it. Everything felt wrong. For the first time since I met Faith, I finally knew in my bones that it was time to let her go.

An odd sensation thrummed through me at the realization. It wasn't even what had happened with Bryan; it was just that she'd grown past the place I had been standing in. We were going in different directions.

She needed to figure out who she was going to be, and maybe one day down the road, we'd find a way back to each other. Maybe.

Or maybe not.

I was adjusting a part on an older Chevy when I heard someone clear their throat.

Tipping my head up, I found Clark Morgan leaning against my tool table, across the room.

I should have punched him, thrown my fist right into his face, especially because I'd never done anything about his betrayal. I'd never gotten revenge, had never even spread a single rumor about him around town. I had gotten him fired, but that was it.

But now, as I looked at him and saw the pathetic mess he'd

become, I realized I didn't need revenge. He'd lost his daughter, and that was revenge enough.

"I should have apologized a long time ago," he started, shoving his hands into the pockets of his slacks.

I waited, silently wiping my tools with a clean rag.

"What I did was wrong. I shouldn't have blackmailed you, shouldn't have betrayed you the way I did." His chin wobbled, just like his voice.

It did something to my chest.

Seeing my worst enemy apologize did something to me, something strange and chaotic, like a torrential downpour in the middle of a desert.

"I was wrong. Whether or not my daughter ever forgives me, I'm so sorry."

I watched him as he tripped over his words and they caught in his throat. I didn't say anything; I couldn't. I didn't even know what I would say. I hadn't forgiven him yet, and what he'd done wasn't okay. So, I merely nodded at him. He tightened his jaw then walked out of my garage, leaving behind him a piece of hope I didn't understand. Why did it feel so good to hear him say he'd fucked up? Why did it matter at all? My mind wandered to Faith, and to him being tied to her, how this was something that'd always stood like a pillar in our way. I hated her father, so in my mind, we would never work in the long term.

It should have made me happy. It should have made me pick up my phone and call Faith. I tossed the rag in my hand down to the ground and went back to work, because him showing up, saying sorry...it didn't actually change anything.

She was still lost to me.

The sting of giving Faith up, the confusion around her father showing up, and her stealing the locket back was ruining the excitement about my new house. I was all alone in my brand-new home, the empty walls, sparse furniture, and impressive views all reminding me of my past.

"I might have to sell this place," I muttered to Trevor over my bottle of beer. I was staring out my back window, looking over my empty back yard to where, down the hill, McGrady's orchard started. My yard still hadn't been touched. I wouldn't get to it until after spring, but I wasn't in a rush.

The sound of someone unlocking my front door startled me. I narrowed my eyes, set my bottle down, and realized too late that Trevor wasn't barking. Instead, he was excitedly wagging his tail. I moved around the corner, closer to the door, and I heard...

"Hey, sorry...ugh, could you come help?" Faith's muffled voice echoed from the foyer. She was carrying a box...one that, in black marker, said *Kitchen.*

"Faith...what are you..."

"I know, it seems odd. I should have just had you load up your truck, but I fit almost everything besides the furniture in my Rover. Isn't that great?" She smiled at me, set the box down, and put her hands on her hips.

What the hell is happening?

"I...uhh...what is..." I tried again, but she merely turned on her heel and smirked over her shoulder.

"You helping or what?"

I stalked forward, gently grabbing her arm to stop her. "Faith, what the hell are you doing here?"

I searched her face, which was void of any makeup. Her lips only had a sheer gloss over them, but she was perfect. She was more than perfect...she was...*home.*

"I'm moving in." She pulled her arm free.

I let out a laugh, because this girl...*fucking hilarious.* "You're what?"

"Thought it'd be obvious..." She smirked again, pulling the door open.

"You are not moving in. This is my house," I said, feeling those words settle on my tongue like a Pop Rocks in soda.

She laughed as she moved toward her open back hatch; she'd reversed her car into my driveway.

"Look, I get it. You're a little surprised, and that's fine, but this is happening. I'm moving in, and if you need me to sleep in a guest room, or the basement...whatever you need to help you adjust is fine. But..." She groaned loudly as she lifted another box. Her Dwight Schrute method of lifting nearly made me laugh, but her appearance tempered the urge. "I *am* moving in."

I moved forward to take the box from her, shaking my head to clear whatever misunderstanding this was. Meanwhile, my heart was doing fucking Olympic flips in my chest. I set the box down and gently tugged on her hand, pulled her into the house, and pinned her against the wall.

"Explain this to me," I whispered, resting my forehead on hers.

She caressed my jaw, her lips curving up as she smiled. "I love you, Jace Walker. I have loved you since I knew what love was. I am going to keep loving you, so I suggest you get used to it. I plan on proposing to you one day, may even give you a necklace to wear."

I laughed, couldn't help it, but I also felt tears start at the edges of my eyes.

"But you're married..." I choked out.

She shook her head back and forth. "I'm not."

"So...you're..." I tried again, but I needed her to give me the words. Bryan's lies were still stuck like glue inside my head, her marriage and her father...it was just too much. I was finally ready to let her go because it was the right thing to do...yet here she was, shoving her way back in.

"I'm stayin'," she quipped with her Southern accent.

I stood back and tried to process what exactly that meant.

Faith

Jace hadn't stopped looking at me strangely since I arrived, which was two hours ago. After we silently carried my boxes inside, he awkwardly headed to the kitchen and made dinner...in silence.

I knew he was overthinking something, and I hated that I didn't know what Bryan had told him. I knew he'd told enough damaging lies for Jace to consider giving me up, so it must have been a hot mess in his mind, but he wouldn't let me in.

The only way I could show him I was serious about this, about us, was to do something drastic—like move in uninvited.

I chewed on a snap pea while watching the muscles in Jace's back shift under his shirt. This was more awkward than I had imagined it would be. I'd thought...I guess I'd assumed he'd see my gesture and sweep me off my feet, take me to bed, and we'd be together, officially. But this...this was so much different.

Is he going to let me stay but never talk to me again?

"I'm afraid of you," Jace declared suddenly, breaking up the silence and startling me.

"What?" I sat up in the stool, clearing my throat.

He flipped the burner off and turned. Blue, dangerous eyes met mine.

"Fucking terrified," he added, moving closer.

I pushed my fingers so hard into my palm, I worried it'd draw blood.

He was finally giving me words.

"I'm afraid you might wake up one day and realize you could do better. I'm afraid we won't last, and it'll ruin me...again. I'm afraid you're going to leave." He moved around the island until he was towering over me.

The pad of his finger danced along my collarbone, as light as a feather. His words were thread, knitting us back together.

I tipped my head back as he continued.

"He said you were pregnant...said you two were working together to buy me out." He shook his head as if to clear the lies away. "I may not have taken his money, but a part of me believed him...not all of it, but that you were maybe playing me."

I held my breath as Jace continued.

"I fear you, Faith, because I'm so fucking in love with you. I've always been in love with you. There is no one else for me." He lowered his lips, nearly touching mine, his other hand caging me in against the island. His breath washed over me, hot and wanting. He kept his lips hovering just above mine, letting me decide.

He was addressing our relationship in its entirety. While I had been willing to hatch this scheme to get him to let me back in, I had buried some of my own pain, the things we'd never settled.

But the old hurt I carried inside me like an extra set of useless organs began to unfurl, expand, and beg for release. Tears slipped down my flushing face as I reached up to grip his shirt. I wasn't strong enough to resist him. The love I had for him was a tidal wave—powerful, terrible, and beautifully destructive.

I wanted us both to sink under its weight.

"He had threatened you and Jessie...your house, your business... her college...all of it."

Jace's brows drew together in confusion.

"It's why I agreed to meet with him, without you, why I was keeping it from you. I just...I didn't want you to leave me because of your pride or do something stupid. I'm s-sorry," I stammered, feeling guilty that I hadn't just trusted him.

His eyes softened with my confession, his finger tracing a trail around the shell of my ear.

I pushed up off my seat, capturing his lips, hoping to reclaim his heart.

He pulled me up until I was flush against him. I stood, wrapping my arms around his neck, pouring every fear we had about us into this kiss, igniting and lighting it all on fire. Our tongues didn't dance; they warred for the things we had been cheated of.

He grabbed me by the thighs, lifting me, and I wrapped my legs around his waist as he carried us toward the stairs.

Once he pushed open the bedroom door, I watched his azure gaze focus on me as he lowered me to the bed. Only the small lamp was on in the bedroom, giving off a soft glow. He'd set up a king-sized bed with a dark grey duvet.

The mattress dipped as Jace crawled over me. I wanted to take a second and relish the softness of the mattress...it was magnificent, and the pillows were all down, fluffed to perfection.

"You like it?" Jace laughed as the rough pads of his fingers pushed my shirt up. I blinked, trying to remember the boy I once knew and liken him to the rugged man who peered down at me now.

I let out a useless lilt of laughter. "I love it. It's perfect. You're perfect."

He responded with a smile, the kind that stretched across his face, crinkling his eyes.

My heart melted.

He leaned down, frantic lips dancing along my skin. His firm hand wrapped around my rib cage, tugging me closer until I was under him. He held himself up while he devoured me, his left hand winding down my body, finding purchase under the waistline of my jeans.

His coarse caress against my wet, aching center was pure bliss, causing me to arch my back and grind against his hand. I closed my eyes as white light crackled along the blackness behind my eyelids. Heaving out a heavy moan, I moved my hips to a desperate rhythm, wordlessly begging him to give me more, even if it ruined me, even if it was the end of me.

"Jace," I whispered.

"We aren't in your parents' house, Pip—no need to whisper anymore." He removed his hand only to pull my jeans down the length of my legs, followed by my panties. His hungry gaze made me brazen.

He stood, removing his shirt, revealing that perfectly sculpted chest, the small trail of dark hair traveling down his stomach. Next went his jeans, leaving him in only his black boxer briefs.

I bit my lip, sitting up, and tugged my shirt off, then unhooking my bra.

"I haven't slept with anyone in over a year," he rushed out, slowly moving his hand to grip his erection through his boxers. I nodded my head, giving him the green light, he was looking for.

"I don't want anything between us tonight," I whispered, husky and hungry.

That was all the permission he needed.

His boxers came down. Free and ready, he crawled toward me and, locking eyes with me, he slowly entered me. Closing his eyes, he waited there, for just a second, letting out a shuddering kind of breath. Like this was as perfect and painful for him as it was for me.

So much time had passed, and I knew as he sank further into me, his mind was wrestling with my past. I wouldn't have any of that tonight. I pushed my chest against his, hard and demanding, bringing my hips up hard against his length. He groaned, finally letting himself go. He pulled out, and entered me again, harder this time.

"Jace," I moaned, clinging to his shoulders, digging in with my nails. It wasn't enough.

Pulling out again, he thrust even hard, pushing me back an inch on the bed.

"I've missed you so fucking much, Pip." He rasped, with so much need it nearly undid me.

I tangled my fingers up into his hair and pushed against him in a frantic rhythm.

His forceful thrusts were what I needed. He leaned back, until his gaze locked on mine, he was challenging me with the slightest lift of his lip, and fuck if that didn't turn me on. I leaned up, pulling his lip into my mouth and sucking as hard as I could, forcing him to drive his hips deeper into me.

"Fuck, Faith. Fuck!" He yelled.

"Yes," I hissed on a throaty moan.

Sex with Jace was always an experience. He made love with what felt like his entire soul, shards of every emotion making their way into each thrust and moan. I'd never felt him like this, though—bare, nothing hindering our connection. It was just us, together when everything tried to keep us apart. I brought my nails down, along his back as he rocked into me.

He sank deeper, groaning into my ear as he pressed hot, hurried kisses to my neck, trailing down to my aching nipples.

I met him thrust for thrust, as though we could heal the broken pieces in our hearts with each slap of skin. Every whispered confession, he continued filling me, pushing against me, until we were nothing but two spent, languid bodies, roaring our release and gasping for breath. Sweat drenched my back as Jace trailed a line down my skin, watching me with a peace in his eyes that I hadn't ever seen before.

I blinked, trying to create an internal scrapbook of looks, sounds, images—everything Jace and I were, saved inside my head. I didn't ever want to forget the look on his face when he tried to pull out and I locked my ankles together behind his back, begging him not to. I knew it was crazy, but I didn't want to waste any more time. I wasn't kidding when I told him he was my dream. Him, our future kids, whatever else life brought to us—as long as it was with him, it would be a part of my dream.

"Tell me something true," I whispered, turning my head to watch him.

He smiled. "I love that you stole your locket back *and* somehow managed to get a key to my place."

I laughed, rolling until I fit under his arm. He gently picked up my locket, stroking a finger down the design.

"That was no easy feat. It took some guesswork, a solid brainstorming session with Jessie, Gemma, and your dad, and then, of course, Jessie loaning me the spare key you'd given her."

He shook his head, that crazy huge smile in place. Mentally I taped the edges of the photo to a creamy page with the word *Forever* printed underneath.

"Marry me, Pip. I know you just got divorced. I know it's not ideal for couples to get engaged after sex, especially makeup sex, but it's my truth, my deepest truth that exists. I want you next to me, for all time, for all the rest of time we have, and to make up for the time we don't." His blue eyes caught the glow of the room, making him look ethereal.

I leaned in to kiss him. "I think we're way past that."

"Oh, we are?" He laughed, pulling me on top of him.

"Well yeah, I mean...I just moved in, but I saw my ring in that box, and I was tempted to put it on instead of the locket. I'm yours, Jace. I won't ever not be yours."

Epilogue
Jace

A few months later

I LEANED AGAINST THE COUNTER, eating an apple. Trevor was curled around Faith's legs, his nose planted in her lap against her stomach. He was always touching her, close to her, especially now. Even with Trudy here, there wasn't any chance he'd leave her side.

I didn't hate it, but at night, when I was trying to make love to her, it got old.

"Jace, it's nice to see that you're doing so well." Julia Morgan smiled at me, a genuine smile with no hidden meanings or secret anythings. I heard Clark straighten his newspaper in the other room, probably a silent request for me to leave the women alone.

If I could have yelled through the kitchen that I didn't want to be in here and I would have much rather been watching the game that was on, I would have, but Faith needed me close, so I stayed.

"Thank you, Julia. I am doing well. The best, actually," I replied, taking another bite of my apple. Faith patted Trevor's head, playing with his ears.

"Do you mind giving us some privacy?" Julia asked kindly, folding her hands in front of her.

"No, he stays," Faith said quickly. I flicked my gaze to Julia's thinned lips and the back of my wife's head. She put her hand out behind her, summoning me to get closer.

I loved my wife, but she was being clingy as fuck right now, and while I loved that about her literally everywhere else we went, her parents' house wasn't the place I wanted to show PDA or be her security blanket. Even so, I wasn't about to give my bride the *Be brave and do this alone* speech.

I interlocked my fingers with Faith's, pulling up a chair to sit next to her, then settled our linked fingers in my lap while I pulled my cell out. I'd give Julia the illusion that they were alone by pretending to check out of their conversation.

"So..." Julia cleared her throat, spreading her hands out in front of her, careful not to touch the black and white sonogram picture mere inches from her fingertips.

Faith's eyes flitted down to the picture that sat between them, like she wanted to yank the image back toward her side of the table.

"So..." Faith drew the word out, huffing out a breath.

Holy shit, this was going to take all day at this rate.

"You're pregnant?" Julia asked, her voice rising.

Faith straightened her spine, tilting her chin up. "And married."

Shit.

I eyed my wife, silently begging her not to rub salt in the wound. We hadn't invited Julia to the wedding, although it had been small enough that there wasn't much to miss. Just Gemma, Seth, Tom, Jessie, my dad, and a few other people attended our tiny backyard wedding.

Clark, however, was one of the people who'd made the guest list. He'd been relentless with pursuing his daughter's forgiveness, taking her out to coffee at least twice a week. He'd eventually worn her down, but Julia hadn't made the same effort.

Things between them were still icy. It wasn't until Clark and I double-teamed Faith, asking her to do this now that we were expecting a child. Enough was enough.

"Congratulations, sweetheart," Julia softly replied, flicking her eyes from her daughter's down to the table. There was no mistaking the pitch and shudder that ran through her as she said it. It must have killed her to miss her only daughter's wedding...although, she had been present for at least one of Faith's weddings, a fact I tried to ignore more often than I cared to admit. But this, the pregnancy, was like a stick of dynamite to all that shit that was in the past. It was new for both of us, something neither of us had ever walked out, so we were blissfully embracing it.

"Thank you." Faith's tone was curt.

I squeezed her fingers to get her talking, and she let out a sigh then relented.

"Mama, I want you to be in this baby's life. *We* want you to be there." Faith leaned forward, sliding the picture toward her mother.

Faith was twelve weeks along, so there wasn't much on the image, just some white swirls and tiny shadows of limbs and where a head would be.

"I would like that very much." Julia let out a small sob, putting a quick hand to her chest while she stared down at the picture of my kid.

And just like that, the invisible wall was down. Faith started sniffling, and tears were streaming down her face as she released my hand. She stood at the same time Julia did.

They both stared at each other for a moment, Trevor adjusting to his new place on the floor.

Then, like magnets, they drifted closer until they were hugging, crying, and sobbing. It was a lot...but even I had to admit it warmed my heart a bit.

Faith had her own reasons to be angry with her parents, but when I'd told her I had found a way to forgive her father, to move on for the sake of our family, the sake of our child, it had made her finally see reason.

Julia was going on and on about how she had just been waiting for Faith to thaw a bit before she attempted to talk to her, saying she'd known what she did was wrong, but she'd also known Faith was so upset there would be no getting through to her.

She wasn't wrong. Faith was stubborn, and once she set her heart on something, there was no changing her mind. That said, this baby changed everything for us, although, I guess it had all changed when we'd given up on fighting each other.

I watched as my wife hugged her mother and smiled, ready for happiness, ready to embrace the future, whatever it held.

Faith

My little reunion with my mother was emotional, more so because of my hormones, but also because it was long overdue. Honestly, I had missed my mother fiercely, and I think Jace knew that, especially when I cried uncontrollably at our first doctor's appointment. I couldn't tell him why I was so emotional, but he could tell my tears weren't happy ones.

They were because I wanted to run into my mama's arms and tell her I was going to be a mother. I wanted her smile, her arms; I wanted her to be my mother. In order to have those things, it required me to talk to her.

After our hug-fest in the kitchen, we sat and actually talked, and I explained my issues with her. What she saw as letting me fight my own battles, I saw as her being distant and cold. It broke her heart, and she cried, begged for my forgiveness, and told me things would be different going forward.

I softened and decided to believe her. Ever since, we'd met at least once a week to talk, to shop, to laugh and gossip. She finally abandoned her two-truffle rule and just lived in the moment, talking, laughing, and loving.

It was a nice reprieve for Jessie, too, whom we included in our trips and dates as often as we could. Jessie had hugged me recently with tears in her eyes, thanking me for fixing it all. I'd laughed and cried because hormones, but I had ensured she knew it wasn't me who fixed anything.

"No, it was. Faith, you could have run, could have left again. You could have run away from Jace when he pushed you away, but you stayed. You fixed it. You fixed everything," she had sworn, hugging me fiercely. When she put it like that, there was a tiny part of me that allowed myself to agree.

I had grown. I had fixed some things that needed fixing.

I couldn't even grasp that this was our life now.

After Jace married me, we traveled for our honeymoon. We started in Mexico, went to Brazil, and then headed to Europe. We still had a million and one places we planned to visit, but after a few weeks, Jace pressed a gentle kiss to my forehead and said he wanted me in our bed, at home, starting our life together.

As the weeks passed, the press lost interest. Tom wasn't hired to help, but he often stopped by to check in, which moved my heart. He relayed once, privately, that Bryan had sought help, honest help with his anger and drinking issues, and he'd done it without the press knowing, which made me think he meant what he'd said. He was truly sorry. It was good to hear that he was taming his demons and finding peace.

Our house, the one Jace had built, was completely finished now, landscaped and complete with security, something to put us both at ease now that our baby was coming. I still spent most of my days at the interior design company I was interning at, learning everything I could and putting the knowledge toward the classes I was taking online.

It was a struggle to keep up with the companies I had inherited, so I sweetly asked my best friend if she was any good at business law, and if she could please find me someone to run the businesses without bankrupting them or running them into the ground. She squealed, threw her arms around me, and said she'd give me two years, then she was going back to civil cases and working pro bono.

I decided I'd take what I could get; besides, my husband owned and operated a company, so I was sure he could help me with a few of them.

I gave the keys to my apartment to Jessie. I'd purchased it and I told her she could pay rent if she wanted, or she could go to college and just focus on her studies. She cried and decided to continue with her studies, entering a veterinary program.

Jace allowed me to buy his father a nice house by the river where he could fish, and he even agreed to retire.

Things in our life were perfect, but I had one last thing to do to show my husband how much our future meant to me. With a rather big bump protruding from my belly, I tugged Jace's hand as we waddled along the turf.

"Look," I said, tilting my head toward the weeping willow and the massive headstone underneath it.

Jace stopped mid-step. With his eyes wide, he slowly strolled forward, taking careful steps toward his mother's grave.

"H-how?" he stammered, running a finger along the glossy white stone.

"I ordered it a while ago, but it was finally finished over the weekend. Your dad came first, and Jessie, but I knew you'd want your own time anyway. So, I'm going to walk for a bit, because that masochist of a doctor said I have to. I'll be near the Rover when you're ready."

I was about to walk away when he stopped me. "I want you with me. I want our baby here. I want to show her my family, let her know her prayers worked."

His eyes glittered with tears, and I sank into his chest, so insanely grateful for second chances and for truth.

"Okay," I whispered, settling down on the earth, basking in the sun as the man I loved began to talk to his mother about our life.

It was glorious, perfect, and mine, and I was never letting it go.

If you enjoyed this book, please consider leaving a review on Amazon. Not only does it encourage me to keep writing, but it helps others decide if they want to read this.

Want more small-town feels? I have two other standalone small-town romances, with all the feels, you can read them for free with kindle unlimited.

The Rest of Me: A widowed, single mother moves to small-town Wyoming to start over. However, her new neighbor makes her new start more challenging by being the only local horse instructor for her kids, and the only man to make her feel something other than her late husband.

Only Once: Set in a small tourist town, Bexley starts a second job at a local resort to help cover the lapse in her child support. There, she runs into the man she left ten years prior, who has become one of Hollywood's elite. Once he recognizes Bexley, he requests that she cater to his every need. It's only a matter of time before the truth of what happened comes out, and they're forced to move on...or go back.

Also By Ashley

Mount Macon Series

Resisting the Grump

Tempting the Neighbor

Saving the Single Dad

The Stone Riders Motorcycle Club

Where We Started

WWB

WWV

WWE

Standalone Small Town

Only Once

The Rest of Me

Tennessee Truths

Romantic Suspense Series:

Glimmer

Fade

College Romance Series:

Wild Card

King of Hearts

The Joker

Anthology/ CoWrites

What Are the Chances

Vicious Vet

Sign up for updates, book news, and more with Ashley's newsletter.

www.ashleymunozbooks.com

Acknowledgments

As always, my gratitude is first and foremost for my creator, without whom I wouldn't have the ability to tell stories or the passion for it.

To my husband and kids. We've been through a lot this year, more than I care to ever go through again, but we made it and we keep making it.

The timing of this book was odd and toward the end, quite challenging. I couldn't have completed it all without your loving support.

To my mother. I thought I knew your strength, but you keep surprising me. You are the most selfless person I know and I can only pray that one day, I become as gracious in walking that out.

Eric, I love you and miss you always.

To my beta readers, Rebecca, Brittany, Gladys, Amy, Krystal and Joanna- thank you so much for your input and appreciation for my words. Thank you for helping me perfect this story.

Brit- thank you always and I can't wait to see you and hopefully meet Connor this summer.

To Tiffany, my PA- I couldn't do this without you. I say that a lot, but I mean it. I couldn't imagine doing any part of this author thing without you in my corner. Thank you for your book recs and your friendship.

To Brandon from Herringbone Books: I thought I'd put it in print, so it's official- if I ever make it big, you're my first stop and I'll never forget your kindness toward a debut- indie author.

To my amazing readers and Book Beauties, you have no idea how much you mean to me. Every tweet, IG mention, facebook tag, comment or share- it just all makes such a big difference in my life. Thank you for loving my words and always coming back for more.

About the Author

Ashley is an Amazon Top 50 bestselling romance author who is best known for her small town, second-chance romances. She resides in the Pacific Northwest, where she lives with her four children and her husband. She loves coffee, reading fantasy, and writing about people who kiss and cuss.

Join her reader group for random life updates, giveaways, and more!
Book Beauties

Printed in Great Britain
by Amazon